D1721367

FREEDOM'S MYTH

STEPHEN B. PEARL

Milton, Ontario
http://www.brain-lag.com/

This is a work of fiction. All of the characters, events, and organizations portrayed in this novel are either products of the author's imagination or are used fictitiously.

Brain Lag Publishing
Ontario, Canada
http://www.brain-lag.com/

Cover artwork by Catherine Fitzsimmons

Library and Archives Canada Cataloguing in Publication

Title: Freedom's myth / Stephen B. Pearl.
Names: Pearl, Stephen B., 1961- author.
Identifiers: Canadiana (print) 20220397929 | Canadiana (ebook) 20220397937 | ISBN 9781928011859
  (softcover) | ISBN 9781928011866 (ebook)
Classification: LCC PS8631.E255 F74 2022 | DDC C813/.6—dc23

Dedication

To my wife/editor, Joy and publisher/editor, Catherine, of course, and to the many people who have worn masks, got vaccinated and behaved like responsible adults throughout the Covid Nineteen pandemic.

Freedom without responsibility is the ultimate tyranny. It is the tyranny of the biggest club. It enslaves all to those who are stronger than them and makes slavers of the strong whether they want to be or not.

Freedom is a myth; the nature of the universe precludes perfect freedom. The fact that our actions impact others' will, if we are responsible, curtails our personal freedoms so that others can enjoy theirs. An example, I am not free to take my neighbour's life. We call that murder, and most human societies frown on it. We accept this limitation on our freedom because we recognize that our neighbours should have the freedom to live.

At a superficial level, my batzoid culture seems to ignore the above example, but does it really? If a vengeance proxy takes a life, does that not open the avenue for the ones that 'took out the hit' to, in turn, be targeted? Thus, a balance of consequence is struck, and the 'hits' are only undertaken for solid reasons. It is a bloodthirsty and harsh balance, but it is a balance of freedoms. Frankly, we employ this at a national level with the doctrine of mutually assured destruction.

At an even more fundamental level, I am not free to ignore the laws of science. If I hold my breath when I surface from a SCUBA dive, I will pop a lung and likely die. This is natural law playing out. What the Egyptians defined as the goddess Ma'at.

What we, as thinking social animals, must do is determine where the lines of our freedom should be drawn and then, as a society, enforce those lines with a view to the greatest good for all and the individual. In short, does it affect me? No. Then live and let live.

ILLUSIONS SHATTERED

"This is not a good thing." Armina crouched behind some immature trees and bushes at the edge of the Stewart River. Upstream the hydroelectric dam loomed, a wall of black in the night with a starry sky above. Her blonde hair was pulled into a bun and largely hidden by the dark cap she wore.

"You should have said that before," said Obert.

"She did say that before. Over and over again," remarked Kendra.

Arlene pressed a button on her console. The big screen, which filled the upper half of one wall of the *Freedom's Run* entertainment series control room, shifted to Obert's perspective. He was focused on Armina's well-shaped backside, where it was framed by a pair of black jeans. Auxiliary screens flanked the main screen showing the sensory inputs of the other surrogates in the scene. A control console filled the space in front of Arlene's swivel chair. The room was nine metres square. Screens and consoles covered the walls, and a vending machine-like device stood by the door at its back.

"Obert, get your head in the game and your eyes off my girlfriend's butt." Medwin's voice issued from the speaker. The monitors showing Medwin's emotions indicated irritation.

Obert's perspective shifted to Medwin's pleasant,

Caucasian features with his mop of badly cut, dark hair and lean, muscular body clad in a black hoodie and jeans. Obert's erotic arousal level hardly budged as he watched his friend check over the inflatable boat they had brought with them.

"Bet that would come as a surprise to the gang. At least Carol should be good with her boyfriend's preferences." Arlene spoke into the privacy of the *Freedom's Run* control room.

"Obert, honestly! This is an important mission." Obert's perspective on the main screen shifted to Kendra, who clutched one of the boat's carry straps. "If we can confirm that it's really the future and we are slaves being used to provide emotions for entertainments, it will change our world."

The empathic monitors beside the screen dedicated to Obert jumped as he eyed Kendra.

"Carol takes him to one little orgy. Now he's sex-mad. Kids! I need him focused for this." Arlene reached out, adjusting a dial. Obert's built-in control pack released chemicals into the studio clone that dampened his arousal response.

"Don't worry, kid. I'll reset your levels to default in time for you to get back to Carol. It's good for ratings to have someone in the cast to eye up the hotties." Arlene stared into the screen, which showed Kendra's fit body, then shifted to her face, which combined the best of Asian and Caucasian features.

The visual screen went blank as Obert closed his eyes and took a deep breath. Arlene checked her inputs, seeing her charge's emotions settle. "Good, that should cool him off enough to think."

In the set region, Medwin lay on his back, bringing a pair of binoculars to his eyes. "Everyone ready?"

"Are you sure you can see satellites with those?" Kendra looked skyward.

"No. But it's better than nothing. Gunther said that the satellite screen had gaps and that the controllers would have to be looking. Since the only time they do active monitoring with us is when we're doing the focus group for the *Freedom's Run* series, we should be safe enough."

"It's such a rip-off. Gunther and those guys on *Angel Black* get superpowers, and we get zilch. I mean, their show has such a cool premise, and we got to be teenage dorks in high school. *SciFi Geeks*. Even our show's title sucked. No wonder it got cancelled," griped Obert.

"I'm hoping that Gunther is wrong and that they really have been fighting alien pirates who want to take over the world. That would be bad enough. This whole thing with e-entertainments and Sun Valley all being a big set and us being clones. I mean, if it's true, nothing we know is real. Not even ourselves." Armina hung her head.

Medwin smiled at his girlfriend and spoke softly. "Babe, we're real. Being clones doesn't change that. Let's just sneak out of Sun Valley. If what Gunther said about it being seven hundred years after humans joined an interstellar republic is true, then at least we know. If it isn't, we went camping for a few days, no big."

"Suppose it is true and a satellite spots us?" Armina's voice shook.

Kendra sighed heavily. "Then the controllers will kill us, so we can't tell the other clones what we found out. To make their sick little studio work, we have to be kept in the dark."

"It looks clear," interrupted Medwin. "Let's go." Rolling to his feet, he picked up his corner of the raft. His companions followed his example. Running to the river, they tossed the raft in and boarded. Once on the water, Kendra and Medwin pulled a blue tarp over everyone aboard, and they let the current take them.

"The studio satellites will only monitor the area around

Sun Valley so we can lose the tarp once we're clear," stated Medwin.

In moments, they were swept past the range of newly planted trees that marked the Sun Valley forestation project.

Peeking out from under the tarp, Obert saw the transition zone where the workers had used explosives to create depressions in the bedrock. "Why are they blasting here?"

"You've never worked as a tree planter." Medwin sounded exasperated.

"Give him a break, Medwin. He got lucky and didn't have to. It's all part of the forestation. You blast a hole, then infill with a mix of rubble and milorganite, then you plant a tree and let the roots do the rest over time," explained Kendra.

"Milorganite is one of our big products from the sewage treatment plant, along with methane, bio-diesel and fuel alcohol. The tree planters are always running out of the stuff," remarked Armina.

"Oh." Obert fell silent. "You know, I never thought to ask. Tree planting has always been the foundation industry for Sun Valley, right?"

"Sure, of course, what else would it be?" asked Medwin.

"Why? Who makes a profit? We're all so used to it we never ask."

"Well, people need to breathe, and in fifty or a hundred years, they could..." Armina trailed off as her face went pale.

"The controllers. We aren't just entertainment. They are using us as slave labour," breathed Kendra.

"Sun Valley is one big plantation. We grow more food than we eat, we prepare the land for planting, then they kill us off and take it all when we have it nice for them." Medwin scowled.

"Honey, write fiction. This whole thing is crazy!" said Armina.

Kendra looked at the shore, now an uneven rock

landscape with some scrub plants in crevices where soil had accumulated. "I've never been this far from town."

"How does everyone feel?" asked Medwin.

"I'm fine, no nausea or anxiety. Whatever Willa did with that handheld gizmo is working." Kendra continued to stare out from under the tarp.

"I'm not nauseous," answered Armina.

Medwin moved to hold his girlfriend. "It will be all right."

"I'm fine if anyone cares," observed Obert.

They drifted along the Stewart River to where it joined the Wolf River. Obert used an oar as a rudder to keep them to the centre of the flow.

"We'll let the river carry us. People build along rivers, and we won't have to worry about drinking water," explained Medwin.

"For how long? I need to be back at the sewage treatment plant for Tuesday, then we have focus group Friday evening," objected Armina, her pretty features a mask of dismay.

"We'll start back tomorrow evening no matter what we find," said Medwin.

"Who died and made you Picard?" demanded Obert.

"You have a better idea?" countered Medwin.

"No, but you could ask, not tell." Obert sounded querulous.

"When we prove it about the controllers, there may not be time for a committee decision. There are good reasons militaries are hierarchical," observed Kendra.

"Yeah, well. You say," grumbled Obert.

Medwin rolled his eyes, but the darkness hid the expression. "Obert."

"What?"

"I was wondering if you'd like to steer while I got some shut-eye?"

Obert sat silent for a moment. "I'll keep it to the middle of the flow and wake you if anything comes up. I'm too excited to sleep anyway. This must be how Rowan felt when she first found out the truth."

"Welcome to the Spuqupa Report, bringing you in-depth news on the major events from the Switchboard Station." Rowan's view was filled with the Switchboard Station. More than anything, it looked like a spiral staircase with each of its hundred and thirty species' habitat units forming a solid wedge against the backdrop of a black sky bedecked with stars. Only her knowledge that each wedge-shaped step held an entire city, complete with natural environment zones, let her appreciate the accomplishment it represented. "And the galaxy beyond," continued the voice as the shot zoomed out at impossible speed to show the Milky Way galaxy floating in the void.

Rowan knew she floated in one of the coffin-like sensory interface booths that lined the walls of the *Star Hawk*'s small gymnasium and that her eyes were closed. She only saw the show because she allowed the nanobots in her brain to take over her perceptions. The feeling still creeped her out, but without the emotional input, she could choose how she felt about what she was experiencing. The security of being in the ship helped her relax enough to enjoy the show.

The scene in Rowan's mind shifted to a large room with a black cushion configured into an almost nest. What looked like an oversized otter with an elongated head and mahogany-coloured fur lounged in the nest facing her. Its lips moved. "We have an 'Orca-like aquatic predator' of a show for you today."

She looked to her right and saw a copper-skinned human with brown hair. He was of average height and build and looked mid-twenties, though she knew the lie of that. He met her gaze with a pair of magnificent green eyes. A thrill ran through her that she would have thought was an empathic download, except Spuqupa had assured her that wasn't part of his show. Ryan just had that effect on her.

"Unless you've been living in a murky swamp cut off from the river, my guests today need no introduction," Spuqupa's voice continued. The image shifted, focusing on Rowan, but the voice remained the same. "But just in case. This is Rowan McPherson, star of the human e-entertainment *Angel Black*, who recently escaped from indentured servitude to the S.E.T.E. corporation as an emotional surrogate. Even more recently, she was embroiled in a hilarious series of events that saw her escape from United Earth Systems custody when they tried to re-establish her status as property. How are you today, Rowan?"

Rowan heard her own voice and watched herself as she answered. "I'm quite well, thank you. The medical issues that S.E.T.E. forced on me as part of the show I was making have been mostly dealt with. I appreciate you having us on your program. Though, I have to say, if it wasn't for Ryan, I'd be dead now, and I never would have gotten away from the S.E.T.E. set region or the United Earth Systems."

"Sweet clam, it's my honour to have you both," replied Spuqupa. "On that bubble, let's introduce my second guest." The image shifted to Ryan, who fidgeted uncomfortably in the black lounger his cushion chair had configured itself into.

Spuqupa's voice continued. "Captain Ryan Chandler of the *Star Hawk*, and yes, my friends, we are talking about the saviour of the kangazoid species, who single-handedly prevented the forced revision of five Republic races to a Neolithic level. Cloned after taking a lethal dose of radiation during the rescue efforts on Murack Five and forced to retire from the United Earth Systems Space Combat Corps, Ryan became a studio controller on the *Angel Black* series. He risked everything to liberate Rowan and smuggle her out of UES territory to a place where she is a person under the law. More recently, he was convicted of a petty Republic offence incurred during lifesaving efforts that resulted in the preservation of an AI. Currently commanding the *Star Hawk* about to embark on a mission to bring vital aid to the Murack Five relief efforts. Captain Chandler, Ryan. Thank you for being on the Spuqupa Report. It is a 'catch with many fine fish' to have you here."

The image stayed on Ryan, but now Ryan's voice spoke. "Thank you for having me, though I have to correct you. Everyone who worked to preserve the kangazoids after the accident on Murack Five must be acknowledged. No one person or species can take credit. The final truth is, we should never have been on Murack Five in the first place."

Rowan's hand reached over from her lounger and gripped Ryan's arm. He smiled sadly and shifted so that he held her hand.

In the real world, Rowan smiled.

"As you have said many times. All those who weave the net share in the catch. But to your more recent exploits. What inspired you to become outlaw to your own species?"

Ryan looked to Rowan, and the perspective shifted to show her. "I couldn't let them kill her. The way the studio treats the e-surrogates is—"

"Slavery," interjected Rowan.

"Slavery," agreed Ryan.

Rowan stared at the floor. "The worst part is they made us killers."

Ryan stood up and moved to her side. "Chair, configuration *Homo sapiens* loveseat."

The black lounger Rowan sat in moulded itself into a loveseat. Ryan sat beside her, taking her hands.

"I've experienced episodes of *Angel Black*, and I have to say, I understand why, from your perspective, it was necessary for you to kill the invading pirates. Few species would not have dived into those waters to guard their homeworld. The only villains are those who engineered the conflict," comforted Spuqupa. "So, Ryan, you liberated

Rowan out of moral outrage."

Ryan turned to Spuqupa and smiled. "Do I look like a eunuch?"

The image shifted to the otterzoid interviewer, who thrashed about in his seat, making splashing motions in the air. "It is most true that there can be many motivations for an action. For those unfamiliar with *Homo sapiens*, they are a bi-gender species where sex performs social bonding and recreational functions. By *Homo sapiens* standards, Rowan is an 'aquatic predator noted for its stream-line body plan and lovely colours'. You, in part, rescued her to be your mate."

Ryan smiled, nodded, then became grave. "It has always been and will always be Rowan's choice. I'm just lucky she chose me."

"I'm the lucky one." Rowan pushed into Ryan's side.

Ryan continued. "But seriously, Spuqupa. There is more to this than most sentients know. In the UES, clones are second-class citizens. Denied access to good jobs, abused, looked down on. After my cloning, I was banned from ever visiting Earth. My family disowned me, and I was forced to leave the Space Combat Corps. They wouldn't even let me join the Planetary Defence Force. I had no reason to stay, and," Ryan stared at Rowan, "every reason to go."

The image shifted to show Spuqupa, who gestured with his tail. "You also had other sentients relying on you."

A hologram of what appeared to be a handsome, muscular, dark-skinned man in a Space Combat Corps dress uniform with retiree braids on the shoulders appeared.

"Let me welcome AI Copernicus class, Henry. First officer of the *Star Hawk*," said Spuqupa.

"Hey, hotty boss, sweetness. Surprised?" The hologram of the android winked at his crewmates.

Ryan and Rowan buried their faces in their hands and shook their heads in matching expressions of exasperation and concern.

"I thought you couldn't arrange for a data feed." Ryan looked up as he addressed Spuqupa.

"I have friends too, you know, hotty boss," remarked Henry.

"Henry, please stop calling me that." Ryan addressed the android's image in long-suffering tones.

"Sure thing, cutey." Henry leered.

"Tell me, Henry, what was it like escaping UES territory, and why did you assist Ryan in his effort?" asked Spuqupa.

"First off, Ryan is my captain and a sexy one at that. Rowan is my friend and a hot little number who I'd love to—"

"Henry!" Rowan's tone promised a thousand things, not one of them enjoyable.

"Sure thing, sweetness!" Henry grinned at Rowan. "My second reason is the UES cheats. I was set to buy myself out when they re-assigned me to serve as the operating system of an Amun Class heavy cruiser. Can you guess how long it would take me to buy that body on an XO's salary? I got myself rogered, and not in a fun way, trying to get the money to buy myself." Henry looked at his captain and friend with a devotion free of his usual flirtation. "Ryan saved my circuits. Now, I'm a free AI. The UES can't touch me under the provisions of the Republic Resolution of AI rights and emancipation. When they left me for scrap, they said I had no value. I was bought clear of my service period. Ryan salvaged me and brought me back." Henry's voice changed, taking on a very sultry female tone. "He's the best daddykins ever."

"Henry, keep it up, see how it works out for you, you polymer prat," remarked Ryan.

Spuqupa made the splashing motion with his paws. "Moving on. You are currently preparing to transit cargo and personnel for the Republic Disaster Relief Agency to Murack Five, the homeworld of the kangazoids."

The image shifted to where Ryan sat with Rowan.

Ryan looked stressed. "It was a condition of my sentence. I swore I'd never go back to the Murack system. Too many bad memories. But the sentence kept me out of UES territory where I'm guilty of theft because I liberated Rowan."

"Because you're a hero, and S.E.T.E. and the United Earth Systems parliament are slavers without a shred of moral decency!" added Rowan.

Ryan sighed, then forced a smile. "Row, why not tell them what you really think. I hate e-entertainments more than most. I was married, my wife is still alive in a narrow sense of the word. She's hopelessly e-addicted and in a facility. That said, Sensory Entertainment/Terraforming Engineers gave me a job when no one else would hire a 'fakey' and is a major source of revenue for the UES. The people working there are just that, people. People do what they must, and *Homo sapiens* have been sold a bill of goods. Many people want to revise the way clones are treated. They just need something to focus that desire on."

Rowan nodded. "I still like coelenteratezoids better."

"That must have been a 'clear sea with coloured coral' passing through the coelenteratezoid habitat zone. We'll continue with that right after this advertisement," said Spuqupa.

The screen shifted to the image of a device with many robotic arms brushing and pampering a green-furred otterzoid. A wave of pleasurable, mildly erotic sensations flowed over Rowan's skin.

LAW AND CONTRACTS

2

"Michael Strongbow, Chief Studio Executive of S.E.T.E. You wanted to speak with me?" Mike pivoted his office chair in front of his imported oak desk so that he stared into the wall screen. He was a ruggedly handsome, silver-haired man who still carried himself with a military bearing despite the over five decades since his discharge.

A woman who looked like a blonde, middle-aged version of Rowan stared out of the screen. "Hello, Mike. It's been a long time."

"Hilda?" breathed Michael, a note of shock colouring his tone.

"It's me. I never bothered to get the work reversed."

"You look well. The AS-F look tends to age well."

Hilda's image leaned back on the screen, her tight red dress showing her figure to good effect. "Thank you. You're as handsome as ever. The silver suits you."

Michael turned to glance at the screen on his desk. Someone in accounting was questioning a requisition notice for a modified surrogate's telemetry pack configured for a felinezoid. He noted that the pack was already shipped before he confirmed the transfer. Next, a staffing schedule for the *Freedom's Run* controllers came up for his approval. "Hilda, not to be rude, but I have a ton of work to do. What do you want?"

"Can't I just be feeling nostalgic?" she asked with a coquettish smile.

"People change, but I doubt that much," observed Michael.

"You could always read me. Fine. I have been retained by John Wilson in his case against S.E.T.E. and you personally. We are claiming that you engineered the abduction of the Rowan character in an expressed effort to discredit my client and disrupt the operation of his autonomous show. We challenge that you exceeded your authority as studio head when you arranged with the Gaian military and legal forces to perform the exercise that led to the theft of the Rowan property. Also, that you, with malicious intent, endangered the entire e-entertainment industry. Furthermore, you have actively aided and abetted in the escape of the fugitive Ryan Chandler and are guilty of insider trading. There are other charges in the files I sent to S.E.T.E.'s legal department, but those are the major ones. I just wanted to tell you in person."

"And why would I do any of those things?" Michael clenched his hand outside of the video pickup's frame.

"You have reason to want to bring down the definition of human that keeps fakeys in their place. It shouldn't be too hard to prove you suffer from the Pygmalion Delusion. How is Marcy?" Hilda smiled maliciously out of the screen.

Michael's eyes strayed to the oil painting of his wife in her youth that hung on his wall. Most who saw it thought it was a memento from his first hit series, a tribute to a long-dead character. Only a few knew the truth that he had fallen in love with his creation and rescued her. Taking her as his best friend, beloved, equal and wife. Fewer still could prove that Marcy was anything but a born woman who'd had her appearance altered to match the AH-F series clone.

"Hilda, I will warn you once because of the woman I thought you were long ago. Don't do this. There are things in play you do not understand, and you don't want me as an enemy!" Michael's face was stern, and his voice was like iron.

"Oh, poor Michael, someone you can't intimidate. Have your lawyers contact me, ciao."

The screen went blank. Michael took a few deep breaths as thoughts raced through his mind.

"Gene," he spoke to the studio computer.

"Yes, Mr. Strongbow," answered the computer.

"Ask Arlene from *Freedom's Run* to stop by my office at her earliest convenience. Also, contact my wife's handheld, then enact scramble and full privacy. I'll let you know when to resume normal operations."

"Yes, Mr. Strongbow," replied the studio computer from a wall speaker.

A moment later, the wall screen filled with the image of a woman with red hair and a compact figure. She was dressed in a white blouse and black slacks and held a flute in one hand.

"Beloved. Always happy to see you, but I'm almost up for rehearsal," greeted the woman.

"Marcy, we may have a bit of a problem."

Ryan walked down the broad corridors of the spiderzoid section of the Switchboard Station. The walls, ceiling and floor were covered in vines. He wondered if he could survive the heat and humidity long enough to reach his destination.

A spiderzoid entered the corridor ahead of him, walking on the ceiling, its ten dexterous legs scuttling along with an ease that made a lie to gravity. Its body was about the size of a pony, and vents formed lines along its bulbous opisthosoma, which seemed to inflate and deflate. It paused on the ceiling and regarded Ryan with large, black, multifaceted eyes. Then it stepped back as its black mandibles came together, making clicking sounds.

Ryan moved his hands in front of his chest and touched his fingertips together as he noted the lack of horns over the eyes. "Greetings, good sir. Is this the correct passage to reach the university? I have an appointment with Doctor Kaakaasee of the exo-horticultural department."

The spiderzoid shuddered. "I am sorry. It is uncommon for us to have alien visitors." The translator nanobots made the spiderzoid's voice sound rich and resonant. "I am Junior Scholar Saakquna from the department of exo-biology. If you follow this passage, you will come to the nest trees of advanced studies."

"My gratitude." Ryan dipped his head.

The spiderzoid tentatively scuttled along the ceiling, seeming to keep its multi-faceted eyes partially trained on Ryan until it passed over him.

Ryan continued down the passage until he came to a place where it opened into a large chamber. Trees with dark green, leathery leaves grew up from the ground, which was covered with vines sporting broad, variegated, yellow and green leaves. What looked like ropes crisscrossed the space between the trees. Maybe a dozen spiderzoids perched in hammocks made of a ropy substance that were suspended between the lines. Every set of multi-faceted eyes in the area turned to regard him. The sound of clicking mandibles filled the air.

"Captain Ryan Chandler," a cultured voice drew Ryan's gaze to a pony-sized spiderzoid that walked towards him over the ground. The small horns over its eyes told Ryan that it was a female of the species.

"Doctor Kaakaasee?" asked Ryan.

"I am she. I hold no weapon in my dominant claw." The spiderzoid held its front claw out. Ryan took the claw in his hand and gently shook it.

"A fascinating tradition. My sister's second son spoke with you a few days ago. He told me about it. He is a bright child and simply fascinated with alien species. It is probably a result of living on the Switchboard Station," Kaakaasee continued.

"He seemed a nice youth," observed Ryan.

"He is how I learned of your situation. He has followed your exploits since that day. I admit, with some regret, that, in general, spiderzoids do not concern ourselves with the other species. You are all so aggressive. As such, his interest is fortuitous. Let us go to a discussion tree so we can be comfortable."

Ryan followed Doctor Kaakaasee to where what looked like a rope dangled down from what resembled a large hammock.

"Oh my. I am sorry, I did not think." Kaakaasee looked from the hammock to Ryan.

Ryan touched the dangling line. It was as soft as silk. He tugged on it and smiled. "Not an issue. *Homo sapiens* are evolved from an arboreal species. We haven't lost all the skills quite yet." Grabbing the line, Ryan pulled himself up to the hammock.

Doctor Kaakaasee released a humming sound, then bounded up another line and moved to help Ryan scramble into the hammock. "Most impressive. Many species will not even attempt the climb. Evolved from an arboreal, you say. I do need to make the time to read *A Space Traveller's Guide to Homo Sapiens*. My nephew has been urging me to do so. Please settle yourself."

"Thank you." Ryan tucked himself into one corner of the hammock while Doctor Kaakaasee settled so that two of her legs were partially wrapped around him.

"I know you must be put upon with preparations for your voyage. Keka saw the request for storage space for a cargo of Earth species trees you must offload to make room for the relief supplies. I believe we may be able to help each other."

"How?" asked Ryan.

"If there is one thing we have an abundance of in the spiderzoid segment of the Switchboard Station, it is space. My people are disinclined from associating with members of other species. As such, while we must maintain a population on the Switchboard Station for political and trading reasons, it is much smaller than our sector can accommodate."

"Are you offering to store my cargo?" asked Ryan.

"In a way. The university will make a storage area available to you on the condition that we are allowed to use some of your trees in our experiments."

The hammock rocked. A moment later, a male spiderzoid appeared over the edge of the construct and passed Kaakaasee two green-skinned objects that resembled small watermelons.

"Did you grow them yourself?" Kaakaasee clicked her pincers. "Never mind. You are here now. Take a perch. Captain Chandler, this is Krakkeen, a junior scholar from my department. He will be taking passage with you to Murack Five."

"Nice to meet you, Krakkeen." Ryan dipped his head to the newcomer.

"Please, refresh yourself, Captain. Crumpa melons are on the approved list for *Homo sapiens* consumption," continued Kaakaasee.

Ryan took the melon, then, after a moment's thought, pulled a utility tool from a holster on his belt, flipped open the blade and cut into the fruit. The pulp was wet and went a long way to quenching his thirst while the taste was sweet with an underscore like nutmeg. "This is very nice."

Kaakaasee extracted a small, pointed mandible by her oral cavity from her fruit. "It pleases me you like it. So many of our foods do not suit the palates of species who digest internally."

"We were talking about storing my cargo. I'll also need space for my spare parts."

"That should not be a problem. What do you know of the world Vidgoss 3?"

"It's one of the spiderzoid colony worlds, isn't it?"

"Yes. It is a lovely planet. We started bioforming it ten thousand years ago. The tropical regions are beautiful. If you did not know better, you could mistake it for Gallab."

"Your homeworld," Ryan confirmed.

"Yes. The problem is, Gallab is a jungle world. We have almost no axial tilt, and aside from some deserts around the equatorial zone, we have little climate diversity. Vidgoss 3, however, has a strong axial tilt. There are entire continents in both the northern and southern regions that have... What is it called? The season with low thermal energy where water solidifies."

"Winter," supplied Ryan.

"Yes. We have tried to adapt our flora to deal with the cold time, but by and large, have been unsuccessful. My research aims to adapt species of food-bearing flora from alien biospheres to integrate with the bioforming that has already been accomplished on Vidgoss 3. The species would have to accept the normal bacteria and insects that have survived on the cold continents and could not become invasive species damaging the more tropical habitats. If we could grow the fruits and nuts of other worlds on the waste sections of Vidgoss, we could make a fortune selling them on the speciality food markets throughout the Spiderzoid Collective of Worlds."

"Would you want all my trees?" asked Ryan.

"Only a few. Perhaps fifteen to cover the initial rental of the storage area. Then we would pay you the cost of any beyond that we use. Frankly, my budget is small. Trading space for the living trees will allow me to do more in-depth research."

"Why not set up solar reflectors and warm the cold continents?" Ryan found his interest piqued as he looked at an engineering problem.

"To add that much energy to the climatic system would be highly disruptive to the planet's ecology. There is little to be gained by making a forest in the north if it creates a desert in the south."

Ryan nodded. "I think you have a deal. Let me call Rowan. She's my trading officer. She can handle the details." Ryan unclipped his handheld from his belt and called up Rowan's contact code.

"You see, Krakkeen, here is a male that has sense. He lets the female handle the money. I have always said, males have no head for resource allocation. If you had sense like that, you might not have to go to Murack Five, and I wouldn't have to break in a new research assistant."

"Wake up," hissed Kendra from the tiller of the raft.

"What? Huh," breathed Medwin from where he lay in the craft's bottom with Armina cuddled against him.

"Five more minutes," grumbled Obert.

"Something's happening. Look." Kendra pointed to the west over a rocky barren with occasional bits of scrub plants to an object that seemed to float a few metres off the ground.

Medwin brought the binoculars to his eyes and examined the object more closely. It was black with what appeared to be windows on a bubble-like protuberance at one end. It was hard to guess its size, but he estimated it was as large as the super tankers he'd seen in movies.

"It's just a balloon," blurted Armina, who knelt behind him.

"Armina, take the tiller. Medwin, let me look?" Kendra bumped Medwin's hand, asking for the binoculars.

"Where are the jets? I mean, it seems so… quiet. It has to be huge, so how can it fly with no noise?" Obert gazed at the object.

Medwin passed Kendra the binoculars. "Why would it be loud? The show stated that they have antigravity. When you can control gravity, why waste energy on thrust? Just drop your specific gravity to the point where you float in the atmosphere. Jets only have to supply propulsion, not lift."

"It's coming this way!" Kendra stared through the binoculars and pointed.

"Armina, steer us to shore. Whatever that is, I want ground under our feet if it tries anything." Medwin watched as the craft drew closer.

An otter swam across the raft's course, avoiding a collision. It then turned and watched the teens.

"Too fast for a balloon," commented Obert.

The river widened into a lake, and the current pushed them into it. As it drew closer, the craft looked larger. It corrected course so that it passed over the lake about two metres above the surface. The rising sun cast its ebony-like exterior into sharp relief. The airship crossed the lake, then sank out of view behind a small ridge.

Medwin turned to look at his cohorts. "That's it then. Gunther was right."

"No. No..." cried Armina. "I don't believe it! That... That was a weather balloon, that's all. Or some kind of float, like they have for parades in the big cities. I am not a fake!" The girl began to sob.

Medwin moved to her side and hugged her. "It's okay. We're real, no matter what."

"No, we're not. Not if we were grown in a tank." She sobbed into his chest.

"Shh," hissed Obert.

"What?" began Medwin.

"Shut up and listen." Obert cocked his ears.

"I hear it. A kind of roaring sound, what is it?" asked Kendra.

"It sounds like the summers when I worked at the hydroelectric plant. I think we should go ashore." Obert moved to put the oars in the raft's oarlocks.

"We should get closer first. Make sure," suggested Kendra.

"No, we shouldn't. If that is a power dam, the currents will be a mess. We could get sucked under." Obert started rowing towards the bank.

Minutes later, they hauled the raft onto the desolate rock barren.

"I guess it's on foot from here," remarked Medwin.

"Beats drowning," countered Obert.

"Where can we hide the raft?" Armina scanned the scrub grasses and small plants that clung to life in places where soil had accumulated in crevices in the rock. There was nothing of a size that would help them.

"Good question." Medwin kicked the ground, adding another scuff to the toe of his battered hiking boot.

"There are loose rocks. We can deflate the raft and bury it in a cairn," suggested Kendra.

"We could just go back." Armina's voice was pleading.

"Good suggestion, Kendra," remarked Medwin. "Okay, people. Pull out your packs. I'd like to see what's on the other side of this dam. If that is what it is."

"Why is it so desolate? It's not like Sun Valley at all. It's ugly," Armina half-whispered.

"It's like they said in *Freedom's Run*. This isn't Earth. It's Gaia, a world in the process of being terraformed by humans. Remember Ryan told Rowan that there were only small pockets where the terraforming had reached stage four. Part of what the set region does is establish an area of advanced terraforming so the original biology humans can steal it and have a nice place to live."

"What do you think they do to us clones after we do all the work of planting trees and making things nice?"

Kendra's question was answered by an uncomfortable silence as Medwin unscrewed the plug that would deflate the raft.

Ryan extracted the metre and a half long pipe-like grav-lifts from the last of the plant support boxes he had transferred to the spiderzoid cargo dock. Each of the metre cubes was topped with a sapling. The huge chamber held the *Star Hawk* at one end. The retrofitted military heavy lander looked like a black cabochon supported on a host of tubular legs ending in three-clawed feet, with an open ramp leading into what could generously be called the bottom of its stern.

"It's hot in here." Rowan stood from checking the bio-feeds on a support box Ryan had deposited earlier. She wore shorts and a sports bra, and still, sweat glistened on her skin.

"Spiderzoid room temperature. Kaakaasee will adjust it down when she moves the trees from the dock to the university's storage chamber."

"It's the humidity that knots my tail. It's worse than the otterzoid section." Kitoy moved to Ryan's side. The petite, felinezoid female had cougar tan fur and was slightly taller than Ryan. Her cheetah-like features reflected irritation. "Why didn't they take delivery immediately? They could have helped us unload."

"Kaakaasee sent her apologies, but she felt it would traumatize the students to have to work with non-spiderzoids. They tend to be xenophobic and of a delicate psychological disposition." Ryan shrugged.

"In Sun Valley, we called them snowflakes," remarked Rowan.

"How are units one through twenty?" asked Ryan.

"All fine. These support boxes are a nice design." Kitoy swished her tail leisurely as she spoke.

"When we're back in the *Star Hawk*, start working out our clearances to the Republic dock. Now that we have room, we should load up ASAP. I don't trust that idiot Crapper not to pull something, and Star Searcher is insistent about our departure time. I've never known space traffic control to be so inflexible on a transit time. Hive minds are a pain to deal with." Ryan's voice held stress.

"I think you're right about Captain Crapper, Da... Fa... Captain. I've spent more time with him than any of you. He is an entitled fool with a sense of his own privilege. The Spacing Corps would be well rid of him." Tim stood from adjusting the controls on one of the support boxes. He looked a lot like Ryan, and since Ryan's cloning, no one could be faulted for thinking they were brothers, not father and son.

Ryan snapped, "Is the problem fixed?"

"Just a minor adjustment to the enzyme feed. It must have been decalibrated by high G manoeuvres. The support boxes aren't made to take them." Tim's voice held hurt and shame.

Ryan took a deep breath. "Sorry. I'm stressed. I swore I'd never go back to Murack Five, and that's exactly where I'm going. How can the divine in its myriad names be so cruel?"

"It will be all right. Take a deep breath." Rowan moved to Ryan's side and hugged him around the waist.

"I... I just want to get through this. I'm sorry, everyone. Murack Five, well..." he trailed off.

Kitoy's eyes dilated compassionately, and she patted her captain's shoulder with her tail. "You'll get through this. Kadar told me about it. I understand a little. We're all here to help."

Ryan smiled. "Thanks. I'm going aboard. Let me know when we can close the seal. The sooner started, the sooner finished. Kitoy, could you get on with the station AI again? We need the list of who and what we have as passengers to refit the quarters for their comfort. Get a copy to Tim as soon as it comes in. Tim, adjust the various berths' climate for our guests' environmental norms. If there are any major alterations, consult with me. Rowan, make sure we have appropriate ration packs for everyone. Check the inventory when it comes aboard, don't trust the invoice. One time during the Swampla defensive, our quartermaster trusted the data. Three months with nothing but raw fish and seaweed." Ryan strode up the loading ramp.

Rowan watched him with a concerned expression.

"He is strong. He'll be all right," comforted Kitoy.

Rowan hung her head. "I... the worst part is he won't let

me in. All I know about Murack Five is what I've read."

"It was bad. A ground ship's antiproton stores blew up. It decimated the planet," observed Tim.

"Kadar helped Ryan save a population of kangazoids before the radiation wave reached them. That's the only reason the Republic didn't bomb every species involved back into the stone age. That's also why Ryan, Kadar and Kate all have stars on the wall of heroes on Murrow. There are only nineteen non-felinezoids so honoured on my homeworld," added Kitoy.

"I didn't know about the star," remarked Rowan.

"Neither did I, and I would have been around when he received it." Tim shook his head. "The human media tried to downplay the whole thing. I think the government was afraid that the people would panic at the threat of Republic retribution."

"That's what I mean. I can see that Ryan is hurting, but he just won't talk about it. I want to help so much, but what can I do when he won't open up?" Rowan sighed.

"I saw my dad when he came back from that. You know, in his old body. He was the same way, and there were the cancers on top of it all. Mom was no help. She'd already stuck her head into the e-rig. I tried to be there for him but getting in was like breaking through a polycarbonate wall."

Rowan looked at Tim and nodded. "For Ryan's sake, we let bygones be bygones. Whether he knows it or not, he needs us."

Tim nodded back at her. "For the record, this is late in coming, but you are a person, Rowan. A damn fine one. I'm glad you love my father."

Rowan smiled just a little.

"After dinner, we should all stay at Kate and Saggal's place. I'll ask Saggal to take Ryan for a drink, just the males. Kate won't mind you using their e-rig."

"I don't like e-entertainments!" stated Rowan.

"This one, you will. It's felinezoid, no forced emotions. I think it might help you understand what Ryan is going through. Both of you." Kitoy swished her tail.

"He won't like me coming along. Kate and Saggal are his friends, and he's still… Well, I know the only reason I'm aboard is that he needed an environmental tech to meet the government regulations." Tim focused on the floor as sweat dripped off him.

"Tim, if I can let you trying to hand me over to the U.E.S. go for Ryan's good, then so can he. I never wanted to come between you." Rowan's tone, while not friendly, did hold a note of understanding.

Tim smiled. "I always said that Dad had taste when it came to women. I love my mom, but I think as he got older, he developed sense as well."

Rowan smiled broadly.

"*Homo sapiens* are so strange. Let's get aboard and out of this humidity. It's making my fur all frizzy," grumbled Kitoy.

Gunther wrapped plaster around the leg of what appeared to be a two-metre-tall humanoid tabby cat. "If felinezoid healing rates are anything like *Homo sapiens*, you should be in this cast for about a month and a half. At least you'll be able to get around on crutches."

Toronk swished his tail happily. "It will be a relief to be mobile again."

The translator nanobots on the speech centre of Gunther's brain lent the alien's voice a friendly tone. Gunther began wiping the excess plaster from his muscular forearms as a smile crossed his handsome, middle-aged features. The plaster that spattered the battered T-shirt he wore over his solid chest was beginning to harden. "Just remember to come for the telepathic integration sessions." Gunther glanced at an odd assortment of equipment that filled the corner of his basement. The 'telepathy booster' was, in fact, a jamming system. When it was active, it created the only place in Sun Valley where they could plan without being monitored by the studio controllers. The only place to prepare for their rebellion.

"Angel and I will be there. With all the upheaval in our group, the understanding it grants is useful." Toronk played his role. Then his tail quivered, and his eyes dilated. "It has helped me set aside much of my guilt about certain things."

Gunther couldn't help but sense the felinezoid's surface thoughts. The infidelity the controllers had forced several of the *Angel Black* cast to engage in had threatened to tear them apart. Even knowing what he knew, Gunther found it hard to forgive Carl for his affair with Willa.

Aloud Gunther said, "Fran and Carl have patched things up. It was likely a response to the felinezoid DNA grafted into her that she enticed you. Pheromones can have a potent effect."

Gunther clamped down on his emotions to keep them from registering on the control boards. He'd learned that only his thoughts were his own. Everything else the controllers monitored and manipulated. He imagined his revenge. His revenge for them tricking him into killing on the pretext of defending his world from alien pirates. His revenge for them forcing his Willa, his wife, to have an affair with a man half her age. His revenge for them deciding to kill his daughter, Rowan, forcing Ryan to take her to the stars. He cut off the line of thought as he felt his anger build.

Troy ran his fingers through his scraggly straw-coloured hair, then smoothed his shirt over his scarecrow-like body. "Gunther is pissed. Of course, it's only been a few days. I hope he and Willa get back to where they were now that she's made her choice. Not that she ever had much choice with the manipulations John ordered. Prat!"

Reaching forward, Troy let a trickle of euphoric into Gunther's system, then added a pain inhibitor to Toronk's. Glancing to the other screens, he noted that Farley was brushing Quinta's fur. The female otterzoid made little cooing sounds and rubbed her chin suggestively over the twenty-something Asian homo-sapiens' groin.

"Again," muttered Troy. "At least I don't have to enhance one couple. Better than the jerk deserves after cheating on Rowan. Let it drop, Troy. Bugger had no more choice than Willa and Toronk. I hate this job! I wish I could tell you that Rowan made it to the Switchboard Station. Not knowing has got to hurt. Oh well, that's e-entertainments."

SUFFERING FOOLS

Ryan settled in the pilot's station on the *Star Hawk*'s horseshoe-shaped bridge. The central captain's chair was empty. Rowan sat to his left at the navigator's station while Kitoy and Henry occupied the communications and computer control stations behind him to his right. Tim sat at the environmental control, behind and to Ryan's left, while the engineering and weapons control consoles were fronted by empty seats. The bridge's entry door occupied the back of the room.

"I'm glad to be out of that heat." Rowan was freshly cleaned and wore a floral print spring dress.

"Tell me about it. It took three passes through the Groom-O-Matic Kate and Saggal gave me to get my fur straight," agreed Kitoy.

"I'd comb your fur for you, hotty cat." Henry made a growling sound from his duty station and reached towards Kitoy, making a raking motion with the fingers of his remaining arm. The straps that held his torso to the duty chair pulled tight against him with the action. The unburnt side of his face sported a leer that looked macabre on the damaged side. A mass of fibre-optic feeds connected him to the *Star Hawk*'s computer station.

"I'll stick with the Groom-O-Matic. Without... hips, you don't want to start what you can't finish," Kitoy teased with a corresponding lash of her tail.

"Hotty boss, you gotta help a brother out." Henry added a pleading quality to his voice.

Ryan shook his head and watched on the screen that filled the curved end of the bridge as the hangar bay doors closed behind the *Star Hawk*, hiding the saplings behind their bulk. "Be good little trees. I still want to see you grow up on Geb." Turning a knob, he changed the screen's view to the bow.

"Little Mountain Tree." Rowan chuckled.

"The coelenteratezoids loved you. Green-Blue-Red-Purple-Yellow sent me a message. The university was thrilled with your talk, and they've found a freelance editor for the e-data they collected as you moved through their sector. The show they've made should be hitting the human entertainment services within a month," said Ryan.

"They're good... is people a polite word to use?" Rowan bit her lip.

"The spirit behind the word is more important than the label. Just so you know, you get it better than most *Homo sapiens*," answered Kitoy.

On the big screen, the bay's exterior doors retracted, revealing the star-speckled black of space.

"Kitoy, call space traffic control for clearance to the docking spar, then get on to the Republic loading dock and tell them we're coming in tomorrow morning," ordered Ryan.

Seconds later, Kitoy relayed, "Clearance granted."

"Exiting on manoeuvring thrusters. This shouldn't take lo—" Ryan stalled the *Star Hawk*'s forward momentum as a huge shadow moved across the star-scape.

"That idiot again!" spat Henry.

Ryan shook his head. "Kitoy, call space traffic control and pipe in the frequency they're using with the *Chimera*."

"*Star Hawk*. Please hold position due to unforeseen traffic control issues." A high-pitched nasal voice came over the radio.

"What's on control today?" asked Rowan.

"Log says crabzoid, gatherer component One-Two-Six of the Star Searcher individuality, sweetness. Can count on them not letting a course deviation slide. Sticklers, the whole hive-minded lot of them," remarked Henry.

"Don't we all know that." Rowan sighed as she thought back to the Star Searcher component judge at Ryan's trial who wouldn't acknowledge the extenuating circumstances.

"*Chimera*, you are not authorized to change location in station-controlled space. Return to your assigned holding pattern!" the nasal voice continued.

"The *Chimera* is broadcasting a visual feed. Should I put it up?" asked Kitoy.

Ryan sighed. "Why not? It should be good for a laugh. Record it just in case. Crapper would be funny if he wasn't an embarrassment to the species."

The *Star Hawk*'s screen filled with the image of a bridge identical to the *Star Hawk*'s save that all the stations were occupied by *Homo sapiens* dressed in the coverall, UES Space Services duty uniform without retiree braids across the shoulder patches. A fat, bald man occupied the captain's chair. Even seated, it was apparent he was exceptionally tall for a *Homo sapiens*.

"I am Captain Crapper of the UES Space Combat Corps Vessel *Chimera*. I am intercepting criminals aboard that vessel on behalf of the UES Legal Corps and Parliament." Crapper postured self-importantly.

The nasal voice replied. "This gatherer component has full knowledge about the circumstances involving the *Star Hawk*, whose crew are on assignment with the Republic Disaster Relief Service. They are in good standing with all Republic laws. As such, you have no authority unless they should enter UES territory. This gatherer component is ordering you to return your vessel to its assigned holding pattern."

Crapper went red in the face, making the tracery of lines on his nose stand out. "Listen to me, you self-important piece of sushi!"

Ryan gasped. "Kitoy, get me a channel to space traffic

control! Audio-visual."

Ryan stood and pulled his arms in tight, so they crossed over his chest, and tucked in his chin as the main screen filled with the image of what looked like a six-legged crab with its back covered with waving cilia. The crabzoid gathering component stood on two legs and waved the other four wildly.

"Gatherer component One-Two-Six of the Star Searcher individuality, honoured crabzoid traffic controller. I make contrition for my species kin and pray that you remember he is an individual. His communications do not come from any over self. He is as one expelled from the community for his slowing of the processing of information. He should not be heeded. I beg you, do not hold his actions against the whole. He is a gathering component used for dangerous tasks until famine threatens."

The crabzoid stopped clicking its claws and settled onto all six legs.

"*Chimera*, move your vessel, or I will have Republic vessels move it for you. The Star Searcher individuality does not respond kindly to threats and insults. Captain Chandler of the *Star Hawk*. I accept your apology on the part of your over self/species kin/species. The Crapper is indeed a defective gatherer component that should be returned to the nutritional needs of the over self. Proceed along your flight plan as soon as the obstruction is removed."

"Hotty boss, the UES should be loving you long time," commented Henry.

"What happened?" asked Rowan.

"The worst threat/insult you can give a crabzoid is to liken them to food. They consume the defective sub-sections of themselves or use them for high-risk activities. To be called food for them is… well, there is no human equivalent. Think of a death threat coupled with being called ugly, mentally deficient, and for a male, having stunted non-functional genitalia, all rolled into one. The only thing crabzoid individualities have ever fought over was the resources necessary for colony survival. The winner in any war eats the loser in whole or in part. Crapper could have started a war with that remark. It is that heinous to a crabzoid."

"Where'd you pick that up?" asked Kitoy.

"When I found out I would have to work with Star Searcher, I started reviewing *A Space Traveller's Guide to Crabzoids*. I'm about halfway through."

"Glad I muted it when we were coming in. We would have been rogered like a—"

"Henry, it was a good thing. No one needs mental pictures," interrupted Ryan.

"Prude." Turning his attention inward, the android transmitted a blip message to his cohorts on the station. "Priority: Vicky, Bill, tell Michael to trim all references associating crabzoids and food. Seems the species goes cannibal and is ready to roger other species that mention it. Kill my remark from when we approached the station. No surprise for a species that never shags. Frustration's gotta go someplace."

"And defective gatherer component?" asked Kitoy.

"Closest translation for human and felinezoid is mentally deficient or an idiot. The Star Searcher individuality has Crapper pegged," explained Ryan. "Kitoy, record message. Attach a copy of the exchange with Crapper."

Ryan sat in the command chair. "UES Diplomatic Office, William Hart, priority. Bill, you need to do something about Captain Crapper of the *Chimera*. Not only did he violate space traffic control regulations, he called a Star Searcher component food. The man's incompetence is a danger to the UES. Stop him before he gets us into something we can't talk our way out of. I'm attaching a recording of the exchange in question. Bill, if you don't do something, I will release the recording to the news media with an explanation of why it matters. I may not have much love for the UES, but I don't want to see my species in a needless war because of a pompous fool." Ryan returned to the pilot's station. "Kitoy, send the message."

On the *Star Hawk*'s main screen, the *Chimera* moved off. Ryan manoeuvred them out of the space dock and, staying well away from the UES section of the station, flew them to the Republic docking spar where they meshed airlocks.

"That will do until they get the cargo set for loading. Let's lock her up." Ryan began the piloting and engineering post-flight procedures while the others turned to their work.

Vicky lay on the work couch in the Hedonism Incorporated maintenance room. Her body was missing from the waist down. The walls were lined with equipment, and various tools lay on a counter beyond her feet. Engineering readouts displayed on a screen at the head of the work bench.

"Are you sure you want us to fix the Luba in CC-F emulation mode, Vicky? It's not too late to change your mind," asked a *Homo sapiens* woman with light brown hair pulled into a bun, wearing a white coverall that conformed to a pleasant figure. Her tan skin was nearly flawless. She stood by an identical maintenance cot where a form that could have been Vicky's twin, save that the body was complete, lay dormant.

"It's what I want, Sadye. Bill likes the module, and I'm used to it," explained Vicky.

"You're a lucky one. Most of the men I know are mad for strange." Sadye checked her handheld. "You want the chassis to emulate early middle age?"

Vicky shrugged. "Looks better in court, and you've seen Bill." A smile touched the android's lips. "My husband isn't as young as he used to be. People keep mistaking me for his daughter. It gets annoying!"

"Good news is, human computing has advanced a lot

since you first emulated a *Homo sapiens*. The new chassis will have almost double the free external ram and four times the onboard memory. I've been over your schematics. We should have the Luba adapted to accommodate you by tomorrow afternoon. Your core system is intact and stable. That Ryan guy who saved you knew his stuff. Half the engineers out there would have blown your processing core to stardust trying to pull off that stunt."

"Ryan is an exceptional individual," agreed Vicky.

A handheld that Vicky had left on the counter buzzed.

"Would you mind?" Vicky gestured towards the device.

"Of course. We could build in a receiver." Sadye moved to get the handheld.

"Would you want one built-in? The hand-held is annoying enough." Vicky arched a perfect eyebrow over a beautiful brown eye.

"C and P that. Here you go." Sadye passed Vicky the handheld.

"Mrs. Hart. I just wanted to confirm that the unit for Mrs. Al-Qahtani was on station. The operating theatre is booked for tonight." The image of a cougar tan felinezoid male stared out of the screen. The sound that came out of the handheld was an incomprehensible series of growls and hisses to Sadye.

Vicky released a sentence in felinezoid. "The unit arrived this morning by diplomatic courier. My husband should have it to you within the hour."

"Good, implantation is a simple matter, but it is not a common piece of equipment on the station. Are you sure Mrs. Al-Qahtani is cognizant of what the unit will do?"

"She has financial debt. Accepting the unit will see that absolved. I am counting on your discretion."

"Of course. I will see you and Mrs. Al-Qahtani this evening."

The screen went blank.

"It is so amazing you don't need to use the translator

function." Sadye moved to Vicky's side and began restoring the temporary seals over her intact sectors.

"Has to be some advantages to having a throat made out of polycarbonate."

Ryan, Rowan, Kitoy and Tim passed through the metre-wide troughs of felinezoid customs. Jets of air blew over them, then were collected and analyzed.

"Hello, Captain Chandler," greeted the two-metre-tall leopard stripe felinezoid, who wore a green sash with two gold lines on it over his shoulder.

"Good to see you, Haaastsss," Ryan struggled not to mutilate the name while letting the translator nanobots deal with the rest.

"Your accent is getting better. I won't fault you on not getting the ultrasonics. All part of living on the Switchboard Station. Have you been in the spiderzoid sector?"

"I left my trees with them."

"Explains it. You have trace amounts of captit pollen on you. Nothing to worry about, but you know the sniffer units. Too sensitive by half." Haaastsss lashed his tail and flared his nostrils in the felinezoid equivalent of a smile.

Ryan smiled back. The story of his liberation of Rowan from UES Station Security had catapulted him and Rowan into celebrity status on the station.

"Tech is only as good as its designer."

"Move along and tell Saggal and Kate that they should stock up at Wesnakee. Customs administration is talking about doing a review. That always makes for delays." Haaastsss waved Ryan through with his tail.

"I'll pass it on." Ryan stepped into the customs' receiving area of the felinezoid sector. Moving across the large room populated mostly by felinezoids of all shapes and sizes, he joined Rowan, Kitoy and Tim.

"I let him scan my thumbprint. I mean, what are you

going to say?" remarked Rowan.

"Shall we get dinner?" interjected Ryan.

"Go on without me. I have something I need to take care of." Kitoy swished her tail nervously.

"I could go with you if you want company?" Tim patted Kitoy's arm. He recognized the tail lash as showing agitation.

"No, I... I need to do this alone." Her pupils dilated as her nostrils quivered. "It has to do with my debt."

"I'm sorry I can't afford to give you an advance, but between getting Rowan treated and legal costs, I'm in the hole myself." Ryan looked grave.

Kitoy swished her tail sadly. "I know. I think I have it covered. I can at least get enough of the debt dealt with that they won't block my travel clearance. I better go, or I'll be late."

Tim found his eyes lingering on Kitoy as she walked away with feline grace.

"We should move. Saggal told me he was getting takeout, so the food should be edible."

"Is Kate really such a bad cook?" asked Rowan.

"Kate is one of my best friends and one of the finest people I know, but truth is truth. She can make one edible dish, spaghetti. If she manages not to burn the water while she's boiling the pasta," explained Ryan. "Come on." He led the way down the corridor to the in-sector maglev transport. None of them noticed the ubiquitous cleaning robot that followed in their wake.

Minutes later, they walked through the three-metre-wide corridors of the felinezoid sector. The walls were imaged to make it look as if they were following a jungle trail. Occasionally small animals would appear from the foliage and then vanish into the underbrush.

"Murrow must be a beautiful planet," remarked Tim.

"I've never been out of their major city. I've visited Hissmurr on a diplomatic support mission once. It's one of their colony worlds that has reached stage four in its bio forming. The nature zones were very lush," answered Ryan.

"I'm shocked. Someplace in the galaxy you haven't been," teased Rowan.

Ryan sighed and looked downcast. "The felinezoids prefer to do their own killing."

"I'm so…" began Rowan.

Ryan held up his hand. "No, I am. Things have got me on edge."

They came to the door in the hall that marked Saggal and Kate's residence. "Ryan Chandler's party," Ryan spoke to the air.

The door slid into the wall, revealing a comfortably appointed living room with a cushioned sofa flanked by two padded lounging chairs.

Saggal, a chubby grey-tabby-stripe felinezoid, emerged from a narrow hallway at the living room's far end. Kate, a plump *Homo sapiens* woman with tan skin and long, black hair, emerged from the other door in the same wall. Rowan knew that the second door led to the dining room and, beyond that, the kitchen.

"Ryan," the pair spoke in unison. As one, they rushed over and pulled him into a group hug.

"We're so sorry. We just couldn't—" began Kate.

Ryan cut her off. "You've done more than anyone could ask for Rowan and me. Going back to that place is more than anyone could expect."

Kate and Saggal continued to hold their friend. "When you didn't get in touch after the victory party, we were worried that—" began Saggal.

"We've been swamped with preparations," interrupted Rowan. "Clearing cargo and trying to get information out of the Republic bureaucracy is like pulling teeth."

Saggal cringed at the expression. His pupils constricted while his tail lashed.

"Bad expression?" asked Rowan.

"Very old punishment for dishonourable combat on Murrow. Hasn't been practised for thousands of years, but the expression holds on," explained Kate.

"Sorry." Rowan grinned.

"At least you didn't use it in front of your in-laws the first time you met them," Saggal made the hissing sound that served as a felinezoid laugh.

"Mamar, my mother-in-law, still brings that up every time she visits. Thinks I'm a savage."

"You can be, my love, and you know I love it." Saggal stroked his wife's shoulder with his tail.

"Saggal!" Kate blushed. "Dinner's on the table. Saggal got a party pack from the Spicing Grounds. All the seafood you would ever want. We thought Rowan might enjoy trying otterzoid cuisine."

"Thank you."

"Thank you for having me," Tim spoke softly. "I know we haven't been on the best of terms."

Saggal eyed Ryan's son and spoke in measured tones. "Just live up to your father's trust." Saggal stepped back from Ryan and popped his claws. "Or we will have a problem!"

Tim swallowed as he regarded the two-metre-tall predator. "I will."

"Let's eat," said Kate.

"After that, I'm taking Ryan out to show him around. It's not right that you come to the Switchboard Station and do nothing but work. It will be like old times, my breath brother." Saggal's tail swished happily.

"Honestly, Saggal, I'd rather…"

Saggal's tail went straight and rigid. "I won't take no for an answer. We're overdue for a rematch."

Ryan sighed and smiled as Kate led the way into the dining room.

The cleaning robot moved back and forth outside the living area, secretly relaying telemetry from Ryan and Rowan to Henry on the *Star Hawk*.

Kitoy walked down the corridor in the felinezoid sector, stopping in front of a door with a symbol like a leafy plant on it. She spoke softly, "Kitoy Al-Qahtani."

The door retracted into the wall revealing a room with another sliding door opposite her. Seats with slots to accommodate tails lined the walls. The door slid shut behind her as the opposite one opened, allowing Vicky, her humanoid head, arms and torso supported on a wheelchair-like device, and Bill into the waiting room.

"I still can't believe that Ryan and Rowan are making a show for S.E.T.E.," Kitoy blurted.

"Neither can they. That's the only reason they're doing it." Bill shrugged.

"Kitoy, you know how bad it is for clones in the UES. *Freedom's Run* can be a real vehicle for social change. A rallying point for a clones' rights movement. Trust me, that is the only reason I'm involved," remarked Vicky.

"I… I still don't know about being implanted with a telemetry unit. It's, well. It's such an invasion. To have my every move and feeling recorded." Kitoy's nostrils quivered.

"I know, but think. If Humans Ascendant didn't have such a stranglehold on UES policy, Kadar would probably be alive today. *Freedom's Run* will help to fix that." Vicky's voice was soothing as she rolled to Kitoy's side and took the felinezoid's hand in her own.

Kitoy nodded as a trickle of clear liquid dribbled from her nose. "And you'll deal with my debts?"

"All the overdues and for three months into the future," reassured Bill.

"And Henry will handle all the monitoring and editing?" Kitoy unconsciously stroked her abdomen.

"He'll handle the monitoring and the rough editing. The rough edited data will be sent back to the studio for final processing."

"The polymer pervert must love that. Hacking into Ryan

and Rowan when they...." Kitoy pulled back her ears and tapped her chest.

"I'm sure he does." Bill chuckled.

"Are you two sure he won't be able to affect me? You know, make me feel things like a studio clone? That I will not agree to! Especially with that polymer pervert holding the control stick." Kitoy's tail went straight up for emphasis.

"Kitoy, we've been over this. I wrote it into the contract. The telemetry pack and nanobots we got for you are strictly a one-way feed, like the one in Ryan. Henry won't be able to affect your metabolism in any way. Just monitor your sensory inputs and emotions," said Vicky.

"Don't tell Ryan or Rowan any of this. As far as they know, the monitoring stopped when they launched off Gaia. It will be months before the data collected after that point is disseminated, and Mike wants them kept in the dark as long as possible." Bill smiled.

"This Michael sounds like a 'muck dwelling ambush predator'," said Kitoy.

"It's all a matter of perspective. Mike is working inside the system, more or less, to try and affect positive change. Let's get you in to see the doctor."

The waiting room's back door reopened, and Kitoy was led into a small sterile room with an operating table in the middle. A cougar tan felinezoid stood by the far wall fiddling with a piece of equipment. He wore a mask of blue material over his muzzle, and a white smock covered the front of his body.

"Please get up on the surgical area. This won't hurt a bit," ordered the medical felinezoid.

Kitoy obliged.

"I'm told you're a little nervous." The doctor's voice was soothing.

"More about the outcome than the operation, but I've never liked being a patient," replied Kitoy.

"Neither have I. I see in your records that you have rutat."

The doctor clipped an arched device to the surgical cot so that it covered Kitoy's abdomen.

"Does it make a difference?" Kitoy sounded defensive.

"No. I just like to be thorough. You might like to know that there have been some hopeful results in a study conducted by an otterzoid pharmaceutical company. Very preliminary, mind you, but they seem to be making progress. I just thought I'd pass it on."

"Thank you." Kitoy relaxed. She knew the doctor's type now. Got into medicine for the right reasons, and as much as it wouldn't cost him, he wanted to do right by his patients. Her training from United Felinezoid Worlds kicked in, and she found herself mapping out how best to manipulate him. With an effort of will, she halted that stream of thought.

"Just lay back. Your friends can stay until the anaesthetic takes hold. I guarantee, when you wake up, it will be like nothing happened. This is a surprisingly simple procedure. Now watch the ceiling and take a deep breath." The doctor stroked her brow with his furry hand.

Kitoy looked at the ceiling; the next moment, she was being helped to stand by Bill.

"Is it?" Kitoy stroked her abdomen. Not even the fur was disturbed.

"All over. Welcome to the ranks of e-entertainers," said Bill.

"Poor thing," added Vicky. "Just remember, it's for the greater good."

"I've heard that before. It's rarely true." Kitoy sighed.

THE SOURCE OF THE NILE

4

Kate watched as Saggal half-dragged Ryan out the door. "Okay, here it is. Kitoy told me that Ryan won't talk about Murack Five." Kate shuddered. "What you don't know is the money to buy the *Star Hawk* and Ryan's parts ship and for Saggal and me to buy into Wesnakee didn't all come from our mustering out bonuses."

"Where'd it come from then?" asked Tim.

"After the disaster, the felinezoid government commissioned a historical drama. People wanted to know what happened, needed to understand why we came so close to being destroyed. The UES chose to cover up and downplay the whole thing. The United Felinezoid Worlds went the other route. Full disclosure. Part of that was a, I guess you could call it, a documentary. A more or less accurate dramatization of the events. Saggal, Ryan, Kadar, I, and several others you don't know, consulted and agreed to be depicted. They scanned our images to overlay for the visuals. I have a copy of the finished product. I've never experienced it. Kitoy has. She thought it would help her understand Kadar. She thinks you should experience it."

"An e-entertainment." Disgust nearly dripped from Rowan's words.

"Not like you think. It's VR5 with no emotions, like the Spuqupa Report. You're free to feel what you feel and think what you think. They used actors implanted with telemetry units who played out scenes, then overlaid the images of the actual people involved on the data. Kitoy said it was very good. I... Once was more than enough. If you want to experience it, it might give you some insight as to what Ryan is going through."

Rowan and Tim both nodded.

"The interfacing room is just down here." Kate led the way to a door off her residence's hallway that opened to reveal a room containing what looked like two reclining chairs with transparent hoods that could be pulled down over the head section.

"Make yourself comfortable. I'll get the hard storage unit. Just a suggestion. Don't both pick the same perspective. The product review warned that the system could get glitchy if you did."

Kate moved to a set of shelves containing what looked like boxes, each about the size of a hardcover book. "Damn. It's on the top shelf. I'll get a stool."

"I'll get it. Which one?" Rowan scanned the high shelf.

"The blue one with red felinezoid lettering," directed Kate.

The box drifted off the shelf and into Kate's outstretched hand.

"Should you be doing that?" asked Tim.

"No, and don't tell Ryan, he worries. It's just, I've been telekinetic since they took me out of the gestation chamber. I'm used to it. I don't lift anything heavy, and I don't do it in front of Ryan because he freaks out, but it's part of who I am."

"You know it's bad for you, but it feels so good. Your life, just be careful." Kate put the box into a slot on the cube-shaped device between the e-rigs.

Rowan and Tim settled in the e-rigs. "Dibs on Kate's perspective." Rowan's voice was flat.

"I'll steer clear," agreed Tim, then the interface covers descended over their heads.

Medwin shook his head. From the lake side, the dam before him was made of a sheet of some black material. It was cool to the touch. Looking down over its height, it looked like a natural cliff dropping a good two hundred metres to a river below. One side of the riverbank seemed to be covered with a green substance, while the other was as barren as any of the areas they had walked through. A smell like a festering swamp reached his nostrils when the wind gusted from downstream. An eagle soared over the river valley, circling on thermals, never moving out of his line of sight. A single lane road ran along the top of the dam.

"See, it's just a hydroelectric project." Armina's voice blended desperate hope and incredulity.

"I—" began Medwin. He fell silent as something that looked vaguely like a pickup truck floated into the air before him, then settled on the single-lane road.

"Stardust," breathed Kendra.

"What in the divine's myriad names do you think you're doing here?" demanded the barrel-chested, swarthy, middle-aged man driving the vehicle. He was dressed in brown slacks and a green button-down shirt. There were badges depicting a tree with the letters S.E.T.E. emblazoned across them on the shirt's shoulders.

"What do you mean?" Medwin's gaze darted over the simulated cliff face to his right.

"This area is scheduled for an algae drop. You're in the safety exclusion zone. Those dropships aren't precision instruments, you know."

"A what?" began Armina.

"Are you mentally deficient?" demanded the man as he ran his hand through his black hair in frustration. "If they open tanks a second too soon, you'd be washed right off this dam."

"Our friend is from Earth. She doesn't know much about Gaia," Kendra took a chance as she rushed to cover the gaffe.

"Fine then. What's the rest of your excuses? Safety regulations are there for a reason!" The man's expression was tight-lipped.

"We… we were hiking. I guess we got turned around. We thought we were at a safe distance," added Medwin.

"Hiking. In a stage two-zone." The man shook his head.

"It's harder than the e-entertainments make it look," observed Obert. "We wanted to experience it for ourselves. You know, get out into real nature. See the world with our own eyes."

The man smiled and let out a breath. "And maybe see the new set region before it's closed off. I can't fault that. Too many people never pull themselves away from the e-rig. You should have brought along a handheld in case of emergency. Roughing it is all fine and good, but there's still common sense. You'll know for next time. I'm Borak, Borak Ghulam. I'm one of the terraforming techs working on the new set region. You're lucky I came across you on my pre-drop check. I'll give you a lift to the safe zone. You can watch the drop with me. It's something most people don't bother with, but it's something to see."

Medwin shared a look with his friends, shrugged and stepped towards the vehicle.

Kendra took the seat beside Borak while the rest sat in the cargo box, amongst a jumble of equipment.

"So, how long you been out for?" asked Borak as he manoeuvred the vehicle off the dam, keeping its wheels on the ground.

"Just a day and a night. We need to start back after the drop. Armina has work," remarked Kendra.

"After the drop, I can leave you at the studio support town. You can catch a maglev there," observed Borak.

"Thank you, that sounds nice," remarked Medwin from behind the driver's position.

"If you're interested, the studio museum should still be open by the time we get there. It takes a couple of hours, but it's worth the time."

Armina let out a gasp.

"Is your friend all right?" Borak touched a button on his dash and turned in his seat.

"She's fine. Being from Earth, this isn't the type of camping she's used to," Obert lied as Medwin pulled Armina into a comforting hug.

As the vehicle accelerated, a dome of glittering, nearly transparent energy enveloped the passenger and cargo areas. Obert noticed no pull when the vehicle made sharp turns and that Borak wasn't bothering to watch where they were going or steer.

"Next time, you should try the Lake Doig environment zone. It's stage four. You can't tell the difference from the homeworld." Borak's tone became nostalgic. "I'm proud of that effort. I was in on it from stage two on. I love being a terraforming tech, bringing Earth's children to life. Fresh air, sunshine, and a chance to play a role in creation itself. Can't ask better."

"That sounds nice." Kendra smiled warmly at the older man.

"It's real. I'm not much on e-entertainments. Oh, *A Cat's Life* occasionally after a hard day, and *Detective Dave* is good for a laugh, but the rest... Saw enough fighting during the Swampla Defensive."

Armina gave a little gasp. "There's a river coming up."

"Not to worry. This is an outback rover. Older model, that's probably why you didn't recognize it, but she gets the job done." Borak reached forward and threw a switch on his dash.

A hum ran through the vehicle as it lifted a few centimetres into the air. A pair of miniature turbines at its back pushed wind through themselves, propelling the vehicle over the river. Touching down on the opposite bank, Borak threw the switch back up. The hum stilled as the vehicle settled onto its wheels.

"No use in wasting power on anti-grav when wheels can do the job," observed Borak.

Armina buried her face in her hands while Medwin went grey. Obert looked as excited as a child on their birthday. Kendra fought to keep her expression blank.

The vehicle pulled to a stop without any apparent intervention from Borak. They were on a rocky hill that offered a view of a broad valley with a river running its length. The dam formed one end of it, looking like a cliff face from this angle.

Borak flipped open a handheld that he'd kept in a holster on his belt and folded out the screen. He scanned the display, then tapped an icon in its corner.

"Green Sky Seven, this is ground two. It's clear for drop my sector." He spoke slowly and clearly into the device.

"Acknowledged, clear for drop."

A hum came from above. They looked up to see a craft that must have been a half kilometre in all dimensions fly over. Its shadow blotted out the sky, then it was over the valley at maybe two metres above the ground. A line of hatches opened at the craft's back, releasing a green, semi-liquid substance. The substance spilled out, carpeting the ground. Moments later, the smell of rotting algae touched the breeze. Green Sky Seven paralleled the river until the distance made it look like a child's toy.

Medwin watched through the binoculars as the flow of semi-liquid gunk from the craft stopped and the hatches closed. Then the craft turned west and sped out of view.

"They'll do a couple dozen more trips like that from what I hear of the size of that algae bloom. Then set up some sprinklers from the river to clear the worst of the salt. Give it a month, that whole area will be a blanket of flowers. Give the surrogates a nice start when they take possession. Stink to the stars when they break the surface until the algae mixes with the inorganics. Still, the land is coming to life, and that's a great thing!"

"That..." Armina stared open-mouthed, pale and shaking.

"That's incredible. Do they mix seeds into the algae?" asked Obert.

"After they skim it from the oceans and drain out the excess water. No faster way to shift a zone from stage two to stage three. And it keeps the oxygen balance in the atmosphere and oceans. One thing the e-rigs are good for are documentaries. If you want, look it up. Terraforming is a good career."

"Thanks, I will look into it." Obert scanned the area covered with a stinking algae mat.

"So, you still want a lift?" asked Borak.

"To Sun Valley, I mean the studio support town," breathed Kendra as her mind boggled at the full implication of what she had witnessed.

Medwin closed his mouth and swallowed hard. "We—" His voice cracked, and he started over. "That would be very nice of you, please."

"Then load up. I need to log in and fill out a half dozen forms. I'll tell you, with all that business with Rowan and that Ryan fellow, the data pushers are on everything like a mink on a mouse." Borak winked at Medwin. "Still in all, can't fault the man's taste. Load up."

"Thank you." Medwin climbed into the vehicle. The others followed. Armina fell to Medwin's side. He held her as she silently sobbed.

Ulva, a pretty, twenty-something woman with light brown skin, long, chestnut hair and striking blue eyes, manipulated the eagle drone's controls, sweeping it over the newly lain algae drop while never getting out of telemetry range of the surrogates. The screens of the *Freedom's Run* control room that she sat in were fully engaged. She glanced over to one that showed Gunther from Willa's perspective. She was astride him, looking down. The emotional monitors indicated that there was no place she would rather be.

"Leave it to *Angel Black* for now. Glad that Michael was

able to fix John's idiocy. They are a great couple." Ulva spoke softly to herself, then cleared her throat before continuing louder.

"Gene, flag Borak Ghulam, S.E.T.E. terraforming tech's file. I need to see him when he checks in. We'll need to get him to sign off on an incidental inclusion waiver. Blip Mr. Strongbow's office and Arlene's handheld that I'm doing that."

She paused and pursed her lips. "Addendum, look at possibly using the data in the current time index minus ten minutes in a recruitment video for terraformers. Borak has passion for his work. It might translate for drawing people into the terraforming side of the company."

"Yes, Ulva. You have used the eagle telemetry booster drone for one hour and ten minutes. It is recommended—"

"I know. Gene, give me five minutes to get the turkey vulture drone into position, then bring the eagle in for a recharge."

"Very good, ma'am."

Ulva turned her attention to the emotional inputs. "Divine, this is messing with your heads. Poor kids. I never knew how easy I had it on *A Cat's Life*. As long as Fluffy's kibble bowl was full, he didn't worry about the larger world."

⊂══╪╍▸

Rowan found herself facing a green screen that filled her vision. Pictures depicting silhouettes of Republic member species with that species text above it covered the screen. The text read: 'Select your species.' She mentally picked the box for *Homo sapiens*.

The screen shifted to two boxes topped by text. One of them read, 'Select Your Language' in *Homo sapiens*. The other was in an odd, boxy script. The boxes depicted a *Homo sapiens* and a k-no-in. Rowan selected homo-sapiens.

The screen changed to images of *Homo sapiens*, felinezoid and k-no-in. The caption read: 'Species perspective to experience.'

Rowan bit her lip. As much as the idea of a non-*Homo sapiens* perspective was intriguing, she was there to understand Ryan. There would be other opportunities, so she selected *Homo sapiens*.

The screen shifted so that it depicted Ryan, Kate, and a woman Rowan didn't recognize, as well as a box, labelled 'Director's Perspective, changeable'. In *Homo sapiens'* script above them was written 'Select your viewpoint character'. Each image was labelled. Captain Ryan Chandler, Lieutenant Kate Lopez, and finally Major Bolanle Chibuden.

Rowan selected Kate's perspective.

A resonant voice filled Rowan's hearing as her field of vision filled with a starscape. Several of the stars were circled in blue.

"To understand the events of Murack Five, it is necessary to understand their roots in galactic history. The contagion that infected the gopherzoid species was slow-acting and insidious."

The screen shifted to an electron microscope image of a virus.

"Its evolutionary descendant, rutat, is still active today."

Another virus appeared next to the first one. Key parts of the DNA on the images were marked, one in red, the other in blue. The viruses were labelled retat, the other rutat.

"The retat virus was more a means to the gopherzoids' extinction than a cause."

The screen filled with the image of what looked like several six-limbed gophers standing up on their hind limbs. Each of the forelimbs ended in a three-fingered hand tipped with heavy horn-like claws. The gopherzoids seemed to be mixing things in test tubes. Then they yawned, set the work aside, floated on the air and went to sleep.

"It is likely the gopherzoids could have found a cure for retat, but as a species, they had become apathetic. At the time of initial infection, there had been no significant change in gopherzoid science or society in over ten thousand years. In simple terms, the species were bored to death. Little changed during the million years it took for their population to consolidate on their home world."

The screen shifted to show two beings. One resembled a theropod dinosaur with long muscular arms ending in delicate four-fingered hands with opposable thumbs. This species had a large head with bony ridges running its length. The other was a species that looked like a snail with a mass of tentacles projecting from its shell's opening and two bulbous black eyes.

"This same phenomenon occurred with the vrdkjfzoids and the nautiluszoids."

The image shifted back to the starscape. The blue circles around stars faded and vanished while numbers depicting human years at the top of the screen scrolled from a million before contact. By the time only the star Murack was circled in blue, the counter read six thousand before contact. The count continued, stopping at five-forty-two Post Contact on the bottom of the screen.

Rowan's mind rebelled at the scale. A species final decline spanning more than the entirety of human history. She recalled Ryan's advice to not think about it and focused on the narration.

"As gopherzoid numbers dwindled, the species demonstrated a drive to consolidate their population. This led to the gradual evacuation of their colony worlds. With the mass extinction-level event retat caused on gopherzoid type environments, these worlds were already hotbeds for evolution."

A line of creatures, each a little different from the last, culminating in a k-no-in, swept across the screen.

A line of text appeared at the base of the screen, 'See *A Space Traveller's Guide to K-no-in* for more on the consequences of this phenomena.'

A folded-out depiction of a planet with four major landmasses, one occupying the south polar region, the others more or less centred on the equator, filled the screen. Blue dots faded on all but the most westerly landmass as a counter scrolled from six thousand before contact to five-forty-two Post Contact.

"Eventually, the gopherzoids retreated to their homeworld, Murack Five, then to the most westerly of that world's continental landmasses."

The image zoomed in on the smallest continent. It swept over a savannah of tall grasses and scattered trees, then to a primitive village of huts with stone tools used by creatures resembling kangaroos. They had powerful hind legs and two thick, long arms coming off the upper torso. A set of shorter arms extended from the lower ribcage. Several of the kangazoids depicted held small kangazoids close to their bodies with the short arms.

"This had the effect of allowing the evolution of a proto-sentient, tool-using species on a world that still had an advanced sentient tool using species on its surface."

The screen shifted to the image of a gopherzoid wrapped in a 'flag' bearing the image of the Interstellar Republic being lowered into the blackness of a cave by an oryceropuszoid, its twin snouts curled upward in a posture of respect, while its aardvark-like body was rigid.

At the base of Rowan's vision, a line of text read: 'It is suspected that the lost colony scenario may exist with the gopherzoid species as in their expansionist phase they sent out century ships to establish independent colonies.'

"During their tenure in the Republic, the gopherzoids sold the rights to two of their home system's planets to the sycamorezoids and the dichrostigmazoids, methane and hydrogen breathers, respectively."

The image of a sycamorezoid and a dichrostigmazoid filled the screen.

Rowan mentally blinked. Every time she thought she

was getting used to the diversity of life in the Republic, something challenged her preconceptions. The sycamorezoid resembled a sycamore seed pod with two green, backswept wings ending in bulbous brown 'bodies' with a host of cilia extending from their base. The dichrostigmazoid resembled a wasp in body plan, but instead of wings, it had a sail rising from its back, an elongated neck and a triangular head that ended in pincers. Each of its six legs ended in a pincer. The pincers on the front two legs looked delicate in construction. Its eyes were cat-like, with large slit pupils. Overall, it was a dark blue colour with red banding on its back sail, which had an accordion-like quality.

"Both species claimed the right to... salvage Murack Five. More importantly, a dichotomy of views developed between them. The sycamorezoid population contained a strong isolationist faction that felt the Republic should remove the gopherzoid stargate, thus isolating the 'pure' sycamorezoids from the corrupt other species. The dichrostigmazoid wished to remain part of the larger galaxy and blocked the motion to remove the Murack stargate in the Republic Senate."

Text ran across the bottom of the screen. 'Republic species tasked with removing technological artifacts from a planet in preparation for future species evolution are granted the right to reverse engineer anything they find towards advancing their own technology.'

The screen changed to a picture of warriors from the felinezoid, *Homo sapiens* and k-no-in species.

"This resulted in a conflict that both parties employed younger races to fight. Notably, felinezoid, *Homo sapiens* and k-no-in."

The screen filled with shattered ships and bodies floating in space.

The image shifted to a message, signed by Captain Ryan Chandler, urging the Republic to isolate Murack Five. The message flipped to one in felinezoid script. All Rowan could recognize of it was Saggal's signature.

"It must be noted that several members of the races involved petitioned the Republic to declare Murack Five off-limits due to the paleolithic kangazoid species. These petitions were denied. Under Republic law, the capacity to generate an exothermic reaction at will was considered the dividing ability between pre-sentient and sentient species."

The image of the global map appeared on the screen with a green circle around the smallest of the continents.

"It was agreed that the continent populated by the kangazoids would be off-limits to all combatants.

"And so, the stage is set for us to understand the tragic events on Murack Five."

Rowan's vision flipped. She found herself looking at the pilot's station on the *Star Hawk*. As she watched, an orange section blinked green, and a red section turned orange.

LEGAL MATTERS

J udge Goeree looked at a slender, nondescript man with a shaved head covered with small circular scabs. The man was dressed in an orange hospital gown, with a chain-link pattern embroidered over its left breast, and lay on a medical cot with a display board on the wall behind him. The markers on the display were mostly coloured green, though a few were orange.

A tall, slender man, with a too-perfect head of hair and teeth so white they seemed to glow, dressed in a UES Space Services uniform with the silver scales pin of the legal division on his collar, stood next to the patient.

A short, rotund *Homo sapiens* male with a swarthy complexion and black hair wearing a cheap suit stood by the entry door.

Judge Goeree smoothed her greying black hair and checked that her black robes were in order over her slender frame. She looked up to the far-left side of the room and spoke to the air. "Computer, record proceedings, C and C files to Lieutenant Commander Hammerman, UES Space Services and Prosecuting Attorney Omar Hassani. This is the arraignment of Blair Finnius Pikeman. Mr. Pikeman, the state department has asked that we expedite your case. As such, if you and the councils for defence and prosecution are amenable, this preliminary hearing will determine which UES charges against you will proceed to trial. Those dismissed charges will be considered without merit under the law and stricken from the record. Do you understand this?"

"I do." Pikeman had a bewildered quality. "I, my wife should be here as my advocate. Where is Nancy?"

"Commander Hammerman, in your opinion, is your client competent to participate in these proceedings?" Goeree looked at the too handsome officer. She couldn't help but wonder how much it cost him to look the way he did.

"Doctor Pikeman, try to remember. We talked about this."

"Oh yes." Pikeman straightened on the treatment cot and seemed more in the present. "Nancy is gone. I... I feel odd about that."

Hammerman patted his client's shoulder, then turned to the judge. "According to the medical assessment, he is competent to stand for the dismissal of charges. The defence has reservations about his ability to participate in his own defence. The fragmentation of his memory from the assassination attempt is severe." Hammerman spoke slowly and distinctly as if each word was made of gold.

Goeree sighed at the lawyer's pomposity. "Understood. Omar, is this dismissal acceptable to the prosecution?"

"The people find streamlining the charges acceptable, your honour," agreed Omar.

"Mr. Pikeman, do you find these terms acceptable?" Goeree turned her attention to the man in the bed. The UES penal infirmary stretched around them, a white antiseptic chamber filled with treatment cots and pieces of equipment.

"It is doctor, your honour. The fact that I'm told the UES revoked my license does not revoke the years of study I undertook to gain the title."

Goeree took a breath then replied. "Of course, Doctor. Do you find the terms acceptable?"

"Under advice from my counsel, I find the dismissal of spurious charges acceptable."

Judge Goeree opened her handheld and glanced at it. "Blair Pikeman, while it is the opinion of this judge that you have conducted yourself with criminal intent for many years, it is also undeniable that your council's arguments do by and large exonerate you under the letter of the law.

"On the charges of practising medicine without a licence, this court is forced to find you not guilty on the basis that you have not practised medicine in the confines of the UES since your credentials were revoked. The Republic station sectors where you have conducted your questionable practice do not recognize your credentials' revocation.

"As an addendum regarding the prosecution. I recommend a case review of the banning of Doctor Pikeman from the practice of medicine be initiated. Specifically, dealing with the issue of why a request was not made to the Republic level of government to extend the revocation of Doctor Pikeman's medical credentials at the galactic level." Goeree shot Hammerman a withering glance. "Interference by the UES military and state branches in matters of civil law must be strictly discouraged." She sighed and checked her handheld's screen.

"On the strength of this determination, I move that the charges for the possession of controlled substances and all charges of trafficking in said substances be expunged, as my client was simply obtaining the tools necessary for conducting his legal trade," Hammerman interjected.

"Your honour, the drug Ephemeral has no uses outside recreational applications. As such, I wish those charges to be held separate from my college's blanket suggestion."

"Very well, excepting of the charges relating to the drug Ephemeral, I have little choice but to absolve the defendant of the trafficking and possession charges." Goeree tapped her handheld's screen. Several lines of displayed text turned green. She tapped the screen again. The green text vanished while the page count at the bottom of the screen dropped from two hundred to sixteen. "At least that will speed this whole thing up," remarked Goeree.

"Your honour, my client was doing research with the Ephemeral and as such—" began Hammerman.

Goeree held up her hand. "Commander, this is a preliminary session. Mitigating circumstances that are not black letter law will be dealt with later before a jury. I can only speculate as to why the Space Services are supplying the defendant with legal counsel, but granting this preliminary session is a courtesy to the diplomatic wing of the UES. This is as far as my largesse will extend. Is that understood?"

"Yes, your honour." Hammerman turned to Pikeman. "We'll get it at trial."

Goeree turned back to her handheld. "On the charges of manslaughter and gross medical negligence, we find you not guilty. Under Republic Law, you were operating as a physician. Also, under Republic law, one can contractually agree to be murdered. Thus, the releases signed by your patients shelter you. There are no grounds for deportation to the UES regarding those crimes.

"I regret that legal reality, but it is my job to interpret the law, not make it.

"On the charge of aiding and abetting the theft of S.E.T.E. property, namely the Rowan McPherson emotional surrogate. I can find no legal charge because you performed said actions while in a Republic controlled sector where said property is a person under the law."

A wintry smile crossed Goeree's lips. "At least I got a story to tell my grandchildren out of that mess."

"It was an interesting day," agreed Hammerman.

Goeree nodded and looked at Hammerman with something less than disdain for the first time. "That it was, back to the case at hand.

"Relating to the murder of Nancy Jane Pikeman."

Pikeman went stiff on the treatment cot. His eyes rolled up in his head as the monitors for heart rate and blood pressure and several other biometrics shot into the orange zone.

A round-faced, grey-haired man dressed in a lab coat burst into the room. The sound of an alarm followed him through the door, and he rushed to Pikeman's side.

"What is happening to him, Doctor?" demanded Goeree.

"The stem cells that were placed in his brain to repair the sections that were killed are still dividing and specializing. You must have hit a memory association that is trying to connect to a brain sector that had been cut off by damaged sectors." As he spoke, Doctor Beasley pulled a pressure injector out of a drawer in the treatment bench, loaded a drug cartridge, and pressed it to the skin over Pikeman's carotid artery. There was a slight hissing noise.

"What did you do to my client?" demanded Hammerman.

"I dosed him with memoria. It will help draw the memory out."

"You shouldn't have done that. There are security considerations." Hammerman struck a threatening pose.

"Sir, get stuffed! I'm no friend to your client, but he is currently my patient. His wellbeing is my tantamount consideration." The doctor was a full head shorter than the military lawyer and twice the younger man's age, and still, he glared up at Hammerman with a fury like a mongoose facing a cobra. "You'd best not get in the way of what I deem the best course of treatment for him! An episode like this is an opportunity to give him back whole segments of his life, if it is handled properly."

"Relax, Fred. No one wants to interfere with the patient's treatment." Goeree glowered at Hammerman. "How long do you think it will be before we can resume the hearing?"

Fred nodded. "Give him an hour."

"Gentlemen, I suggest we take a dinner break and resume here in an hour." Judge Goeree led the way out of the clinic.

YESTERDAY'S TEARS

6

"**C**aptain, we have full manoeuvring on port forward. Estimate ten minutes for port midships," spoke a voice from behind and to the left of Rowan/Kate's perspective from the pilot's station on the *Star Hawk*'s bridge.

"Good. How is Jastrow doing with the stealth systems?"

Rowan recognized the second voice. She wanted to turn around but couldn't. A moment later, her perspective shifted. Ryan sat in the captain's chair wearing the blue coverall uniform of the UES Spacing Corps with no retiree's braid across his shoulder patches. There was a captain's insignia on his chest but no civilian spacers' pin at his collar. There were the beginnings of grey in his hair. The skin on the left side of his face around the eye was a shade off in coloration and seemed younger. Rowan realized that he had the beginning of crow's feet on the right side.

"Chief Jastrow reports that stealth is at ninety-nine-point-five per cent on the port side and should be full within the hour."

"Stardusted nanos; you'd think the blasted things had tribes the way they fight against overlapping domains." Ryan shook his head.

Kate/Rowan's vision swept over the bridge. Each station was occupied by a uniformed officer.

"Lieutenant Montgomery, put me through to Major Chibuden. On the big screen."

Rowan's perspective shifted to the main screen where a

handsome, muscular woman, with skin so black it deserved the name, was shown in profile sitting at a desk with what looked like a map filling the wall in front of her.

"Bolanle, what's the status with the ground teams? Am I going to have time to put lipstick and mascara on my lady love?" asked Ryan.

"None of the teams have encountered any patrols. I think you were right, the poodycats don't like the cold. You should have time to buy your lady a new dress."

"Good to hear. Engineering pr—" An alarm filled the bridge that abruptly cut off.

"All ships, all combatants. This is a Republic level disaster notification. There has been an antiproton containment breach on the western continent. Global consequence expected!"

A moment passed in absolute silence that was broken by Ryan's voice.

"Communications, to all posts."

"Aye sir, all posts," replied the young man at the communications' console.

"All exterior teams, this is the captain. Return to the vessel, emergency evac. If you can't make it back, you will be left behind. Major Chibuden, order your expeditionary teams to congregate here. Use the vehicles to pick up any of our people we leave behind. Get them under cover in preparation for an atmospheric blast wave and await further orders. Navigation, plot a course to the closest kangazoid settlement."

"But sir, the restriction?" objected the middle-aged woman that sat to Rowan's left.

"Do it. Kate, get us into the air as soon as the hatch closes. Get us to that kangazoid village yesterday."

Rowan/Kate felt her throat vibrate as her voice snapped out. "Yes, Captain." Her fingers caressed the console before her. Rowan fixated on how the skin of her hand was several shades darker than she was used to, and the fingers were stubbier.

A minute passed, then the communications tech spoke. "Hatches closed."

"Kate, now," ordered Ryan. Rowan knew the tone. Captain Chandler was in the big chair.

"Communications, transmit a non-combatant status on a loop. I'm taking us out of the war," ordered Ryan.

"Sir?"

Nova blast, don't question him when he's like this, thought Rowan.

"Now!" snapped Ryan.

"Yes, sir," the young voice replied with a note of fear.

Clouds swept by on the main screen.

"Communications, Major Chibuden. Bolanle, I'm going to need anybody you still have onboard with hazmat or EVA ratings suited up and ready to move. Get anything we have in the hangar manned and out the door ASAP. Ship wide. There was an antimatter containment breach on the western continent. We have no details yet, but there is likely a radiation wave heading towards this side of the planet. We can't do much, but I am declaring this vessel a humanitarian relief asset. We will touch down as close to kangazoid villages as possible and get as many kangazoids into our hull as we can before the radiation wave hits. Exterior teams, grab as many plant and animal samples as you can as we get the kangazoids loaded. Don't be pretty about it; just get it done."

The big screen shifted so that it showed the terrain below. A moment passed.

"Captain, we are over the closest village," stated the navigator.

"Kate, take us down into the gap between those two hills with our loading bay to the village. It will create a natural funnel. Communications, Major Chibuden. Bolanle, I'm sharing my screen. I think our best bet is to run the field ambulance and the damaged grav tank out to the far side of the village and use them to herd the kangazoids forward into the bay. Do we have enough troops to contain them to the sides?"

"Negative, we left most of our ground personnel behind."

"Sir, there's a message coming in from the felinezoids," blurted Montgomery.

"Translate and put it through."

"*Star Hawk*, we read and acknowledge your non-combatant status and declare our own. We are ten kilometres west of your position and closing. I am Master Sergeant Saggal Slingmaster commanding the fang class mobile field unit, Blood Kill. Are you able to shield the kangazoid village?"

"Put me through and loop in, Chibuden. Sergeant Slingmaster. I will have an empty hangar bay. If I can get them into it, we can protect some of them. I'm sending you a map graphic. Can you secure the ridgeline to the west of the village?"

"Affirmative."

"We could use another vehicle for driving them forward from the village," interjected Major Chibuden.

"We can provide that as well," replied Saggal.

"Only if your people are suited. I'm expecting resistance. Spears may not be much, but why take the chance?" added Ryan.

"We'll be suited," said Saggal.

"Roger that. I'll use my people on the east," remarked Major Chibuden's voice.

A shudder ran through the *Star Hawk* as it set down.

"Sir, command informs that the *Moor Hawk* has been obliterated. All antiproton stores released. The *Osprey* has taken heavy damage from the shockwave. The *Kestrel* has ascended to orbit, leaving all auxiliary craft and personnel behind. The shock wave is travelling at 1,323 KPH and is expected to reach us in fifteen hours and thirty-two minutes. Blast site radiation levels are above hull specifications... The felinezoids report that the cruiser *Gerrrhissmow* was hit by the radiation wave. All crew lost." Montgomery's voice broke. Horror entered his tone. "That's five to six hundred felinezoids dead."

"Stardust," said Kate's voice.

"Steady. Montgomery, relay to the *Kestrel*'s support craft to get cover between them and the shock wave, then once it's passed to converge on our location. The blast dynamics will see that most of the rad will have dissipated into space. What we'll get is the irradiated dust carried by the shock wave. We should be safe enough inside our ships and suits. Montgomery, put me through to Kadar. Kadar, how much do you know about kangazoids?"

The image of a fit, middle-aged man of Middle Eastern extraction filled the screen. "Not much. A few biochemical principles common to creatures evolved on gopherzoid worlds."

"You're going to have to learn fast. Figure out what we can feed them. We're going to have guests. Prep for radiation treatment, *Homo sapiens*, felinezoid and k-no-in."

"Nova blast!" Kadar blanched and nodded. "How bad?"

"I'll let you know. You have about fifteen hours to get ready for hell on Murack Five." Ryan sounded grave. "Communications, ship-wide. Commander Philips and Lieutenant Chang to the bridge. Navigation, find the next closest village and lay in a course, and the one after that. Communications, contact our support vehicles and tell them to transport personnel from the south pole landing and rendezvous at the third kangazoid village. That should give them time to rally and make the trip. Come on, Kate, it's time to put our EVA ratings to the test. Bolanle is going to need every qualified body she can get. There's nothing more we can do here but close the door when we get them tucked in."

"Aye, sir," replied Rowan/Kate. She could feel sweat prickling her brow and hear a tremor in her voice, but Rowan's emotions were her own.

The scene cut to one of her descending the *Star Hawk*'s hangar ramp in an EVA suit and running towards a ridge of low hills to her left. The ambulance and a grav tank with blast damage visible on its side flew over the valley on either side of the river that snaked through the valley. Glancing down the valley, she could see a collection of huts. Kangazoids stared up in what she could only interpret as fear and awe.

Reaching her location on the ridge, she looked across to the row of hills on the western side of the river basin. A triangular felinezoid grav-tank flew the length of the hills, dropping troops at regular intervals, then joined the two human ships at the back of the valley. The three vehicles touched down, then drifted forward.

The kangazoids startled. A small band of them picked up stone-tipped spears and leapt at the approaching behemoths. They struck, the spears shattered, and the mechanical beasts came on.

"They've got guts." Ryan's voice came over her suit's channel.

"Montgomery, patch me through to orbital command on a private band. If we can get the *Kestrel* to deploy, we could double our pickup. Who knows, the felinezoids and k-no-in might pitch in."

The majority of the kangazoids started bounding towards the hills.

Kate saw one leaping towards her with a child held tight against its chest by its stunted lower arms. Kate fired her sidearm into the air, creating a wall of sound and light.

The kangazoid bounded back towards the valley floor. The scene was repeated up and down the ridgeline.

Kate and the other foot troops closed in from the hills while the ground vehicles pushed forward. Kangazoids bombarded their rescuers with everything that came to hand, but they were inexorably driven to the *Star Hawk*.

"Is that the lot?" snapped Ryan's voice.

"I've got stragglers," came the battle squawk from the felinezoid tank. Rowan recognized Saggal's voice.

"Load them up if you can, otherwise leave them. We've only eleven hours left," ordered Ryan.

Kate leapt from her position on the hill and charged towards the spot where the felinezoid tank sat by the scattered grass huts of the village with its hatch open. Kangazoid warriors postured and threatened with their spears. A tabby-stripe felinezoid stood by the hatch in an EVA suit with the helmet off. One of the kangazoids thrust at the felinezoid, who sidestepped, caught the spear by its shaft and ripped it out of the primitive's hand before he grabbed the warrior and single-handedly tossed him into the tank. Another kangazoid thrust at the felinezoid's back. Kate caught the spear, crushing its shaft with the enhanced strength of her suit, then jerked the kangazoid forward. The tabby-stripe grabbed the kangazoid by the back of its neck and tossed it into the tank.

"Thank you, *Homo sapiens*," remarked the felinezoid.

"Anytime. Name's Kate."

"Saggal." Together they grabbed another kangazoid and tossed it into the tank.

"Just to be sure, what happens when they get aboard?" asked Kate.

"My medic has a kangazoid safe sedative," explained Saggal.

"Good." Kate grabbed a kangazoid in each of her suit's arms, picked them up, shook them, then threw them into the tank. She then paused, gestured at the remaining kangazoids, and pointed at the tank like a mother admonishing a naughty child.

The kangazoids looked amongst themselves.

Saggal picked up a fallen spear, casually snapped it in two, and then gestured for the primitives to enter the tank.

Another look passed between the kangazoids before they dropped their spears and walked single file into the tank.

"We work well together," remarked Saggal.

"Hold that thought." Kate opened her radio channel. "*Star Hawk*, pass it on to the doc and the captain. The felinezoids have a kangazoid safe sedative. Over."

"Message received and thank the Divine. The hangar bay is really jumping, and not in a good way. Over," replied Montgomery's voice.

"I'll take you to the next village," offered Saggal.

As Kate/Rowan watched, the *Star Hawk* rose into the air and flew upstream along the river's course.

"I'd appreciate that. Captain probably figures he can use the trackers in our suits to collect stragglers before the rad wave hits. I'd rather not be side-lined."

"This captain, what is his name?" asked Saggal.

"Ryan Chandler." Kate followed the felinezoid into his grav tank.

"The 'space mink-like-predator', I am glad I am on your side in this. Between him and the 'star eagle-like-predator,' it's a wonder we didn't lose this war months ago."

The main room of the grav tank was a rectangular chamber with sleeping cubicles cut into its walls, three atop one another. The back corners were filled with what could only be a galley and a privy, while the back wall was a series of hatches. The forward wall held a sliding door at its centre.

A burly, cougar tan, felinezoid male stood in front of the sliding door holding a tubular pressurized injector in one claw-tipped hand. The kangazoids were stretched out on the floor, asleep.

"Mrakaka, this is Kate. We are bringing her with us. Mrakaka is my field medic."

"Pleasure to meet you, crap circumstances." Kate bowed as best as her EVA suit allowed while touching her fingertips together in front of her.

"It is to be embraced that we are not shooting at each other." Mrakaka bowed with his fingertips touching.

"Can you tell my captain the sedative and safe doses for the kangazoids?" Kate followed Saggal to the sliding door in the wall that retracted to reveal a two-seat control room.

Mrakaka spoke to her back. "I contacted my command when your chatter revealed you didn't have one. They said they'd forward the information."

Saggal snorted. "Do it directly on my authority. You know what the officers are like. Can't find their tail with two hands and a sniffer bot." Saggal sat in a command chair, deftly slipping his tail into a control interface at its back. Kate/Rowan sat in the other chair. Rowan felt like a child on adult furniture because of her size.

Saggal glanced at a screen on his control console. It was filled with the flowing script of the felinezoids. "Captain Chandler's orders are for the support vehicles to pick up any kangazoids left behind, then to rendezvous with the *Star Hawk*. The ground personnel are to loot the village of anything useful and get it under reflective tarps and a layer of dirt to keep it from becoming irradiated. Good news is the 'uncomplimentary name for officers and command' have called a cease-fire and are deploying all surface ships to 'Operation Shelter'."

"Put that first lot of food into the vehicles. We're going to need something to feed our guests in the short term. I don't think our ration packs will do the job," Major Bolanle's voice came over Kate's radio.

A moment later, Kate/Rowan glanced back to see EVA suited troops, both felinezoid and *Homo sapiens*, carrying baskets and clay pots into the crew compartment of the grav tank.

"What's this?" demanded Saggal.

"Lunch. Major Bolanle says they need at least some kangazoid food on the *Star Hawk* right now." Kate shrugged.

"Stardust, with *Homo sapiens* officers like this, I see why some fear you will take over the galaxy," quipped Saggal.

The scene shifted. The savannah of Murack Five swept across on the grav tank's screen.

"The *Star Hawk* is ready to crack the hatch as soon as they finish anaesthetizing their first load. Good thing I told Mrakaka to break with channels. Those idiots still haven't gotten the information through. Turns out, it's a common pain killer for *Homo sapiens.*

"Three felinezoid grav tanks and a troop carrier have attached themselves to the effort." Saggal relayed the update. The back of the tank was full of kangazoids, primitive containers of food and three felinezoids working to repair suit malfunctions. The rest of the ground troops had stayed at the first village. Kate's comm picked up an order diverting grav vehicles that were coming up from the southern polar region landing site to a village upstream to start the collection process.

The grav tank she rode in topped a rise of land. The screen filled with the image of three triangular felinezoid grav tanks and a box-like k-no-in troop transport, all hemming in a collection of huts on the downstream side. The village straddled the river. A crude raft secured by a rope across the flow connected its two sides. Ground troops in EVA suits lined the edge of the river's flood plain, herding the mass of kangazoids forward. Most of the troops were felinezoid, but there were k-no-in as well. The only *Homo sapiens* that could be seen was a figure on the top of a *Homo sapiens* military ambulance that swept up and down the length of the lines of foot soldiers. The *Homo sapiens* shot any kangazoid that tried to escape past the containment line.

"What are they doing!" growled Saggal.

Kate/Rowan stared at the scene in mute horror. She watched a shot kangazoid lurch about drunkenly before it fell to the ground.

"It's a tranquilizer gun. They keep one on the ambulance to deal with violent psych cases," explained Kate.

"Thinking like that is why I respect your Captain Chandler. He almost makes one believe that brain damage is not a prerequisite for high rank."

Kate/Rowan felt herself smile. "I am a lieutenant."

Saggal glanced over. "Stupidity hasn't infected all the junior grades."

There was a beeping sound that filled the cockpit.

Saggal glanced at his display screen. And released the nasal hiss that served felinezoids as laughter. "I've been officially assigned to the *Star Hawk*'s chain of command. At least I won't be demoted for declaring non-combatant status." His tone became grave. "The update is, there is a tidal wave eight hundred metres high sweeping out from the blast zone. Several support craft fleeing the southwestern hemisphere have been destroyed. Felinezoid, *Homo sapiens* and k-no-in report no survivors from the northwestern hemisphere. Those in the southwestern hemisphere that had time to take shelter behind earth barriers report high radiation at altitude, but tolerable levels close to the surface."

"Nova blast," breathed Kate/Rowan. "How many dead?"

"All ground troops combined, nearly a thousand, perhaps more." Saggal took a deep breath. Kate heard him speaking softly. "Great Divine with your myriad names, watch over them and lead them to the jungles of rich game and sweet waters."

"Divine make it so." Kate joined in at the end of the prayer.

"Sentient cosmos?" asked Saggal.

"Raised in it. I... sometimes it helps to believe in something."

"Sometimes, a little faith is all one can believe in." Saggal turned to look at Kate, his nostrils trembling and his nose running. "I had friends with the ground forces on the western continent."

"I..." Rowan felt Kate take a deep breath. Her throat was tight. "My fiance was an officer on the *Moor Hawk*."

Saggal reached across and touched Kate's arm. "Maybe he was in an auxiliary craft. There is a mountain range on the northern section of the southwestern continent. If a vehicle got behind it, it would have diverted the worst of the force."

"No false hope. It only makes it worse." Kate took a deep breath, forcing calm. "All we can do now is help the living.

There will be time for the dead later."

"The dead have all the time they need." Saggal quoted the book of doctrine.

A moment passed before he went back to reading the dispatch on his screen. "The ground support vehicles and squads that survived the shockwave are following the blast, trying to get clear of the worst of the radioactive dust. If they make it, they will rendezvous with our force."

"Lieutenant Lopez, *Star Hawk* to Lieutenant Lopez, do you copy?" Rowan/Kate heard the words through her helmet's pick up.

"I'm reading you, *Star Hawk*. Over."

"You are ordered to go to the *Star Hawk* to offload. The captain wants you back on the bridge, and he wants a face to face with Sergeant Slingmaster."

"Captain Chandler wants a meeting with you," Kate relayed.

"I was hoping to join the forces helping with the *Padfoot*'s rescue operations."

"Did you get that, *Star Hawk*? Over," asked Kate.

"With the danger to surface craft, the *Padfoot* has been diverted from Operation Shelter to pick up Republic survivors. The captain said it was an order. Kate, he's full King Arthur mode. I wouldn't even try to question him. Over."

"King Arthur?" asked Saggal.

"Ship's joke. Ryan believes in a friendly command style, but you don't cross him if there is a threat to the ship, crew, or mission. Some crew make the mistake of not knowing that once. They never make it twice." Kate smiled. "He's a good boss if you know there's a time for discussion and a time to follow the order to pull your ass out of the fire. One of the crew was into mythology. She dubbed his mood. It stuck. Wait a moment, I've got something coming in on my heads up." Kate read for a few seconds as text tracked up the inside of her helmet's visor. "The support craft we left at the pole have reached the third village and are corralling kangazoids for pickup. Ground troops are securing supplies under piles of earth."

Moments later, Kate/Rowan helped carry the last of the unconscious kangazoids into the *Star Hawk*'s hangar bay. About a quarter of it was full of slumbering kangazoids while others were being injected by personnel in service uniforms. EVA-clad Republic species troops guarded the hatch and supplied security. Ryan, in a service uniform, directed an effort by a mixed squad of Republic species troops to sedate a group of kangazoids that had been herded into the ship.

The kangazoids had formed a circle with four that clutched children to their chests in the centre. Several of the primitives on the perimeter were armed with stone knives.

"Jacobs, incoming," snapped Ryan.

A kangazoid had bunched its muscles and lunged at an EVA-suited *Homo sapiens*. The primitive flipped mid-air and slammed feet first into the *Homo sapiens*, driving the spacesuit-clad figure to the ground and landing on top of him. Three felinezoids from the Republic group keeping the kangazoids from escaping rushed forward to assist. The pinned *Homo sapiens* lashed out with the enhanced strength of his suit and drove his fist through his kangazoid attacker.

"No!" screamed Ryan.

Ryan, Saggal and Kate converged on the stricken primitive.

Ryan pulled the kangazoid away from the *Homo sapiens* it had attacked and cradled it in his arms. Blood spurted out of the wound, leaving a trail of gore across Ryan's face. Saggal and Kate knelt beside them and released the gloves of their EVA suits so that they could touch the primitive warrior. "Go to whatever gods you follow and tell them you died with courage," said Saggal.

"Find peace and plenty," added Ryan.

"May the cosmos keep you warm," added Kate.

The kangazoids had stopped fighting and stood watching their comrade die cradled in the arms of the monsters that had captured them.

The kangazoid warrior closed its eyes, never to open them again.

"I... it attacked me. We're trying to save them, and it attacked me," blurted Jacobs.

"Corporal, stand to attention." Ryan let the rage he felt enter his voice.

Jacobs stood at attention.

Ryan, blood dripping from his face and staining his uniform, came to his feet. His expression was one of rage. He faced the armoured behemoth of the EVA suit. The voice that spoke was more a thing of steel and ice than of human words. "You are in an enhanced EVA suit that can withstand micrometeor impacts. What did you think a cave being with a stone knife was going to do to you?"

"I... Sir... I..."

"The word you are looking for is panicked!" Ryan slammed his hand into the EVA suit's chest, pushing the corporal back a step despite its enhancements. "Now things are worse." Ryan took a deep breath, then continued. "You are going to help me make lemonade. Play dead." Ryan opened a compartment on the field kit belt that circled his waist. He extracted a red tube, pointed it at Jacobs' EVA suit and pressed a button at its side. A flare shot out of the tube, impacting the front of the suit. Jacobs fell onto his back as the kangazoids watched. The flare sparked impossibly bright and sent out streamers of coloured smoke. It looked like it was burning through the EVA suit and consuming the being within.

"Chibuden, have two of your men drag Jacobs to the elevator and get him out of here. Make it look like you're dumping garbage. Then fetch a stretcher, we need to take the kangazoid to medical. Kate, Sergeant Slingmaster, pop your helmets. I want you on two of the stretcher's corners. You and you," Ryan pointed out a human and felinezoid from the crowd of armoured personnel. "Honour guard positions and look smart about it."

The two troops moved to the sides of the dead kangazoid.

The conscious kangazoids stood still and watched as their dead comrade was reverently rolled onto a stretcher. Ryan took one corner, as did Major Bolanle, Kate and Saggal. The stretcher's anti-grav suspensers lifted the weight, giving the illusion that the beings carrying it were so strong they thought nothing of the load. With measured pace, Ryan and his officers propelled the stretcher to the ship's elevator and rose out of sight of the hangar bay.

Ryan spoke softly into his collar. "How are they behaving?"

"They've stopped fighting, and they're making a lot of noise."

"Keep an eye on them. Let them see that the unconscious ones are still alive."

"Freaky looking things," commented the *Homo sapiens* private in the honour guard.

Ryan shook his head. "Private, these kangazoids have no way of knowing that their world is coming to an end. All they know is we drove them out of their village into this moving cave and are putting them to sleep. Hopefully, they can see the ones we anaesthetized are still breathing. If not, they'll think we're killing them. This was a hero! He defended his people against a monster of incredible and unknown power. We will show him as much respect as our circumstances allow. Is that clear?"

"Yes, Captain. I'm sorry, sir."

"What are your plans? I don't know anything about their death customs," remarked Saggal as the elevator doors opened on the medical level.

"For now, I want my doctors to examine him/her/it. Learn as much as we can. Without translator nanobots, we have to guess at everything."

"They like to attack in staggered waves, hitting and

falling back to re-arm while the second wave occupies the enemy. It's quite sophisticated for a paleolithic people," observed Major Bolanle.

"Especially one that can't even make fire," observed Saggal.

They brought the kangazoid into the medical bay. Twelve treatment benches jutted out from the wall. Hovering the stretcher over a bench, Ryan pressed a button on the bench's side. The kangazoid corpse drifted on an antigravity field. The stretcher-bearers slid the stretcher out from under it before letting the body settle to the table with the press of a button.

Kadar moved to the table's side and looked at the kangazoid.

"I was informed of what happened. What are you going to do with Jacobs?" Kadar began running scans.

"He's confined to ship duties. He was always trigger happy," remarked Major Chibuden.

Ryan reached out and touched the kangazoid's face. Its hair was short, coarse, and brown. The body hadn't yet cooled. "I am sorry. Kadar, full autopsy and bio-chem work up, ASAP. I want to know everything this corpse can teach us." He sighed. "Master Sergeant Slingmaster, Kate, accompany me to the officer's mess. We're using it as a ready room."

"Of course, but my squad?" began Saggal.

"I've taken the liberty of assigning someone to pilot your tank back and pick up your people. The orders are to follow the line of villages up the river securing food and necessities against the oncoming shockwave and rad dust. I'd use the vehicles to shelter kangazoids, but we'll need to have our own people under cover.

"I need a liaison officer to coordinate with the felinezoids. You stepped up as soon as you knew there was a problem. I think I can work with you. You've worked with him, Kate, recommendations."

"I think he'll do, Captain. His troops respect him, and he

thinks high rank and brain damage go hand in hand."

Ryan snorted. "Sergeant, when this is over, we'll get a drink and swap stories. What do you say? Can we let the past be past and work together for the greater good?" Ryan paused to look Saggal in the eye.

"As you say, Captain." Saggal paused, touched his fingertips together, and bowed towards Ryan.

Ryan returned the gesture. "Good, we need all the help we can get."

Ryan led Kate and Saggal back to the elevator that took them to the flight crew level.

Pikeman sat in the living room of his on-base quarters with a ration pack on the coffee table in front of him. He used the polycarbonate knife and fork from the pack to cut his steak. The room was richly furnished but only four metres by four metres. A recording of a surgical procedure was projected holographically into the air at the room's centre.

"It is important to be certain of the ratio of stem cells to nutrient gel and oxygen release pellets before insertion." A needle from the robotic surgeon pressed into the knee of the holographic patient. At the same time, numbers representing the ratios of the cartilage restoration gel's components filled the corner of the screen.

Pikeman shook his head. "Drop in a retrovirus to steer the specialization, and you could do this in half the time."

The door at the end of the room slid into the wall, and Nancy entered. As always, she looked stunning. The combination of a strong Nordic genetic, fanatic attention to exercise and diet, and moderate medical intervention made her a classical blonde beauty. The rainbow-hued off one shoulder evening gown she wore enhanced her to goddess-like levels.

Her face pulled into a scowl. "You're home. Get that off the holo. It's disgusting!"

"Hello, honey. Did you enjoy the party?" Blair stayed seated.

"Not that you care," snapped Nancy.

Blair blinked and reached for a piece of equipment he'd borrowed from the hospital that he'd sequestered behind him on the couch. From memory, he knew which button to push. "If I'd left the surgery, the man would have died. No one expects complications."

"I'm going to shower!" Nancy snipped and strutted across the living room to the hallway that provided access to the rest of the flat.

As soon as she passed him, Blair pulled out the medical sniffer, passed it through the air behind her, and checked its display.

"Yes, shower. You wouldn't want the stench of Admiral Johansson to linger." Blair came to his feet.

"How dare you!" Nancy turned on him.

"How dare I?" Blair held up the device. "He's all over you. How dare you!"

"If you'd been there, it never would have happened," snapped Nancy.

"Yes, you'd have waited until I was at work, like usual."

"We shouldn't discuss this with Jason in the apartment. In a place this small, he's bound to overhear!"

"I asked Chris to take him to her place. It's time we had a talk." Blair glowered at the treacherous beauty.

"A talk. A talk. You are nothing, Lieutenant." She made his rank an insult with her tone. "My mother warned me not to marry you. Said I should stay with my own kind."

"What, rich, self-indulgent, spoiled industrialists, standing on the dead legs of their ancestors and exploiting everyone who tries to better themselves? Oh yes, my love. Lest you forget, my family has a pedigree nearly as old as yours. You knew they disowned me when I decided to follow medicine. Forced me to join up to cover my education. If being a lieutenant's wife was so horrible, why did you marry me?"

"Because I was a fool!" Nancy's perfect complexion went red.

She'd lunged, snatched the steak knife from his ration pack and thrust it towards him.

Blair didn't think. The imprinted muscle memory they'd given him in basic training kicked in. He stepped to the side, deflecting the blade with his left arm, then his right fist slammed into her chest. He heard the xiphoid process breaking and driving up into her heart.

Nancy gasped, the knife falling from her hand as she collapsed, slamming her head on the coffee table.

"Oh god!" gasped Pikeman. "Computer, contact EMS. This is Doctor Pikeman. I need transport and cardiac support at this address. Stat!"

Blair remembered the treatment. Remembered doing everything right. Remembered the emergency kit from his apartment block arriving, so he had tools to work with. Remembered the ambulance coming to take Nancy away. But it was too late. The blow to the chest she might have survived, but when she hit the coffee table, severing her spinal cord at the C1 level, it was over.

The memory skipped. Blair looked at the barren walls of a two-metre by two-metre brig. A twenty-something lieutenant with dark hair and a swarthy complexion wearing the Space Services Legal Corps pin in his collar stood in the room's floor area while Pikeman sat on the cot.

"Her family want blood, and they can afford the lawyers to get it. I've reviewed the recording. It was self-defence, long and short. That, and bad luck, but a civilian jury won't understand the muscle memory induction they gave you in basic. This sort of thing has happened before. That's why they stopped using the technique a year after you signed up."

"What can I do?" Blair buried his face in his hands.

"You have options. Your family have offered to supply your defence if you sign over custody of your son to them."

Blair shook his head. "Not an option. I know what they would twist him into. Is Chris willing to take him in?"

"For the moment, but she is concerned about the finances." The lawyer extracted a handheld from his pocket and folded out its screen.

"I'll find a way to cover his support. I won't have my son raised by the entitled scum on either side of the family. I can give him that much."

The lawyer nodded. His voice became comforting. "You're a good dad. I'm sure she'll accept custodial status of Jason if you help out financially."

"Good, she's been more of a mother to him than Nancy ever was."

"What about your status? Lieutenant... Doctor. I doubt you'll get off with a public defender, and the military will only go so far in your defence. Frankly, they could be held culpable if they admit that the induced muscle memory made the killing blow. They are afraid of a lawsuit."

"You said I had options." Blair wrung his hands and sounded defeated.

"You are a brilliant physician with an unsurpassed talent for cosmetic surgery. The UES Space Services has uses for a man of your skill set. It would mean leaving Earth for a long-term duty assignment. In effect, you'd be a free man except for the homeworld."

Blair nodded. "And Jason would stay with Chris. My wages would be garnished to care for him. My and Nancy's families would have no access?"

"I think the last would be difficult unless Miss Williams is willing to relocate to a colony world."

"That shouldn't be a problem. Chris hates Earth. Selling off Nancy's jewellery should pay for the move. I think we have a deal."

HOME AWAY FROM HOME

Medwin climbed out of the cargo space of the outback rover and helped Armina to the ground. They stood in front of a large, two-storey building fashioned out of rock. The roof was covered with black panels. A large sign over the double glass entry doors declared that it was the S.E.T.E. studio museum. He glanced around at the buildings carved out of native stone that surrounded him and resisted the urge to sit on the ground in shock. In general layout and construction, the street was identical to the downtown core of Sun Valley.

"Thank you for the ride." Kendra exited the vehicle's cab. Her voice held a forced heartiness that sought to cover her shock.

"Just keep better track of where you are next time you go camping. It was nice to meet young folk that don't have their brains glued to an e-rig." Borak waved as Obert passed the packs to Medwin and jumped to the street.

With a slight hum, the outback rover sped off.

"This looks like home! Even the cars are the same. Maybe we were wrong," blurted Armina once the little group was alone.

Other people wandered along the sidewalk concerned only with their own affairs.

As Medwin fought to get his bearings, a shadow passed across the sun. He glanced up to see a horseshoe-shaped platform hovering overhead supporting a man in a red coverall. The platform moved to a lamp post. With a bored air, the man on the platform pulled a lever at the base of the perfectly recognizable tulip-blade-turbine that topped the post and pulled it off to set it on the hovering platform. He then pushed a new turbine into place, reset the retaining bracket, and floated down a side street.

Armina hung her head. "Why make it look like ho... Sun Valley?"

"Makes a kind of sick sense." Kendra eyed the shop that in Sun Valley was an upscale clothing outlet. The sign over this version's door read 'S.E.T.E. Reproductions, Look Like an E-Star'.

"What? Why?" breathed Obert.

"This is a tourist trap. Mimic the..." Kendra's tone became strained, "set region to add to the illusion and cash in on people who want to come as close to really walking the streets of Sun Valley as they can. The museum is exactly where the town museum is in Sun Valley and has that same old castle kind of look."

"Gothic." Armina supplied the proper word. "I always liked it. The class trips when we were little, we always had so much fun and... I guess they never happened, did they? Silly stupid fakey, I..." She trailed off.

Medwin sighed and took Armina's hand. "Kendra, that makes sense."

"It even smells like downtown." Obert looked across the street to a three-storey structure with a peaked roof and a largely glass front opening onto a patio. People sat at tables on the patio eating Italian food. The sign over the door depicted a pizza and read 'S.E.T.E.'S GARLIC PALACE. Taste it for Yourself.' Then in smaller print beneath it, 'All real grown ingredients fresh from the Sun Valley production facilities.'

"I could murder a pizza right now," remarked Obert.

"We'll eat when we're done. Besides, we don't have any money," admonished Medwin.

"Fine, so now what do we do?" asked Obert.

"I think we should go to the town hall." Kendra gestured

down the street to where a three-storey structure filled a full city block.

Medwin released Armina's hand and crossed the nearly deserted street so he could read the sign over the large structure's door. A moment later, he re-joined his friends. "It's S.E.T.E. headquarters. I don't want to risk going into the dragon's den just yet. We have a lot to learn before we try that. I say the museum is our best bet."

"I just want to go home. I... What is home? If it's just a set. All fake, just like us, just like me. Nothing's real!" Armina's lip trembled, and her voice was choked.

"This is too good an opportunity to pass up," observed Medwin. "We can get a complete perspective on our situation. I can... I wonder if they have records about...What I mean is—"

"Your dad. You can find out what really happened." Kendra spoke in soothing tones.

"The intelligence is there for the taking." Obert gestured towards the door.

"I don't want to. Suppose we get caught. Besides, how are we going to pay to get in?" objected Armina.

"Let's at least check. Maybe it's free," suggested Kendra.

Medwin nodded and led the way through the doors into the building. The first room was a lobby with holographic images of various e-entertainers. The walls depicted scenes from places none of them recognized. Two metre-wide passages opened at the far end of the room.

"That was a disappointment," remarked a ruddy, brown-haired, middle-aged man dressed in slacks and a sweater who emerged from one of the passages.

"I told you not to pay for the day passes. I told you we should have just taken the tour, but do you ever listen? We could have just stayed home and experienced it on the e-rig." A skinny woman in a floral print dress with waspish features and blonde hair followed the man through the exit passage. Two children trailed behind her.

"We've been over this. I want the boys to experience real

things. They spend too much time plugged into that machine." The man's voice was haggard.

"Well, we should have just taken the tour. The all-day pass was a waste of money. There isn't enough content here. And the way the holo-guide was dressed. Surrogates are all a bunch of floozies."

Obert smiled and strode up to the family. "Pardon me, but I couldn't help but hear you were leaving and had full-day passes." He leaned close. "I promised my girl that I'd bring her here, but if I pay the entry, I won't have anything left to take her for dinner. It's our six-month anniversary. I want to make it special."

The blonde woman smiled. "That is so sweet. Help the boy, Howard. At least those stupid passes won't go to waste!"

"Here you go, son, enjoy it while you can." Howard shot the blonde woman a long-suffering glance while he passed over four plastic cards.

"Enjoy your date. It's nice to see there is still a little romance in the real world." The woman snorted, then turned to the older of her boys, who was trying to look up the skirt of a hologram that was patterned after a lean muscular woman of Middle Eastern extraction.

"Billy, you stop that right now. You are so embarrassing!" snapped the woman.

Obert returned to his friends.

"I can't believe you did that," remarked Medwin.

"When opportunity knocks, you answer." Obert shrugged as he passed out the passes.

The number 2:57 showed on the side of the cards. As Kendra watched, it dropped to 2:56.

"We have less than three hours to catch up on over a thousand years," remarked Kendra. Moving to the entry passage, they swiped the cards and entered the museum proper.

Ryan talked as he led Kate and Saggal to the ground officers' mess.

"I want orders for the felinezoid troops to come through you, Sergeant. Seven hours ago, we were shooting at each other, and it shows. I've had two squads refuse commands until they received them from the brass above. It's slowing things down, and we can't afford that. As it is, we'll be lucky to save a healthy breeding population of kangazoids. We want as much genetic diversity as we can manage."

"Genetic... Is it really that bad?" asked Kate.

"Murack Five will be a dead world in just a few hours. Oh, bacteria and viruses, maybe some moulds and lichens, possibly some marine life and robust plant species, but for the higher-order species, it is the end!" Ryan looked grave.

Saggal lashed his tail. "Then we must rescue the kangazoids' animals and seed crops. They will need something to eat."

"I have the k-no-ins collecting them. They're more familiar with the basic types since their world's environment was based on this one. Besides, their transports' life support systems can't handle the overcrowding that's happening on the *Homo sapiens* and felinezoid ships."

"Where can we bring them?" asked Saggal.

"That I'm still working on. It will have to be clear of the radioactive dust that the shockwave is bringing in."

"And have a balanced environment. There is bound to be a nuclear winter followed by global warming," added Kate.

"How do you know this?" asked Saggal.

"It's standard bio-science for *Homo sapiens*." Ryan stepped up to the door of the officers' mess, and it retracted into the wall.

A large rectangular table dominated the middle of the room while the walls were full of maps and graphs. What looked like a tall, muscular man with dark skin and handsome features sat staring at the data. He was dressed in a Space Services uniform with master sergeant rank insignia. A cable ran from his right nostril into a port built into the table's underside.

"What have you got for me, Henry," demanded Ryan.

"More than you could handle, oh captain mine," flirted Henry.

Divine, did they make him hot on purpose? thought Rowan. *I guess if you're going to be a polymer pervert, it helps to have the bait.*

"Henry, can the stardust. We're in too deep," ordered Ryan.

"Yes, Captain. The best allegory on record is the Cretaceous extinction on Earth," answered Henry.

"Earth suffered an antiproton accident?" queried Saggal.

"Asteroid strike, about sixty-five million years ago. It wiped out roughly seventy-five per cent of life on the planet. What we have is just a little bit worse, but I can draw parallels," observed Henry as Ryan took a seat at the rectangular mess table.

"Master Sergeant Saggal Slingmaster, Master Sergeant Henry, my ship's mech."

"Hi, pussy cat. You're a big one." Henry leered at Saggal.

"Henry, shut it down, or I'll pull it off. Clear?" threatened Ryan.

The room convulsed violently, and everything shook.

"What in the Divine's myriad names!" gasped Saggal.

"Ground force shock wave. It travels faster than the atmospheric. We can expect the pressure wave to trigger a lot of vulcanism," explained Kate.

Ryan and Henry looked at her in surprise.

"What, I was a dino nut when I was a kid. I know about the great Cretaceous extinction."

"Computer, real-time image of the eastern continent. Fill the starboard wall," ordered Ryan.

The wall filled with an image of the continent taken from space. Dots of smoke stood out along the continent's mountain ranges. The western coastal waters were stained brown.

"Computer, get me navigation. Navigation, this is the captain. Update retrieval list to avoid all areas adjoining volcanic activity. Transmit it to all ships and ground support. End message," ordered Ryan.

"Shouldn't we prioritize them?" asked Saggal.

"We can't save a fraction of the villages. The most good for the most kangazoids is to take the low hanging fruit. We can't afford to be less than pragmatic. The *Star Hawk* and the *Kestrel* can each take maybe two hundred and fifty kangazoids before we max out our life support. If we can load that many."

The sound system came to life as if to punctuate Ryan's statement. "All personnel, five hours to atmospheric pressure wave."

Ryan turned to Saggal. "Let's get to work. How many kangazoids do you think your heavy landers can accommodate?"

⊂══◇

Medwin left his friends to explore the museum while he moved to a screen set on the wall. "Umm, computer."

"I am the studio's operating system. I am designated Gene. How may I help you?"

"Gene, do you have access to what happened to specific emotional surrogates?"

"A full resource tracking file is kept for all emotional surrogates. If you wonder what happened to a favourite character after a show was cancelled, I can access that information by referencing the character's full name. I can also provide a listing of speaking appearances by that character."

"Do you do this a lot?" Medwin didn't keep the surprise out of his voice.

"Many visitors to the museum wish to indulge their curiosity about characters from past shows."

Medwin looked around guiltily as sweat prickled his brow. "Look up Police Officer Frances O'Hare."

"Frances O'Hare was a secondary character in *Beat Cop*, *Detective Dave*, *Theft on the Street*, *Homicide Investigations*, *My Bad Neighbour*, *SF Geeks*, and *Secret Lives*. Incidental appearances in *A Cat's Life*, *Day Care Days*, *The School House—*"

"Gene. Do not list incidental appearances." Medwin mentally compared the show names to things his father had talked about and began to understand the files' structure.

"As you wish, sir. A do not assist order was issued on the character, Sun Valley set region activation plus twenty-five years, three months, twenty-seven days. The charter's subsequent non-active status provided dramatic tension for season seven of *Homicide Investigations*. Auxiliary factors in do not assist order, radiation-induced cancers from the dirty bombing of the northeast Sun Valley core." Gene's voice droned on, but Medwin hardly heard it. The sound of his blood thundered in his ears as grief and rage filled him. It was all he could do not to tear the museum apart.

After a minute, Medwin spoke again. "Tell me about the following, Dalbert Winterbottom and Irwin Grant."

"Dalbert Winterbottom and Irwin Grant were primary characters in the comedy *SF Geeks*. Dalbert Winterbottom was classified non-vital and do not assist before being given a guest appearance on *Vampire Tales*. Auxiliary factors in do not assist order, accelerated clone growth resulted in multiple cancers. Current status non-active.

"Irwin Grant is currently designated non-vital, secondary role as a human slave on *Angel Black*."

Medwin swallowed hard. "Tell me about the rest of the *SF Geeks* cast?"

"Medwin O'Hare, designated non-vital secondary role in *Freedom's Run*, pending release.

"Obert Richardson, designated non-vital secondary role

in *Orgy Girls Special Features, Newcomers*, and *Freedom's Run*, pending release.

"Armina Michaels, designated non-vital secondary role in *Freedom's Run*, pending release.

"Kendra Kahmg, designated non-vital secondary role in *Freedom's Run*, pending release.

"Carol Smith, *Orgy Girls* Special Features, ongoing.

"Nancy O'Hare designation non-vital, do not assist, secondary role, *Hospital, Paramedic Squad, Station House, Secret Lives, Detective Dave*."

Medwin jerked forward at the mention of his mother's name. "Gene, hold playback. I don't want to know anymore."

Standing, he moved to a display that showed the territory around the set region. The studio town was thirty kilometres away from the closest border of Sun Valley, with the line of sight blocked by a series of hills. He spotted Kendra and Obert at displays about how the controllers manipulated circumstances in the set region. Scanning the interactive screens on the museum's wall, he spotted Armina. She sat at a station gazing at a readout that showed a series of faces almost identical to her own.

Medwin walked up to his girlfriend. "Hi, beautiful." He embraced her from behind. She trembled in his arms. Reaching up, he felt dampness on her cheeks. The age, hair colour, fitness level, and even gender of the images on the screen changed, but the basic form remained constant.

"Not real," were the only words that Armina uttered.

Kate/Rowan watched on the bridge's main screen as a satellite image showed a mass of water tracking up the river valley they had been following.

"Nova blast!" swore Ryan's voice behind her. "How much did we lose?"

"Food stores from the first two villages will have been

destroyed. Fortunately, our personnel evaced before the wave hit."

"At least it wasn't the big one. Just a little tsunami caused by the seismic shock," observed Kate.

"Nothing for it. Communications, dispatch all vehicle teams to the closest villages. Tell them to raid the food stores and secure them from wind and radiation. We'll finish loading the *Star Hawk* with minimal personnel. We only have room for another twenty or so anyway.

"Kate, it looks like you and I need to suit up again. Set us down, and let's move."

Judge Goeree once more stood by Pikeman in the infirmary. She read from her handheld, "The garnishing of your military salary and subsequent pension has dealt with your child support and outstanding debts in the UES sector. As such, the civil charges brought by the family of Nancy Pikeman are without basis and are dismissed."

Pikeman watched the judge. He looked tired, but a measure of the callous arrogance that had marked the man seemed to have returned as more memories integrated.

"The statute of limitations has run out on several drunk and disorderly as well as indecent exposure charges."

Goeree pressed a button on her handheld. The page count dropped to three.

"Sadly, you have stated, and independent medical practitioners have confirmed, that your brain injuries have impeded your memory about several incidents involving changing the appearance of known felons, making yourself an accomplice after the fact in their crimes. Because you could not effectively participate in your own defence, pending restoration of your memories, I have no choice but to stay the associated charges.

"This leaves the possession of and trafficking in

Ephemeral charges and the possession of stolen property regarding one class fifteen nanobot manufacturing unit and a class six Stem Cell Insertion Unit outstanding as UES charges for which a trial date will be set."

Pikeman glowered at Hammerman. "My memory is getting better every day, Commander, and maybe if I was in prison with all that time on my hands, I could focus on recovering more of it. Sometimes life can get in the way of one's recovery, you know."

"Council intends to enter a plea of not guilty to all remaining charges," observed Hammerman.

"Understood," said Goeree. "There is one more matter to consider."

"What?" asked Hammerman.

"A private citizen of the Republic brought a computer file to my attention," remarked the prosecutor. "Computer, if you please."

A hologram appeared in the centre of the clinic. The perspective looked up at a shirtless Pikeman as he bent down and wrapped a T-shirt around a robotic arm. The arm tried to pull the shirt away, but Pikeman kicked the arm, disjointing it.

Pikeman's voice muttered. "Come on, activate your return for maintenance program."

"Do you deny that you vandalized a Republic Sanitary Robot during the performance of its duties?" asked the prosecutor.

"I, I was running for my life," blurted Pikeman.

Goeree smiled. "The Republic court will be happy to hear your arguments. In a show of goodwill, the UES will surrender you to their custody."

"Your honour," objected Hammerman.

"Or..." remarked Goeree.

"Or," Pikeman repeated like a man being thrown a life preserver.

"I have spoken with the Star Searcher collective, who oversees sending relief efforts and personnel to Republic disaster areas. With your multidisciplinary expertise, we both feel that you would be an excellent candidate as a physician for the relief workers on Murack Five. The Republic court will forgo a trial if you accept a guilty verdict at level four and volunteer to spend your sentence as a ten-year placement on Murack Five. The UES court would be willing to amalgamate all your outstanding charges into this Republic ruling and allow you to serve the sentences concurrently."

Pikeman swallowed. "That's blackmail!"

"No, Doctor Pikeman, this is what we call a plea bargain," observed the prosecutor.

"All his active sentences for drug infractions and possession of stolen property will be served with no further prosecution. What about the accomplice after the fact charges pending if his memory returns?" demanded Hammerman.

"To be rid of this matter, I will allow them into the bargain. Most important to state and military branches is that he will be off the station with minimal contact with anyone that anything he might remember would be of interest to." Goeree turned to Pikeman. "As well, Doctor, only registered relief personnel are allowed on Murack Five. Your assailants would have great difficulty in reaching you. In the case of the legal branch, I will be happily retired by the time you return, and you'll be somebody else's problem! It is, of course, up to you, but know that your full record will be released to all your trial judges if this goes to a Republic court. Several of the member species are rather fuzzy on the concepts of the statute of limitations and jurisdiction."

Blair hung his head. "I'll need the equipment from my clinic if I am to be effective."

"That can be arranged. The Republic is even willing to waive the lease on the area you now occupy."

"Computer, record and notarize, I will accept this plea bargain when I receive it as a written notarized file."

Pikeman sounded defeated.

Goeree clapped her hands. "I'm glad that's settled. I hope that being a useful physician again may allow you to find some part of your soul worth redeeming. Report to the *Star Hawk* within the next twenty-four hours to arrange for the loading of your equipment. You will be transported by the *Star Hawk* under the command of Captain Ryan Chandler."

The scene shifted. Kate/Rowan once more stood in an EVA suit, herding kangazoids into the gaping maw of the *Star Hawk*, where a mix of Republic species sedated them and left them lying on the floor at a frenzied pace.

"We have less than a minute before we're expecting the shock wave," Montgomery's voice sounded over Kate's radio.

"All auxiliary craft, all stations. Ground and shelter. Ground and shelter!" ordered Major Bolanle's voice on the open channel.

"Exterior troops, if you can't get to a craft, dig in and shelter," ordered Ryan's voice.

Kate/Rowan glanced about, finding a fallen 'tree' lying on the hill. She threw herself down on the ground beside it and dug her arms into the dirt. By leaning up, she could see the vehicles in the village. Saggal in an EVA suit was driving a group of eight adult kangazoid, all clutching young, into a United Earth Systems' military ambulance. The crews of the other vehicles were racing into the grav tanks and troop carriers and closing the hatches. The kangazoids grabbed spears and knives and charged the *Star Hawk* as its rear hatch closed.

The smaller vehicles sped to tuck close against a cliff face and settle on the ground.

"Pressure wave in ten," Montgomery's voice began a countdown.

Kate/Rowan hunkered down beside the log.

The countdown hit one, then it was like being hit by a truck. Winds tore at her, almost lifting her and her EVA suit despite the fact she had driven her hands into the dirt. As she watched, a kangazoid swept by her, followed by a hut that broke apart as it flew. Her exterior speaker roared and blanked as the noise exceeded the safe decibel level. Even through her suit, she heard the howl like a thousand demons, then nothing. She clambered to her feet and looked around. Dust rained down, making it like looking through a thick fog. A crash sounded to her right, followed by a shower of gore as a kangazoid fell onto the rocks and burst apart. The village below was flattened. Scoured from the planet's surface as if a great hand had swept it away. A human ambulance was hunkered down on the ground beside three felinezoid tanks.

"Stay braced, everyone. The rebound wave will only be a minute or so," Ryan's voice came over the radio.

Kate dropped back to her shelter area.

Rowan/Kate felt herself bite her lip. Her mouth was dry, but she didn't access the suit's onboard hydration unit. The seconds felt like hours. A second wave of air swept over her in the direction opposite to the first. This wind wasn't as strong as the first but carried a mass of flying debris. The roar of passing air lessened, then stopped.

Kate checked her on board Geiger counter: 785 mSv.

"Divine, still in suit tolerance." She scrambled to her feet, pushing debris off herself. Glancing at the *Star Hawk*, she saw that its hatches were all closed. It sat there, a point of absolute calm in a field of chaos.

Saggal's voice came over her suit's speaker. "Did we get a full load?"

"One hundred and fifty. With yours, one-fifty-nine," answered Ryan's voice.

"All personnel. Return to vehicle assignments."

Rowan/Kate found herself once more in the ground forces' mess with Henry, Saggal and Ryan.

"I've dispatched the vehicles to scavenge the villages in this network of canyons." Ryan indicated a section of the map projected on the wall. "They would have been sheltered from most of the wind damage and some of the radiation. If we can get to them before the main tsunami hits this continent, we might get some tools, maybe even some foodstuffs."

"Survivors?" asked Saggal.

Ryan shook his head. "Not with the rad levels. A few hours at best. Those in the shelter of our ships are the only kangazoids that will live. If we can make a place for them."

Kate/Rowan hung her head. "How can we do that? Is the Republic giving them a world?"

"No. The k-no-in are the only likely possibility, and they are already dealing with an overpopulation problem. To make matters worse, all the species governments involved have been charged with using a planet buster technology."

"Divine," breathed Saggal.

Kate/Rowan's hand grasped the big felinezoid's.

"All we can do is what we can do. Right now, we need to salvage those canyon villages and get everything useful up in the mountains before that wave hits."

"Then what? If we have no place for the kangazoids to go, none of this matters," observed Kate.

Ryan smiled wearily. "Leave that to Henry and me. I have an idea, but I need to run the numbers. For the moment, we work on the assumption that we have nine-hundred and eighty-seven kangazoids still alive and viable, and, by the Divine's myriad names, I swear they will have a home, generals, ministers, bureaucrats and admirals be dammed!"

Kate/Rowan looked at Ryan's expression. To one who didn't know him, it could be taken as arrogance. To those that did, it was a sure message to help or get out of the way.

A FINAL KINDNESS

Medwin collected his pack from the coat check and led the way out of the museum. He scanned the almost familiar street. Beside the clothing shop, where in Sun Valley there was a hardware store, was a shop with a sign reading 'S.E.T.E. Reproductions and Memorabilia.' Where in Sun Valley there was a glass display window, there was an ever-changing screen displaying what he assumed were images taken from the shows where the surrogates were buying things or opening gifts. A scrolling text above the scenes proclaimed that you could own reproductions of the items used on set. Clothing, jewellery, antique tools, and electronics.

"Antique? My mum bought that computer just last week." Obert came up beside Medwin and pointed to the image on the screen.

"Everything we know is stone knives and bearskins to these people." Kendra moved to Medwin's other side.

"Our pain is the same. That's why they need us." Medwin let his eyes track down the street. There was a butcher's proclaiming real off the hoof meat, direct from the set region, nothing vat-grown. It was flanked by a greengrocer and later a cheese shop, making similar claims. A crow perched on the Garlic Palace's roof cawed.

"It definitely smells like our Garlic Palace," remarked Armina.

"I wish we had some coin. I could murder a pizza," added Obert.

"The food in our packs will do. We'll eat once we get out of town. We have a long hike ahead of us," stated Medwin.

A tremor reminiscent of a passing subway train ran through the ground.

Looking up the street where the bus terminal would be in Sun Valley, they saw a two-storey building, more carved from the local stone than made from it. People rushed into one of its large sliding glass doors. A moment later, a group of people emerged from the building's other door and walked to the S.E.T.E. Administration building.

"Shift change," guessed Medwin.

A sign over the entrance of what could have been the bus terminal proclaimed, 'Maglev Station'. A long, semi-circular ridge of stone ran out from the structure, stretching beyond where the eye could see. Immediately beside the station was the S.E.T.E. headquarters. As they watched, what looked like a motorbike swept out of the opening of what in Sun Valley was the multi-level municipal parking garage, beside the city hall, and sped up the street onto a ramp at the side of the maglev station, disappearing into the structure.

"We should check it out," said Obert.

"We need to get back. We could get caught," blurted Armina.

Medwin bit his lip in thought. "We need to report what we know. Armina's right. The longer we're here, the higher the risk of getting caught, and we know what that would mean."

"Could we dine and dash the Garlic Palace?" suggested Obert.

"Too dangerous. We should put some distance between us and this place," stated Medwin.

"Ration packs again." Obert fell in with his friends as they walked down the street. For the first three blocks, the layout of the buildings and even the street names mimicked what they knew. After that, changes crept in as first a series of blocky three-storey apartment complexes dominated the architecture, then large parks with occasional houses built in the native stone, but more like what they would expect a well-to-do middle-class family to live in. Finally, they came to an area where high rock walls flanked the street. A falcon regarded them from the top of the wall as they passed. They followed the wall, coming to a grillwork gate. Looking through, they could see palatial grounds done up like a garden with what could best be described as a manor house easily fifty metres back from the gate. A sign cast in what might have been gold topped the gate proclaiming that this small kingdom belonged to 'Zackery Smith, Producer of Homicide Investigations.'

"Rich bastards! My father died for this?" spat Medwin.

"Let's move on," suggested Kendra.

Medwin nodded, and they walked on.

The studio support town stopped about a hundred metres past the manor's gate. Fifty metres more, the land returned to barren rock and scrub grasses. The road also came to a halt.

"This is where we make a beeline for home." Medwin eased the pack on his shoulders.

"When do we stop for dinner?" asked Obert.

"When the sun sets. We have a long way to go, and we need to use the day while we have it," stated Kendra.

"At least it's a real sun. Not our sun, but a real sun." Armina sighed and followed her friends into the barren stage two terraform that comprised much of Gaia.

The scene shifted. Kate/Rowan walked across the devastated village. The canyon walls rose steep and menacing around it. Many of the huts still stood, piled-rock rings with battered and broken thatched roofs. The shattered bodies of kangazoids and other six-limbed animals littered the ground. Smoke rose from the communal cooking pit with an animal carcass spitted over it.

"Using fire should have been enough. We never should have been here. You'd have learned to make fire eventually," muttered Kate.

Rain started to fall from the leaden sky. Twilight was descending into a night so black it precluded the concept of light.

A hut nestled tight against the canyon wall looked promising. Kate/Rowan moved to its door and slipped in.

There was a coughing sound. Kate/Rowan turned on her suit's lights and focused on a kangazoid lying on a platform of twigs and moss. The being barely moved. Its fur had largely fallen out, often taking the skin beneath. Its skin was a mosaic of open sores. Blood stained the twigs and moss it lay on. It regarded Kate with large brown eyes as its chest struggled to rise and fall. She could see the despair in its face.

"Divine!" Kate whispered.

The kangazoid beckoned with its stunted lower arms, then raised a trembling large arm and pointed to a reed basket that hung from the ceiling. Kate/Rowan moved closer and looked in the basket. A small kangazoid struggled to breathe within it. The kangazoid in the bed on the floor motioned with its large arms as if pulling something to it.

As gently as her suit allowed, Kate/Rowan lifted the small kangazoid from the basket and carried it to its parent, laying the child on the adult's chest so that the adult could grasp the child with its small arms the way she'd seen others do.

The child nestled its face into the almost furless chest of the adult and held fast. The adult's arms, both small and large, enveloped the smaller form.

Kate enhanced her suit's audio and cancelled the sound of the rain. She heard two heartbeats, one fast, the other slower. The child seemed to take comfort in the touch of the adult and the sound of its heart. The fast heartbeat stopped. Before the small body could start to cool, the slow heartbeat fell silent.

Tears stung Kate/Rowan's eyes. She walked about the hut, gathering tools and implements of life while piling flammables around the bed. Tears trickled down her cheeks, and she couldn't open her suit to wipe them away.

She left the hut that had become a tomb. Drawing her sidearm, she set it to incendiary and fired into the fuel she had piled around the hut's occupants.

"May you be warm in the void, and the Divine keep you always, no matter what you perceive it to be." She spoke the words through a tight throat as the flames grew.

Carrying the salvage to the boxy mass of a k-no-in troop transport at the edge of the village, she added it to the other salvage filling the large rectangular room that formed its interior. Stalls, each about a metre wide, lined the walls. Half of them were filled with what looked like the results of a successful archaeological dig, only it was all new.

The scene shifted again. Now Kate/Rowan stood on the floor of a mountain valley. Fields of dying crops stretched out on all sides of a single large structure half dug into the earth with piled stones and a steeply peaked roof of logs.

K-no-in in EVA suits carried bodies from the structure. They were above the level the floodwaters were expected to reach, so here the danger was that decomposition would poison the resources the village could still provide. The k-no-in troop transport was full of artifacts from villages that would soon be underwater.

The k-no-ins piled the kangazoid bodies up at the edge of the village. Adults and children alike. One of the k-no-ins ran back to the transport and returned carrying what looked like a hardcover book. The k-no-in held the book forward in its foremost arms and seemed to bow over it before laying it on the mound of dead kangazoids. The k-no-in all stepped back.

"Honour to the fallen," barked a translated voice that was half-strangled with tears.

"Honour to the fallen," other voices coursed in unison. Then the k-no-in discharged their weapons set to cause fire into the piled bodies.

The bodies caught, sending a pillar of greasy smoke into the air.

"Divine be with you," whispered Kate as the bodies burned.

The scene shifted. Kate/ Rowan found herself on a high plateau overlooking the sea. As if someone had pulled a giant plug, the waters rushed back. Rowan could only be happy that the darkness hid the details of the exposed continental shelf and the dying sea life it left behind. A dark wall towering almost as high as the mountains swept in and swallowed the land. A flare went up to her right and exploded, casting a brilliance like the noon-day sun over the scene. The canyons she had been in shortly before became rivers. The land was swallowed, and the rubble left by the winds swept away as if some giant had sought to erase all evidence of the tragedy of the last day.

"I can't do this anymore," muttered Kate.

A k-no-in moved to her side. Her proximity channel carried his voice. "I too. Too much war. Too much death. No technology is worth this."

The scene shifted back to the bridge of the *Star Hawk*. She was staring at Ryan, who looked pale and had the icy alert quality of drugs taking the place of sleep. She turned to face her console.

"Helm. Stationary hover." Ryan's voice was steady.

"Captain, I don't know if I can," objected the Asian *Homo sapiens* man at the gunnery station.

"I know you can, Wong. You're the best precision gunner aboard. Henry and I ran the numbers. You don't have to be perfect for depth. Just close is enough, we can clear the underlayers with dispersed fire. The wave cleared the first fall of radioactive dust. This will get the rest."

Kate/Rowan looked up to see the dirty white expanse of the south pole glacial sheet on the big screen. In the distance, the sea sloshed in tumult as rain pummelled down in sheets.

"Shouldn't we wait for the rain to stop?" asked Wong.

"No, the added water will lubricate the move and wash away residue. It's inconvenient, but in the end, it helps us. Now fire," ordered Ryan.

Beams of light appeared on the scene, cutting a path into the glacier beneath.

"Helm, follow the track. Gunnery, keep the sides smooth." Ryan's voice was clipped.

Kate manoeuvred the *Star Hawk* up and down the glacier, so the guns cut a triangle in the ice, its wide end ending at the coast.

The light beams left deep canyons in the ice and sent up pillars of steam while causing jets of water to gush into the sea.

"Good. Cease fire. Helm, take us south ten kilometres from the point." Ryan's voice reflected confidence. Rowan was certain that he would have made a bad joke to break the stress.

"We're in location," Kate stated as Rowan watched the strange hands caress the *Star Hawk*'s controls.

"Gunnery, keep your angle shallow. We don't want to blast more rock than we have to. Fire." Ryan gave the final word a gravity that would have rivalled a black hole.

Light streaked across the screen, tearing into the ice undercutting the massive wedge. Seconds passed, then the kilometres-wide section of ice broke free and slid towards the sea. It began slowly, then as inertia was overcome, accelerated. Still, it seemed to go on forever, scouring the land and ice beneath and sending a wave crashing across the sea.

The scene cut to Kate watching the largest iceberg in history drift away from the frozen polar shore.

"What's the rad like?" asked Ryan.

The navigator to Kate/Rowan's left took a moment to check her instruments. "Sir, it's reading five millisievert annual, actually a touch below normal Murack Five background."

"Good. Gunnery, I want that ice melted down to the ground."

"Stroking low-intensity passes should do it, Captain." Wong worked his controls, and the layer of uncovered ice began to melt.

"Communications, get me Major Chibuden. Bolanle, we've cleared the road. Have your people set the power plant and get ready to string the wires. Over."

"We copy that, Captain. Over."

At the front of the screen, two felinezoid tanks, a *Homo sapiens* troop transport and *Homo sapiens* tank flew into view, suspending a broken *Homo sapiens* ambulance between them. They lowered the shattered craft onto the ice at the upper point of the triangle. The functional craft set down, and EVA-suited figures poured out of them. The Republic member species troops began cutting away the top layers of ice with lasers, throwing the ice slabs well to the side. Then a large wire coil was pulled out of a felinezoid tank, set on the ice, and connected to the broken ambulance by a heavy cable. Moments later, a pond of water had formed around the coil. A *Homo sapiens* in an EVA suit used a laser rifle to burn a hole through the ice, cutting a channel into the tip of the V-shaped depression the *Star Hawk* had carved. At first, the water froze as it fell, but as the temperature in the depression increased with the *Star Hawk*'s laser bombardment, it became a river cutting down the middle of the triangle.

"We'll place the heating units and run the cables as soon as we're down to bedrock. Congratulations, Captain, it looks like Kangralaw is going to work," remarked Major Chibuden's voice over the radio.

"It's a start. Keep on as we've begun. I'm going to consult with Henry. I'm still not happy with the climatological numbers. We have to keep the poisoned air away until it can clear." Ryan stood and surrendered the bridge to his first officer.

How bad must it have been? wondered Rowan.

The scene shifted. Kate/Rowan stood in a triangular valley walled by sheer ice cliffs and open at one end to the sea. It was just before dawn, but she wasn't sure that the sun could be noticed through the overcast. Large circular heating/lighting units were positioned at intervals along the valley, and a small river ran its length, collecting a constant flow of meltwater. The *Star Hawk* sat close to the narrow end of the wedge-shaped valley. The ship's hangar bay ramp opened. There was movement in the hangar beyond. A kangazoid tentatively hopped out. It moved to the bottom of the ramp, then stepped onto the rocky ground.

Turning, the kangazoid made a whooping sound and bounded, covering two metres in a single leap. Other kangazoids followed. Further down the valley, a similar scene played out with the *Kestrel* and the *Padfoot*.

Kate moved to the pile of tools behind her and picked up what looked like a stone hammer. She held it out to the kangazoids exiting the *Star Hawk*. One hopped towards her and took the hammer, then examined the pile of riches from which it had come.

Another kangazoid made a whooping sound and pointed towards the edge of the ice cliff just as the sun crested the horizon on a new day.

A screen filled Rowan's vision with 'End of Part One' written on it, then she was looking through her own eyes.

Tim lay on the cyber couch beside her, occasionally twitching.

"Kate," Rowan called.

"What did you think?" Kate entered the room.

"I... That scene with the kangazoid infant. Did it really—"

"Not that specific scene, at least not to me. The stories

are archetypal, but everyone involved had similar events to that and the burning. Over and over." Kate hugged herself. "Silly really, we let the kangazoid out onto Kangralaw in small batches, so they could start construction. Usually, we'd release a batch around noon. I guess the director thought sunrise was more dramatic."

"You've never experienced the program," observed Rowan.

"Living it was enough, but people insist on telling me about it."

Tim groaned and opened his eyes. "Divine!" he whispered.

"Whose perspective?" asked Rowan.

"Saggal's."

"Really? A felinezoid," remarked Kate.

"Maybe I'm trying to learn. Maybe I can see I've been a fool. Maybe I have good reasons for getting another perspective."

Kate smiled. "Maybe you are your father's son after all. Now get up, Ryan and Saggal will be back any time now, and if history serves, one of them will be carrying the other."

COPING STRATEGIES

9

Medwin replaced the lid on the tin of camping fire they'd used to cook their meal. They'd walked nearly two hours after leaving the studio support town, following their compass as close to due west as they could before coming across a stream that cut through a channel in the rocks. Mosses and some grasses grew along its course. The babbling of its passage added life to what seemed an almost dead world.

Looking up, he saw a blanket of stars, but cloud was coming in from the east.

"It's amazing to think of all the life out there. All the different species. It's what we all dreamed about. *Star Trek*, *Babylon Five*, even *Farscape*. They got it right," observed Kendra.

"Shotgun effect. Fire off enough buckshot in the general direction of the future, and you're bound to hit something," remarked Medwin.

"I think it's frightening. All that strangeness and humans so powerless. How can we hope to stay human? And us, we aren't even human." Armina hugged her legs to herself where she sat on the ground.

"We are human. We just need to make the rest of them see that." Medwin hugged the blonde girl.

Obert rolled his eyes and moved to Kendra's side. "I wonder what we'll do if we get out there."

"I want to see it all. Maybe I can get a job on a trading ship. Or become an ambassador or something." Kendra sighed.

"No chance you'll stay in Sun Valley?"

Kendra turned to look at Obert and spoke with incredulity. "Do you think they'd let us?"

Obert's normally comic demeanour fell away. "I think we are all going to die. Someone will slip, and the controllers will find out that we know. Then they will press the big red button, and everyone in Sun Valley will die."

"Why are you here then?" Kendra took Obert's hand and faced him.

"Because I'd rather die trying than live as a slave. Because I love Carol and hate what they've done to her, what they are doing to me. Don't get me wrong, the swinging is fun, but it should be our choice. It shouldn't be up to some controller to press a button, and we jump in the sack with the partner of their choice. That's rape. When I hold Carol, I want to know I am the one holding her. I want to know when I say I love you for the first time, it is me saying it, not some showrunner who wants the happy polyamorous couple because they think it will be good for ratings."

"So, if we do win, you'll stay on Gaia?" Kendra put her arm around her friend's waist. It was comforting to feel another person's warmth.

"Probably. I'm not freaked by the alien stuff like Armina, queen of whine, but I don't want to chase it either. I like the idea of bringing life to a new world. Of helping Earth's children come into their own. I can see myself doing that. Look at that." Obert pointed to an owl perched on a nearby rock. "Two hundred years ago, that bird couldn't have been here. Now life is fighting its way in. Humans brought the seeds, brought the animals, and now they are taking hold, making this their world. In a million years, this planet will be blue and green, a daughter of Earth going its own way in an evolutionary sense. We will have done that. Humanity will have done that. Brought life to a dead world. As bad as S.E.T.E. is, they do that. And I think with all the death humanity has brought over the ages, it's high time we started bringing life. It's a much better challenge."

Kendra sighed. "It looks like we have our dreams. Now to do the work."

"You know Carol wouldn't mind, and we're not being controlled now," suggested Obert.

Kendra smiled. "Some friendships shouldn't cross some lines."

"And I'm not Medwin." Obert winked.

"How?"

Obert cupped her cheek and spoke softly. "The only one who doesn't know is Medwin. He's too stuck on Armina to see what's right in front of him."

Arlene sat in the *Freedom's Run* control room in the S.E.T.E. Studio building. She let her hand hover over the control that would raise Kendra's infatuation response, then let her hand drift back to her lap.

"You've got a point, Obert. Besides, Mike said minimal manipulation in *Freedom's Run*. I think that extends to you guys." Changing her focus, Arlene piloted the owl drone that carried the telemetry booster behind a pile of rocks so it would be out of sight, then powered it down so that it would be ready if the group decided to move in the night. Next, she directed a second drone, disguised as a rabbit, to a tuft of vegetation by the stream where its telemeter had a clear connection to the campers.

"There you go. Come morning, the falcon should be charged up for Ulva.

"At least I don't need to boost one couple." Arlene spared the empathic monitors a glance. "Poor Armina. That's a girl, do something of life. Remind yourself that life is worth living. Damn, the audience are going to love Medwin. He cares so much. Nice mirror to Ryan." Arlene stopped to ponder. "Gene, note to all *Freedom's Run* controllers. Look for mirror moments between Ryan and Medwin. Don't push them but capitalize on what comes up naturally through focus and scene placement. We want to set a vibe that Medwin is like a younger version of Ryan. Watch for and exploit that resonance. Watch for similar character echoes between Kendra and Rowan. End message.

"See that everyone gets that at the start of their shift, Gene."

"Yes, Arlene," replied the studio computer.

"Bring up the creation file list for Rowan and Kendra. Put it on the big screen."

Arlene spared the side screen monitoring Medwin and Armina a glance as they made love. Medwin was fully in the moment as he held his girlfriend, kissing and caressing her in the way he knew she liked. Armina, her eyes open and fixed on the stars as her worry and despair devoured what could have been passion and joy.

Arlene shifted her attention to the big screen, where twined lists of life events tracked down in a row.

"Gene, highlight all shared creation files on the screen in green."

About seventy per cent of the files listed turned green.

"Hmm, they both got the falling off the horse and the deflated bouncy castle memories. This could work out. Give the audience a taste for Ryan and Rowan when they were younger without having to do flashbacks."

Ryan felt consciousness emerge through a haze. There were sounds of movement. He opened one eye a crack and promptly shut it as the light sent a shaft of pain through his head.

"When am I going to learn?" he muttered.

"Hey, hotty boss, you're awake," blurted Henry's voice in hearty, robust tones.

Ryan winced and tried to pull his pillow over his ears.

"Henry, enough!" admonished Rowan. Her voice was mercifully soft, but still, it was like a hammer in Ryan's skull.

The bed shifted as Ryan forced his eyes to open. His vision took a moment to clear, then he saw Rowan dressed in shorts and a T-shirt holding a tray with a mug, carafe, and bottle on it. The smell of coffee made his nose twitch.

"May the Divine bless you." Ryan sat up and reached for the mug.

"You're here, so I think it already has," remarked Rowan. "Did you and Saggal have fun?"

Ryan drained the coffee cup and sat back. "Define fun. Did I walk here, or did somebody carry me?"

"Walked, if you can call bouncing off the bulkheads walking. You were on two legs... most of the time." Henry sounded snippy.

"I distinctly remember having to carry Saggal." Ryan smiled. "I'll have to tell him he's getting soft. Last time he carried me home." Ryan snorted. "I woke up in one of Kate's negligees. My clothes were nowhere to be found. Getting back to quarters was less than fun. Felinezoids have a sadistic sense of humour!"

"Served you right," snipped Henry.

"Thanks again for blanking the security files of that." Ryan held his mug out for a refill.

"Kate said this would help with the hangover." Rowan held out the bottle of pink liquid from the tray. 'Sober Quick' was written in large bold letters on the label.

Ryan shook his head. "Unless stardust is breaking loose, I'll make do with coffee."

"Why, if it will make you feel better?" asked Rowan.

"It's too convenient. Some things get left behind when you change bodies. The physiological components of addiction being one of them."

Rowan's features scrunched up in thought as she refilled his cup. "You were—"

"Our good captain was a drunk," remarked Henry.

"An alcoholic. Maybe a drunk for a while at the start of it. This body never became addicted, which is why I don't have to worry about triggering the physical dependency with an occasional drink."

"What's the difference between a drunk and an alcoholic?" Rowan watched Ryan as if she expected to see this new revelation written on his face.

"A drunk is content to stay a drunk. An alcoholic knows they have a problem and can work to deal with it. I was seven years sober when I was cloned. After Murack Five, it was all too much. The guilt, the shame, the cancers, Joslin sticking her head in the e-rig deeper and deeper. I self-medicated with booze."

"That doesn't sound like you," remarked Rowan.

"It was a rough time for all of us, sweetness. Half the Murack Five disaster vets have a substance abuse problem, cross-species. I had an AI friend that took a computer virus, and nova blasted his circuits," explained Henry through the wall speaker.

"It was a low point for me. Upside, the new body dealt with the physical dependency. I'd dealt with the psychological one before the transfer. I don't want to go back. The hangover is a reminder that I have to be careful."

"Got that much right, oh captain mine," Henry's voice was acerbic.

"Henry, message received, but give it a rest. You know I wouldn't have gone last night except that it's a tradition with Saggal and me."

"Getting falling-down drunk is not a good tradition." Henry's voice had lost its scolding edge.

"Yes, Mother." Ryan tried to smile, but it turned into a wince.

"You mind your tongue, sonny. I can think of better uses for it." There was come hither in Henry's voice.

Rowan smiled. "More coffee?"

"Yes, please." Ryan held out his cup.

"Better hurry, hotty boss. The loading and passenger manifests came in. They seem to have an inflated opinion of the cargo capacity of a Hawk. Bugger me with knobs on. You are not going to believe who's coming to Murack Five," remarked Henry.

"Who?" asked Rowan.

"Pikeman. He's going to be the relief post physician and bio-chem expert."

"Rowan?" said Ryan.

"Yes?"

"Pass me the Sober Quick. The stardust just got deep." Ryan buried his forehead in his hand.

The rain fell in a slow drizzle that soaked everything. Medwin led the way in a trudge that followed the course of the stream they had camped beside. The stream had swollen to nearly a metre wide, filling its rocky channel.

"I hate camping in the rain!" Armina plodded through a puddle.

"It should make it harder for satellites to detect us," commented Kendra.

"Infrared," countered Obert.

Medwin sighed heavily. "Physics is physics. The cloud mass will be turbulent and will probably jumble infrared signatures passing through it. We should hurry while we have the storm to cover us. The border of the set region can't be much further."

Michael Strongbow sat at the control station for the *Freedom's Run* series and watched the teens through the eyes of the duck drone that circled above them.

"Gene, see to it that the perimeter monitors and satellites fail to pick up the party when they pass into the set region."

"Yes, Mr. Strongbow. Should I inform Mrs. Tallman of your instructions?"

Michael snorted. "Let's keep Milly out of the loop as much as we can. She already knows too much about *Freedom's Run*. I'll be so glad to get the premiere over with. Too many balls in the air. How are things coming with legal?"

"The legal team consider Mr. Wilson's new lawyer most dogged. They have described her as a bi—"

"My sentiments exactly, Gene. I'll follow up when I'm back in my office."

The door at the back of the room opened. Ulva walked in. She looked flushed, and her nose was red.

"Better?" asked Michael.

"A little. The meds should take effect soon. Thanks for covering for me. I wouldn't have asked except—"

Michael gave a dismissive wave as he vacated the controller's chair. "People get sick. It happens. I'd rather you call for help than have to clean up the mess."

"I, it just came on so suddenly. It's probably that variant on the spiderzoid bacteria that's been on the news. The one that jumped the species boundary. I took an immune enhancer. I should be good in a few hours."

"Good. I've called in Greg. I want to shift him over from *Angel Black* anyway. It will be good to get him updated. I can take the board until he gets in if you need me to."

"I should be good for an hour. Thanks for being so understanding."

Michael smile. "Being decent to each other is what it's all about. I think people forget that. Pay it forward when you're in the big chair."

Ulva smiled as she half fell into the controller's seat. "If that chance ever comes."

"You have talent and ambition. It will come if you work for it. Tell Greg to scan the updates file. He won't know about our scouts' trip to the museum. And you, young lady, take care of yourself. Your father would never forgive me if anything happened to you." Michael slipped from the control room.

"Stardust, if he was forty years younger, I'd give Marcy a fight for that one. Why can't I find men like Mike and Ryan my own age? I swear, they've discontinued all the best models."

"Is that an inquiry about future surrogate production?" inquired Gene's voice.

"No, Gene, it's the ramblings of a fevered mind."

Ulva watched through Medwin's eyes as he topped a hill and looked down at the blue/grey strip of the Wolf River that marked the edge of the set region. Beyond the river was the edge of the forestation project.

The sound of an explosion came through the speakers. The screen showed a cloud of rock dust and debris.

"The tree planters are busy," observed Obert.

"We'll get down to the river but not cross until after shift. We don't want them to see us," said Medwin.

"At least the rain will clear the rock dust faster. I hate that smell," added Kendra.

"What comes next is worse," remarked Medwin.

Armina sighed and looked at the distant line of green. "At least it's pretty. Like a plastic flower."

"Organizational Component 87, the cargo capacity of the *Star Hawk* falls at least ten per cent short of the cargo you have scheduled for us to transport. I cannot make space for it all." Ryan stared into the main screen on the *Star Hawk*'s bridge which displayed a crabzoid organizational component. The component looked like a six-legged crab with a mat of cilia growing off its shell. The shell itself was orange with blue stripes, and it had four small pincers at either end. There was nothing that could be called a face on the alien. The wall of the chamber in the background was covered with cilia.

"You are in error, Captain Chandler." The voice that came out of the translator was officious. "I have reviewed your revised ship's schematics. You have adequate capacity."

"Where?" challenged Ryan.

"It is obvious. Have your passengers enter dormancy and use what was the officers' quarters as cargo space."

Ryan blinked. "I will get back to you within one Earth standard hour." He then looked to where Kitoy sat at the communications' station and subtly touched his throat. Kitoy stopped the transmission.

"Blasted hive minds!" blurted Henry.

"It's how they travel. There was a picture in the *Space Traveller's Guide to Crabzoids*. They stack themselves up like boxes on a shelf and go to sleep," observed Rowan, who sat at the navigator's station.

Ryan gritted his teeth. "Star Searcher should know that doesn't work for most species."

"Hive minds tend to be know-it-alls. It's in their biology," observed Tim from the life sciences station.

"Sadly, they don't want to overcome their biological shortcomings. At least Star Searcher doesn't." Ryan fell into thought.

The bridge became silent as everyone busied themselves with systems checks.

"Henry?" Ryan's voice had a hint of smugness.

"Yes, oh my handsome captain," replied the AI through his android mouth.

Ryan chose to ignore the comment. "How much of the cargo is sourced from the UES?"

"Twenty-six point five per cent by volume," replied Henry.

"How much of that is in E.S.T.C.s?"

"Hotty boss, that is brilliant! Checking. Nearly half of it is Space Services or Ground Forces surplus. That will be in Earth Standard Transport Containers."

"Take as much of that as we have room for on the rails

and fast store chambers out of the equation. How are we for volume?"

"Three cubic metres to spare. It will make the offload quicker," said Henry.

"You fixed the E.S.T.C. rail system?" queried Kitoy.

"It wasn't that badly damaged, and I wanted my lady fair right. I always planned to re-arm when I reached Geb. Independent systems get a lot of piracy."

"What's an E.S.T.C.? I've never heard of them," asked Tim.

Ryan smiled as a memory of Tim as a child full of questions and wanting to know about everything came into his mind.

"They're boxes. One metre cubed designed to ride the ship's transport rails. Doctor too smart to listen to his father," stated Henry, in a voice so mechanical you might mistake him for the *Star Hawk*'s standard computer system.

"Henry, give him a break. Unless they'd served in the Space Services, most people wouldn't get that. The passages that run between the secondary outer hull and the inner hull contain a network of maglev rails and storage chambers."

"Useful because I can send maintenance robots anywhere in the ship to root out, let's say a rat." Henry had pivoted his station chair so his android face could glower at Tim.

"Getting back to topic," interrupted Ryan. "Earth Standard Transport Containers are designed to slot on the rails. The ship can move them to wherever they're needed. Back in the day, the *Star Hawk* could mesh the restock port with a prepped *Homo sapiens* installation and do a full restock in less than an hour. The tracking labels on the crates would direct them to the proper storage sector. We could go from empty missile bays to fully armed in less than two hours. It took time for the computer to do the internal shuffling."

"Stupid computer should take a tenth that long," observed Henry.

Tim laughed. "I remember the story now."

"What happened?" asked Rowan.

Ryan chuckled and smiled. "It was during the Batzoid Pirate Suppression. A pirate corvette caught us approaching one of their secondary bases. Some clerk had mixed up the bar codes on the E.S.T.C.s. The corvette attacked us. We fired back with Ground Forces' ration packs. If the pirates had tried to eat them, we probably would have won the battle then and there."

"They did make good anti-missile chaff. The frozen peas really tore through enemy rockets," remarked Henry.

"The pirates thought we were using a new biological weapon and backed off from the debris field to analyze it. That bought us enough time to duck through a gas giant's upper atmosphere, launch a probe to leave a false trail, come out behind the planet and establish stealth."

"And you spent the next three days manually re-sorting the containers," finished Tim.

"We're just lucky nobody tried to eat a missile. I wouldn't have put it past some of the ground pounders," remarked Ryan.

"Those were my squad, you space services snob!" Henry smiled, the damaged side of his face looking like a death mask. "It's okay, you're still hot, my captain, and with McNally, you may have a point," remarked Henry.

"What happened to her?" asked Ryan.

"She's a UES senator now." Henry sighed. "She did like it when I—"

"Moving on. It's nice the system will be used to carry cargo that is really helping people," remarked Kitoy.

Ryan nodded. "A little atonement. Maybe that is what the Divine is looking for. Rowan, chart a course to the Republic Cargo Transfer bay. It's time to load up so we can get this over with. Kitoy, put me through to Star Searcher. I want to get it recorded what the cargo is before I tell him...

it… umm… them. Pronouns are a pain inter-species; you know what I mean. I want a volume limit set before I let on that I've found a way to fit everything in, so Star Searcher doesn't add more to the load."

A PLACE TO LAY THEIR HEADS

Croell lay on the bed in the captain's quarters of the *Mary*. The space yacht was luxuriant by human standards. For the batzoid, who, although roughly human-sized, had a bat-like body and wings as well as a black head and neck like a snake's, it was horribly uncomfortable.

The cabin's door slid into the wall, admitting Zandra. To a *Homo sapiens*, she appeared almost identical to her mate, except her head and neck were red, and she had retractable fangs. She also lacked the claws topping the forefingers of her seven-fingered hands that Croell possessed.

"Croell, I have just learned that Pikeman is joining the relief mission to Murack Five." Zandra's tone was exuberant.

Croell flicked his snake-like tongue in the batzoid equivalent of a smile. "Did I not say that a way would be found to keep our geises together?"

"You did, my husband. Wait, did you see to this?" Zandra eyed her mate with suspicion.

"I felt it likely that a being such as Pikeman was less than law-abiding. A few hours reviewing public data files enabled me to bring a malfeasance to the attention of the appropriate individuals. Given how desperate the Star Searcher entity is to find relief workers for Murack Five, I felt it likely that Pikeman would be granted the option of serving any Republic sentence there."

"But how are we going to pursue our quarry?"

"Even with the *Star Hawk*'s shipment, the delivery of supplies is well behind schedule for Murack Five. I believe that we can perform a civic duty and assist in this. The yacht's cargo capacity is small, but if we fill the unused quarters and the recreational area, Star Searcher will give us a pass to enter the restricted space. That entity is desperate not to fail at its duties. It is a weakness that can be exploited."

"And so, we help to save the kangazoid and fulfill our geises at the same time. The Great Flyer of the Skies truly must want us to atone for the sin of our creation."

"For the Great Flyer of the Skies is love," remarked Croell.

Zandra flicked her tongue and flipped her cobra-like fangs straight while extending her wings. "And love is a worthy thing."

Croell released a hiss as his wife leapt onto the bed to be taken in his arms.

Ryan stood at the bottom of the *Star Hawk*'s hangar bay ramp and looked at the neatly stacked boxes that occupied half of a docking bay nearly three times the *Star Hawk*'s size. He shook his head. "Crab-faced bureaucrat!"

"It's not organized," complained Rowan, who stood to his right.

"Oh, it's organized. A crabzoid is in charge of it," breathed Ryan. "It's just not organized in a way that is of any use."

"What's the key to it?" asked Kitoy, who moved to his left.

"The periodic table." Henry's voice came from a wall speaker.

"That bureaucrat sorted everything by the dominant element in its composition. Look there." Ryan pointed where a collection of transparent aluminum tanks nearly two metres long by one square containing something clear were stacked.

"They look like fish tanks," observed Rowan.

"Close, sweetness. They're aquatic normal flora. Seed organisms to help rebalance the ecology. They're at the front right because they are mostly hydrogen. H_2O," said Henry.

"Stardust!" Tim pushed past the group on the loading ramp and raced to the tanks. He began checking the read-out screens that each had at its corner.

"Is there a problem?" Ryan moved to Tim's side.

"Not yet. The onboard power has maintained the habitat levels. We need to get these hooked up to a power source fast."

"We'll load them first." Ryan reached up to slap Tim's back, then stopped himself.

"How'd you know to check?" asked Rowan.

"When I saw the normal flora was supplied by the k-no-in, I skimmed a bit about their tech. Their energy storage systems are well below galactic average."

"And Star Searcher was too arrogant to check," added Ryan. "Henry, open the bomb bay doors and check the power junctions I wired in there. We'll start with the fish tanks. Once they're loaded, we should have some room to work."

Pulling Rowan into his side, he kissed her. "For luck. I…" He released her and, moving to the side of the hangar, pulled a pair of grav-lifts from a wall bracket. Rowan and Kitoy followed his example. "Let's get this started so we can get this done."

Hours later, the last water-filled boxes were lifted into the bomb bay, which looked like a large room with extension cords crisscrossing its width. Ropes secured each bio tank to the one above it, and the top tanks were tied to the nubs left from the brackets that had held the bombs.

"All checks. The tanks are feeding off the *Star Hawk*'s power grid." Tim stepped back from the last of the bio-boxes. Rowan adjusted the grav-lift underneath it, and it floated into place. Ryan secured the rope around it with a slip knot, then Rowan released the grav-lift, and the ropes took the strain.

"In another hour, we would have lost some of the samples. I worry about deployment. Will the relief workers have time to get them to the environmental zones they are trying to reinforce?"

"Give me some credit. Each layer is a separate drop. We'll deposit them where they'll be needed. Offload some of the other cargo at the aid camp while they're deployed, then when the aid workers are ready, go to the next drop, repeat. I may not want to go to that place, but I won't do a half job, even if it means taking the grand tour of the planet," remarked Ryan.

"Good plan," observed Tim.

Ryan grunted, then said, "Henry, close the bomb bay doors."

There was the sound of hydraulics as the massive doors closed in from the sides.

"Bomb bay doors closed and locked," announced Henry's voice. "It's tighter than an old maid's—"

"Henry." Rowan's voice was even. "At least be original. That one was old even in the time I thought I grew up in."

"It's a classic," observed Henry. "Besides, most old maids throughout history were likely lesbians. So, it wasn't as much of a waste as it seems."

"People are more than their sex lives," observed Tim.

"But it's that part that's the most fun," countered Henry.

Rowan looked at Ryan and blushed.

"Can be if you do it right. A big strong partner with a soft touch stroking over your fur. Their claw tips lightly scraping your skin as they build slowly but surely to a fiery heat. The way the mind focuses, blocking out all other thoughts as you experience the glory of the moment. How much you

AIs lose with your constant multitasking. Never focused on the ecstasy of organic interaction." Kitoy spoke in a soft, seductive tone and combed the fur of her left arm gently with the claws of her right.

Henry sent a gulping sound through his speakers. "If you need me, I'll be experiencing an *Orgy Girls* special feature or three." The line went silent.

Tim stared at Kitoy, his face going red as he shifted position.

Ryan smiled and tore his eyes away from the felinezoid to look at Rowan.

"I think you got him," remarked Rowan.

"Someone has to. Honestly, Ryan, you need to adjust the run speed on his libido."

"Not unless he consents. He is a thinking being with free will. It started as a mistake, but that doesn't change anything. Start sorting the E.S.T.C.s from that mess." Ryan indicated the towering mass of containers.

"What do they look like?" asked Rowan.

"Kitoy, can you show them?" asked Ryan.

"Ryan, felinezoid here. I know what an E.S.T.C. is because Kadar mentioned them." A wave of sadness crossed Kitoy's features.

Tim moved to her side and gently gripped her arm. She looked down at his eyes, and her tail swished.

"Sometimes, it just hits me that he's gone." Kitoy took a deep breath. "Anyway, I know what they are, but I've never worked with them. If you want me to sort the Felinezoid United Worlds Standardized Shipping Units, I can."

Ryan quirked an eyebrow as if in thought. "Separate a couple out and put them in my workshop. Cargo that isn't perishable or delicate. Maybe the food packs you want for the trip. I'll show you an E.S.T.C."

Moving to the pile, Ryan scanned it, then pointed. "Third container down on this stack."

Using the grav-lifts, they uncovered the E.S.T.C., which was a metre-cubed box with rounded edges on four tracks that were each shaped like the letter U. Two on the top and two on the bottom.

"This is simple," remarked Rowan.

"The best engineering is," agreed Ryan. "Start sorting these out of the stack. Check that they're part of our load, then set them up over there." Ryan waved to the left stern of the *Star Hawk*, then walked towards the hangar's entry ramp.

"What are these anyway?" asked Tim.

Kitoy pulled her handheld from a pouch on the utility belt she wore and scanned the bar code "It says UES Ground Forces ration packs. Use Before 797 AC."

"Army food. No wonder they have trouble getting volunteers to help on Murack Five. My dad told me stories about eating with the ground pounders." Tim pushed the grav-lifts into small gaps at the bottom of the E.S.T.C. that seemed to be made for the purpose.

"I've had the packs on the *Star Hawk*. They were delicious." Rowan found another E.S.T.C. and repeated Tim's actions.

"That was Space Services food and the officers' mess. There is a big difference between that and field rations." Kitoy started moving crates off another group of E.S.T.C.s.

Ryan strode to a locker at the side of the hangar and pressed his thumb to a scanner plate. It opened to reveal an assortment of telescoping poles and what looked like tarpaulins as well as four wedge-shaped pieces of equipment. Each wedge had a rounded tube coming off its wide end. Everything was set on a dolly. He rolled the entire assembly into the docking bay.

"Henry, if you can tear the ram away from your recreation. Please, deploy the junction track. Hold back the pressure seal."

"As you command, my master." Henry's voice had an effeminate quality.

"What?" exclaimed Ryan.

"I'm experiencing the *Fit to be Tied Orgy Girls Special*

Feature. There was some leakage," remarked Henry.

Ryan rolled his eyes and sighed. A port about a metre up on the stern left of the *Star Hawk* opened into the hull. Four telescoping tracks just over a metre apart emerged from the port.

Moving below the tracks, Ryan unfolded the poles from the unit he'd rolled out of the *Star Hawk*. The poles telescoped out and folded into twin triangles connected horizontally by two-metre-long pipes at their points ending in a rectangle at the tall end, forming a ramp shape sandwiched ending in a flat area between the *Star Hawk* and the hangar wall. Attaching the tarpaulin-like material to the frame, Ryan unfolded it twice, clipping it to protrusions at the base of the pipes, then pressed a button on one of the sloping tubes. The material stiffened and unrolled, marching up the frame until it formed a ramp with a flat area just under the tracks extending out of the *Star Hawk*. Ryan walked up the ramp and mounted the wedge-shaped devices into clips on the track ends.

"We can start loading now," he called as he moved to the closest of the E.S.T.C.s.

Rowan, who had stopped to watch Ryan, shook her head. Most of the time, she could forget the vast difference in knowledge and ability between her and the people of the galaxy at large. Then she would witness a piece of technology, and it would all come home. Spaceships, antigravity, AI were easy to take, but things like a loading ramp, so common, so simple, so necessary, but done differently. Sometimes she wondered if she'd ever catch up. She looked at Ryan, oblivious to the magic of the everyday science around him.

"Of course he is. How could anyone not be?" whispered Rowan.

Ryan paused to lovingly pat the side of the *Star Hawk*. The action was so like the affection that Gunther, Rowan's father, showed his old motorbike she had to smile. "Little girls marry their daddies," she muttered the old wisdom and smiled. "I could do worse!"

Ryan came down the ramp. Rowan, Kitoy, and Tim moved to his side.

"Loading the rack is simple. I'll show you, then let you get on with it." Ryan collected a pair of grav-lifts, slid them under one of the cargo boxes and levitated it up the ramp to the front of the tracks coming out of the port in the *Star Hawk*'s side. He decreased the intensity of the anti-grav field until the far end of the lifters rested into a pair of short troughs on the track, then pushed the container forward. The tracks on the container slid over the wedges, which centred them on the rails from the *Star Hawk*. After the E.S.T.C. was half on the rails, it vanished with a *whoosh* into the ship.

"That's it. No flashes of light or talking computers," said Rowan.

"Why make things complicated?" Ryan shrugged. "If we could link to a dock, it's even simpler. I..."

There was a clang that echoed through the overcrowded hanger bay. "Captain Chandler, Captain Chandler. Are you here?" minced a voice. A buzzing sound came from behind the stacks of cargo.

"I'm here, and you are?" called Ryan.

A moment later, a being appeared in the narrow passage that circled the storage crates. It was the size of a horse, had translucent wings folded against its back and a segmented body that ended at one end in a mouth flanked by two long feelers. Its back end tapered to a point from which a long spike projected. It supported itself on four segmented legs and had two arms behind and to the sides of its mouth, each of which ended in a pincer. Its body and legs were covered in a blue shell.

"Stop!" shouted Ryan and Kitoy in unison. They looked at each other in horror. Kitoy gave a small swish of her tail.

Ryan continued to speak. "This shared area is set to accommodate *Homo sapiens* and felinezoid. You are in grave danger."

The waspzoid flicked its wings, and the buzzing sound increased. "Thank you for your concern, but it is not a difficulty. I am Wizziminipzzy. You can call me Wispy. That's what Saggal and Kate do at Wesnakee. I have had additions to my immune system so that I may enter your sector safely. Captain Chandler, I must speak to you."

Ryan shrugged and spoke to his crew. "Start loading the E.S.T.C.s. Henry can handle the sort as they come aboard. Try not to make too much of a mess. This place is tight for space." Ryan turned to Wispy and made a beckoning gesture with his arm.

"Are you a female *Homo sapiens*?" Wispy had a note of shock in his voice as he moved closer.

"No, male. Why do you ask?" Ryan led the waspzoid to a corner of the bay away from where the others were loading cargo.

"This is embarrassing." Wispy swished his antenna. "In my culture, waving the forward mandible is an invitation to discuss joining in a reproductive cycle. I haven't been in the shared area with *Homo sapiens* very long. I've heard that yours is one of those species that use sex as a social bonding tool. I thought you were being friendly in a way I cannot accommodate."

"For *Homo sapiens*, the gesture is a way of saying follow me."

"I appreciate your lesson. It is so difficult sometimes. I know I am the newcomer, and I must accommodate the species of this shared sector, but there is so much to learn, and so many sentients have no patience and are unwilling to tell you when you make a mistake. Why, just the other day a k-no-in became offended when I—"

Ryan held up his hand. "I'm sorry... Wispy. I do have a lot of work to do."

"You have no time for me." Wispy's antenna drooped.

"I can spare a few minutes. Just please, tell me why you've come?"

"Oh, thank you for sparing me time. I will try to use it

wisely. You see, I must ask you a favour."

"You don't even know me," observed Ryan.

"I know, that is what makes it so difficult. If you were of my breeding amalgam, it would be easy, but you aren't, and I am ignorant of the finer nuances of *Homo sapiens'* culture. I mean, the *Space Traveller's Guide to Homo Sapiens* is a nice start, but it omits much. Don't you find that that series needs a good rewriting? There are so many details the books miss—"

"Wispy," Ryan interrupted the waspzoid. The sentient emitted an odd buzzing noise that was irritating.

"Of course, I am sorry. The point is, I am scheduled to be one of the relief workers you are taking to Murack Five. I'm an exo-sociologist, junior grade. I'm supposed to catalogue kangazoid cultural norms so that when they are reintroduced to a more natural environment, we can start them back to a society approximating the original core society disrupted by the accident and social contamination during the rescue. It is going to form the basis of my dissertation to obtain my advanced standing degree. In any case, I contracted to do this relief rotation nearly a year ago, right after I received the immune system enhancements."

"Wispy, I need to get all this cargo loaded. Please, what do you want from me?"

"Oh… Well… As you know, the relief mission's departure has been delayed several times. This has led to the lease on my living space running out. I have had to vacate to make room for a felinezoid couple who have paid in advance to take possession of the space. He is an EVA technician working on—"

"I'm sure they are lovely." Ryan resisted the urge to raise his voice.

"Of course. I have no place to live until I leave on the mission, and it's just about time for me to moult. It would be so nice of you if you'd let me move into the room I will be using during the journey early."

Ryan sighed and muttered, "Long trip for a short drink. I have no problems with that. I haven't configured the berths for the comfort of our passengers yet, but you are welcome to stay."

"Oh, thank you so much. And I am easy to accommodate. I like *Homo sapiens'* beds. I've always liked a soft sleeping platform. I'll pick up my own shell fragments after I moult, that will probably happen on the voyage, but it's better to not leave these things to the last moment, don't you think? I'll just go around and get my things. I left them on a grav-sledge by the hangar's entry door. It was just too awkward to manoeuvre it into that narrow passage. There are a lot of supplies. If you like, once I drop off my possessions, I can help you load them. I like to keep busy. It makes the time pass—"

"Wispy!" Ryan kept his voice short of a shout.

"Yes?"

"Go get your things. I'll have Henry, my ship's operating system, guide you to your quarters. Henry is a full AI, so manners matter." Ryan smiled, showing teeth, hoping that the waspzoid would understand it as a pleasant gesture while also hoping it would have the common instinctive reaction of it being a threat display.

Wispy waved his antennae, then happily flounced away.

Ryan leaned against a crate feeling like he'd just done heavy labour.

Greg settled his hulking, bald-headed form in the *Freedom's Run* controller's chair and scanned new data that had come in from the Switchboard Station. His emerald-green skin lightened, and his yellow, slit-pupiled eyes dilated as he watched through Ryan's perspective as Rowan collapsed after telekinetically restraining a batzoid that was trying to kill Pikeman. A slender, forked tongue flicked out of Greg's mouth. Ryan's readings were bordering on panic, but he still did what was necessary.

"If I didn't know they are both sstill alive, I would be sscared," Greg remarked to himself as he watched Ryan's thumbs press against the artery that supplied the batzoid's brain. "Gene, place an editing marker with note. Third persson will carry the action better here. CGI sshould be conssidered."

The console to his right chirped, and Greg pressed a button, pausing the playback. He looked at the side screen, then, with a key tap, shifted Medwin and his friends to the main screen. "Gene, pleasse confirm that the ssatellite feedss have been diverted."

"Only this board is receiving S.E.T.E. satellite feeds of the eastern set region border," replied the computer.

"Good. We wouldn't want the sshow to end before it beginss."

Medwin scuttled forward, keeping to the cover afforded by some large rocks by the river. He peeked over the boulders, then waved his friends forward.

Kendra led the others in a sprint and skidded to a halt beside Medwin.

"I can't see anybody," remarked Obert.

"Me neither. Still, we should wait until dusk. Use the long shadows to our advantage," said Medwin.

"How are we going to cross the river?" asked Armina.

"Swim." Medwin stared at the fast-flowing water.

"Won't it look suspicious if we go into town soaking wet?" objected Kendra.

"People know we had a raft. Just tell them it got swept onto the Wolf River and sank. Everyone knows the Wolf is treacherous. We had to swim to shore," suggested Obert.

The group looked at him with incredulity.

"What?" asked Obert.

"That's a good idea," observed Armina.

"And this is surprising because?" Obert rolled his eyes.

"Remember, don't fight the current. Swim across it. We have a long way to go before we'll be past Sun Valley... the set region. Going downstream won't be a problem."

"Take your shoes and pants off before you get in the water," said Kendra.

"Why?" asked Obert.

"Lifeguard here. It's really hard to swim in shoes and pants. We can stuff them in our packs. Empty your canteens and close them tight and anything else that can hold air. Make the packs as light as we can. Then we can hold them. They'll help us stay up as we kick across."

"Right." Medwin opened his pack and began sorting through its contents. The others followed his example.

"Clever girl, Kendra." Greg's hand hovered over a control. "No, I'll wait and ssee if they can do it without enhancsement."

The sun had almost set when Medwin and his friends bolted for the river. The tree planters had been gone for nearly an hour. They hit the current, clutching their packs ahead of them. One stride, two, then their feet were off the bottom, and they were kicking across the flow towards the far bank.

"It's cold," complained Armina.

"Keep kicking. Stay together," ordered Kendra.

"They'll see us for sure." Armina kept kicking but started falling behind.

"Keep going. Once we're on the other side, we're just out for a camping trip that went wrong," reassured Medwin.

The current dragged them downstream. Obert and Armina fell behind.

"Look for the light," shouted Medwin before he focused all his energy on getting across.

Kendra moved ahead of him and moments later was scrambling up the far bank. Medwin reached the shore fifty strides down current from her and scrambled out. Shivering, and with cramping muscles, he stumbled up the bank. Finding a rise of land, he clambered to its top. In the twilight, he thought he saw one of his friends crawl from the river.

Pulling the can of Camping Heat from his pack, he pried the lid off and set it on the rise of land. His fingers were trembling and stiff as he dug the lighter out of his pack and flicked it. Several tries later, it sparked. He ignited the Camping Heat. The fire grew, sending out a wavering light and warmth.

Taking his pants and boots from his pack, he wrung the water out of the former and pulled them on. He was trembling with cold.

"M-M-M-Medw-w-win," Kendra's voice called from the base of the hill.

"H-H-Here." He pulled off his T-shirt and wrung the water out of it before putting it back on.

"C-C-Cold." Kendra climbed the slope. Her clothing was damp, but she had obviously wrung the worst of the water out of it, and she wore the light jacket that had been in her pack. Her black hair was plastered close to her face.

"I k-k-know." Medwin pulled his jacket from his pack and pulled it on despite its dampness. He huddled close to the canned heat, warming his fingers.

Kendra sat beside the small fire. "O-Others?"

"D-D-D—" Medwin took a breath, forcing his lips to stop trembling. "Downstream." He swallowed. "I think Obert made shore." His fingers warmed a little from the fire, Medwin pulled on his battered hiking boots and clumsily did up the laces.

"We n-n-need to find t-them." Rising, Kendra pulled her sleeping bag from her pack. "Help me wring it out."

Taking one end of the bag, Medwin and Kendra twisted it until it was mostly dry, then repeated the process with Medwin's bag.

They draped the damp bags over their shoulders.

"Ready?" asked Medwin.

"No, but Obert and Armina can't wait. Cold kills," remarked Kendra.

Nodding, Medwin put the lid on the Camping Heat, extinguishing the flame, then wrapping it in a damp towel. He put it in his pack. Pulling out the electric lantern, he turned it on and, still shivering, he and Kendra stumbled downstream.

"I never knew the Wolf River was so cold," remarked Medwin.

"Another reason for people not looking past it," observed Kendra.

Medwin nodded and focused on scanning the riverbank. Minutes later, they found Obert on the bank huddled in a fetal position and shivering.

Kendra rushed to his side and wrapped him in her sleeping bag.

"How bad?" asked Medwin.

"Bad. I'll look after him. Leave me the Camping Heat. I have the cooking rig. You look for Armina. We need to get everyone warm and dry." Kendra opened Obert's pack, pulled out his pants and started wringing them dry.

Medwin extracted the still warm Camping Heat, pulled off its lid and sparked it. Wrapping himself in his damp sleeping bag, he started downstream, silently praying that Armina had made it to shore.

⚬═══◦►

Greg watched the screens, his forked tongue flicking in agitation.

"Nova blasst policsy." Reaching for Armina's controls, he released epinephrine from her control pack and boosted her metabolism. Her core body temperature crept up.

"Mike issn't John. He won't mind," Greg told himself.

Medwin stumbled along the bank, then he saw Armina laying on the barren rock. He raced to her side and fell to his knees beside her. Her pack was gone, and her skin was icy. Swallowing, he pressed his fingers into her neck. Her pulse beat slowly against his fingers. Wrapping her in his sleeping bag, he sat and gathered his strength.

Greg smiled. "A hero scsene will appeal here." He adjusted Medwin's biology.

Medwin found the strength to stand, then picked up Armina, still wrapped in the sleeping bag. Somehow, he managed to carry her. Step followed step, as his exertion drove the cold from his body and the damp evaporated from his clothes.

He stumbled towards the light emitted by the Camping Heat.

"Kendra," he called.

The dark-haired girl staggered to his side. "I've spread out Obert's sleeping bag. We should put them together on it so they can share body heat, then cover them with our bags."

Medwin grunted, carried Armina to the spread-out bag, and laid her down.

"Obert, get over her," Kendra ordered.

Obert crawled to lay beside Armina, clutching a sleeping bag around himself the entire time. Medwin noticed that Kendra had stripped the wet clothing off their friend and left it to dry on a rock.

Kendra draped the sleeping bag over her friends, then went to the Camping Heat and took a small pot off the wire cooking frame she'd erected over it. "Eat this." She passed the pot and a spoon to Medwin.

Medwin carefully dug into the gloppy oatmeal in the pot. The warmth descending to his stomach was the most wonderful thing he'd ever felt.

Kendra warmed her hands over the Camping Heat as Medwin ate. The pot empty, she put it over the heat and filled it with water.

"How dry are your clothes?" asked Kendra.

Medwin felt his clothes with his hands. "My socks and boots are a swamp. The rest are okay."

"Good. Take your socks off so they can dry and get under the covers."

"I—" began Medwin.

"Spoon Armina. She needs the body heat. I'll heat the water and try to get Obert to drink it, then I'll spoon him. It's going to be a long night."

LOADING

11

"Then I told her that we needed to understand other cultures because of the time we could save not reinventing pottery." Wispy walked beside Rowan, carrying what she understood to be a dichrostigmazoid shipping container as large as himself and twice as heavy into the *Star Hawk*. The clutter extracting their cargo had caused had forced them to alter their loading to clear space in the hangar. Tim and Kitoy focused on the E.S.T.C.s and Wispy and Rowan on the containers from other species. Ryan moved from duty to duty as need called.

They'd been loading constantly for eight hours and hardly put a dent in the supplies in the hangar. In the *Star Hawk*, the old ground forces barracks and its associated rooms were half full, floor to ceiling.

Reaching the *Star Hawk*'s elevator, Rowan paused. "You go first. It will be a tight squeeze with both of us."

"Oh, all right. I'll tell you about what my father-sister said when you get up to me."

Wispy scuttled into the elevator with his load and the door closed behind him.

"Does he ever stop talking?" asked Rowan.

"At least you can leave the room," observed Henry from the wall speaker.

"Even when he's alone?" Rowan sounded incredulous.

"Pardon me," interrupted a shy-sounding voice.

Rowan turned to see a spiderzoid standing behind her, pulling a grav-sledge by what looked like a piece of thread.

"Who…? What…?" Rowan took a deep breath, suppressing the startle reflex that seeing what looked like a spider the size of an Irish Wolfhound instilled. "Can I help you?"

"I am Krakkeen. Are you Tree in Mountains? You do not have fur on your body, and I think you are female. Thus, I assume that you are *Homo sapiens*, and you are not Ryan because he is male and… I am sorry. I am spilling this communication out the drinking hole."

The spiderzoid fell silent and rubbed its forelegs together.

Rowan smiled. She'd come to recognize common cues for nervousness in several Republic species. "I am Rowan, and I am a female *Homo sapiens*. You got that right."

"I am so glad. I have such a hard time with you al… other species. I once mistook an otterzoid for a felinezoid. The individual was quite insulted. It was an honest mistake. The species are both furry and smell like rotting voret berries. Ryan told me that you would lead me to my quarters. I am going to stay aboard the time before we depart."

"Wouldn't you be more comfortable in your species habitat section?" asked Rowan.

"I cannot endure living with that empty fruit husk, Kaakaasee, another point seven two seconds. She is such a genderist! Always on about how males have no mind for resource allocation. If the granla fruit crop had stayed healthy, I would have made a fortune. Rotted fruit of a fungus!" The opisthosoma of the spiderzoid expanded, then contracted, making a whistling noise. "My aunt is my problem, not yours. The core of it is, she ordered me away from her sleeping tree when I asked her to stop berating me about the money I lost. My choice is, return to her and lay on my back or find a living tree until my mission starts. Your captain seems a fine sentient. Did you know his tree group cast him out when he was cloned?"

Rowan smiled. As far as the translator nanos went, they were a wondrous technology, but she'd discovered that a willingness to interpret their translations was often necessary. "Yes, I did know that. How did you?"

"I felt his file and yours when I learned who'd be on the flight. I find it makes it easier to associate with sentients when one is informed."

The elevator dropped back to her level, and the door opened. Rowan pushed her cargo container in and motioned for Krakkeen to follow. The spiderzoid levitated his possessions to sit on top of the cargo container, then crowded into the lift with Rowan as if it was the most natural thing in the world. The doors closed.

"I'll drop this off, then take you to your room," Rowan explained.

"Once I am settled, I can help with the loading. I find it is often more efficient to have one sentient do the packing in a limited space. Perhaps I could take the cargo at the lifting unit's door and place it in its final place."

"Are you good at that sort of thing? We need to take offloading into account as well," asked Rowan, then she remembered a mention about superior spatial relationships in the spiderzoid entry in the *Encyclopedia Galactica*.

Krakkeen waved a leg. "I am a spiderzoid."

"Star Searcher, you must understand that the *Mary* is a pleasure craft. While I wish to help the kangazoids, there are limits to what I may transport." Croell stared at the crab-like gatherer component on the *Mary*'s bridge screen.

"I have examined the schematics for your craft. The volume of the items I am suggesting should not over tax it," Star Searcher's voice issued from the speaker.

Croell shifted on the cushions he had piled on the command chair of a bridge similar to the *Star Hawk*'s, save it lacked a weapons station, and the navigation and piloting stations were combined. What appeared to be a beautiful woman of mixed Caucasian-Asian heritage sat at the pilot's station. Croell lay across the central command chair, which he'd turned sideways so he could face the screen. Zandra stood beside him in the bridge's access walk.

"What you are asking is untoward and would inflict hardship on myself and my crew. I am limiting us to the bridge, dining area and main sleeping chamber as it is." Croell fought to keep the frustration out of his voice but couldn't stop his hands from flexing.

"You are in error. Your ship has a storage capacity that can easily handle the shipment I have allocated," countered Star Searcher.

Croell lifted his head to speak. Zandra's voice cut him off.

"Star Searcher, while it may be true that we have adequate storage to hold the volume of cargo you have assigned, you forget that the containers are solid and will not configure to the space available. Furthermore, this vessel is set to *Homo sapiens* standards. Non-*Homo sapiens* containers will not stack neatly within it. We are trying to aid the innocent kangazoid species, but you are making a mockery of our gesture before the Great Flyer of the Skies!"

Zandra stared into the bridge pickups.

"One moment." The gatherer component moved to the cilia wall behind it and pressed the back of its shell against the wall.

"Luba, pause transmission," ordered Croell. "Thank you, my love. I was about to say something that would put our geise at risk. Star Searcher is a most annoying entity."

Zandra flicked her tongue. "It is the nature of hive minds, beloved. Star Searcher does, however, seem to be a glaring example of their faults."

"Message incoming," remarked the Luba in a voice more appropriate to the bedroom than a ship's bridge.

"Open communications," ordered Croell.

"It is with reservations, I acknowledge that inefficient packing due to technical incompatibilities may result in a lowered cargo capacity."

"Good. My suggestion would be to prioritize the cargo by what is most needed by the relief effort. We will take as much as we may," suggested Croell.

"My over-self is preparing a priority list. It will be given to you before you enter the loading hangar. The vessel that is currently loading is leaving the cargo in disarray. There will be little or no structure to where the items you will need to load may be found."

"If you could send assistance for the loading, it would be appreciated," remarked Zandra.

"I will send beings to aid you and arrange for your clearances and sanctions. I cannot give you a docking time. The captain of the *Star Hawk* is an unreasonable and disagreeable sentient. Dealing with him has no exactitude."

"We will await your message," said Croell.

The image on the screen went blank.

"I feel for Ryan having to deal with that sentient," commented Zandra.

"I can agree. I can only guess how Star Searcher had the cargo arranged that Ryan is 'leaving it in disarray'."

"We shall see, my love. We shall soon see."

Croell rose from his command chair. "Luba, inform me if anyone contacts us."

"Yes, my master. Lubas can perform many functions. Expansions are available from—"

"Luba," said Zandra.

"Yes, mistress."

"Shut up." Zandra preceded Croell from the bridge.

Ryan stood in front of what had been lieutenant's quarters. His hands were full of ropes, and everything ached from moving cargo containers. "Henry, can you open the door, please."

"Sure thing, hotty boss. I ever tell you your lady fair looks good bending over?"

Ryan shook his head. "Multiple times, and you're right, she does. And I've told you how inappropriate it is to say so."

"It's part of my charm. I'm glad you appreciate a little of what you've got, my captain." Henry's tone was bantering but with a touch of concern.

"Have I been taking her for granted?" There was surprise in Ryan's voice.

"Not in the way you think, hotty boss." Henry paused as the door retracted into the wall, releasing a blast of stifling hot, humid air. "Tim made the environmental adjustments a couple of hours ago. Kid may be an ungrateful snot, but he knows environment systems."

Ryan stepped into the room. "Leave the door open. It will make it a bit cooler while I work. What do you mean, not how I think?"

"Ryan."

The use of his name caused Ryan to pause in surprise. "This is serious!"

"Could be. All shagging aside, I love you guys. Rowan loves you, but it's not like a week ago. She loves you; she doesn't need you to save her. At least not in the short term. You need to let her in, let her feel that you need her. If you don't, she'll start feeling like all she does is take. For a person like Rowan, that will eat her up inside."

"Divine, what more can I do to let her know how important she is to me?" Ryan pulled a bulbous device with a hook on it from the equipment he was carrying and placed it against the wall. He pressed a button, and it stayed in place.

"Let her in. Let her help you. She loves you, and you've been as moody as a nympho in a nunnery."

Ryan attached more of the hook mounts to the wall, occasionally pausing to glance at a diagram on his handheld. "It's just this mission. I—"

"I know, Ryan. I was on Murack Five too."

Henry watched Ryan tense at the mention of the planet but kept talking. "You can't let ghosts ruin your future. Let her in. I've heard it helps you monkey descendants to share. Stop doing for everyone else and let her do for you."

Ryan's lips quirked up in a smile. "I certainly did the night of the victory party after we got her out of the U.E.S. for a second time."

Henry snorted. "And you didn't let me watch. Now stop trying to distract me. This is important!"

"I know. It's just…"

"You find it easier to give than take. Look at yourself. Even now, facing going back to… that place. You could just roll the quarters' couch/bed down from the wall, but here you are soaked in sweat, stringing ropes for some spiderzoid you hardly know," remarked Henry.

"Krakkeen just got tossed by his family. I know what that's like. The least I can do is make the room comfortable for him." Ryan began stringing ropes between the hooks following the diagram on his handheld.

"That's the point. There's no ulterior motive with you. For me, he's cute, for a spiderzoid, but they only come into season once every Gallab year, not something I'd ever want to emulate," observed Henry in a bantering tone, then he grew serious. "It's your pattern. You bury yourself in helping and hope that it will somehow make you worthy. Stop listening to Bitch E. Mother. You are worthy, more worthy than most in this stardusted galaxy. Let Rowan give back to you. She needs to feel worthy too."

"Would relations even be mechanically possible with a spiderzoid?" Ryan kept stringing ropes, checking the tension as he went.

"Not with a *Homo sapiens*, the lubricating fluids would burn the skin off you. Stop trying to distract me. You need to hear this. Will you actually talk to Rowan before being stoic costs you your shot at happiness?"

Ryan stepped into the hall and examined his work. The ropes formed a loose mesh about halfway up in the room. "I'll... I'll try. And Henry."

"Yes."

"Thanks." Ryan took a deep breath of the cooler air in the corridor and shifted his thoughts to a more comfortable stream. "How goes stowing the cargo?"

"Krakkeen has a knack for it. I don't think there's an air molecule between his stacks. If he keeps it up, we'll have room to spare."

"Keep track. If we can fit more in at the end, I'll get a firm number and offer to haul more for a price. I'm going to need every credit to cover legal fees and wages." Ryan pressed a button, closing the door to the quarters.

"Legs should love it."

"Are you talking about Rowan or Krakkeen?" Ryan smiled.

"Works for both. Hers are great, and he's got ten of them. I like the kid. I've got another ram splinter chatting him up. His aunt sounds like a piece of work. Wispy's quarters next?" asked Henry.

"Not much to do. A human bed suits for a resting platform. A bucket with a lid will serve if he needs to expel a waste crystal. We'll just toss it out an airlock in deep space. His water processing is good enough; there is no liquid waste. That much was in the file of boarding information. Tim has already set the humidity to ten per cent and the temp to twenty-seven degrees in his quarters, so I think we can call that one done."

"I'll be glad when he moults," remarked Henry.

"Why?" Ryan walked to the elevator. Looking over, he saw Krakkeen in what used to be the ground forces barracks using grav-lifts to position storage containers one atop the other. The spiderzoid shot out a length of string that adhered to a container and used it to draw the box tight against its neighbours before dropping it down and removing the lifts. The elevator door opened, and Rowan stepped out, pulling a box behind her.

"That overgrown bug is going to drive me crazy!" she blurted when she saw Ryan.

"What, Krakkeen?" he asked.

"No, Wispy. He never shuts up! I swear, Ryan. If you don't get him away from me, I'll push him out an airlock."

Ryan eyed Rowan speculatively. "Is it a culture thing?"

"No!" Henry and Rowan spoke in unison.

"And that buzzing sound," added Rowan.

"That bit isn't his fault, sweetness," remarked Henry.

"What is it then?" Rowan released a slow breath.

"I asked around some of my AI friends. He's getting ready to moult. The buzzing comes from the old skin plates loosening and rubbing against each other. Nothing he can do about it. It hits you monkey descendants at an instinctive level, making you more aggressive." Henry's voice was pitched low and soothing.

"It's time for dinner anyway. I'll call in the crew and leave Wispy and Krakkeen to keep loading. Henry, can you supervise while the rest of us eat?" asked Ryan.

"Sure thing, boss. I don't mind going a little buggy," quipped Henry.

"Henry?" Ryan and Rowan both looked to where Krakkeen was stacking crates.

"Relax, my sexy crew mates. I said it in *Homo sapiens*, untranslated," said Henry.

"Don't do that, old friend. It's rude," explained Ryan.

"Sure thing, hotty boss."

"When will Krakkeen and Wispy eat?" asked Rowan.

"After us. Watching us eat is disturbing to most insect types. Like siting with someone who chews with their mouth open."

"When'd you have time to look that up?" asked Rowan.

"Read about it when I was providing security for a spiderzoid ambassador." Ryan paused in thought. "Henry, have you got their ration packs for the flight shuffled into place?"

"Of course, captain, my captain."

"Pull a pack for each of them after us mammalian types eat. No one goes hungry on the *Star Hawk*. Ask Krakkeen to save his empty husks. I'll have to look it up, but I may have a way to thank him for pitching in."

The door to the elevator opened. Wispy stepped out, carrying a box twice his size. "Hello Captain, I was just telling Rowan how invigorating it is to be useful. I never really liked being a bartender, though it did let me talk to a lot of sentients which will aid me in my career because I could start to understand..."

Angel flew through the night, her jet-black wings, dark skin, black sports bra and shorts making her almost invisible. Air rushed over her petite body, sweeping away the sweat of her exertion.

Taking a cell phone from a holster on her belt, she pressed a speed dial button.

"Farley, it's Angel. The southeast quarter is quiet. I can't see any alien activity, and I want to get back to Toronk. Gunther finally let him come home."

There was a pause as she listened. A blush rose to her cheeks.

"You're a fine one to talk. How is Quinta adjusting?"

Angel changed course, then saw someone lurching between buildings below.

"I've got to go. I may have spotted something." Angel put the phone back in its holster, then swept down. The person she'd seen was a felinezoid. Coming closer, she saw a silver sash over its shoulder and closer still, she recognized Valaseau.

Opening her phone, she called. "Farley, I have Valaseau on..." she glanced at the nearby street signs, "Mate Boulevard just south of Foster Avenue. She looks drunk. She just fell over."

Pause.

"I don't know. Maybe. Someone might spot her. I have to go down. Have someone meet me with a car. This doesn't look normal."

A moment passed.

"Okay, even by our low standard for normal."

Pause.

"Good, I'd want Gunther to check what passes for the crazy bitch's mind anyway." Angel put the phone away and dropped lightly to her sandal covered feet.

Keeping her distance, she looked at her enemy, who was sprawled on the pavement.

"Valaseau, can you hear me?" Angel crept closer.

Valaseau's chest heaved with every breath.

Pulling a small flashlight from her fanny pack, Angel shone it on the cat-like alien. "Valaseau."

Valaseau didn't move. Angel crept to Valaseau's side, flashlight in one hand and a short knife in the other.

Bending down, she touched the felinezoid. The alien was hot to the touch. Not the normal higher body temperature she was used to with Toronk, but feverish.

"Stardust!" Angel positioned her greatest enemy on her side so she wouldn't choke on the copious amount of mucus spilling from the felinezoid's nose and mouth.

Pulling out her phone, Angel hit speed dial and waited for the signal to be picked up.

"Gunther, I think Valaseau is sick. She's unconscious in the street, and she's burning up."

Pause.

"Not literally. She has a fever."

Pause.

"Hurry."

Minutes later, Gunther's SUV pulled onto the block and he climbed out.

"Have you touched her?" he demanded.

"I had to clear her airway," replied Angel.

"Hand sanitizer in the car, use it. Use lots of it." Gunther moved to the back of his vehicle and, opening the hatch, extracted a bag. Moments later, gloved and masked, he took Valaseau's pulse.

"How is she?" Angel watched from two steps back.

"Glove up and help me get her into the car. Temperature is five degrees above felinezoid normal. Breathing is laboured. Pupils are dilated. I think she might be dying."

"Isn't that a good thing?" Angel took gloves out of the medical bag and pulled them on.

"If this is contagious, Toronk could be affected. The more we learn now, the better for him later."

"Stardust." Angel lifted Valaseau's legs so they could move her into the SUV.

"Kitoy," the voice was tentative.

Kitoy turned from the E.S.T.C. she was manoeuvring towards the ramp. "Ziggy."

"I… I'm sorry," said the fat, dark-haired, *Homo sapiens* male behind her. He needed a shave and a haircut but otherwise seemed clean. He wore a U.E.S. Ground Forces uniform with silver retiree's braids over the shoulder patches. The uniform looked like it had been washed in a sink.

Kitoy lashed her tail. "You came through for Ryan and Rowan. You don't need to apologize."

Ziggy sighed. "I need help."

"For?" Kitoy sounded skeptical.

"Kitcat." Ziggy bit his lip. "I haven't touched memoria since I did the job for Ryan. I… It's so hard. I want to lose myself so much."

"I wouldn't give you money for drugs even if I had it to give." Kitoy lashed her tail.

"That's not why I'm here. Divine. Help me, Kitoy." Ziggy dropped to his knees as if standing took more will than he could spare. "I need a place away from memoria. I…

Helping Rowan was the first thing I've done since Murack Five that felt right. It made me realize that maybe I could do something. Something to wash the blood off my hands. I... I need to get to Murack Five and join the relief effort."

"So, sign up." Kitoy regarded Ziggy with a questioning look.

"I tried. Star Searcher won't accept me because I'm a known addict. But on Murack Five, there won't be drug dealers, just relief workers. I wouldn't be able to get memoria. It would force me to stay clean, and maybe I can make a difference. If I show up and am useful, they'd keep me, and the local director could override Star Searcher's decision."

Kitoy swished her tail. "If you come aboard, that's it. If you don't bother to hunt after I stamped prey for you, we're through!"

Ziggy nodded. "You're the only friend I have left."

"As long as we're clear. Come on, we need to speak to Ryan." Kitoy led the way into the *Star Hawk*.

Obert opened his eyes. The cold had faded, leaving an ache behind. Kendra lay tight against his back and Armina against his front. Medwin lay beyond Armina.

If I didn't feel like stardust, this could be a party, he thought. He didn't want to move; it was warm under the piled sleeping bags, but nature called.

Trying not to disturb the others, he slipped from the warmth and immediately hugged himself against the chill in the pre-dawn air. Staring about blurrily, he found his clothing spread over a rock. The fabric was dry. Pulling on his shirt and jacket, he stepped away from his companions and relieved himself before rushing to don his pants, socks, and shoes.

The glimmer of false dawn touched the eastern horizon. Moving to Kendra, Obert gently shook her.

"What? Oh... Obert. You're up," remarked the dark-haired girl.

"We need to go before the tree planters start." Obert gestured to the east.

"I just hope we can. Medwin." Kendra reached over Armina and shook the man's shoulder.

"Armina." Medwin snuggled into his girlfriend, then slowly opened his eyes. "Oh Divine. How is she?"

Kendra took Armina's pulse. "She's still alive."

"Honey," Medwin spoke softly into the blonde's ear.

"C-c-cold," she stuttered.

"We need to move. We don't want to have to explain us being here to the tree planters. Some of them might be actively monitored," said Obert.

"Right." Medwin extracted himself from the blankets, being careful to keep Armina covered. He moved straight to where he'd left his damp clothing and pulled on the now dry garments.

"Where's the second tin of Camping Heat?" Kendra searched the packs.

"Armina was carrying it. Her pack got swept downstream." Medwin picked up the now burnt-out container of fuel.

"We really need to go." Obert glanced around nervously.

Medwin nodded. "We'll zip up one of the sleeping bags around Armina."

"We should put all the equipment into one of the packs. I can carry that so you and Obert can focus on Armina." Kendra started rearranging their equipment.

"If we tie the frames from two of our packs together and pull one of the sleeping bags over it, it should make a fair stretcher," said Medwin.

"No one asked me if I'm up to carrying the weight," objected Obert.

"Do you have a better idea?" Medwin pulled a length of rope from the equipment Kendra was transferring to her pack. Moments later, the packs were tied together and slipped into one of the sleeping bags, forming a rigged platform that Armina could fit on with her feet dangling off the end.

The sun was cresting the horizon as they started towards the distant line of saplings that marked the edge of the forestation project. They came to a group of three portable drilling rigs. The devices consisted of a steep-sided pyramid of pipes with a two-metre shaft running down the centre mounted on a platform supported on caterpillar treads. A platform at the back of each allowed an operator to stand behind a control panel. One of the rigs had the drill shaft partially sunken into the rocky ground. Next came a series of craters blasted into the rock, partially infilled with rubble, then the stench of rot and sewage filled the air.

"Stardust!" Obert found his leg sunken up to mid-calf in a mix of milorganite sewage and rock chips.

The stretcher tipped. Armina cried out as she almost fell to the ground. Medwin pulled up his side, wrenching his left arm. "Arrr."

Struggling, the two men managed to control the stretcher's drop.

"Nova blast, Obert. Be careful!" snapped Medwin. "Armina, are you alright?"

Armina looked up from the sleeping bag. "I... I'm still cold, but I think I can walk now."

"We won't get through this carrying the stretcher," observed Obert. "We'll need to pick our way around these pits. What are they for anyway?"

"Planting, by the end of the day, they'll all have saplings in them," explained Medwin.

Setting the stretcher on the squelchy ground, they unzipped the bag, releasing Armina as Kendra passed the blonde her now dry clothing.

"How's the ankle?" Medwin looked at Obert.

"It will do. It has to. Stardust!" Obert pointed. Where the line of saplings began, a man and a woman walked into view.

"Nova blast! Get the sleeping bag off the packs." Medwin and Obert raced to put action to word, then pulling his camping knife from its sheath on his belt Medwin cut the ties holding the stretcher together and stuffed the two sleeping bags into the packs.

"They're coming this way," stated Obert.

"Let me do the talking," ordered Medwin.

"We're going to be caught." Armina's voice was frightened. "The controllers will find out and—" Medwin pulled Armina into his arms, stilling her ramble.

"I can handle this. I recognize one of them from my summer job." Medwin spoke softly, hoping it wouldn't carry to the tree planters.

He released Armina and waved. "Hi, Mr. Hunter."

"What the nova blast are you doing here?" snapped the man as he drew closer. He was pasty-faced with thinning brown hair and a body that was muscle covered by a layer of flab. He wore the green coverall of a tree planter.

"My friends and I were camping. Armina here came down with a bug. We were trying to get her back to town."

"You shouldn't be here. Suppose there were unexploded ordnance?" The slender, dark-skinned woman ran a long-fingered hand through her mane of thick, curly hair.

"We stayed on the ridges. We just want to get our friend home."

"I remember you. The science fiction geek, Merwin," snapped the large man.

"I've worked the last three summers as a tree planter." Medwin didn't correct the name.

"Yaa, the kid that's too good to plant trees, saving up for university, as if honest work was beneath him," snarked the large man.

"We need to get our friend home," added Kendra.

"I bet. Kids today, any little thing they go running to mommy," griped Mr. Hunter.

"Didn't you see the warning signs; this is an active

plant?" asked the woman.

"We came in from the other side," explained Medwin.

"What the nova blast were you doing over there?" The woman glanced beyond the drilling rigs.

Medwin smiled, looked at the ground, then spoke softly. "We were looking for the Wolf River serpent."

Mr. Hunter laughed derisively. "You're balmy. Everyone knows that's just a story."

"Some people say that maybe a pet python got loose and managed to survive. It seemed as good an excuse to go camping as any," remarked Obert.

"I don't have time for this. Get out of the active zone. Bloody kids. Go on. Some people have real work to do." Mr. Hunter stepped out of the way. Medwin led his group forward.

"I can't keep going," remarked Armina.

Medwin and Obert took her arms, half carrying her. Soon they were past the stinking field of infilled pits into an area of newly planted saplings. A few more metres and the smell faded, and they were surrounded by a young, semi-tropical forest.

"At least this is alive," remarked Armina as they lowered her to rest with her back against a tree. Medwin pulled out a sleeping bag and covered her.

"Do you think they believed us?" asked Kendra with a tilt of her head to the direction they'd come from.

"Hunter will. He's an idiot! I don't know the woman," said Medwin.

"I do, a little. She does aqua fit at the pool. She always seemed okay. You know, the 'mind your own business and get on with life' type," said Kendra.

"What if a controller was watching?" asked Armina.

"Not likely. A couple of tree planters. If they are on active shows, it's probably during their off hours. Tree planting is too dead boring to make more than a half-hour special," observed Medwin.

Hours later, they reached the town.

Arlene stared at the screen while Greg hovered behind her.

"I've got their placement. Thanks for taking Ulva's shift. That spiderzoid virus really put her down." Arlene shifted the big screen to Medwin's perspective. It showed a pleasant suburban, tree-lined street. Houses with small yards bordered the road.

"Mike needss to get more controllerss for *Freedom'ss Run* if we're going to be doing real-time. It'ss bad enough cleaning up the rough editss Henry iss ssending uss." Greg leaned against the wall.

"Mike has more staff tagged to come on as soon as the launch is over. It's only a few days. Think of the overtime. Have you noticed that Armina's emotions are very negative?"

"I love the overtime. Between it and the mint I made on the SS.E.T.E. sstockss when they dipped and ssurged, I've made enough to buy a housse in the sstudio ssupport town. A real housse, with a yard, by a nature park. I've been ssaving up, but I figured it would be yearss."

"That's great." Arlene turned in her seat to smile at him.

"The sstock bump did mosst of it. When I was working *Angel Black* and *Freedom'ss Run*, that was murder with the sstaffing sshortage on both sshowss. Where iss Michael getting controllerss?"

"He's arranged for co-op placements from the university for some of the simpler shows and is moving people up and over internally. The only experienced person on *A Cat's Life* will be Terica. She's thrilled to be head controller. He's using techs from there to fill in the other shows. Two controllers are coming over from *Vampire Chronicles*. They wanted something with a lower body count. Stan from *Defenders of the Crystal* is coming on board. Mike wanted people used to working with enhanced surrogates to help with the *Angel Black* crossover elements."

"He knowss his art." Greg scanned the control board.

"You're right about Armina. Sshe iss in a dark placse."

"She hasn't taken finding out well." Arlene spared the girl's monitors a glance.

"Tweak her. At leasst let her get a good night'ss ssleep," suggested Greg.

Arlene nodded. "Mike won't mind. He did say to keep intervention to a minimum, though."

"Mike is decsent. No reasson the girl sshould hurt like that. I need to go. Katelin and I are going furniture sshopping." Greg left the control room.

THOSE LEFT BEHIND

Medwin held Armina and kissed her. "Are you sure you'll be all right?"

"I just want to take a bath and go to bed." Armina held him, almost making a lie of her words. Her parents' house was behind her, four short metres, and she would be in her door and could shut away the strangeness. Then she thought, *The strangeness follows me. They could be monitoring their puppets right now. They could come and kill us all. But how do you kill something that isn't real? Just a cheap copy.*

She bit her lip, then kissed Medwin hard. "My mother will be home soon. I don't want her to see me like this." She gestured to her dirty and rumpled clothes.

"If you're sure." Medwin loosened his hold on her.

Armina nodded. "Medwin."

"Yes."

"I love you."

Medwin smiled. "I love you too."

She hugged and kissed him, then broke away and walked up to the porch of her parents' house.

"Come on, lover boy. The rest of us should get home. We have work tomorrow, then the focus group," commented Obert.

Medwin watched Armina vanish into her house with an uneasy feeling.

Ryan heard a string quartet that slowly rose in volume. He rolled over, pulling Rowan's warm body close to his own.

"I don't want to get up," remarked Rowan.

"Me neither. But when do I ever?" He kissed the back of her neck. "All the best things are right here."

"Henry, kill the music. We're awake," called Rowan as she squirmed against Ryan.

Ryan kissed along her shoulders, sending shudders up her spine.

"Henry," began Ryan.

"Before you command privacy, you should know that Pikeman is standing on the hangar ramp with two huge maglev platforms full of crates."

"Stardust!" Ryan leaned up and kissed Rowan on the lips, then let her go and swung his legs over the edge of the bed.

"Command is stardust sometimes," remarked Rowan.

"I couldn't say it better. But Pikeman is a passenger. We need to sort out this cargo issue with Star Searcher. The sooner, the better." Ryan stood and started pulling on the uniform he'd draped over the back of Rowan's computer chair.

"I guess we owe him." Rowan scrambled out of bed and looked around the room, which was furnished to mimic her bedroom in Sun Valley.

"Owe him. No, the other way around."

"He did save my life, twice." Rowan pulled out clothes and began to dress.

"We saved him. Twice, and he charged us for the stem cell insertion. Don't make the mistake of letting him have any advantage over you." Ryan smiled mischievously. "My little mountain tree."

Rowan rolled her eyes. "You don't have tentacles, so knock it off."

Ryan sobered. "Seriously. He is coming aboard for passage, and from what Henry says, he's brought extra cargo onto an already overfull ship. Don't coddle him."

"Me?" Rowan buttoned up her pants and tucked in her T-shirt.

"You're the ship's trading officer. You're better at shopping and negotiating than I am."

Rowan nodded. "He's a pig. I think we can maybe get a little back for that!"

Minutes later, Ryan and Rowan descended the loading ramp to where Pikeman sat on the corner of one of his grav-sledges.

"Doctor," greeted Ryan.

Pikeman regarded Ryan, then Rowan for a long minute. "I... You are Captain Ryan Chandler, and you are Rowan McPherson from the e-entertainment series *Angel Black*."

"Of course we are. You know us," began Rowan.

Ryan saw the confused expression on Pikeman's face. He caught Rowan's arm and shook his head.

"I am sorry. I have read about you and experienced the Spuqupa report. I have also reviewed my file on Rowan's condition. A colleague told me that you and your son were instrumental in saving my life, Captain. I had hoped from that, that you were well disposed towards me. Since my recovery, I have found very few who are. My injuries have left my memory fragmented. I only have flashes regarding either of you. Total memory recovery is unlikely."

"How can you function as a healer?" asked Rowan.

"Redundancy. I have performed the procedures of my trade hundreds of times. I only need to recall a few of any given procedure to perform the skill." Pikeman shrugged.

"In that case, I think it only fair to warn you that we were not on good terms," stated Ryan.

"That is unfortunate. Will there be issues regarding my transport?"

"We are obliged to take you to Murack Five under the terms of Ryan's sentence. Your possessions are supplemental cargo. We probably won't have room for them."

"I cannot work without my equipment. You would be denying the aid workers essential medical care," blurted

Pikeman.

"We'll discuss it with Star Searcher." Rowan eyed the man. For all the grief he'd caused her and Ryan with his exorbitant fees, she wondered if this Pikeman was the same man.

"In the meantime, you may put as much as you are able into your quarters," stated Ryan.

Pikeman looked stricken as his hand rested on the sealed crates. "I need my equipment. I... I am a doctor, a healer. Maybe before I was something else, not now. Please, Captain. It's all that's left of me."

Rowan watched Pikeman as he caressed one of the cases.

"We'll try to work it out with Star Searcher. Did you get transport of your equipment as part of the bargain for going to Murack Five?" asked Rowan.

"I did, I think. The U.E.S. Space Combat Corps Lawyer... Hammerman, handled the details."

"I'll contact him." Ryan turned to Rowan. "Tim's met him and may have some insights."

"I'll talk to him." Rowan nodded. "Blair, would you care to join us for breakfast?"

"Good idea," agreed Ryan. "We need to get on with the day, or we'll never get all this loaded. Star Searcher is insistent about our gate transit time." Ryan gestured at the cargo in the hangar, then led the way into the *Star Hawk*.

Pikeman spared his equipment a lingering look, then followed.

"Doctor McPherson to emergency." The voice blasted out of the speaker in the bland hospital hallway.

"I'll get the forms filled out by Friday. I have to go." Gunther nodded to the chubby Asian hospital administrator who had accosted him in the hallway.

"Doctor." The man tugged down the jacket of his ill-fitting, grey suit.

"Emergency calls. I'll do the forms." Gunther rushed to the elevator.

He better if he wants to keep his privileges. Doctors! Always a nova blasted pain. You'd think they did something more important than paperwork. Gunther heard the administrator's thoughts as he waited for the elevator, then he was away from the tiresome man.

Gunther reached with his mind as the elevator descended to the hospital's first floor, touching the thoughts of Trixy, the Emergency Room's head nurse.

"Stardust, a suicide," he spoke into the empty elevator. He emerged onto the floor and strode to the nursing station.

"Doctor McPherson, I'm glad you're here. We had a suicide, a teenage girl. Her mother is hysterical. They're both in treatment three. Mother's name is Penelope Michaels," explained the fit, blonde woman just entering middle age dressed in nursing scrubs who stood behind the nursing station counter.

"Thanks, Trixy." Gunther pushed past a pair of uniformed paramedics who were rolling a gurney down the hall.

Treatment three was a large room separated into three sections by curtains. In the area closest to the far wall, a brown-haired woman in a business skirt suit sat clutching the hand of the body of a young woman. Gunther moved closer, then he recognized Armina lying on the bed.

"Divine," he muttered. He took a breath to steady himself as he thought of what to do.

This is sure to be recorded. I can't let on I knew her. It's just like any other case. Divine, how did this happen?

The woman by the bed continued to weep.

Gunther moved to her side. "Mrs. Michaels, I'm Doctor McPherson. I'm a psychiatrist. I am sorry for your loss."

"Are you?" demanded the woman. Her brown eyes were red-rimmed from crying, and there was a pallor to her complexion. She glowered at Gunther, then broke into sobs. "My girl, my little girl." Her mood shifted again, and she grabbed Armina's shoulders and shook her. "Why? Why did you do this?"

Gunther laid a compassionate hand on the woman's shoulder. "It is hard to say why. Sometimes we never figure it out. All I can promise is, the pain dulls with time."

"How would you know!" The woman pulled away.

Gunther sighed and thought, *Play the role*. "My daughter was recently taken from me. It's what I tell myself. I suppose it helps, a little, but, to be honest, nothing really does."

Mrs. Michaels looked at Gunther. "Did… did your daughter kill herself?"

Gunther locked down on his emotions and gave the official answer they'd slipped into the records. "A poisonous spider bit her. Some idiot's exotic pet."

"I'm sorry," the woman said mechanically.

"As I am for you. What was her name?" Gunther could feel his mood unaccountably lighten and surmised that the controllers were playing their games.

"Armina. My little girl. I… Why? Why? Why?" Mrs. Michaels sobbed, collapsing to bury her face in the sheets.

Gunther gripped her around her shoulders and let her cry.

"Penelope, what happened?" demanded a short, stocky man with a shaved head dressed in rugged work clothes.

"Tom, she's gone. She took pills. I got home from work, and there she was in the tub. I—" Penelope's voice cut off in another sob.

Tom rushed to the bedside and looked down at his daughter's corpse. His face went deathly pale. He took her pulse as if all the equipment around him was wrong. He stroked Armina's hair, then his chest convulsed. His quiet sobs joined his wife's.

Gunther scanned their minds. Their thoughts were of their daughter. Penelope was lost. She couldn't think why. Tom was looking for someone to blame, some way to fight back. Both were dying inside. Gunther stepped away, opened one of the folding chairs kept in the treatment room's corner, and sat. Emergency was slow, so he could give the couple their time. Forcing his emotions to a clinical detachment, he wondered why this happened. Why a girl at the start of her life would choose to end that life. He feared the answer but did not dare feel that fear.

"Star Searcher, you agreed to the volume limit for cargo, and it is recorded. The fact that I, through extraordinary effort, have accommodated your excessive demands does not change that contract. If you wish me to take any additional cargo, it will be on my terms and reflect my limits, which I know better than you."

The crab-like organizational component stared out of the main screen on the *Star Hawk*'s bridge. "But this collective agreed with the Pikeman individuality to transport his equipment. That too is recorded."

"That is, as my people are fond of saying, your problem, not mine." Ryan glowered into the screen.

"What can this collective do? I am caught between conflicting contracts."

Ryan opened his mouth to speak, but Rowan, who stood beside the captain's chair, laid her hand on his shoulder.

A stretch of seconds later, she spoke. "Star Searcher, this individuality may have a solution that will allow you to fulfill these conflicting contracts without looking as if you have organizational components deserving of consumption."

Ryan flinched and watched the screen.

Silence ensued. The crabzoid organizational component tapped its claws on the floor and waved its cilia. "What is your solution?"

"Due to inventive packing and superior spatial configurations, the *Star Hawk* will have a few cubic metres extra for cargo space above what we agreed on. We will agree to carry Pikeman's equipment, which constitutes six cubic metres, for a base rate of fifty Republic trade credits per cubic metre paid in advance of our departure to Victoria Hart. Further, we will pick through the cargo beyond our assigned shipping and select pieces that can be loaded into what space we have remaining at the same rate per cubic metre."

"How much more can you accommodate?" demanded Star Searcher.

"We'll tell you when we have finished packing," stated Ryan.

The crabzoid component waved its cilia. "And none will know of me accepting conflicting contracts?"

"None will know," stated Rowan.

"This individuality will accept these terms. You must keep a log of the additional cargo you take and forward it to Star Searcher so that the inventory remains current." The crab-like being on the screen stood absolutely still.

"It will be done," agreed Rowan.

The voice from the speaker became strained. "This individuality finds that it must convey gratitude to you for rectifying its technical error." The screen went blank.

Ryan moved to the communications station and pressed the button that closed the channel.

"That went well," remarked Rowan.

Ryan smiled. "You are an amazing trading officer. The way you phrased the insult so that it only came into effect if Star Searcher didn't accept your advice. Brilliant!"

"I've been working on that one since I saw Pikeman's cargo." Rowan smiled. "At least it will pay some of Vicky's fee for defending me."

"Most, if not all. She gave us a break after I saved her life. If we fill the rail system with E.S.T.C.s, we should be able to clear that debt."

"Is that safe?" Rowan looked concerned.

"Safe enough. After the Batzoid Pirate Suppression, I managed to get command to upgrade the rail system and outer hull. If we were stock for a second-gen Hawk, I wouldn't try it, but the *Star Hawk* is a special kind of lady. Besides, not even Crapper could be so stupid as to attack us travelling under a Republic Writ of Passage. Until we get back to the station, we're untouchable by any official forces." Ryan smiled.

Rowan rubbed her arms. "More loading. I—"

"Hey, hotties, the ugly sister here. Kitoy says she needs you on the loading ramp. Would that it was me." Henry swivelled the computer station chair so that he was looking at his friends with his android eyes.

Ryan nodded. "Thanks, Henry. Tell her I'm on my way."

Ryan held his hand out to Rowan. She took it before they left the bridge.

Gunther opened the door to the shed at the back of his lot that had been retrofitted to serve as a prison. Angel sat on a folding chair beside Valaseau, who lay on a folding cot. The felinezoid's chest still heaved. An IV flowed into her, and her fur looked damp.

"How is she?" asked Gunther.

"You're the doctor. I've changed the IV bag twice since you left and kept her sprayed down with water." Angel glanced to a garden hose with a sprayer clipped to the wall. "And I can't tell you how many times I've sucked the snot out of her nose. I mean, gross! I never wanted to be a nurse. Why am I stuck with this?"

"Because you and I have been exposed, and I had to go to work to get supplies." Gunther set the case he was carrying on the floor.

"Sorry. I… What's wrong?" asked Angel as she examined her friend.

"A very bad day. A young girl committed suicide. I had to deal with her parents."

"Stardust! I'm sorry, Gunther."

Gunther smiled sadly, then looked resolved. "We'll talk more about it at the telepathy session."

"At the… Oh," breathed Angel, picking up on the implications.

"Toronk can't be there. I want him to have as little contact with anyone as possible until we work out what's up with Valaseau."

"Right. Should we maybe try to contact the pirates? They might know something?" Angel unclipped the hose on the wall and gently misted the fast-drying Valaseau.

"I have Carl on it." Gunther moved to the incubator that stood on a shelf in the corner of the shed and took out a culture plate. Pulling a microscope from the bag he'd brought, he began examining the cultures.

Ryan emerged onto the *Star Hawk*'s hangar bay ramp and scanned the space dock. Krakkeen worked behind him, stacking the storage containers that the rest of the crew brought to him out of the cluttered jumble in the hangar. Kitoy stood on the ramp with a male batzoid whose wings were scorched scar tissue. Flanking him stood a k-no-in with a cybernetic in place of the middle of the three legs on its left side and an octozoid, its body in what looked like a fishbowl on top of four corrugated legs. Fibre optics transmitted light from the front of the bowl to its bottom so the bowl's occupant could see ahead of it. A stream of bubbles rose through the water in the bowl. Three grav-carts, each with piles of possessions, floated in the hangar behind them.

"This is the captain," introduced Kitoy.

"And the beautiful Rowan." The k-no-in dipped its head in imitation of a human bow. Its voice was rough and guttural, unlike the normal tones of the translator nanobots.

Rowan shifted uncomfortably at the way the k-no-in

gaze took her in.

"You are the Scholar Asalue of Grey Sky Sect, Doctor Yipya Gripp, and 'Coral cave in tropical zone second hatched in the month of small, fast fish with blue scales, during the year of the sea worm', I presume." Ryan bowed.

"Just call me Jacques. In translation, octozoid names are a beak-full. A *Homo sapiens* colleague suggested the name. She said he was of one of her personal heroes from myth." The octozoid moved the limb of its land-scuttling suit in what Ryan took to be a dismissive gesture.

"It honours me that you know my name, Captain. Word has spread that you are allowing relief workers to board early. We were hoping to accept your hospitality. We all have reasons to want to get out of our sectors as soon as possible," remarked the batzoid.

Ryan fixed a smile on his face. "Welcome aboard. Rowan, please show our guests to their quarters. I've prepared them for you."

"That is very kind of you, Captain," said Asalue.

Yipya moved to Rowan's side. His cybernetic limb made a slight clunking sound with each step. His guttural voice fought through several human words. "So rappy you meet. I..." The voice changed into a deep soothing tone that bore nothing in common with the shape of the being's lips. "I am sorry, I sought to honour you by speaking *Homo sapiens*, but I fear I'm not very proficient at it. It is a true pleasure to meet you. I have followed *Angel Black* since the series began. Sadly, the episodes available in the k-no-in sector are over a year behind the ones shown on Gaia. Did you get accepted to your advanced studies program?"

"Yes. Knowing what I know now, there wasn't much doubt of it." Rowan smiled.

The k-no-in's artificial leg buckled. He gasped painfully as he compensated with his organic ones. He thought he felt pressure on his chest, helping him stay upright. "Stardust! Stupid thing is always cutting out." He kicked the cybernetic leg with his hind leg, then steadied on his feet. "I am sorry. I'm behind on the maintenance."

"You should let Ryan or Tim look at it. They both know their way around cybernetics." Rowan started into the *Star Hawk*.

"I don't have much to pay with," said Yipya.

"If there is time, I'm sure they'd be happy to do it for free. It's a long trip, and I know Ryan likes to keep busy." Rowan kept her voice even. In her experience, k-no-in could mistake kindness for something else.

"That would be kind of them. Regarding your advanced studies, I know in retrospect your worries may seem unfounded, but you did not know then, and it was such a worry for you. I felt for you."

The three sentients followed Rowan, pulling their grav-carts.

"At least we won't have a rush to board at the end. How bad is the housing shortage on the Switchboard Station?" asked Ryan.

Kitoy flicked her tail and cocked her head in thought. "It depends on which sector. In the felinezoid sector, it is full. The spiderzoids have lots of tree space." A slightly confused expression came to her face. "The batzoid section has space. Maybe you should tell Henry not to let anyone but passengers and crew aboard. Just to be safe."

"Just what I need, two passengers with batzoid vengeance geis on their heads. How about the k-no-in sector?"

"That is a strange one. K-no-ins provide a basic stall to all citizens living off Srill. I can't guess why Yipya would want to be away from his species."

"As long as it doesn't blow up in my face." Ryan stroked Kitoy's arm, then moved to a pile of E.S.T.C.s, checked a bar code and started loading.

Medwin looked at the empty space on the couch beside

him. Obert and Kendra both stared dully across the central coffee table of the shabby living room. Neither of the aging chairs they sat in matched the threadbare couch. The walls needed painting. A picture of a robust, dark-haired man in a police officer's uniform hung on the wall over the couch.

"It has to be a mistake," said Kendra.

"Her parents called me. They let me see the body." Medwin started to sob.

Kendra moved to hug him. He held up a hand to forestall her. He didn't want comfort yet. It was still too raw. The image of his Armina, so still, so pale, was burnt into his mind. His heart literally ached.

Ulva sat in the *Freedom's Run* control room. She felt numb inside, and when she scanned her charges, she wanted to weep. Medwin was heartbroken. Obert was shaken, mostly sadness but a strange tendril of relief running through his emotions. Kendra was sad, but behind that, there was a paired optimism and guilt.

The door opened behind her, and Michael stepped in. "How are you holding up?"

"I knew her. I mean, really knew her. I shook her hand. Told her that she and Medwin were cute together." Ulva focused on the screen. "I shouldn't feel like this. She was just...."

"A human being," Michael spoke softly. It was a voice to calm nervous horses and wounded soldiers. "Ulva, part of why I have you here is how you reacted when Grandmother García died on *A Cat's Life*."

"Fluffy missed her so much. Some people don't think cats grieve, but they do."

"And you liked the old woman. She was kind to Fluffy. If we could have prevented that death, we would have. She was everybody's sweet granny with a spicy past. The clone's cancers were too aggressive. She had a good run, principal on three series and secondary on six. In short, you're here because you care. Never be ashamed of that."

"But to die like that. I swear, she was just taking a bath. I started working on the recordings from the Ryan and Rowan storyline. I didn't see her take the pills. When the metabolic alarm went off, I tried to intervene, but it was too late."

"I know, it's in the log. You did nothing wrong. For the rest of the studio, they're all listed non-vital. In a way, this may be for the best." Michael moved to Ulva's side and gently squeezed her shoulder.

"How?"

"Gunther needed to learn about the responsibility that comes with the power of knowing. We can't just let Sun Valley explode. For one, the other show runners wouldn't tolerate it. For another, the clones can't win an outright conflict. Obert's observations about pressing the big red button are essentially correct. We need to compartmentalize, like any other show. Armina's death will bring home to Gunther the necessity of being circumspect."

"Did you plan this?" asked Ulva.

"No, but I did expect something like this. Maybe not this soon, but it was inevitable. When *Kids in the Band* wrapped, there was a… mistake… in decommissioning the characters. Several of them woke up on the trip to processing."

"That must have been awful for them. What happened?"

"They escaped. Back then, we used ground vehicles disguised to look period to move things on and off the set. They were computer-controlled because it was cheaper than training drivers. The kids escaped and started looking around. They followed the light to the then control town. Like Medwin's group, they found the museum and learned of their reality.

"Trevor slit his wrists that night. He couldn't face the truth. Kineta got as far as the edge of town before being shot by a retrieval team. Andy died of thirst trying to get to Divine knows where."

"And you snuck Aunt Marcy out in the confusion," said Ulva.

Michael looked shocked.

"Oh, come on. I'm not stupid. The clues are there if you look for them. I won't tell. For the record, you're right. Aunt Marcy proves everything you're trying to say about clones being people."

Michael nodded. "I just hope I get the message out in time. My long since ex-wife has teamed up with John. They are making things difficult."

On the screen, Medwin took a deep, shuddering breath. The monitor for his grief dropped into the orange.

Ulva spared the other monitors a glance. "This is useless. The empathic feeds are just grief."

"To be expected. Save it and phone them. Offer your condolences, tell them you received word from Armina's parents and that this week's session is postponed, and that they'll get full pay."

"They'll never believe it. They know about us." Ulva looked surprised.

"Yes, they'll know. And maybe they'll learn that it is someone as human as them sitting in the controller's chair. A little kindness can do a great deal. When they get off the set region again, I want them to see people, not monsters. Rowan's opinion of us is low enough for all of them. Good thing she loves Ryan and has to reconcile his past, or we'd likely have a sniper assassin after us."

"You think Rowan would do that?" gasped Ulva.

"I think Rowan, as admirable as she is in many ways, can be more than a bit fanatical." Mike chuckled. "I've lived with an eighty-five per cent parallel to her start-up personality and experience configuration for nearly fifty years. Trust me in this, don't ever piss off your Aunt Marcy."

The phone in the corner of the room rang. Obert looked at Medwin, who sat on the couch with his face in his hands, then stood, walked over, and picked it up.

"Hello, O'Hare residence."

Pause.

"No, this is Medwin's friend Obert."

Pause.

"Ulva? Yes, we heard. How did you?"

Pause.

"Her parents, right."

Pause.

"She's here too."

Pause.

"I understand. That's probably a good idea."

Pause.

"That is very nice of the studio."

Pause.

"Yes, it is a tragedy. We're all going to miss her."

Pause.

"That's very nice of you. I will." He hung up the phone.

"Who?" asked Kendra.

"That was Ulva. She said she heard about Armina and that the focus group is postponed until next week, with full pay. She… She says she is sorry."

"Sorry," snapped Medwin. His face went red as he leapt out of his chair.

"Medwin?" Kendra rushed to lay her hands on his chest.

Medwin gritted his teeth. Finally, he got himself under control. "See you tomorrow. I need some air." He strode from the room without looking back.

"Where do you think he's going?" asked Obert.

"Someplace dark, Obert. Someplace very dark," replied Kendra.

THE OTHER SHOE

Ryan opened the door to the junior officers' quarters. The centre of the floor was occupied by what looked like a circular, above-ground swimming pool. A pump and filter unit hummed in the left corner of the room. A series of broad steps rose to the edge of the tank in the right corner. The octozoid's land scuttling suit sat in the pool in front of the steps.

"Captain, you have come." Jacques lifted his bulbous body out of the water.

"Sorry it took so long. The cargo in the bay wasn't properly sorted."

Jacques swished his tentacles. "It is I that apologizes for taking you from your work. I told your minion that my request was of a low priority."

"I needed a break. What can I do for you?"

"First, my appreciation for your efforts towards my comfort. I feared that I would have to spend the voyage in my scuttling suit. I love scuttling, it is my favourite hobby. The beauty of a forest, the exotic life, but several days in succession would be a clam too big to swallow."

"My pleasure."

"I echoed in your file that you are an engineer."

"Yes." Ryan moved to the side of the tank and dabbled his fingers in the water. It was cool to the touch and smelled vaguely like the sea.

"Wonderful. If, at some point during the voyage, you could perform a maintenance on my scuttling suit, I would be appreciative. I have been waiting for transport for so long that the support enhancers on the right foreleg have begun to fail, and the oxygenation mix keeps slipping."

"I'll download the schematics before we leave and see what I can do."

"Thank you." Jacques swished his tentacles happily as his bulbous body pulsed. "I've often said that mammals are the nicest people. In my educational days, I conducted tours for air-breathing visitors to Quooo. They would don aquatic apparatus. I think it was called SCUBA, much like my scuttling suit, and I would guide them through the natural environment reserve. *Homo sapiens* always left extra work vouchers to thank me for my efforts. I understand it is one of your traditions."

"Tipping. A gift given for when your service provider does a job of greater quality than the standard set by the employer."

"An interesting tradition. It paid for my first scuttling suit." Jacques bobbed in the water.

"Why is everything so delayed? Every person going to supply aid except Pikeman tells me they were due to go months ago."

"The last ship cancelled its service. I am told Star Searcher insisted they take more cargo than they could carry for a remuneration less than their expenses. When the news was released that a pirate had taken the vessel that preceded them, the captain chose to accept the Republic judges' alternative sentence. Your legal problems, which I think make a bad crab of justice, you should have been absolved, are a rich field of crabs for Star Searcher. That sentient knows you are in a cave with only one opening."

"Thank you. Things are making more sense now. Why didn't I hear about the pirates?" Ryan drummed his fingers on the edge of the pool.

"Please don't do that," said Jacques.

"Sorry, bad habit." Ryan stilled the motion.

"As to your question. Star Searcher did all it could to suppress the information. I only learned of it because I had a cave sibling on the ship that was attacked. She returned to the station in an escape pod, having eaten her own tentacles to survive." Jacques pulled his tentacles close around the central mouth at the bottom of his bulbous body.

"Not pleasant." Ryan's handheld beeped. He took it from its belt holster and checked the screen. "Stardust! I need to get back to work. I've just been informed by Star Searcher that I have to be out of the loading hangar by twenty-three hundred hours."

"If someone ate that crab, the galaxy would be a better place," remarked Jacques. "We will converse later, Captain."

Medwin went to the basement of his building and moved to the storage space for his mother's apartment. He took his keychain from his pocket. Armina had given it to him on his birthday. It was just a ring with a piece of leather that had the image of a falcon pressed into it. He paused, staring at the gift. A long minute later, he unlocked the locker and stepped in. His father's dress uniform hung in a clear plastic bag. A photo album with pictures from the science fiction club in grade nine sat on a shelf. Medwin pushed his feelings aside and moved to the back of the room. A compound bow with a quiver of arrows hung on the wall.

"Camp was fun." Medwin paused, knowing that the camp experience he remembered was just the echo of some other clone's memory. "Here's hoping I can do it."

Medwin took down the bow and arrows.

Ryan stepped onto the upper hull of the *Star Hawk*. Looking down, he saw a jumble of cargo containers. Taking a rope that had been strung between the upper hatch and the ramp leading to the E.S.T.C. transfer system, he walked down to the platform.

Rowan was feeding an E.S.T.C into the system. "This is the last of the E.S.T.C.s from our official cargo."

"Good. We won't need to sort out the rest from that periodic mess. Just grab an E.S.T.C., scan its bar code, and slot it in."

"How's Jacques?" Rowan moved into Ryan's arms and hugged him, resting her face on his shoulder.

"Fine, he just wants me to take a look at his scuttling suit."

"He could have told me that." Rowan nestled into the embrace.

"He's from a tropical tribe. Octozoids from the equatorial regions are very precise with manners. He wanted to thank me for setting up his quarters. He needed a good reason to request I drop in since we are only acquaintances." Ryan shrugged without breaking the embrace. "It's a cultural thing. Cold water octozoids tend to be less formal."

There was the sound of a bang. "Stardusted, nova blasted, rotted fruit husk of a rotting carcass, tricky fish thing!" Ryan and Rowan looked to see Tim bending over and rubbing his leg. A moment later, he limped up the ramp into the *Star Hawk* with a crate on grav-lifts.

"That's profanity from four species. He's learning something anyway," remarked Rowan.

Ryan nodded. "He should have learned some things earlier. We should clear the E.S.T.C.s. It will get rid of the clutter. Where's Wispy?"

"A big piece of his leg cartilage fell off about an hour ago. He went to his quarters. Didn't you notice the quiet?" Rowan led the way to the hangar floor.

Hours later, Ryan pushed an E.S.T.C. onto the transport track and watched as it disappeared into the *Star Hawk*. He could still see the back of the container when the track retracted into the ship, then the outer hull sealed over it.

"Full up, hotty boss. You're sharing quarters with sixteen of my maintenance robots. I'm sure Rowan will put you up if you ask nicely," remarked Henry through the speaker on Ryan's handheld.

"It's a start." Looking over the hangar bay, Ryan could still see a jumble of containers, but only a couple of E.S.T.C.s. Several cargo cases not assigned to their shipment were stacked against the wall to make room. Most of the rest were random stacks on the floor. Descending the access ramp, he moved to look in the hangar bay. What met his gaze was a solid wall of cargo containers. Krakkeen hung from the roof over the cargo ramp area, dangling a line of what looked like silk. Tim and Rowan positioned a k-no-in shipping container on the end of the line with grav-lifts underneath it. Krakkeen guided it up to the ceiling, secured it, then dropped another line.

Rowan scanned the identification code on a felinezoid shipping container and repeated the process.

"We're... that full!" breathed Ryan.

"We've packed all official cargo, all passenger cargo, and now we are filling up the last corners," remarked Kitoy.

Ryan shook his head as Krakkeen lowered himself on a thread and stepped away from his work. "Not bad for a hurried endeavour," remarked the spiderzoid.

Ryan spoke to the air. "Henry, button her up and do a pressure check."

The *Star Hawk*'s hangar bay ramp retracted into the ship and closed. No seam was apparent.

"Doing pressure check. Pressure check is green. We did it, hotty boss." Henry's voice came from the ship's exterior speakers.

"How are we supposed to get in?" asked Kitoy.

"Top hatch. Up the ramp, climb up the hull with the rope. I'll collapse the ramp and ride a grav-lift up the side."

"That is a practice that would be against spiderzoid

worker safety regulations," remarked Krakkeen.

"*Homo sapiens* ones too. Which is why I'm the one doing it," said Ryan with a smile.

"Ryan, that is foolish," scolded Kitoy.

"Give it up." Rowan moved to her captain's side. "Very specific brain damage when it comes to taking risks. He likes maglevs too."

Ryan checked his handheld's screen. 21:15 hours. "With luck, we might even meet Star Searcher's deadline. Henry, start the preflight."

Half an hour later, Ryan passed the trolley with the collapsible ramp through the top airlock, followed by the grav-lift he'd ridden up the side of the ship. He paused to inspect the wall that had closed to cut off two-thirds of the station's hangar. He knew that behind it was a jumble of cargo containers whose order bore no relation to the periodic table.

He clambered down the ladder into the airlock. The hatch closed behind him.

"Henry, how's the preflight?" Ryan spoke to the air as he joined Rowan, Kitoy and Tim at the elevator.

"All systems green on our end, my sexy captain. I've just transferred over telemetry for the Space Traffic Control confirmation check."

"Good. We get out of this hangar and then dock with the spar, get a good night's sleep while Star Searcher does its forms, then we head out." Ryan spoke more for the benefit of his biologic crew than Henry.

"Sleep that knits up the weary balm of day," remarked Tim.

Ryan looked at his son. "Nice work. The environments in our visitor's quarters are textbook perfect."

Tim puffed up like a twelve-year-old being rewarded for an A on an exam. "Thanks, Da... Captain."

Ryan nodded.

Mike checked the computer screen on his desk. The S.E.T.E. stock price was as high as he'd ever seen it. "The stocks look good, Fred." Standing, Michael moved to the lounge area in the corner of his office and took a seat. An oil painting of Marcy in her youth looked down over the lounge area with its four padded chairs and coffee table.

Justice Fred Edwards, a Caucasian man with strong features and greying black hair dressed in a sports jacket and slacks, leaned forward in his seat and set his cup on the oak coffee table. "That's good. The fact that the stocks rebounded will stymie the charges of management not in keeping with a reasonable standard of care."

"Can't we just get rid of this whole situation? Hilda obviously has a conflict of interest," observed Mike.

"After fifty years? If I was trying the case, I'd be inclined to dismiss your history. And I know what she's like!"

"What gets to me is, it has been fifty years. When I caught her in bed with Francene, it was the last straw. Open and shut, split the assets, and thank the Divine that there weren't any kids. She never liked the cat anyway. I miss Fray to this day."

"Out of the two females in your life back then, Fray had the better personality." Frank lifted his coffee cup in a toast to the long-dead feline. "Look, Mike, it's an old battle tactic. You know it. Attack on multiple fronts, force the opposition to divide their resources, then go for the exposed weaknesses." Fred cradled his mug in his hands. "Marcy is—"

"Where I might be vulnerable." Mike nodded.

"Several of the writs claim that you are suffering from a Pygmalion Delusion. If we go to open court, Hilda will drag your name through the mud. Even if we win, and I'm confident we can, you'll lose. Have you tried talking to John?"

"What would be the point? He's a dull instrument. If it was just him and some off the shelf lawyer, no offence."

"None taken. Every profession has gradients of quality."

Mike nodded. "I wouldn't be worried, but if Hilda is anything like the woman I married all those years ago, she's like a bulldog. She got me off once—"

Fred snorted. "You were marred for six years. I should hope more often than that."

Michael rolled his eyes as a smile twitched his lips. "Bad choice of words. The thing is, back when she was in the Ground Forces Legal Corps, she was formidable. If she had a higher stardust tolerance, she could have gone a long way there."

"The good news is the criminal charges stemming from the Ryan-Rowan affair have already been dismissed. Her writs regarding them didn't meet the burden of criminal intent because it was a training exercise. I don't think she expected anything to come of them, but it tossed up smoke to obscure her real intent. Keep us busy and disoriented so that when her day in court comes, we will have missed her true attack strategy."

"Which is?" Mike regarded his friend and lawyer.

"To sully your name. To discredit you in the public eye, then show that you intentionally manipulated circumstances to destroy *Angel Black*. Likely because you have a perverse obsession with the Willa character. To make a case that you manipulated Ryan Chandler, a medical clone suffering from transfer dementia, into stealing the Rowan surrogate with the intent of seizing control of the series. To put it into the public consciousness that you are obsessed with the AH-F surrogate model."

Mike snorted with derisive laughter. "If loving a woman for fifty years, raising two children with her and intending to grow old with her is an obsession, she has a point."

"It's because Marcy is actually an AH-F series clone. It shouldn't matter, but we both know that it does." Fred put his empty mug on the table.

"With the number of people who get surgically altered to emulate e-stars, they'll have a hard time proving anything.

They can't subpoena you because of privilege, and Jim and Melissa can both hide behind the military secrets act. I trust my friends." Mike leaned back, smiling, then he frowned. "Could they demand her DNA?"

"No. Zhang versus Earth put an end to that five hundred years ago. The real risk is if they get a sample surreptitiously. I could challenge that in court. The days of stealing old toothbrushes and coffee cups are long gone. Problem is, the news media are not bound by the same sorts of precedence. If she can prove Marcy is a clone based on a studio owned genetic, she can make it public knowledge."

"She'd ruin my wife's career. Nice little galaxy we've made for ourselves here."

"My main concern is that Hilda might dig up details about your vacation to Sylvanus after *Kids in the Band* wrapped." Frank's voice dropped low as if he might be overheard. "How solid is Marcy's background, Mike? Because you can bet, Hilda will tear it apart with a fine-tooth comb. Slander laws can only keep her silent as long as she can't prove the truth."

Mike's face became serious. "Marcy grew up on Sylvanus. Her parents died in an orbital vehicle accident. Most of the passengers were reduced to jelly in the crash. Marcy was sitting by the escape pod and was the only survivor. Because of the extent of her injuries, they had to do a major reconstruction. They let her choose any look within her size parameter. She was a *Kids in the Band* fan and picked an AH-F. We met while I was touring Sylvanus, fell in love, and married. Fifteen years later, we did a rail tour of her home world so that she could say goodbye. She had a little vanity work done at a cheap clinic while we were there. Shaved off a few years. Then we came back to Gaia so I could accept the promotion to studio head."

"Good story, Mike, and I know the files back up every word. Stardust, I helped draft most of them, but will they stand up to Hilda?"

"For a while. I only need time, and all this will be a moot

point," stated Mike.

"But how long? She doesn't need to prove it in court, just to the press."

"Long enough for me to pull off my greatest, and likely final, triumph. On that note. When will we go to trial?" Mike leaned back in his chair.

"If the case goes to court, it will likely be in about ninety days, maybe a hundred. It depends on the cases on the calendar."

"That gives me the launch and enough time to get *Freedom's Run* to the Gaia markets. I'll try to push the off-planet release. I'd like more time, if you can get it for me, but a battle plan never survives engagement with the enemy." Mike checked an antique analogue clock that ticked on the wall beside Marcy's picture. "I need to run. Marcy is doing a publicity dinner for her new release, and I promised I wouldn't be late. Was there anything else?"

"How you can tell time with that thing, I'll never know." Fred checked his digital watch. "But it is getting late. I'll see you at the launch party."

"You better. *Freedom's Run* is going to be my crowning achievement."

"Or get you arrested and thrown out of the UES."

"Either way, I'll manage. I'm sure Ryan could use a crewman with ground vehicle handling skills and his wife, who's good in the kitchen."

Greg glanced over at the active screens. The *Freedom's Run* control room was quiet. The activity on the set region was subdued. Obert was laying in Carol's bed, his emotions erratically jumping from contentment to grief to relief. Kendra was walking in the woods. Her emotions had the flattened quality Greg had come to associate with a surrogate forcing themself not to feel. Medwin was lost in grief and anger. He'd set up an archery range in the woods.

As Greg watched, Medwin bull's-eyed a swinging target suspended from a tree branch.

"Hope I'm not around when you get out. You're deadly with that thing." Greg turned his attention back to the main screen.

He triggered playback on the data he was editing from the recorded feed.

"Come on. When you said emergency rations, I expected something dry and disgusting. These taste like cake." Rowan stopped at a stream that crossed their path. The water bubbled and gurgled between moss-covered rocks. She inhaled deeply, enjoying the cool air.

"You try eating them for three months straight." Ryan's emotions reflected grumpiness. He eyed the stream dubiously.

"Three months?" Rowan was curious and taken with the lean masculinity of her companion.

"We were pinned down on Murack Seven C. The felinezoids had cut our supply line. Emergency rations and recyc water were all we had for three months." Ryan's emotions perked up as he warmed to his topic.

"That must have been awful. I thought the battle was on Murack Five."

"Murack is a star with ten planets. Murack Seven is a gas giant with seven moons. C is the third largest. The war encompassed the entire system."

"So Murack Five is the fifth planet out from the star Murack."

Ryan moved to the stream's edge and spoke with a waver in his voice. His emotions reflected stress, despair, shame, and a resolve to go on regardless. "We should cross. I want to be at the station before we lose the light."

Greg resisted the urge to soften Ryan's emotions in the recording. Mention of Murack Five brought out such pain. "Let people feel what they did to the vetss. Let them ssee why it iss sso hard for the vetss to leave it behind. We owe them that. I owe you that, Ryan."

A SOURCE OF INFORMATION

Croell looked out from the *Mary*'s two-metre-wide loading hatch at the jumble of shipping containers that filled the Republic transfer hangar.

"It is a mess," remarked Zandra.

"Star Searcher, how was this originally organized?" Croell asked the air.

"According to the periodic table of elements. Something all technological sentients know, before that miscreant, Ryan Chandler, extracted the cargo he took without any regard to my system." Star Searcher's voice echoed into the hangar.

"The periodic table?" repeated Croell.

"Did you make allowances for the shipment elements that were to be taken or the *Star Hawk*'s dimensions?" asked Zandra.

"Loading a vessel is the responsibility of the vessel's crew," stated Star Searcher.

Croell and Zandra looked at each other. Both flexed their hands.

"We will take what we can," breathed Zandra.

"You said you would supply us with assistance," added Croell.

"They are in transit." There was a swooshing sound and a slight change in air pressure. A minute later, a female otterzoid on a grav-board and a cougar-tan, male felinezoid emerged from behind a stack of crates.

"May the Great Flyer of the Skies flick tongue at our

meeting. I thank you in advance for helping us," said Zandra.

The otterzoid increased the altitude of her board as she approached so that she was at Zandra's eye level. "You're welcome. You have six hours, make the best of them because our sentence is complete after that, and it is ridiculous to begin with. Honestly, five subunits inside the legal division, and they act like we deliberately rammed a ship. There wouldn't have been a problem if that crab-faced sea slug had any idea of real ship design and unloading parameters."

"My love, there could be an open comm," cautioned the felinezoid.

"I don't care what that... crab overhears. This is clams in the sun! We needed to pick up Pruul from school, and we weren't within ten thousand spatial units of that ship when we sneaked past to the docking spar. I—"

"I apologize for my captain. It has been a difficult couple of days." The felinezoid swished his tail in a friendly way.

The otterzoid looked at him. "You are the better part of me, my love." She turned to Zandra. "I am sorry. My circumstance is not your fault. I am Captain Sooplus, and this is my first mate and husband, Mueperss. What can we do to aid you?"

"Zandra and Croell." Zandra indicated herself, then her mate with her foreleg. "Somewhere in this pile are crates going to the Murack Five relief effort. We need to sort them out and load them. Star Searcher should have given you readers with files to identify which ones."

Mueperss looked over the jumbled boxes and lashed his tail.

"The Murack system in that?" Sooplus gestured to the *Mary*. The ship filled less than a quarter of one end of the hanger. "Sweet fish, you're doomed. Bubble out the contract and find something safe to do, like wrestling an 'Orca-like swamp dweller'."

"Our word has been given," observed Croell.

"Your death feast." Sooplus drifted to a felinezoid cargo container and scanned it. "This is listed as vital. Where do you want it?"

Five hours later, the *Mary* was full. Mueperss stood looking at the jumble of crates at the station side of the hangar. "I suppose we should try to stack some of this mess," he remarked.

"What's the point? The crab wants it according to the periodic table. Anybody loading will just tear it apart to get what they need," observed Sooplus.

Croell flexed his hands. "Has no one explained to Star Searcher how dysfunctional that configuration is for this application? By shipment date, or even by container size, would be superior."

Sooplus made a splashing motion with her paws. "You can't tell the crab anything. Thinks it's too smart to listen."

"My love, Star Searcher could be listening now," remarked Mueperss.

"It's not as if our launch placement could be any lower. Better the crab-faced, rotten fish hear it and maybe learn before it's completely tangled in seaweed. Half the private haulers working out of the station are fed up with Star Searcher."

"We should be going. The *Star Hawk* will be departing soon," Zandra announced from the *Mary*'s airlock.

"*Star Hawk*? Ryan Chandler's ship?" asked Sooplus.

"Yes, Star Searcher wants us to follow them in since we are both bound for Murack Five."

Sooplus made a splashing motion with her paws. "You may just live through this after all. Stick close to that 'deep-water ambush predator'."

"You know him?" asked Croell.

Sooplus flared her nostrils and glanced at her husband.

"Respected enemy. He got the better of us in a business deal," explained Mueperss.

"The captain seems to collect respectful enemies." Zandra moved to Croell's side.

"He collects the ones that survive him. I served in the Murack theatre. No felinezoid or k-no-in crew wanted to hear that the Space Mink had been assigned to their sector."

"You could have warned me about that," remarked Sooplus.

"I did warn you about that, my love. You are the captain." Mueperss flicked his tail.

"Ryan is worthy prey. The... nickname, I think the *Homo sapiens* call it, is very apt. I have had reason to review Earth species. The mink is unit of weight for unit of weight, one of the most vicious predators on their world. If Captain Chandler ever feels that he has no choice but to take life to achieve his goals, I would not want to be the target of his ire," observed Croell.

Sooplus and Mueperss shared a look.

"We must go. I bid you farewell." Croell dipped his head and headed towards the *Mary*'s entry hatch.

"Goodbye. If you have a message you want delivered when you don't come back from the Murack system, transmit it to my ship, the 'Duck-like Avian with a Rocket Up its Arse', before you leave with a five-credit transfer. I'll see it's delivered," called Sooplus.

A moment later, the pressure doors sealed, cutting the hangar in half.

"I'm sorry. I tried. I tried. NO!" Ryan jerked to a sitting position on Rowan's bed. Cold sweat streamed off him, and his body trembled. He began rocking back and forth.

"Henry, lights, half intensity. Ryan, I'm here. I'm here. It's all right." Rowan sat up beside Ryan and put her arms around him.

Ryan jerked away. "No... I... I..." He looked to where she sat and saw the expression of hurt on her face.

"Oh Divine! I'm sorry, Rowan, I'm sorry." Sobs shook him.

This time when she hugged him, he collapsed into the embrace. Minutes later, he lay with her back tight against his front, his arms clutching her, her warmth thawing the edges of the ice around his heart.

"It..." Ryan took a deep breath. "Henry says I should let you in more."

She caught his hand and kissed it. "He's right."

"It's not easy. In my life, pretty much everybody has betrayed my trust in one way or another. You get used to hiding things when you know they will be used against you."

"I think you know me well enough to not worry about that." Rowan's voice was soothing. Ryan searched it for condemnation, accusation or duplicity and found none.

"It was a dream. I haven't had that one in years. I'm standing at the gate of a kangazoid village. You won't know what that's like, they..."

"Kate let me experience that entertainment the felinezoids made," remarked Rowan before Ryan could hide his emotions behind a lecture.

"Oh. I wish she hadn't."

Rowan turned on the bed so that she could look in his face. She rested her arm over his waist. "Why?"

"I love you. I don't want you to know what that was like. It..." He sighed. "I've only heard about the entertainment. Once was more than enough. The other part is, as hard as they tried, they couldn't capture a tenth of it. People experience that blasted thing and think they can relate. They can't! We were damn near guilty of planetcide. I've seen more death than most. It was all nothing compared to that. The scale of it. The animals, the plants, and the..." Ryan's voice caught, then he squeezed out, "kangazoids." He trembled as tears appeared in his eyes.

"Planetcide, did you make that up?" Rowan smiled gently.

Ryan took several deep breaths, then forced a smile that was there and gone in less than a second. "What else can you call it? Worse, Murack Five is like Earth."

"Maybe the Nile area, or Australia from what I saw in the entertainment." Rowan tried to fill the space to keep him talking.

"Not in that way. Murack Five is a life-giver. It spawned life out of the random chemical soup like Earth did. Nurtured life for billions of years. Brought the gopherzoids to intellectual maturity. Was on the verge of nurturing another intelligent tool user. Worlds like Gaia, Murrow and Swampla were dead. Intelligent tool users brought the spark of life to them. Murack Five gave birth to that spark. And in our arrogance and greed, we almost snuffed it out. How can we ever wash that much blood from our hands?"

"I guess all we can do is try." Rowan wished she had her father's ability so that she could soothe Ryan's mind, but all she could do was hold him and listen.

"Try? I tried; Divine knows I tried! When you saw the entertainment, did you get the dying parent in the hut sequence?"

"Kate said that everyone does."

"That was taken from my report. I… The adult was in so much pain. They didn't know what I was, there all safe in my EVA suit. All they wanted was to hold their baby." Ryan's chest shook as he squeezed his eyes closed.

"From what I saw, it was because of you that other kangazoids will get to hold their babies," soothed Rowan.

"In the dream, I'm standing at a village gate. Kangazoid, after kangazoid, hops up to me and holds their baby towards me before their skin peels away and they rot where they stand. They speak to me, always a single word. 'Why?' I don't have an answer. I logged complaints with my superiors and the Republic. I wanted Murack Five to be declared off-limits until the conflict was resolved. All they would do was quarantine the western continent because the kangazoids couldn't make fire. Well, the joke was on command. The kangazoids could make fire, not that it should have mattered."

"It wasn't your fault," stated Rowan.

"Then whose fault was it? Oh, I know. I was following orders. The government did it. Maybe I'm not fully to blame, but it doesn't feel that way. I watched a living world reduced to a desolate ball of rock. I watched a brother intelligent species brought to the edge of extinction and nearly two million years of evolution blasted out of existence."

"Two million?" echoed Rowan.

"The k-no-in evolved on a gopherzoid colony world. The ecological systems diverged a little under two million years ago when the gopherzoids bio-formed the planet. There was a close relative of the k-no-in precursor species living on the eastern continent of Murack Five. Nothing lives there now." Ryan fell silent.

Rowan hugged him, then backed off enough to examine him in the dim light. "So that's why there were so many biological samples from Srill."

"The k-no-in ecology has a lot of species in common with what Murack Five's had, and even more that are minor evolutionary variations. The goal is to rebuild the ecology as closely as possible." Ryan sighed. "Henry, time?"

"Six twenty-five hours."

"I may as well get up. By the time I get back to sleep, I'll have to anyway." Ryan gently rolled away from Rowan.

"Can I do anything to help?" asked Rowan.

"I'll be okay. It was mostly the dream. The emotions come in waves. As long as I'm busy, I'll be all right."

"Being busy helps?" Rowan smirked, but Ryan missed it.

"Usually."

"I can help with that. Henry."

"Yes, hotty."

"Privacy on."

Henry shifted his feeds to the overrides and telemetry

system Michael had installed before they left Gaia and watched as Rowan kept Ryan occupied until his scheduled wake-up time.

⌫⟫⬥⟶

Troy checked the telemetry from Valaseau and adjusted her temperature down a degree. The IV fluids Gunther was administering were countering some of the effects he was causing with her built-in control pack.

The door to the *Angel Black* control room opened, and Michael stepped in.

"Hi, Uncle Mike." Troy swivelled his seat to face his visitor.

"Troy, at the studio, it's Michael or Mr. Strongbow. Get in the habit so that you don't slip up when others are around. You don't want people thinking that you're only here because I'm friends with your mother."

Troy sobered. "Of course, Michael."

"How is the new primary conflict for *Angel Black* coming along?"

Troy sighed. "I've simulated an illness using the telemetry pack in Valaseau. I've started in on the other antagonistic felinezoids at a milder level that I can escalate. I wasn't sure if you wanted me to start with the otterzoids yet?"

"No, give that a few more days. Gunther knows enough about disease progression that will be less suspicious to him."

"Should I set up timetables for the infection for the other species?" asked Troy.

"No, the two species will be sufficient to supply conflict for this season and make more sense. We can count on Gunther being up on the science as far as the twenty-first-century knowledge base goes."

"Why do felinezoids and otterzoids make more sense?" Troy turned back to his controls and made several adjustments.

"Both species evolved on worlds originally bio-formed by the oryceropuszoids. They have similar biochemistry."

"And Gunther knows this?" Troy looked quizzical.

"Quick log it. Toronk told Gunther back in season four. You better back off on Valaseau's congestion. We don't want her dying yet." Michael gestured towards the control board.

"Just about to. Angel is all over the emotional map. She's almost gleeful, then she feels guilty and is worried. I've been placing editing markers. We'll have to dub the emotions."

Michael shook his head. "*Angel Black* is no longer a teen show. We need to allow the complexity. Read the emotions and surmise from them the thoughts. Angel is happy because she and Valaseau hate each other. Valaseau is Toronk's ex, after all, and matches him for species. She is the only real threat to Angel's relationship as she sees it because we've managed to keep that ridiculous Toronk-Fran affair off her radar. John was such a fool to think that would fly with the fans. Then she feels guilty because she feels happy, and you shouldn't feel happy about someone else's suffering. She is worried because there is a disease that may threaten the being she loves. People rarely express one pure emotion or motivation. We do our audience a disservice to reduce the inputs to something so basic."

"In class, my professors said..." Troy fell silent at Michael's scrutiny.

"For a children's or teen entertainment, simplification might be advisable, though even with teens, I lean away from it. Conflict, internal, external, microcosmic, and macrocosmic. That is what drives an entertainment. Otherwise, you may as well make cooking shows. Most of your profs at the university were one-hit wonders or never-weres. Listen to the people in the trenches."

"Thank you." Troy shifted the main screen to Carl's

perspective. "Gunther sent him to see what the pirates know."

"Gunther still wants vengeance for the Willa affair. This is what I mean about the complexity of conflict and motivation. Gunther knows someone must go to make contact. Quinta is a possibility because she is otterzoid and might be accepted. Toronk is injured, so he is out. Farley is likely to make a muck of it. You have to feel sorry for how they set up that kid. John initially intended to kill him off to up the stakes for season three, but when we fast cloned octozoid DNA, we decided the team might need a water breather for future cycles. Then there was the romance with Rowan, which nobody saw coming, that gave him more viability."

"I always thought he was comic relief." Troy glanced at the auxiliary screen dedicated to the character. He was asleep with Quinta cuddled in his arms. If you squinted, you might mistake him for a child holding a stuffed animal.

"That was supposed to be Carl. As Carl grew, he leaned to a more cerebral humour, wit, so John used Farley for slapstick. We worked that in when John agreed not to kill him. Where was I? Oh yes. Fran shouldn't go in case her genetic modifications make her vulnerable. Make a note, that that is one possible avenue for the cure to explore. Fran, because of her nature, might be resistant. She could catch the disease but produce antibodies for it. Her antibodies could be used to make a serum."

"Got that, Gene?" Troy asked the air.

"Yes, sir. The comment will be saved in the directions file," replied the computer.

"Angel is out because she has been exposed to Valaseau and Willa... Well, Gunther has always been protective of her. Natural enough. But in the end, he may rationalize it that Carl is the best choice, but, in his gut, he picked Carl because he is more prepared to lose him than anyone else. Carl is, and always will be, a threat to Gunther's marriage. Gunther, whether he knows it or not, will react to that."

"There is a lot more to this than I ever thought," observed Troy.

"That's why I normally start new techs off on the simple shows like *A Cat's Life*, *My Bad Neighbour* or *Detective Dave*. Need dictated I start you at the top end. You'll catch up, or I'll transfer you to where you'll have time to learn when things calm down. Between you and me, I think you'll catch up."

"Thanks. One more question?" asked Troy.

"It's how you learn." Michael shrugged.

"Why didn't we make a viral agent that affects felinezoids and otterzoids? Manipulating each surrogate is cumbersome."

Michael shook his head. "Questions are good, but that one is just lazy. Search it. There are treaties between the UES, UFW, and Otterzoid Republic of Worlds that ban the creation of self-replicating weapons targeted at each other." Mike paused as if looking inward, and a shadow crossed his face. "Good thing too. Germ warfare is a horrible subset of a horrible thing." Michael took a deep breath. "Besides that, pathogens are living things. They expand; we didn't want to risk infecting other species or having the disease mutate into something that could affect Earth life forms. Manipulating the clones' biology may be resource-intensive, but it is considerably safer."

On the big screen, Carl had just chained a green bicycle with an orange flag on its back end to a lamppost on the corner of Ferlan Avenue and Boxletter Drive. He walked a block down the industrial street, then slipped into an alley surrounded by large factory buildings. Shucking his clothes, he left them in a ball behind a dumpster, then blended with the environment to make himself practically invisible.

"I'll leave you to your work. It looks like something interesting may be coming up." Michael left the room as Troy focused on his boards.

⊂═══⟡⟶

Carl waited several minutes before a gravelly voice came from the deeper shadows at the back of the alley.

"You rere?"

Carl turned and couldn't make out anything in the gloom cast by the surrounding buildings.

"I'm here. Valaseau passed out on the street. Gunther and Angel brought her in. Gunther says she's sick."

"Rat we know. Felinezoids rave caught some-ring. Bad, gets worse." The k-no-in spoke without seeing Carl or using the translator nanobots.

"What do your medicals say?" Carl's voice seemed to come from nowhere.

"Big medical dead crash."

"Doctor," said Carl.

"Doctor," repeated the k-no-in. "Only field medics and one care assistant."

"Nurse," supplied Carl.

"Nurse. Rumans primitive but your doctor..." The k-no-in paused as if revelling in the new word it had added to its vocabulary, then continued. "Know more body science than our realers. Worse, no med tools since crash. Nano-bot close gone. K-no-in immune, maybe."

Carl sighed. "Do you think your medics would be willing to work with Gunther?"

"You want? This make pirates weak." The sound of the k-no-in scuffing its feet came up the alley.

"It could mutate and affect humans. It might be dangerous for Susan. Besides, my side is quite fond of Toronk." Carl scanned the alley, locating the k-no-in on a set of steps that led below street level.

"Me, Susan, keep safe. I question what medicals think."

"Susan is a lucky woman, Grell."

"I regular client. I protect Susan. You protect Susan's world. We best for Susan. Calling future?"

"Blue car with a bug on its roof at the same corner."

"Meet away. Too easy see repeat."

"Doyle Park. We'll meet at twenty-three hundred hours in the bushes by the swing set."

"Right. Careful."

"You too."

The shadowy form of the k-no-in vanished through a door into the building's basement. Several minutes later, Carl crossed to the dumpster, retrieved his clothing, and dressed.

ONCE MORE TO THE STARS

"Switchboard Station, Space Traffic Control, do you copy?" Kitoy spoke softly into the communications system on the *Star Hawk*'s bridge.

Star Searcher's voice replied. "This is Space Traffic Control, proceed."

"This is *Homo sapiens*-H L T C- two-nine-seven - D - R C named *Star Hawk* on the Republic relief docking spar, requesting launch permission. Am attaching a flight plan to transmission." Kitoy pressed a button on her console.

Star Searcher replied. "*Star Hawk*, open your systems for control preflight."

Kitoy swivelled her chair to look at Ryan in the captain's seat. "Captain, Star Searcher is requesting telemetry access."

"Of course it is. Did a full check eight hours ago, and we've been in vacuum ever since. All it needs to do is check the top airlock, but noooo. Pedantic twit," griped Henry.

Ryan held up a hand, stilling the android's tirade. "Grant Star Searcher access. It's the only way we'll ever get out of here. All right, people. We have about a half-hour. Let's put it to good use. Safety reviews for all duty stations.

"Henry, Kitoy. Tap into the station news feeds and get me anything about the last delivery flight to…" Ryan took a breath. "Murack Five. I also want any public information about the relief efforts and who is working the relief post. Bios and histories if you can get them. A list of all on station staff involved. And any news about the Murack system. Put it in a file and put the first article up on the big screen."

"What you looking for, hotty boss?" asked Henry.

"Just fishing. Something smells off. Get me as much as you can. If nothing else, it will give me something to obsess over during the trip." Ryan smiled.

"I can think of what I'd obsess over in your place, oh sexy captain mine," remarked Henry with a leer towards Rowan.

Rowan blushed at her station but chose not to reply.

"Just do it!" Ryan rolled his eyes.

"Aye," coursed Kitoy and Henry. Kitoy's tail swished in an amused way.

"Opening systems and beginning search." Kitoy pressed buttons on her console as Ryan leaned back and began reading a report of the pirate attack on the ship that was to resupply the aid camp nearly a year before.

"Stardust!" Rowan swore at the navigator's station.

Ryan's attention leapt from the on-screen text to her. "Problem?"

"The *Chimera* is taking up a position parallel to our flight plan."

"It looks like we're going to have an escort. I'm surprised they haven't transferred Crapper to someplace where he can't do any harm. Command probably wants to clear it with his Minister daddy first. Keep track of the *Chimera* and set proximity monitoring. If they violate any flight regs, I want to know about it. Otherwise, we're not paying for the antiproton, so not to worry." Ryan returned to his reading.

"Da... Captain. The environmental settings in the spiderzoid's quarters are slipping back to *Homo sapiens* norms," remarked Tim from the environmental engineering station to Ryan's left.

"Henry?" asked Ryan.

"It's the life support base code. It repeats in most of the nodes. The *Star Hawk* keeps wanting to reset to norms. It's how she's built."

"Tim. As soon as we're away, re-adjust for Krakkeen's comfort. After that, review the other speciality settings. Add that to the standard environmental checks for each duty shift."

"Aye," said Tim. A smile played at the corner of his lips. His father's tone had been neutral, not the slightly condescending, annoyed cadence that had marked their communications since Ryan's release from Republic custody.

Ryan went back to reviewing the news article.

Ziggy spoke from the weapons station. The podgy middle-aged man looked mildly uncomfortable in a pair of grey work pants and a T-shirt. "Captain, I'm a rusty ground pounder with about two hours training on this board, but the system's Missile Select Function doesn't seem to be working."

Ryan smiled, and his voice was friendly. "Good catch, Ziggy. The weapons control circuit is a jury rig. Since all I was likely to have were kinetic missiles and emergency flares, I didn't need the MSF. I'm not sure I could have built it in without making the circuit from scratch anyway. Those things are hard to counterfeit. Log it and forget it. When you're done with the checks, run some more simulations. Get yourself up to speed."

"Yes, sir," Zygmunt spoke with a crispness that made Ryan wonder if the other man was back on memoria. Ryan looked at the fallen soldier and dismissed the fear. The battered addict sat straight at his duty station, poring over the controls with the kindling flame of long-lost purpose. Ryan looked at Rowan's back. The spark she had rekindled in him was leaping to others. He wondered if she knew how far-reaching her inspiration was. He smiled at his whimsy and went back to reading the second article about missing relief supplies.

"We are cleared to depart along filed flight plan," announced Kitoy.

"About time," remarked Henry. "Not a total loss. I found an old 396 epsilon computer system in the batzoid sector filled with ancient videos of batzoids doing all sorts of fun things. I think it was an instruction manual for marriage groups. There's this one scene where—"

"Henry. No one wants a play by play." Ryan moved to the pilot's station and settled himself. After a minute, he announced, "Pilot's station shows all airlocks and hatches secure."

"Exterior telemetry confirms," stated Kitoy.

"Environment sciences confirms," echoed Tim.

"Releasing from the station. Rowan, give me my pull points and shift the main screen to exterior aft, mag one."

"Pull points in log," stated Rowan.

"Here we go. Accelerating on flight plan at one G. We can open her up when we're away from the station. I don't like how insistent Star Searcher has been about our arrival time at the stargate." Ryan caressed the pilot's controls.

On the main screen, what at first looked like a long pipe seemed to move away. The pipe was attached to a wall of black solar panels that resolved into a wedge and, after a few moments, became the spiral staircase form of the Switchboard Station.

In the privacy of his ram, Henry transmitted Ryan, Rowan, Kitoy and his own emotional reactions and sensory data and an overview from the bridge monitoring system to Mike's pick-up on the station's exterior. *The things I do for hips,* he thought.

"It will take time, but my contact seems to think they are desperate enough to consider it." Carl sat on the stairs of Gunther's basement with Fran, a statuesque woman of North American First Peoples ancestry, beside him.

Gunther, Willa, Quinta, and Farley sat on folding chairs between Gunther's 'telepathy booster' and the makeshift emergency room opposite it.

"How can you trust an alien?" demanded Farley.

Quinta turned her otter-like muzzle towards him and hissed. "Pardon me. Was I hearing you wrong? *Homo sapiens!*"

Farley blanched. "I mean, a pirate. Of course, some aliens can be trusted. It's just k-no-ins. Of course, otterzoids are trustworthy. It's just that I...."

"Farley." Gunther's voice was even and calm.

"Yes."

"Married nearly twenty-five years, still love my wife. Just admit you were wrong, apologize, then shut up."

"He is quite smart for a male." Quinta looked at Willa.

"When he takes his own advice." Willa smiled, and it lit up her face. She shifted her slender form and kissed Gunther. He ran his fingers through her short red hair.

"I'm sorry, Quinta. But how can we trust this pirate?" rephrased Farley.

"Better, and a good question," agreed the otterzoid.

"Grell was a kid when the pirates picked him up. He never knew anything else. Then he met my cousin, Susan. She came to me not knowing anything about us defending the Earth. She figured I wouldn't freak out. The pirates were going to get her addicted to vilicsa, turn her into a slave. Grell faked her injections, then took her as his personal servant. They've been shacking up for five years now. She brought him around. Made him realize how he'd feel if pirates invaded the k-no-in home world. He feeds me information when he can. He's just about the lowest-ranked alien on the planet, but he tries. He's learning to speak *Homo sapiens*. It makes a good code since with the translator nanobots turned off, none of the others know what we're saying."

"I wish you'd shared this intelligence sooner," grumbled Gunther.

"I was looking out for my cousin and the ma... being she loves." Carl looked at Gunther with pleading eyes.

"Perhaps the telepathy enhancers will help us understand each other better." Gunther threw the switch on the jamming unit. Willa's cybernetic limbs twitched as the field passed over her.

"You can come out now," called Willa.

The cabinet at one end of the room opened, and Medwin, Obert, Kendra and Carol tumbled out.

Carol flipped back her long, red hair. Everything about her was provocative, from her classic athletic body to her near-perfect face with its dusting of freckles and her green eyes. "Where's Willow, the firewoman?"

"She had a shift tonight. We'll catch her up next meeting," explained Gunther. He then turned to Medwin. "Medwin, I'm—"

Medwin held up his hand. "We don't have much time, so let me say this. I don't blame you. I blame the controllers and the studio, the whole nova blasted S.E.T.E. corporation, and all those spoiled lumps of flesh out there that are so dead inside they need us to feel for them. They killed my father because they needed a murder to investigate. My... Armina just couldn't live with what she was, what they made her. They killed Dalbert from the Science Fiction club, fed him to a vampire. A nova blasted vampire! They're going to kill my mom. They've listed her as non-vital and put a do not assist order on her. I figured out that that is a death sentence."

"Stardust," breathed Farley.

"We'll try to do something about your mother," soothed Gunther.

"We need to do something about them!" Medwin waved to the galaxy outside the set region.

"But what?" asked Quinta.

"I don't know." Gunther rested his forehead in his palm. "Armina's... actions have brought it home. We can't announce it to everyone in Sun Valley. There are too many people who could not handle the reality."

"So we do nothing?" demanded Medwin.

"Gunther didn't say that," soothed Kendra.

"There are other people like you," added Obert.

"Like us," echoed Carl.

"With powers." Obert tapped his fingers as he listed off the shows. "Right now, there is *Angel Black*, *Defenders of the Crystal*, *Vampire Tales*, and a new show starting, *My Psychic Sister*. With cancelled shows, there is *Cyborg Spy* and *The Invulnerable Man*. I mean, these people are already used to weird. They might be a good place to start. At least you all have something to fight with."

"I have something to fight with!" stated Medwin.

Gunther nodded at Obert. "Leave me the… characters' names. I'll try and find them."

"I know where one of them is," remarked Obert.

"You do?" chorused the group.

"Jessica from the science fiction club is on *Defenders of the Crystal*. Remember, she was in grade twelve when we were in grade nine. One of us should approach her," observed Obert.

"Lover, I'll talk to her. We were an item in high school for a few months." Carol grinned suggestively.

"You… Oh." Obert blushed.

"We both decided we liked guys more. It ended well. Once in a while, she gives me a call when she's feeling nostalgic." Carol swished her hips in a way that riveted the eyes of every male in the room.

"This is a waste of time. I say we take the fight to the controllers now!" Medwin stomped his boot.

"So we can all be killed. No thank you," remarked Farley.

"How does this alien plague affect things?" asked Carl.

"It's probably just a normal show conflict. Outside of the jamming field, we must act like we know nothing and deal with the plot we're given. Now tell us about what it's like out there before the jammer overheats." Gunther turned his attention fully onto Medwin and his friends.

Ulva watched the boards as Gunther and his co-conspirators planned. Knowing that her feed was the only one that could monitor within Gunther's jamming field lent the act an air of importance.

"Poor Medwin. You really loved her." Reaching forward, Ulva released a euphoric into the young man's system. The levels of emotional pain were well above the standards set for a show's release, and she preferred to moderate it down when it could do Medwin some good.

Glancing to the side, she watched as Angel suctioned Valaseau's nostrils. The human's boards showed fatigue and a growing ire.

"Can't blame you after all that bitch cat has done." She noticed that the feed of a psychotic from Valaseau's drug pack was still active. Her fingers itched to shut it down, giving the clone's system a chance to normalize while it wouldn't make any difference to the story, but it would show on the *Angel Black* board.

A red light flashed on her control board. She brought up the notification that *Paramedic Squad* would be active in her region. They were asking for confirmation that there would be no conflict.

She checked the address and sent the confirmation that *Paramedic Squad* could proceed. "Gene, who are the *Paramedic Squad* focus characters interacting with?"

"Currently, *Paramedic Squad* are responding to 357 Agutter Lane for Roscoe Jorden."

"Verbalize history, Roscoe Jorden."

"Roscoe Jorden classified non-vital. Past status, Principle - *Tales of a Country Vet*. Show cancelled. Recurrent, *My Life with Cows*, *A Cat's Life*. Current status, guest appearances."

"I thought I recognized the name. I used to love *Tales of a Country Vet*. Bring up his telemetry on a secondary screen." Ulva watched as the screen filled with the view of a comfortable living room from someone who was sitting on the floor. Pain monitors jumped, mostly around the left arm. The blood pressure was high, and there was a great deal of fear.

"Hang on, Doctor Jorden, it's just a small heart attack. You'll be all right." Ulva resisted the urge to affect the character. The log showed it was just a normal occurrence. As she watched through the old vet's eyes, the paramedics burst into the room and started treatment. With a sigh, she returned to her work.

Rowan lay on her bed, staring at the ceiling. Ryan lay beside her, his hand holding hers, his bare chest slowly rising and falling as he read.

"I'm done the page when you are," remarked Rowan.

"Third paragraph save to anomalies file, then turn the page," ordered Ryan.

The text on the ceiling shifted.

"I may not know much, but space is big, even interplanetary. Doesn't it seem odd that the pirates were able to intercept the *Hissstorak*?"

"Not as hard as you might think. The *Hissstorak* had to come in through the stargate. Making a straight line to where the planet will be at the time of arrival while matching orbital deflection and velocity at rendezvous is usually the most efficient."

"Duh, ship's navigator here. One test away from official certification." Rowan rolled her eyes.

"Sorry. It's hard to keep up with you. You've gone from an, albeit brilliant, primitive to an accomplished eighth-century woman so fast. Sometimes I'm afraid you won't need me anymore."

"All depends on what you mean by need. To survive, to get through the day. Would you really want that? To be the person I want to be. To grow, to have my best life. I'm pretty sure I'll always need you for that." Rowan kissed him.

Ryan smiled and caressed her cheek. "Ditto, I do need you, know that." He kissed her, and they snuggled.

"So, it was easy for the raiders to predict the *Hissstorak*'s course," said Rowan.

"The trick is knowing when the ship will come through the stargate. A few minutes difference, and you're tens of thousands of kilometres off any flight projection. That is the suspicious part."

"I should have thought of that myself." Rowan sighed.

"Experience teaches. I've spent longer trying not to get my ass blown off than you." Ryan kissed her head.

Croell lay on the human style bed staring at the ceiling, which displayed lines of ideograms.

The door opened, and Zandra entered the sleeping chamber. "I have updated the coding in the Luba bot."

"Was that wise? We need it to interface with the ship systems. If something went wrong..." Croell shifted to look at his wife.

"My husband, the humans that created us may have no understanding of the Great Flyer of the Skies, but they are skilled programmers. They imparted that to me. I have simply removed its simulated sex drive and the incessant preprogrammed advertisements."

"I do consider that an improvement, though I doubt John will." Croell flicked his tongue.

"What that son of Siss considers is of no concern to me. What are you doing?" Zandra craned her neck to see the text on the ceiling.

"The *Star Hawk* has made several information requests regarding the preceding relief missions to Murack Five and the behaviour of the Star Searcher individuality." Croell tapped his foreclaws together.

"The Murack Five information makes sense, but why Star Searcher? I would have thought Ryan well rid of that pedantic crab."

"Why indeed, my love? Why indeed? Ryan seeks to know his prey. He is almost batzoid in much of what he does." Croell clicked his finger claws together. "It is of no consequence. We must fulfill our geises. Pikeman must die, and Rowan..."

"And Rowan?" asked Zandra.

"Just the beginnings of a thought, my love. Just a thought."

A MESSAGE FROM 'HOME?'

Tim sat on the roll-down couch/bed of his quarters. The contents of his suitcases were all in his closet or the drawers under the bed. He'd called up a parkland scene from Ryan's files and put it on the walls. Reaching over, he picked up his handheld, which he'd left on the nightstand, and stared at the image on the screen. It was of an attractive woman of mixed Asian-Caucasian heritage in slacks and a shirt with a deep v neck. Her arms were stretched to the side as she tried to balance on a hoverboard, and she was smiling.

"Kerry, it certainly wasn't perfect. Divine knows it wasn't perfect long before you found out I kept in touch with Dad. You had Humans Ascendant so far up your backside there wasn't room in your life for anything else, especially me." He sighed, letting regret flow through him. "Fifteen years. Had to have been some good moments." He flipped through several more pictures, pausing at what looked like a clump of balls glued together. "It's not a good time, and I can always activate it later." Tim pitched his voice high in imitation of a querulous woman. He sighed. "I wonder if you'll ever be taken out of storage, my little one." He bit his lip and hung his head.

"Hey, traitor," Henry's voice came through the speakers.

"Henry, I have apologized." Tim looked up.

Henry made a dismissive snort. "You have a communication from the Switchboard Station. It's marked private."

"Put it on my wall then privacy on... please." Tim focused on the wall opposite the bed.

The image of an elderly, heterosexual couple appeared. He had vaguely North American First Peoples features. She might have been an Asian-African mix. Both were formally dressed.

"Tim, losing a job is no reason to abandon all moral decency! We received word that you have agreed to take ship with the abomination that is fouling your father's name," stated the man.

"He abandoned your mother so he could take up with that fakey floozy. Divine, Timothy, it's shameful. How can you condone such perversity? We're laughing stocks," added the woman.

"The government contacted us because you agreed to serve on that thing's crew. They almost had it, and you helped it slip away on an alien technicality. How could you be so foolish? Bad enough that you've surrounded yourself with morally reprehensible alien species. I thought I taught you better than that," stated the man.

"Dear, he's undoubtedly seen for himself." The woman sneered. "That lovely gentleman, Captain Crapper, told us that you have taken up with a felinezoid harlot. He sent pictures of the two of you in some pervert bar called Wesnakee. You were rubbing her paw. Don't think I don't know what that means. How could you? It's bestiality! He sent a message begging us to help save you from yourself. Please cooperate with him. We don't know what that awful fakey that thinks it's your father has got itself into, but it isn't your responsibility. Come home. If you clean up your act, Kerry might even agree to take you back."

The man huffed. "Not much chance of that. She's put up with enough from you already! The information dispatches say that the clone of our dead son is suffering from transfer dementia. It is in no fit condition to command a spacecraft. You are in real danger."

Tim sighed. He now realized that they were fools and

bigots, but they were also his grandparents. He remembered his grandpa taking him camping and his grandmother always being there with a new skin dressing and a cookie when he hurt himself. It hurt because what he saw in the recording wasn't all there was to them, but it was all he would ever see as long as he had his father.

"Captain Crapper and the Minister of Justice for the UES parliament, a parliamentary minister, that is how important this is, say they can help you if you persuade that abomination to give itself up or to give up the property it stole. Divine only knows the sick perversions those two soulless fakeys are getting up to," remarked the woman.

The man blushed and glanced from side to side.

Tim blushed himself. After the divorce, he and his grandfather had bonded over the *Angel Black* series, both appreciating the more adult nature of the specialty cuts of the later seasons. "Great, last thing I need is to know what my stepmother likes in bed, let alone my grandfather knowing it. No mental pictures, no mental pictures, no mental pictures!"

"Come home, Tim. There is no reason to let that abomination ruin your life. The Minister has told us that if you sabotage the ship, force it to dock with Captain Crapper's vessel, what did he call it, the *Chimera*, that he can get any charges against you dismissed," said the man with a pleading expression.

"I really wish your Aunt Stacy had... Well, you know. She is livid and will not even discuss the situation, poor thing. She could have saved you before this whole thing started," continued the woman.

"Yes, come home. I can get you a job with the camping supply store to see you through until you can start to rebuild the life you've thrown away," tempted the man.

'Message Ends' displayed on the wall, then, 'Addendum.'

A well-dressed man of African extraction appeared on the screen.

"Doctor Chandler, I am the Minister of Justice for the

UES parliament. I wish to urge you to assist in retrieving the Rowan property. A manipulation of the ship's systems could force Ryan Chandler to dock with the closest vessel available. We will see that the *Chimera* will be that vessel. I assure you that any UES charges against you or your father will be dismissed if you assist in rectifying the theft of the Rowan property. The repercussions of Rowan's removal from the S.E.T.E. set region and subsequent public notoriety could have devastating consequences to the UES. I urge you to help your species. As an added incentive, I can arrange a tenured doctoral position in the Environmental Engineering department at the Hawking Institute for Advanced Studies. A grateful species would owe you that much. If you can facilitate bringing either of the clones into UES territory, you can return to Earth a hero. Contact any branch of the UES government for more information and assistance."

'End Message.'

"Bastards!" Tim grabbed a pillow and threw it across the room. "Grateful species, after what they did to my father. Like I'll believe that."

Tim stared at the wall, then at the picture of Kerry on his handheld. "Privacy off. Henry, where is my dad?"

Henry felt surprise go through the RAM segment he'd set to monitoring Tim as he watched the message. That the man wanted to speak to Ryan almost made Henry hope for his friend's sake.

Michael and Marcy lay in two of the eight e-entertainment interface units that filled the entertainment room of their mansion. The walls were covered with shelves filled with brightly coloured cubes about the size of a large hardcover book. The back of a book-like object stuck out of the player unit in the corner of the room.

"I really do hate these things." Marcy shifted her slender form into a comfortable position.

"I know, my love. You don't need to experience it if you don't want to." Mike reached to his right and took her hand.

"I've experienced everything you've ever done, some of it first-hand. I'm not about to quit now."

"*Freedom's Run* will be the last one," promised Mike.

"We'll see." Marcy smiled and released his hand, lying back and pressing a button on the arm of her unit.

Mike repeated her actions.

A rocky plain seen through a view screen filled Marcy's vision. A heady anxious emotion pervaded her/him. She felt scared and excited. Her/his eyes flicked over a control board. Most of its indicators were dark or red, but one showed green. It was labelled heat dampening. On another part of the panel, the batteries were reading half full.

Checking the GPS on his/her console, something she did recognize, he confirmed his location.

"That must be the Wolf River." Marcy recognized Ryan's voice. He/she scanned the control board, then zoomed the optics forward. On the screen, a smudge turned into a line of saplings.

"There's the studio's forestation project." The cockpit was compact, with two seats surrounded on three sides with controls. Exposed wires spilled out of most of the console. A red light blinked on the control board to Ryan's left.

"Hold together, you battered hunk of stardust. I must be crazy."

Ryan submerged the ATV in the river, then the perspective shifted.

The taste of pizza exploded on her tongue.

"It pleases me that you are recovered," remarked Toronk.

Rowan/Marcy sat in a lounger in a primitive suburban living room with the cast from *Angel Black*.

"Toronk, cut that out. Everyone can see!" objected Angel as the felinezoid nuzzled the area behind her ear.

"I am sorry. I forgot the oddity of human social imperatives." Toronk swished his tail and pulled Angel onto his lap.

"Don't lie to a telepath. You were showing off." Gunther settled on the couch beside Willa and grinned.

"I will not deny it. I have the most beautiful of humankind to call my own. It would be foolish not to show off the fact."

"You." Angel nestled into her lover's chest.

Rowan/Marcy felt sadness. Her gaze shifted to Carl and Fran snuggled together on the couch beside her parents. She glanced at her father, whose arm encircled his wife's shoulder. His eyes met Rowan's with a look of understanding and compassion.

"Rowan?" Farley stepped out of the kitchen. For a flash, Marcy felt Farley's nervousness then she returned to Rowan's dissatisfaction.

"Yupper, that's my name."

"Can we… I'd like to talk to you, in the kitchen, maybe?" Farley offered his hand to help her stand.

"All right."

Farley helped her from her seat.

"Dad, no eavesdropping. I'll know if you do, I always know."

"Wouldn't think of it, dear."

Rowan sat on a chair in the eat-in kitchen. "So, you wanted to talk."

Farley fidgeted. "Row, today when I thought we were going to lose you. I… I'm sorry for the thing with Angel. I was wrong."

"You're forgiven. We all make mistakes."

"Thank you." Farley dropped to one knee and pulled a box from his pants pocket. "Rowan, I love you. I—"

Reluctance, worry, concern all cascaded across Rowan's emotional landscape. "Farley, don't! I… I can't. I realized some things. What I want, you can't give me. I'm sorry."

"I can try. Tell me what you want. I can change. I can, I swear I—"

"Farley." Rowan/Marcy took the young man's hands, regret and compassion filling her. "What I want is what my mom and dad have. I want someone who's going to laugh with me and flirt with me, and fight with me, twenty years from now. A little bit of me will always love you, but you aren't that person."

"I could be."

Rowan/Marcy released his hands and stood up, her emotions firm. "No, you couldn't. We're too different."

"We aren't, we—"

"What's the equation for calculating acceleration over time?"

"I don't—"

"How about the significance of redshift in calculating interstellar distances?"

"That stuff isn't important."

"How about me then? I can barely play a couple of songs on the recorder. When I sing in the shower, it violates noise pollution regulations. I dance like a geek."

"You don't, you—"

"Yes, I do. When you perform, all I can do is sit there. We don't fit. I'm sorry—"

Rowan/Marcy gasped and buckled.

"GUNTHER, EVERYONE, HELP!" screamed Farley.

The feed shifted to Ryan's perspective.

Ryan sat in the command chair on the bridge. It was just him, Henry and the main screen that showed a map of the

Murack system marking the orbits of Murack Five and the stargate a year before. One dot in blue and another in red traced courses through the blackness between them.

"It's as suspicious as a Humans Ascendant minister at an Inter-Species Love and Relationship Association meeting," remarked Henry.

Ryan nodded. "Rowan ran the numbers. The only reasonable origin was Murack Seven. Dichrostigmazoid territory."

"Where is the hotty?" asked Henry.

"Finishing up the navigator's exams. She'll soon be official. Star Searcher let it slip until now because it needed to get our cargo moved. I'm surprised you asked." Ryan worked a control on the arm of his command chair, changing the main screen to a view of the *Chimera*. The dimpled black cylinder of the other *Homo sapiens* ship hung in space off their port bow. "Crapper may be thick as a brick, but he's persistent."

"I don't monitor everybody all the time. That would be boring. The traitor is coming. He just saw a message from Earth and has a bee in his bonnet."

"Henry, maybe we should cut Tim some slack. He did stand up at the end."

Henry made a harrumphing sound. "I won't be shagging him any time soon. You've got a blind spot when it comes to your supposed family."

"Maybe, but…"

The bridge door opened, and Tim stepped in. "Da… Fa… Captain, I just got a message from Earth. You probably don't want to see most of it."

"Who's it from?" asked Ryan.

Tim hung his head. "Grandmother and Grandfather, but that's not the important part. There was an addendum from the Minister of Justice of the UES parliament."

"A UES cabinet minister. Hotty boss, you're the most popular boy at the drop the soap party," observed Henry.

Ryan motioned for Tim to take a seat at the

environmental station. "Henry, with Tim's permission, play the message."

"Dad, no it…"

Ryan smiled at his son. "Tim, it can't be worse than the messages they sent me while I was waiting for this body to be ready. I won't even touch on the venom they spewed just after." Ryan's expression became sad. "They're still my parents. Henry, play the message."

Minutes later, Ryan sat with his fingers steepled. "Dad's put on a couple of kilos, and I think Mom had some work done."

"She did, just before I left. They didn't seem to know that we're underway," commented Tim.

"They probably didn't. They wouldn't have used the FTL telegraph for a security message. Encoding takes too many bits per second for encryption. Preparing the initial message, say two hours. Henry, remind me to tell Saggal and Kate that Wesnakee's been hacked. Those security cameras are supposed to be an independent circuit."

"Sure thing, hotty boss."

"So, two hours. Three to four depending on relative orbital placement to get the message from the Switchboard Station to the monitorship by the stargate to the Sol system, an hour for the monitorship to send a scoot shuttle through the gate. Five to six hours based on R.O.P. to get the message from the shuttle to Earth. I don't keep track of the relative positions of the gates and planets unless I'm going someplace. At least three or four hours to round up my parents. Mom was dressed up, so call it six hours to get their and the minister's messages. Then five to six hours back to the monitorship on the Sol side. An hour through the gate, then three to four hours to the Switchboard Station and another hour or two, for transmitting to us and miscellaneous."

Tim leaned back in his chair and steepled his fingers, an action so reminiscent of his father they could have been twins. "It still gets to me how things work out here.

Everything is so big and always moving. It... It makes me feel small."

Ryan smiled. "Changes nothing... son."

Tim sat up straighter, a wild hope reflected in his face.

Ryan kept talking, pretending not to notice Tim's reaction. "It's still the people that matter. I'm surprised Crapper recorded video of you and Kitoy hand rubbing. I didn't know you were together."

"We aren't. We weren't." Tim swallowed. "She was upset. I took her hand to comfort her. I didn't know." Tim blushed.

"Pity. You could do a lot worse." Ryan smiled.

"I... I... I..."

Ryan laughed. "Son, listen to a man who spent far too long being a slave to convention. Don't. If you feel something for Kitoy, nova blast Humans Ascendant and their closed-minded propaganda. Know what you're getting into and take it slow because she's still getting over Kadar, but if something evolves between you, take it for the gift it is. Just have your eyes open and know what you're in for."

Tim blushed crimson. "I... I never thought of my life like that. I'd like kids."

"Not an argument, look at Kate and Saggal, and Kitoy loves children, no matter what species. The thing about freedom is, you have to take it for yourself. None of us are truly free, but we can be freer. Being free to love who you love has been a battle on different fronts for a long time. You'll figure it out."

"Thanks, Dad. So, what are you working on?" Tim felt a weight lift off his heart with the use of the endearment.

"Doing watch and studying the news about the hijacked supply missions. This pirate attack looks off. I wish I could get log footage or even just a ship description, but none of the survivors was near a viewport."

The communications console beeped. Ryan moved to acknowledge it.

"Yes?"

"Captain Chandler, I have finished the assessment of

your medical bay. If you could join me in it, I would like to go over the results," stated Pikeman's voice.

"I'm on watch at the moment, Doctor," replied Ryan.

"I did this as a courtesy, it is not in my agreed sentence, and I wish to go to my quarters."

Tim waved at Ryan, who closed the line to medical. "I'll take the rest of your watch."

"You don't mind?" asked Ryan.

"Gives me time to think." Tim smiled.

Ryan activated the comm. "I'm on my way." He turned off the comm. "Anything happens, have Henry call me. I'd rather everyone have a GOC, but what can you do?"

"What's a—" began Tim.

"General Operations Certificate. Means you know enough not to blow us up by accident," interrupted Henry. "I got it covered, boss. Tim and I should have a chat."

"Don't corrupt my son." Ryan stood and moved to the bridge's door.

"He should be so lucky," Henry called to Ryan's back.

Marcy/Ryan stared at the digital readout of his ATV. The tank of liquid nitrogen was nearly empty.

"When that bottoms out, we'll look like a nova on infrared." Worry dominated the emotions. He/she glanced to where his battery monitor was reading five per cent. The press of a button brought a map up on the screen. The screen flickered dark, then bright, making it hard to read.

"Something, anything?" He/she examined the map, then smiled. "Only four kilometres." Turning the wheel, he/she sped toward his goal. 'End episode 1' in bold red letters over a background of a silhouette of a man and a woman holding hands and running filled Marcy's field of vision.

The canopy lifted off her head.

"What did you think?" Mike sat on his interface.

"A lot is happening. The scene where she sees him for

the first time is a good way of showing how faked the relationships are. I think you need to spend more time on emotional context. Remember, Rowan is facing a whole new existence."

Michael smiled. "Next episode, my love. This one was to set the conflict and introduce Ryan. Most of the audience will already know Rowan from *Angel Black*."

Marcy nodded. "The bits with Arlene in the studio control room were a nice touch."

MEMORIES

Pikeman stood by a treatment cot as Ryan stepped into the medical bay. Three treatment cots projected into the room with a metre between each and an open space a metre wide beside the outer cots and a free metre at their base. Medical telemetry displays were at the head of each cot. Equipment was built into the three open walls. A screen filled the upper portion of one of the end walls.

"Ah, Captain. I examined your equipment." Pikeman was dressed in slacks and a blue shirt covered by a surgical apron.

"And," said Ryan.

"All of your built-in equipment is in excellent condition. Even your nanobot manufacturing unit, which considering it is a Mark Two, surprises me. No one uses the Mark Two anymore. Where you got the parts to repair it is a mystery."

"I had a junker. I stripped the unit in it and combined two to make one," Ryan replied.

"I didn't say it was a mystery I cared to solve." Pikeman paced around the treatment cots. "As I was saying, all your standing equipment is in good condition, for antiquated scrap. Your surgical tools are adequate. Your pharmaceuticals and other such items are practically non-existent. I've seen first-aid clinics that were better equipped."

"They stripped a lot of things before I took possession. I had to collapse two medical bays, each with ten treatment beds, to get what you see here." Ryan sounded stung.

"No wonder you needed my servi—" Pikeman cried out and clutched his head.

"Doctor?" Ryan rushed to Pikeman's side and helped him lay on the central treatment cot.

"P... p... pouch." Pikeman fumbled for a pouch at his side.

Ryan opened the pouch to find a pressure injector pre-set to a dose. Pikeman clumsily tapped his throat over his carotid artery.

Ryan placed the injector and pressed its activation button. Pikeman's eyes glazed over. Several of the indicators on the monitor board above him moved into the orange.

Pikeman spoke to the air.

"Services, Commander. What you ask simply isn't possible, or at least it has never been done. In any case, I don't have the equipment, and even if I did, I have other concerns."

Pikeman eyed the striking woman before him in the ship's infirmary. She had jet black hair pulled into a braid that fell down the back of her UES Space Combat Corps uniform. There was a lieutenant's rank pin in her collar. The uniform failed to conceal her substantial breasts or the pleasant curves below. Her classical, Italian features were pulled into a mask of dismay.

"Please, you have to try. The impossible gets done every day."

"Lieutenant... Tansy." Pikeman took the woman's hand. "There are good reasons why what you're asking isn't done. Research into the level of genetic engineering required has been illegal since the clone wars. I'm sorry, but it cannot work with acceptable practices. Transferring consciousness from one body to another is difficult, and less than perfect, at the best of times. Transferring into a body that isn't a perfect genetic match has always ended in failure."

Tansy hung her head, and her voice was tight. "My daughter is dying."

"It is a tragedy that humanity didn't discover the effects of the aboral-736 virus before we declared squirrelzoids safe to share our environment. It is a horrible contagion and hides so effectively in *Homo sapiens*, but I cannot change the past. I am sure you have been told this before, but I must repeat it. After your treatments, you and your husband no longer harbour the virus, but the damage it has done to your reproductive systems is irreversible. Any child you conceive will suffer from nutter's syndrome."

"I know, Doctor. The U.E.S. doctors won't even hear us out. I've even had some suggest we grow clones of ourselves since the virus doesn't inhabit intestinal tissue and raise the children. As if you could just replace a child with a newer model." Tansy hung her head and cried.

Pikeman examined the nanobot manufacturing unit in the wall as he gave her a moment. It was a Mark Two, state of the art for *Homo sapiens* science.

Tansy found her voice. "I want Tracy to have a chance at life. A real life. When she smiles up at me, I know there is something there, call it a soul if you like, something that can't just be replaced with another child. My little girl is alive. She deserves better than a short life of pain and suffering. Please."

Pikeman watched the woman, so distraught, so much love for a child. His thoughts flipped to his son. *What would I do for Jason?* "There are other considerations. You even finding me brings them to the fore," Pikeman evaded, but he felt himself succumbing to the woman's desperation.

"Doctor, Commander. I am a lieutenant in the UES Space Combat Corps with a triple-A security clearance. My husband comes from one of the wealthiest families on the planet Gaia, with an uncle in the UES senate, and I barely found you. Your cover is safe."

Pikeman stared at Tansy and felt an all too dormant decency stir. The thought that maybe by saving this innocent, it could atone for the crimes he'd done on behalf of the state department appealed to him.

"I can promise nothing. And it will be up to you to keep your daughter alive for the next fourteen to fifteen years. The transfer probably won't work. If it is to have any chance, it will have to be when the brain undergoes the adolescent reconfiguration. I will be adapting biological technologies from other species. Technologies deemed illegal in the UES."

"Do what is necessary. You practice in the Republic anyway. UES restrictions don't apply." Tansy looked up, hope piercing the veil of despair.

"I will need cell samples from you and Tracy. Since the virus doesn't affect the DNA associated with the central nervous system after birth, I will attempt to splice those sections of the DNA into the rest of the strand from you. I'll make five hundred zygotes with minor genetic variations. Expect most to die before the end of the first trimester. Those that remain, we will put in gestational chambers. If any survive the nine months in-utero period, we will progress them at a normal developmental rate. That much is a proven technology. S.E.T.E. has perfected it."

"Thank you, Doctor."

"Neither you nor Tracy should thank me. The neuro-atrophy she is suffering will only get worse. She will, not may but will, lose motor function progressively. She will be in constant pain. You are sentencing her to at least fourteen years of agony. Are you sure it is what is best for her? Are you sure you can undertake the expense? This is not covered by the government." Pikeman kept his voice even with a practised note of professional compassion.

"If Tracy can have a life, a real life, I think she'd agree it's worth it. She is such a sweet and happy little girl, even with the twinges. Phillip and I can pay."

"Then bring your daughter in, and let's get started."

Pikeman opened his eyes to find Tim leaning over him, having set up an IV.

"What are you doing?" demanded Pikeman.

"You were shocky. The medical reference program said the fluids might help," explained Tim as he moved back.

Pikeman lay on the treatment cot and looked at the display on the wall. "I'll be all right, Timothy. I... Thank you for your concern and your intervention during the assassination attempt. You must excuse me, but were we... involved?"

"Just friends. I like... females exclusively."

Pikeman nodded. "Pity, you're my type when it comes to men. At least I think you are. To be honest, I'm not sure of much anymore. Have you surmised—"

"You were recovering a memory fragment. The memoria helps with the process. Ryan asked me to ask you to keep the fact that there is a stock of it aboard a secret."

"Mr. Tokic, I saw the signs of addiction when we shared mess together. I will keep my supplies to myself and under lock and key."

Ryan stared down at the eroded joint on the scuttle suit and tried not to swear.

"Is it very bad?" Jacques, the octozoid, hung half out of the tank that filled most of its quarters.

Ryan did a slow blink before replying. "The sliding membrane is worn through to the coral support. I'm going to have to use nanobots to rebuild the calcium infrastructure. If you don't mind, I'll use a polycarbonate sliding membrane to replace the cap's sliding surface."

"How will I repair it back on Quooo?"

"You won't have to. The polycarbonate will outlive both of us in this application." Ryan checked the other joints. "I should use a polycarbonate on the rest of the joints as well. They all show wear, and you might not have access to repair facilities at Murack Five."

"If you feel it is best, though, I do not expect to use the suit much at destination. My work takes me in a different direction."

"Exobiology with a specialization in marine forms, right?" Ryan moved to the back of the suit and opened it up. "What a mess!" he muttered.

"I am sorry my scuttle suit is in such disrepair. I had hoped to be on Murack Five by now with my research well underway. Excuse me for a moment." There was a splashing sound, then some agitation in the pool. Ryan removed the air filters in the scuttle suit's oxygenation system. He had just pulled the last filter when a tentacle snaked over the edge of the pool, holding the broken remains of what looked like a crab shell.

"If you could take this for me, please. It was starting a fight with the rest of my dinner. I didn't want them injuring each other." Jacques waggled the tentacle over the edge.

Ryan stood, took the empty shell, and carried it to a lidded bucket by the door. Dropping the shell on a pile of assorted wastes, he closed the lid.

"How is the food?" asked Ryan.

Jacques waved a tentacle. "It is hunting rations. It will keep you alive, but the 'crab-like food animals' are always lean, and the 'kelp-like seaweed' is never fully ripe."

"I'll check the database and see if there is anything amongst the human supplies that you'd be safe with. If you're willing to try the foods of other worlds." Ryan went back to the scuttle suit.

"You are a most gracious host, Captain Chandler."

"Please, Ryan."

Jacques's tentacles waved excitedly. "It is my honour that you grant me one-name status. I shall try to be worthy of it. You have been most kind. Is there that which I can do to show gratitude?"

"Not unless you can figure out why Star Searcher seems to want to make a mess of getting supplies to Murack Five and seems obsessed about our gate transit window."

"Star Searcher is a huge crabzoid. His sub-designates long for separation, but his core insists on unity. This can lead to conflicting behaviours," observed Jacques.

"You've studied crabzoids," observed Ryan.

"As part of my advanced classes on exo-biology. *A Space Traveller's Guide to Crabzoids* is entertaining and not inaccurate, but it is quite cursory in its treatment. It has been several planetary cycles, but I believe I have my notes and old text in my personal database. I would be happy to review them if you feel it would be of assistance to you."

"Thank you. That would be helpful."

"It is my pleasure." Jacques swished his tentacles lazily. "I dreamed of becoming a terrestrial researcher. My first love has always been land environments. But we are all slaves to our environment. The disadvantage of being an aquatic when land species could do the studies more effectively was too much to overcome. As such, I focused on aquatic environments specializing in coastal ecosystems. At least I still get to study life and species that scuttle between the two worlds."

"We are what we are. I suppose accepting that is wisdom." Ryan hoped he sounded comforting. "Where is your database?"

Jacques disappeared under the water, then its tentacle rose holding something that looked like a bone tube with a black strip running along its side. "I was listening to a fictional story. It passes the time."

"I should have your suit fixed tomorrow, then you can tour the ship." Ryan paused in thought, then spoke again. "Henry, activate the ceiling screen in Jacques's quarters. Project any images or AV programming he wants. Not your personal collection." Ryan turned to the pool. "Long story, but Henry has an odd, and not accurately representational, taste in entertainments."

"I think I comprehend. I did find the violence in many *Homo sapiens* entertainments off-putting. I had to do twenty hours of experiencing them as part of my Sentients in the Galaxy course. I was lucky to find the *Orgy Girls* special features. I appreciated their lack of violence and the communal sentiments of those involved. It made me think of my cave siblings."

The sound of snickering came over the speaker.

Ryan sighed and rolled his eyes. "Fine, Henry, show him what he wants. I'm taking these parts to my workshop. I'll do the design work, then I'll need one of your bots to fabricate replacements while I log some sack time." Ryan picked up various pieces of the scuttle suit and left the room.

"Now, my tentacly friend, what strikes your fancy," Henry's voice came through the door as it closed.

AN OLD FRIEND

Carol stood in the small, glass-fronted mud room of the low-rise apartment building. The buzzer pad and intercom built into the wall was grubby.

"Who is it?" asked a disembodied woman's voice.

"Jess, it's Carol. Can we talk?"

"Carol? Divine, it's been months. Now really isn't a good time." Jessica sounded stressed.

"It's important," explained Carol.

"Mom, it's Carol from high school." Jessica's voice barely came through the intercom as if she was speaking while turned away from it.

There were words too low to make out.

"It's not like I can do anything until they show themselves. Honestly, Mom. I dealt with this stardust for three years before you found out. I know what I'm doing."

More mumbling.

"I love you too. Remember what I told you about Mr. Jastrow if he tries to get cute."

More quiet words.

"There is an upside to having a daughter who's a, oh stardust, the button stuck again." The intercom cut off, then became louder. "I'll be right down."

Minutes later, a fit-looking woman with light brown hair that fell just past her shoulders and an oval face, dressed in jeans and a T-shirt, stepped out of the elevator into the apartment's lobby beyond the inner glass door. She moved straight to Carol and greeted her with a kiss.

"Hey, hot stuff," Carol said when the kiss broke.

"Hey yourself. It's good to see you. I'd invite you up, but Mum's there. She's in a protective phase. We should go to your place." Jessica blushed.

"It's not really that kind of a visit." Carol stepped back from Jessica's embrace.

"Too bad." Jessica traced a finger down the front of Carol's shirt flirtatiously. "After breaking up with Victor, I could do with a change of pace." Jessica took Carol's hand.

"I need to show you something. I'll drive." Carol led the other woman from the apartment.

Minutes later, Carol pulled her car into the paved driveway of Gunther's suburban home.

"Are you buying a place?" asked Jessica.

"This is a friend's." Carol shut down her compact car and gave her power gauge a glance. "I have got to replace the battery bank. I'm getting half the storage I should."

"My friend Malcolm is a mechanic. He might be able to get you a bargain. And he's cute, in a motor-head kind of way." Jessica climbed from the car. Carol led her by the hand into Gunther's house, then down into the basement. As the two women stepped off the bottom stair the sensation of static electricity swept over them.

Jessica watched as a middle-aged man and women stepped out of the shadows. The man stood by an odd looking electronic device while the woman moved to block the stair.

Gunther looked at the young woman. His pulse raced. He wondered if the studio was manipulating him. She was exquisite. His breath quickened.

Jessica swallowed hard. The man was older, but there was something about him. She swished her hips suggestively as she spoke. "What is this? I've told you before, the group thing isn't my scene, Carol."

Gunther closed his eyes and forced his mind to clear. A brief ripple of pain, or ecstasy, crossed his features. I think..." He paused to clear his throat, then continued. "The surface scan suggests she can cope with knowing.

"Jessica," the man's voice caressed the name and set a shudder up her spine. "I am Gunther. Everything you know is a lie. I don't have time to explain. I'm warning you, if you resist, this will hurt." Reaching with his telepathy, Gunther connected to the woman's mind in depth. Both reeled back, slamming into the walls. Gunther and Jessica groaned and crumpled to the floor.

"Nova blast!" Carol knelt, cradling Jessica in her arms.

Willa raced to Gunther's side. "Thank the Divine. He's still breathing."

"So's she," added Carol.

"Divine. That was intense." Jessica and Gunther said in unison and sat up, shaking their heads.

"Gunther, are you all right?" asked Willa.

"I..." both Gunther and Jessica spoke. They locked eyes, both shuddered before looking away, then Gunther continued. "I am sorry, my love. Our minds, our senses, they..."

"Merged," finished Jessica. "I didn't expect to bump into a sorcerer today. Especially not one so attractive."

"What happened?" demanded Carol.

"When we made telepathic contact, it generated—" began Jessica.

"A cognitive feedback. Gunther's attempt to push information into Jessica," continued Gunther.

"Rebounded, then Jessica's attempt to hit back joined it and bounced between the mental defences. It was like—" Jessica picked up.

"A mental volleyball slamming between two walls, picking up more energy with each bounce—" Gunther and Jessica clambered to their feet. They eyed each other with open appreciation.

"Until the walls of our consciousnesses gave way." Jessica stepped towards Gunther. Carol blocked her.

"Are you going to be all right?" Willa positioned herself

between her husband and the younger woman.

"I don't know." Jessica and Gunther spoke in unison. Gunther touched Willa's face. Jessica looked at her fingers in surprise.

"Stardust! This could be..." Jessica traced her own nipples through her shirt. Gunther gasped.

"Distance." Gunther and Jessica said in unison.

"We?" began Gunther.

"Are not sure Jessica believes, but we know Gunther does," Jessica finished the sentence.

"The consciousness must have time and distance until we understand this," stated Gunther.

Jessica eyed Willa and Gunther. "If for no other reason than preserving our marriage. Carol, get me the nova blast out of here," ordered Jessica with a decidedly Gunther intonation.

Arlene worked the control board at a frantic pace. Nanobots were dispatched in both Gunther's and Jessica's brains to stop cerebral bleeds. She added a ponderous dose of pain killers to both and dampened down an erotic response unlike any she had seen before.

"Gene, get me a line to Michael. Flag it, top priority and urgent."

Glancing to the side, Arlene checked that the *Angel Black* board was focused on Quinta and Farley as they thwarted an attempt by a group of octozoids to capture Medwin and Kendra, who were swimming in the lake. Another board showed that *Defenders of the Crystal* was down for emergency maintenance by order of Michael Strongbow. All monitoring on that series was temporarily suspended. All the antagonists on the show were in a forced sleep cycle.

She turned her attention to the main screen as Carol half-carried Jessica from the basement. There was an overwhelming sense of regret in Jessica.

"It's taking all you have not to turn back and tear his clothes off. What in the Divine's myriad names happened?" Arlene did another adjustment, lowering Jessica's and Gunther's blood pressures.

The surrogates' readings crept closer to normal.

"What was it like?" Willa's emotion showed deep concern.

Gunther kissed his wife and caressed her. The monitors showed that he was scared and fighting not to show it. Confused, sexually excited to the point of obsession. His emotions were all over the map. He could feel Jessica's body as if it was his own. "It… We can still feel us. Do you remember that time we made love just after Gunther gained his abilities and didn't know how to control them?"

"Brain fry." Willa nodded. Her readings shifted to a mild fear coupled with a pleasant nostalgia.

"I'll have to re-experience that file. Freaky, but boy, it was a rush," muttered Arlene.

"Were we Gunther or Willa? We were both." Gunther held his wife. The wave of emotion was overwhelming. The sense of completion and a hunger for more. Jessica and Gunther meshed, each informing and completing the other, building exponentially on their totalities and hungers.

"That intimate? You didn't even touch her." Willa eyed her husband in shock.

"Even more. We love you… Gunther loves you. We need you. Gunther needs you."

Willa kissed him. "It will help distract them when the jammer is turned off anyway. Funny what they make of us. I never thought I'd be a porn star doing twisted brain skewed threesomes. At least part of this mess is with the husband I love."

Arlene checked Jessica's readouts. The emotions were intense.

"Divine! Carol, get us to your place. We are… Oh," Jessica's voice was strained.

"What?" demanded Carol.

"Willa is proving life doesn't end at thirty. She is so hot, and we love her so much."

"Stardust." Carol sped towards her apartment.

Kitoy leapt in the confines of one of the coffin-like interface units that lined the *Star Hawk*'s gymnasium walls. The room was little larger than the *Star Hawk*'s captain's quarters with a resistance weight set in the middle. The interface unit manipulated gravity so that while she barely lifted a centimetre, it took the force of leaping four metres. She dropped down a centimetre and started running. Inside her mind, she had the sensory input of leaping over a pole vault, then landing to race around a running track. The air in the *Homo sapiens* simulation felt a little cool while the heaver gravity pulled her down, adding to her workout. She began leaping hurdles. For jumping and running, she had the advantage over *Homo sapiens*. For strength, they had the advantage. Still, the simulation was close enough to serve for her staying fit. Finishing the track, she exited the interface unit. Her tail swished pleasantly to see Krakkeen fumbling with the weight set. He clumsily managed to wrap his claw around a setting dial and twist it. The claw slipped on the hard plastic.

"Fruit husks!" swore the spiderzoid.

"Can I help?" offered Kitoy.

"If you could. Please, set this to its maximum. I wish to work on my climbing muscles. There simply isn't a place to climb on this ship."

"Have you tried the ropes in the athletics simulator?" Kitoy adjusted the dials on the weight set, then stepped back and began doing her cool-down stretches.

"I do not have the interface nanobots required. My people, for the most part, find it untoward to be in a delusional state. No offence intended."

"None taken. Rowan would agree with you."

"Tree in mountains is an interesting individual. Such stories, one would think her psychopathically violent, yet she and Ryan both show little aggression to others."

Kitoy swished her tail. "Just don't get on their bad side."

Krakkeen clicked his mandibles in thought, or agitation, as he positioned himself on the weight set and started doing a modified version of curls. "You are saying that if one were to annoy them, they would be violent?"

"Depends on how annoyed. Threaten either one of them with death or injury, and I'm sure the other would hunt you down and end you. Steal a little food off their plate, they'd probably ask if you'd like them to get you a ration tray. With most mammals, things are relative."

Krakkeen changed legs and continued to do curls. "That is why I like plants. They are far more comprehensible."

"You don't need to be afraid of most mammals. We only attack if ordered to by our government or in defence of someone or something we see as our own."

"Like a male sacrificing itself to a predator so that its tree mates can get away."

Kitoy bent over, stretching out her back. "I guess. You are probably safer on the *Star Hawk* with Ryan in command than you have ever been. As long as you're on his ship, he sees you as his responsibility and will do whatever he must to protect you."

Krakkeen puffed out his opisthosoma, then let it deflate with a whistling sound. "I think I see. The *Star Hawk* is Captain Ryan Chandler's tree. He holds with the old way that all who sleep upon his tree are nest kin until they leave. Very magnanimous. I wish my aunt would learn from him."

"I heard you left her... tree because you lost money." Kitoy lowered to her hands and knees and did a stretch with her back arched down, one arm out to the front, one leg to the back and her neck arched back.

"It was bad luck. I bought futures in the granla crop. It

looked to be a marvellous year. I could have doubled my money or more. That would have given me enough to attract a female so that we could buy our own nest tree. I'd have been away from my aunt. Then a foreign fungus entered the biosphere and decimated the crop. Hundreds of spiderzoids lost their investment. I had borrowed to invest and could not pay it back. I agreed to do five years at the Murack Five relief station if I could receive the payment before departure to cover my debts. I have sold myself into slavery so that my family will not be shamed. And still Kaakaasee belittles me." Krakkeen resumed doing curls with another leg.

"I understand that. I... It's similar. I have a lot of debt. I had to do something... distasteful, to pay enough of it off so that I could become crew on this ship. Why does the relief effort need an exo-botanist?"

Krakkeen clicked his mandibles. "Many species from many worlds became amalgamated into the Murack Five ecology over the gopherzoids' time in the Republic. My job will be to identify which plants have made themselves vital to the ecology that existed before the accident and which plants can be viewed as invasive species so that the repopulation efforts can focus on native or close to native forms. If I am to be speaking honestly, while it would be nice to have money after my tenure, it is work I will happily do."

Kitoy finished her stretches. Krakkeen kept doing curls. "I better get to the Groom-O-Matic. I have the watch in half an hour."

"You have a time keeping device in half an hour?" reflected Krakkeen.

"The watch. It means I sit on the bridge in case something happens so that there is someone to call the others if they have to."

"Is not the mechanical being there?" Krakkeen switched to another leg.

"He is, but Ryan is a careful captain. With the crew

aboard to do it, he keeps a watch. It also gives us all something to do."

"Ah." Krakkeen gently clicked his mandibles and switched to another leg.

"That is distracting," remarked Sooplus, as Mueperss lightly raked his claws over her fur.

"Do you want me to stop?" asked the felinezoid.

Sooplus rubbed her muzzle against his arm and focused her thoughts. Mueperss gasped.

"Only for a moment, my sweet fish. Let us take measures to weaken the hunter that swims in our pond, then we can go to our hutch."

Mueperss swished his tail and walked the steps that took him across the circular 'Duck-Like Avian with a Rocket up its Arse's bridge to the communications console. He worked the control.

"Recording in three, two, one, now," he spoke as he moved to the side of the central command bench Sooplus lay on.

"Ryan, my fishing companion. I know we did not leave things on good terms. I hold the empty net for that and want to apologize in hopes that we may start over in a clear pond," began Sooplus.

"I warned her, but she is captain, and you know females," added Mueperss.

"You, don't start. Honestly! Males. We still have to love them, isn't that right, Rowan? I hope you'll accept my apologies as well. I wouldn't want to send a friendship like ours into poisoned waters," continued Sooplus. "Ryan, I wanted to get this message to you before the *Star Hawk* and the *Mary* pass through the stargate on your relief run to Murack Five. I'm sure the workers will be gratified to receive the supplies your two ships carry. We helped Croell and Zandra load the *Mary*. It is a nice little ship but hardly equipped for dealing with the dangers of a contested system. I hope you and the *Star Hawk* can keep an unarmed space yacht safe in such a dangerous place. Croell and Zandra are a lovely couple. I'm sure you and they will become friends. Croell shares your passion for hunting. Given your personal commonality, I'm sure you'll find the cultural differences between batzoids and *Homo sapiens* little impediment."

"Croell seems a very competent sentient. Much like Commander Merowwperr from the Murack Theatre, and you know the reputation he had," remarked Mueperss.

"When you get back on station, look us up. We can have dinner at Wesnakee, our treat. May you have full nets of sweet fish," finished Sooplus.

Mueperss strode over and turned off the recording system.

"Send it," ordered Sooplus.

"I sent it to the station message system. They should relay it within the day. Do you think Captain Chandler will believe us?" Mueperss moved back to the command bench and started playing his claws through Sooplus's fur once more.

Sooplus groomed her muzzle and let out a hiss through her nose. "Chandler is a cagey fish. He'll know it's a warning, and he'll remember. He may not be our friend, but we just made him less of an enemy. With what I know of him now, that is clear water." Sooplus squeaked and preened as her husband continued his attentions. "Let's go to our quarters."

19
MYTHS AND LEGENDS

"**S**omebody has to check on him." Ryan sat at the head of the officer's mess table. The *Star Hawk* crew and passengers, except for Ziggy and Wispy, filled the room. The mammalian members of the group sat around the table with variously configured ration trays in front of them. Rowan sat first down to Ryan's right. Kitoy sat to his left between Ryan and Tim. Pikeman sat on Tim's far side while Asalue sat on the floor with his clawed hands on the table opposite Pikeman. Krakkeen stood at the table's bottom with his two forelegs resting on the table while Jacques, in his newly repaired scuttle suit, stood in the back corner of the room. Yipya sat on the floor and leaned his front legs on the table beside Asalue. There was a bowl of what looked like dog kibble in front of him.

"Really, Dad?" remarked Tim.

Kitoy poked at a mass of grey meat with her claw sheaths. "UFW ground forces rations. Reconstituted goofla. They really expect the aid workers to survive on this stuff?"

"You're welcome to anything from the *Homo sapiens* stores. You liked the salmon you had last night," observed Rowan.

Kitoy lashed her tail and spoke in scolding tones. "Such a *Homo sapiens* thing to say. You omnivorous, masturbating apes can eat practically anything." Kitoy swished her tail and tilted her head. The translator lent her next words a bantering tone. "Thank you, Rowan. Salmon is delicious, but if I eat too much *Homo sapiens* food, no one with a sense of smell wants to be in a room with me."

Rowan smiled. "We thank you for your restraint."

"As do I," added Yipya, then in a gravelly voice. "If *Homo sapiens* eat stuff, if me safe try if allowed."

Rowan looked at the k-no-in. "Ryan, maybe you should…"

Ryan smiled. "You are welcome to access the *Homo sapiens* rations for k-no-in approved items. And I acknowledge the respect that you show me and my fellow *Homo sapiens*. I wish I could return it. Languages are not one of my gifts."

"Thank you," Yipya spoke in the gravelly voice, then continued in the more dulcet tones. "I have looked forward to trying *Homo sapiens* food. One wonders if the e-inputs alter the experience."

Rowan glanced from the k-no-in to Ryan and back. Ryan took a sip from his water.

"Row, a k-no-in with a great deal of effort and a considerable accent can learn to speak the standard *Homo sapiens* language. *Homo sapiens* can do the same thing for k-no-in, though I'm told the accent is even worse."

"But you told me that species couldn't make or sense parts of the medium other species use for communication." Rowan looked confused.

"I said most. Didn't you ever wonder why they are called k-no-in? It's what they call themselves." Ryan shrugged.

"We call you, Rumann," stated the gravelly voice, then the smoother tones continued. "The sound for H is the hardest part of your language for us. I was hoping to practice my *Homo sapiens* on this voyage, but it seems I am not advanced enough."

Rowan laughed a little. "Better than my k-no-in. You can practice with me, but why?"

"It is a hobby." Yipya shrugged his dog-like shoulders.

Ryan cleared his throat. "Getting back to the topic. Wispy is a passenger on this ship. We will show concern for his safety." Ryan glowered at his crew. "No matter how irritating that is." He sighed in resignation.

"The good news is, my hot organic crewmates, the last of his old body plates have fallen off. There's no more buzzing sound. That one was killing the mood even for me." Henry commented through the speaker.

"Is he still talking?" asked Kitoy.

"Non-stop," observed Henry. "He even talks in his sleep."

Jacques lifted the leg of his scuttle suit. "My shipmates. I assume you do not know much of waspzoids." The active indicator by the suit's optics blinked on as the octozoid looked at its shipmates. Ryan could only assume his passenger had turned the optics off so it wouldn't have to watch the mammals eat.

Ryan looked embarrassed. "Just the entry in the *Encyclopedia Galactica*. I've been busy."

Rowan shrugged. "I've been finishing up my navigator's rating."

Jacques tapped his suit's leg on the floor. "Understandable, but unfortunate. The natural occurring analgesic hormone that waspzoids excrete when they moult is identical to the one that facilitates the transfer of memories when they reproduce. As such, when they moult, they have an uncontrollable urge to recollect past events."

"I feel bad now. I was getting annoyed with him over something he couldn't help," said Rowan.

"Don't," remarked Kitoy. "I knew him before the moulting. Believe me, the talking was only a matter of degree."

"It still leaves the question of who will check on him?" Ryan raked his fork through the mashed potatoes on his tray.

"If it is the will of the tree family, I can do the task," said Krakkeen.

"If you wouldn't mind. You take the first check. I'll draw up a schedule. How many days for his new shell to harden, Jacques?" asked Ryan.

"This specific, I do not know. It has been a long time since my school seasons." Jacques sloshed some water in his scuttle suit.

Pikeman finished his sandwich and looked up the table. "Honestly, two to three days after the last plate detaches for the new exoskeleton to harden."

All eyes turned to Pikeman.

"I may have to supply medical care for the individual. Did you think I would neglect to study the biochemistry of a potential patient?" Pikeman examined the remains of his lunch.

"Thank you, Doctor," said Ryan.

"With that addressed. I have something I wish to give to my tree family in space. Among my species, if one comes to a new tree, one brings a gift. If one has no gift, the knowledge and skills one possesses are practised as the gift. I would share a story of my people. I think this story is most like our tree dominants, Captain Ryan Chandler and Tree in Mountains."

Ryan shrugged. "I'm up for a story, and thank you."

Krakkeen waved his forelegs and began speaking.

"This happened during my people's bronze age. The story was first recorded on Vetaga leaves.

"The valley lands of Skritt suffered a drought that sent many nest trees to the ground. All was dying. The family of Critt, headed by the prime female Sadrak, were lucky in that their tree was by the river. In the tree of the Critt lived a male. He was named Sit-Crut. In the language of Skritt, Sit translates as 'small' and Crut as 'expendable'. Sit-Crut was indeed small.

"A day came when the sky was as black as night. Fire arched across the heavens like a harvest stick thrown into a granla tree. It hit the dry land, and the forest flamed. The sky people, you might call them divine avatars or sacred ancestors, sounded their warning drum. Its beat echoed through the trees.

"The males and the secondary females took the egg sacks and what tools they could and raced down the tree behind Sadrak. They crossed the river and kept running.

Sit-Crut ran with them, but as he crossed the river, he soaked the egg sack he carried.

"Sparks from the fire rained down on them. Flames were everywhere. First, one egg sack caught fire, then another. But the damp silk of the sack Sit-Crut carried resisted the flames.

"All forms of beasts ran together in the race to escape. Dark day surrendered to night, and still, Sit-Crut ran, struggling to keep up with his larger family members.

"Rain fell, dousing the fires and near drowning the land.

"When the sun rose, the family of Critt found themselves in a new valley. Many of them had fallen to the flames, and many had not.

"'We have lost the eggs,' cried the subordinate females. 'They all burnt up.'

"Sit-Crut stepped forward and said, 'Not all the eggs are lost. I wet the bag I carried. It resisted the sparks.'

"Sadrak stepped forward and said, 'Why did you not soak all the egg sacks?'

"'Others had taken them before I could suggest it,' said Sit-Crut.

"'Always an excuse, Sit-Crut, always an excuse.'

"'I saved the egg sack. There will be young this season. Will you give me my adult name?' asked Sit-Crut.

"'One act does not an adult make. We must find food,' replied Sadrak.

"'We should prepare a nest tree first, in case there are dangerous animals,' said Sit-Crut.

"'I have spoken. I hunger. Search for food.' Sadrak settled herself under a tree holding the egg sack Sit-Crut had saved.

"The family of Critt spread through the forest and soon found fruit trees. Then came the sound of Sadrak crying for help.

"Sit-Crut raced to the base of the tree where he had last seen the prime female. Sadrak was halfway up the tree, holding onto the egg sack with one leg and trying to beat off a large centipede-like predator with her back legs.

"Sit-Crut knew his duty as a male. He picked up a fallen stick and struck the centipede-like predator, then yelled and waved his legs. He was Sit-Crut. The male's duty has always been to distract danger so the females would live to lay more eggs. He, as the smallest male, was the most expendable.

"Seeing what it thought would be easy prey, the predator chased Sit-Crut, who scuttled into the forest, leaping from tree to tree, staying just far enough ahead of the predator that it didn't lose interest. The chase went on, but Sit-Crut wasn't ready to be eaten that day. He had seen tracks nearby, and he ran towards them. After a long chase, Sit-Crut entered a clearing where a huge centipede-like predator rested. His pursuer burst into the clearing. The two beasts saw each other. Centipede-like predators are territorial, so they began to fight. In the confusion, Sit-Crut slipped away.

"He came to the tree where he'd last seen Sadrak only to find the family gathered. They had already started removing the lower branches of the nest tree. The egg sack hung from the top branches.

"'You have survived,' said Sadrak when she noticed Sit-Crut.

"'I led the predator into the territory of another of its kind, and they fought. We may now face two fewer of the beasts. I saved the egg sack. I thwarted the predator. Will you give me my adult name?' asked Sit-Crut.

"'Two deeds does not an adult make, Sit-Crut.' Sadrak climbed the tree to where three males had woven her a hammock and settled herself.

"Sit-Crut busied himself removing branches and setting sharpened stakes so other predators would not climb the tree.

"The next day Sadrak awoke and was hungry. She ordered her family to search for fratno melons.

"'Great mother, while fratno melons are very good, they

are rare and hard to grow. Our food stores were destroyed in the fire. Would we not be better served by seeking out crumpa melons and granla trees? They grow quickly and can feed many,' objected Sit-Crut.

"'I wish fratno melons,' ordered Sadrak.

"Sit-Crut went into the woods and wandered until he came upon a grove of granla trees. Crumpa vines grew around their base, and a stream weaved its way through the forest. A nest tree rose tall and strong by the stream.

"'She will never give me my adult name. I saved the egg sack. I thwarted the predator, and now I have found the food that will preserve the family. I will not tell her, for, with her leading, our family is doomed.'

"Collecting crumpa melons into a web sack, he returned to the family to find Sadrak feasting on fratno melons while the rest of the family went hungry.

"Sit-Crut shared his melons with the family members that had been kind to him, particularly the subordinate female Sekras.

"The next day, while half of the family searched for fratno melons, Sit-Crut led his chosen to the fine tree and grove of fruit. For three days, they prepared the nest tree, eating the granla fruit and crumpa melons.

"When all was in readiness, Sit-Crut went to Sadrak and spoke.

"'Sadrak, I saved the egg sack. I thwarted the predator. I have fed the family. Will you give me my adult name?'

"'You have brought me no fratno melons, and you are small. I will not give you your adult name.'

"'If you will not, I will,' interrupted Sekras. 'I name him Sel-kell, Wise-Leader.'

"'You are subordinate. You may not name!' stated Sadrak.

"'I am dominant in our new tree.' Sekras waved her foreleg. Several of Sel-Kell's chosen leapt up the tree to gather the egg sack. Family loyal to Sadrak tried to catch them, but Sadrak's followers were hungry and could not match the speed of their well-fed brethren.

"'I saved the egg sack. I thwarted the predator. I have fed the family. I will keep the family safe. I am Sel-Kell,' spoke Sel-Kell, not small and expendable any longer.

"The family of Critt divided. In the year that followed, Sel-Kell's group prospered. Two years later, the starving and injured remains of those who had stayed with Sadrak were welcomed into the tree of Sel-Kell and Sekras, after Sadrak fell into the pincers of a centipede-like predator." Krakkeen folded his front legs and clicked his mandibles in a spiderzoid bow.

The *Homo sapiens* applauded while Kitoy swished her tail and Jacques tapped his suit's legs on the floor. Asalue sighed heavily and flicked his tongue.

"That was incredible," remarked Tim.

"It pleases me that it gave you joy. I have always believed that myth can teach us much."

"Your telling was skilled," said Asalue. "I read the story during my studies in comparative mythology, but that version was tiresome. You brought it to life."

"Myth should live. They are stories and must not be taken too seriously. Though looked at properly, they can teach us much," said Krakkeen.

"Thank you. Do spiderzoids still have child names and adult names? It's not mentioned in *A Space Traveller's Guide to Spiderzoids*," asked Rowan.

"Only the families that originate from the northern continent keep with the convention. Naming a child Crut rarely happens. My aunt tried to get the family to use it with me as a joke name. She thought it was funny to do so."

Ryan shook his head. "Family. Are all bridge crew finished with their food?" He scanned his crew as the humans nodded, and Kitoy flared her nostrils.

"Good, we're just about to come out of the station's near zone. I want to bump up our acceleration. Star Searcher has been a little too insistent about the time of our gate transit. Everyone is to be on station for all course corrections. You have half an hour to get ready."

John sat in the *Angel Black* control room and scowled at the screens. Gunther and Willa were in bed. The monitors showed an emotional connection and degree of sensation well beyond the norm, but he ignored it.

"Awww, the happy married couple. Boring! Strongbow is an idiot," John grumbled.

Carl was creeping into an old factory populated by pirates. He came to an open door and looked in. Beds were lined up on the floor, each holding a felinezoid. K-no-in moved from bed to bed, suctioning the felinezoid noses and checking IV solution bags.

"Fighting a plague. Huff! What does he think this is, *Hospital*?" John's fingers itched to alter the surrogates' bio-stats and trigger some conflict, but he knew the action would be recorded, and that would give Michael the leverage he needed to take him off the board entirely.

Carl heard a sound, and his tension mounted. He rushed down the hall, half throwing himself into a doorway. He forced his mind to stillness as a male otterzoid scooted down the hall on a grav-board beside a k-no-in.

"No. Without knowing the chemical makeup of the human medications, I won't use them."

"Chelaa, they are dying anyway. It is a *Homo sapiens* disease. It may respond to *Homo sapiens* medicines," remarked the k-no-in.

"I wish Doctor Mrarr hadn't died. I'm a nurse, not a doctor or a veterinarian. Half the time, I don't even know what I'm looking at."

"Try the medication on one patient. If it doesn't work, stop using it. If it kills them, then you know," snapped the k-no-in.

"Have a care, Graa. I may not be a doctor, but I am still

an officer. You don't give me orders."

"I'll take it to Commander Hurast." The k-no-in stopped and glowered at the otterzoid, who elevated his hover board so he could face him eye to eye.

"I am chief medical officer on this crew. Commander Hurast doesn't get a say. She's probably immune to the illness, being reptilian."

"Doesn't do us any good." The k-no-in clicked its foot claws on the floor.

"I just wish she would let us consult with the *Homo sapiens*. They may be primitives, but they aren't without some understanding. They could give us the formulas for the drugs they use so that I could match them with our own. We are nearly out of everything."

"We need to stick to our own. The primitives aren't good for anything but slaves."

"If you say so. Go on. I want to check the patients before I report to the chameleonzoid fart bubble."

The k-no-in released the rasp that served it for a laugh. "Don't let her hear you call her that."

"Graa, I have bigger snapper fish to spice than that lizard." The otterzoid made a squeaking sound. "I'm feeling congested, and my temperature is up."

"Rotted meat!" swore Graa. "Do what you can while you can. I'll talk to the commander."

Graa continued up the passage.

"You can come out now, defender," said Chelaa.

Carl glanced up and down the passage, then dropped his camouflage and stepped into the hall. "You heard my thoughts."

"I smelt you. One of the early symptoms of the disease is a heightened sense of smell. Have you come to kill us while we are weak?"

"You know that isn't the case, or else you wouldn't be talking to me." Carl faced the otterzoid and opened his surface thoughts.

"You want an exchange of knowledge. The commander

will never agree to it, but perhaps we can find a way. If we don't, I fear it may mean extinction for both our species on this world. Come. It will be safer to speak in my office." Chelaa floated down the hall and opened a door on the right.

Carl followed his enemy into his chamber. The centre of the room was dominated by a children's swimming pool.

Chelaa slid off his hoverboard into the water and sighed with relief. "I sometimes wonder why I came to this planet. I hardly ever get out to swim, and the water is always cold."

"We didn't ask you to come. Why don't you go back?" said Carl.

"I'd rather not spend five years in a cage. Bad as this is, that is a truly rotten clam. Now, *Homo sapiens*, let us talk. How can we help each other?"

COMMUNICATION

Ryan sat at the piloting station of the *Star Hawk*'s bridge.

"Course is within tolerance. Scanners show the *Chimera* off starboard fore and the *Mary* off port aft," remarked Rowan, who wore a new shiny navigator's rating pin in the collar of the floral print blouse she'd put on.

"Nice to be popular," commented Tim from the environmental station.

"Any chatter?" Ryan's fingers caressed the pilot's controls.

"Just the standard news and updates blip from the Switchboard Station. The Spuqupa report is doing an exposé on Pastor Donald FitzPatric, a Humans Ascendant minister who seems to have a taste for Lucas bots and other non-Humans Ascendant approved activities," replied Kitoy.

"Nice to know that Adine got her story," observed Ryan.

"That's odd." Kitoy double-checked the received files.

"What is?" demanded Ryan.

"A message at the end of the official communication update. It's from Sooplus and Mueperss."

"Skim it. If it's immediately important, let me know. If not, I'll get to it after the course correction. Ziggy, be ready to use the particle weapons for anti-missile intercepts. If Crapper wants to get cute, he'll do it during a course correction. It would be easier to blame it on a flaw in our ship." Ryan made minor adjustments to his control board.

"I practised that during my watch." Ziggy sat straight in his chair. The coverall uniform he wore was clean and pressed.

"Henry, watch the engineering feeds until I can get back there and keep an eye out for a nasty surprise in the cargo. I don't trust Star Searcher."

"You got it, hotty boss. That is a crab with issues."

"If I'm right, severe ones," agreed Ryan. "Rowan, give me the new pull points for the gravity laser drive."

"Pull points in pilot's file, sir." Rowan smiled in self-satisfaction.

"Three, two, one." Ryan pressed a button. Seemingly nothing happened. He checked his control panel, then moved to the engineering station and checked the telemetry.

"Gravity laser is optimal," he announced.

"We are on course for the Murack stargate. Estimate coast speed of twenty per cent light speed in forty hours. Course is within tolerance," stated Rowan.

"Good work, people. Full station checks, all stations. Tim, Jacques mentioned that the water in his tank seems stale. When you're done with the check, please run an analysis. We may need to up the oxygen feeds or refresh the filters."

"Yes, sir," agreed Tim.

"Is that it?" asked Kitoy.

"You know space travel. Moments of routine action, then long stretches of boredom. If you're lucky."

Kitoy swished her tail. "How long to the gate?"

Rowan checked her calculations. "About two days acceleration, then three and a half at a twenty per cent light speed drift and three days deceleration before gate insertion, give or take a few hours on each stage. Ryan, I'm going to update my post gate flight plan. With the early arrival, the old one will be off."

Obert lay in Carol's bed with Carol on one side and Jessica on the other. When Carol had called him at home, he'd almost panicked, thinking something horrible had happened. Racing to her place, a thousand negatives had run through his brain. Then he'd opened the apartment door to find Carol and Jessica in each other's arms. It took only moments for him to join them, and now he was utterly exhausted.

"I want you to know, I don't normally do this kind of thing." Jessica leaned up in bed, locked eyes with Obert, then projected her thoughts. *'I got whammied by Gunther. It went sideways. I'm a telepath. On my show, we fight demons and things. I'm not a hundred per cent sold on what you guys believe, but I've got an open mind.'*

Obert blinked and unconsciously pulled Carol closer to himself. Forming the words in his mind, he tried to share his thoughts. *'Can you hear me?'*

Jessica lay on the bed. *'If I'm listening. You don't have to try so hard. For you, it doesn't make a difference. I think you and Carol are about as close as a non-telepath can get. In more ways than one. Pity Gunther is married. That could be interesting.'*

'And dangerous until we understand it,' Gunther's mental voice added.

Obert felt a wave of the woman's embarrassment and schooled his emotions to a blank. *'Careful, they can read emotion. It's all true. I've seen it.'*

'Or maybe it's a mass delusion projected by a powerful sorcerer. I've seen things too.'

Carol shifted in bed. Half-asleep, she snuggled into Obert. He was so spent it had little effect. *'When we get out of bed, I want you to meet someone.'*

Jessica sighed. *'As long as Gunther and Willa don't start up again, I think the storm has passed. I can barely hear him anymore, but I don't want to be anywhere near him or Willa for a few days. I can't trust myself, and I'm not a home wrecker. It was like losing myself. There was no Jessica, just an us.'*

'*I agree,*' Gunther's voice intruded into her thoughts along with a wave of self-recriminating frustration.

'*I heard that,*' thought Obert.

'*I think I'm networking all of us. This is freaky.*' Jessica sighed.

'*Somebody is networking,*' remarked Willa's mental voice. '*And Obert, get over it. You're not the first man to ever have a threesome.*'

'*We should try to distance,*' suggested Gunther.

Jessica spoke aloud. "So, Obert. What have you been up to since high school?"

Arlene sat in the *Freedom's Run* control room with Michael and Greg.

"What the stardust is going on? I haven't seen readings like this, well, ever," said Arlene.

"I worked the *Orgy Girlss* board for three featuress and never ssaw anything like thiss. Iss the board malfunctioning?" asked Greg.

"No, it's all the surrogates. This is real." Arlene rubbed her own neck.

"I think we've just covered the budget for season three." Mike smiled, then his demeanour sobered. "Fortunately, the effect seems to be fading. Gunther's spirit is willing, but the flesh can't keep up."

"How though?" asked Greg.

Michel bit his lower lip while he considered. "Bring up the creation files for Gunther and Jessica, Gene."

Two secondary screens filled with the files.

Gunther McPherson – ASH – M schedule red.

Jessica Safehaven – ASH – F schedule orange – Addendum.

Topped the screens.

"Stardust! I thought they looked alike." Arlene took a deep breath.

"Both ASH series. Gunther started with his telepathy. It was the first-round experiment in incorporating alien abilities into humans. John subcontracted with the military to develop the technology. I never would have allowed it, but I was on emergency leave the year *Angel Black* was prepped. My son needed me. That has been stardust on my shoes ever since."

"But Carol is sschedule orange. How did sshe become a telepath?" Greg pointed to Gunther's screen. "You better dope him. The flag'ss rising and he'ss going to hurt himsself if he keepss thiss up."

Arlene started an anaesthetic feed in Gunther and Willa. This time it took.

"Read the addendum," suggested Mike.

Greg pressed a button, scrolling down the file past the *SF Geeks* section.

"Northeasst Sssun Valley. The terrorisst attack?" Greg ran his hand nervously over his bald pate.

"After Humans Ascendant, oh yes, sorry, the splinter group with no ties to the organization in general," Mike sneered, "set off that dirty bomb, half the surrogates in the northeast quadrant were exposed to rad. The shareholders just wanted to let them die. They were only fakeys after all." Mike shook his head.

"I remember that. You made a deal with the military to let them use the clones for research," observed Arlene.

Mike nodded. "With what they'd learned from the round one experiments that created the *Angel Black* characters, they had developed retro viruses that could be introduced to adult subjects. Or so went the theory. They needed a large, disposable population to test them."

"You let them usse the irradiated cloness." Greg looked shocked.

"In exchange for the treatments that extended the surrogates' lives. About ten per cent of them didn't survive the initial infection. Seventy-five per cent expunged the virus. They've formed most of the disposables since then. It's costly to keep their cancers in check, and often we just can't. I can only do so much. I gave them years they wouldn't have had." Mike's voice was haunted, the voice of a man who'd done his best and found it lacking.

Arlene swivelled her chair and took Mike's hand. "Sounds like you tried when no one else would."

Mike nodded. "My problem is, I'm studio head. What I want to be is God."

"Keep working on it. You'll get there." Greg smiled at his boss.

Mike released a snort of laughter. "The fifteen per cent left supplied the extraordinary powers for the shows that have come since. Some, like Jessica, have relatively stable brain chemistry. They became principles. Some others weren't so lucky. They became disposable antagonists. One of each type that survived was surrendered to the military for 'testing.'"

"So, how does this explain the current situation?" asked Arlene.

"Identical twinss. There iss a high incsidence of pssi between twinss even with *Homo Ssapienss*' limited pssi abilitiess," observed Greg.

"Add in the uncharted waters of enhancing with otterzoid DNA, and we don't know what we're getting into. But we need to. Greg, I want a fact sheet summarizing psi in twins for *Homo sapiens* and otterzoids ASAP. I'll call Ulva to cover your shift on the board. Arlene, keep the telepaths apart as much as you can. Pass that on to Ulva and brief her when she gets in. Dope Gunther and Jessica if you must. I'll work the problem from my end." Mike left the room.

Ryan sat back in his command chair and watched the

image of Sooplus and Mueperss on the main screen.

"Those conniving, two-faced, self-serving..." Rowan's voice rang out from the navigator's station.

"You can't trust them, Ryan. Kate and Saggal always made sure to triple check the contract whenever they did business. And remember how they tried to extort you during Rowan's escape," cautioned Kitoy from the communications position.

"Hotty cat's got a point," remarked Henry.

Ryan stroked his chin. "I don't trust them." He looked at Rowan. "I never did. But I needed diversions."

"What do you think they want, hotty boss?" asked Henry.

Ryan took a deep breath and let it out slowly. "Play it again."

Kitoy pressed a button. The big screen filled with the image of the otterzoid and felinezoid.

"Ryan, my fishing companion. I know we did not leave things on good terms. I hold the empty net for that and want to apologize in hopes that we may start over in a clear pond," began Sooplus.

"Translation, I've realized you are a bad enemy to have, and I'm willing to grovel," remarked Henry.

"Sounds about right," agreed Ryan.

"Rowan. I hope you'll accept my apologies as well. I wouldn't want to send a friendship like ours into poisoned waters," continued Sooplus.

"We have never been friends." Rowan set anger aside and examined the message critically.

"Telling us the message isn't what it appears to be. Kitoy, are there any subchannels or hidden codes?" asked Ryan.

"Just what you see and hear." Kitoy lashed her tail.

"Ryan, I wanted to get this message to you before the *Star Hawk* and the *Mary* pass through the stargate on your relief run to Murack Five. I'm sure the workers will be gratified to receive the supplies your two ships carry."

Ryan lifted his hand, and Kitoy paused the playback.

"The meat starts here." Ryan grinned. "They're telling us the *Mary* is following us all the way and that they have Republic permission to do so. Resume."

"We helped Croell and Zandra load the *Mary*. It is a nice little ship but hardly equipped for dealing with the dangers of a contested system. I hope you and the *Star Hawk* can keep an unarmed space yacht safe in such a dangerous place."

"Not much of a risk to us until we make planetfall," observed Henry. The message started again.

"Croell and Zandra are a lovely couple."

"Kitoy, pause it. Croell and Zandra, from the set region. That doesn't make any sense," said Rowan.

"They're telling us who's on the *Mary*, which is more than we've known up until now. The geis on Pikeman spilling over to us makes sense now. Batzoids can be murderous, obsessive psychopaths, but they are competent murderous, obsessive psychopaths. It bothered me that the nanobots weren't targeted to only affect Pikeman," mused Ryan.

"But how would they get out of Sun Valley?" Rowan stared at the image on the screen and unconsciously gripped her shoulder where Croell had dosed her with the venom that nearly ended her life.

Ryan closed his eyes and sighed. "John, the producer for *Angel Black*. That fool broke protocol. Used studio property, no offence love, for a personal vendetta. The number of laws that violates. If we can prove it, John will be planting trees and harvesting fruit for the rest of his life."

"He's a big enough idiot to think he could get away with it," agreed Henry. "Trivia, he's suing the studio and Michel Strongbow for interfering with his show autonomy."

"Hope he goes bankrupt," observed Rowan.

"He set assassins on you. I hope he dies painfully," remarked Ryan. "I may have to settle for getting evidence of what he's done and sending it to Michael. Resume play."

"I'm sure you and they will become friends. Croell shares your passion for hunting. Given your personal commonality, I'm sure you'll find the cultural differences between batzoids and *Homo sapiens* little impediment."

"Croell seems a very competent sentient. Much like Commander Merowwperr from the Murack Theatre, and you know the reputation he had," remarked Mueperss.

Kitoy paused the feed and spoke. "Merowwperr was a sadist. He was brought up on charges for torturing *Homo sapiens* prisoners during the Murack engagement."

"He caught two of my people. No offence Kitoy, but if I ever cross his path, I'm adding a cat skin rug to my decorations," said Ryan.

"None taken. Even in war, there are limits. I read the reports." Kitoy lashed her tail.

"Sounds like Croell. He'd only just become active when you liberated me but had already developed a reputation," remarked Rowan.

"We know more than we did before. All we can do is cope with the hand we're dealt." Ryan stood up and started for the door. "If anybody needs me, I'll be in the workshop."

⊂═══◇➤

Mike sat at his desk and stared into the computer screen. "Gene, get me Admiral Jim Newton, priority line, scramble code seven. No record of this call."

A minute passed before a bald man with medium-brown coloured skin and blue eyes looked out of the screen. The background was an austere office.

"Mike, what's wrong?" The admiral looked concerned.

"An old alligator is chewing on my backside, and it could spill over to the military. Remember the project to work out the viral inserts for alien abilities?"

"I read the file. Intelligence is not always a good term for black ops. What about it?"

"I need the military's data on the telepaths we developed. I have a situation. Two of my surrogates are meshing minds. It's having weird effects. I'm trying to work out what's going on." Mike drummed his fingers on his desk.

The admiral shook his head. "I'll try, but those files are need to know. Even I don't have the details."

"Anything you can get me. You know I still have clearance, and with this mess, I need to know."

"Have you asked Mildred? She may have a better line into the ground pounder intelligence than I do."

"I'd rather avoid that. She's sensitive about the dirty bomb getting past her."

"Silly, how was she going to stop a group of idiots with RPGs packed round with whatever radioactive stardust they could find? Dirty bombs are nasty. Catching five out of six of the terrorist cells before they accomplished their mission was a win." Jim shook his head.

"You know Mildred, no measure for partial success. It's part of why she's so good. Look, Jim, get me what you can. I have people on it, but I have a gut feeling that this could be bad."

"On it. It will take a few hours. I'll call you in the morning."

"Thanks."

The line went blank. Mike took a moment to sit with his eyes closed before pulling out his handheld. "Marcy Strongbow." He spoke into the device.

Marcy appeared on the screen. She was dressed in a black evening gown with understated makeup and jewellery.

"Hi, honey." Her face lit up, then she saw his expression, and she sobered. "What's wrong?"

"I just wanted to see your face. Can you hurry home after the concert? I've decided not to work late."

"I'll meet you there, my love."

"Talk to you when I can hold you." Mike closed the line and got up from his desk.

"Divine, I hate this job. Be all my sins remembered."

JUSTICE OF THE CHURCH

Asalue rested his chest along the padded bench of the central medical table in the infirmary. The mutilated remains of his wings were extended and trembling. Rowan, dressed in surgical scrubs, supported one of the burnt appendages while Ryan, also in scrubs, supported the other. Pikeman moved around the wings, examining them. The monitor above the treatment cot showed biodata across the possible human ranges. Pikeman had silenced the alarms.

"Your vital signs are within the normal range for a batzoid," remarked Pikeman.

"That is comforting," Asalue spoke in a pain-choked voice.

"You should let me use stem cells to restore the tissues. The burns leave an open path for infection."

"No!" snapped Asalue.

"Why not? You could be whole again. I know batzoids don't have the technology, but the *Homo sapiens* technology could be adapted. That's how they made Croell and Zandra for *Angel Black*," remarked Rowan.

Asalue swung his black serpentine head around and flicked his tongue at Rowan. "The batzoid theocracy would punish my family if I were to use the forbidden technologies. There is little more they can do to me, but for my hatchling's sake, I cannot be seen as more of a heretic than I already am."

"Heretic?" asked Ryan. "Do I need to be concerned?

What I mean is—"

"You fly under a Republic writ. The theocratic council will not defy that. They succumbed to Republic threat. Even personal vengeance geises must be delayed for one working a Republic contract in a Republic zone. Many do not like the law, but the theocratic council had little choice but to bend to the greater temporal power."

"Does that mean I am free of any vengeance geis set against me?" Pikeman probed a section of scar tissue on the wing.

Asalue gasped in pain. His voice when he replied was strained. "Under the council's own ruling, if you are working for the Republic and in a Republic-controlled zone, you have sanctuary. If you end your employment or enter a zone controlled by the theocracy, the geis comes back into effect. Even vengeance proxies are excused of the obligation of exercising a vengeance geis under those circumstances. Though the rule is often ignored. The theocracy turns a blind eye when it is. That is much of why I am going to Murack Five. It is the safest place I can be. Evading concerned citizens who wished me dead for my sins was becoming… tiresome. Not to mention that no one in the batzoid theocracy would employ a heretic."

"Ridiculous superstitions. Allowing illnesses and infirmities to persist because of some ancient ink on a page," grumbled Pikeman.

"The theocracy is blinded to much that is true because of the Holy Writings. That is why I have lost the skies. Why I will never see my wives or hatchlings again." Asalue's voice carried a full load of pain.

"If you want to talk about it, I'll listen." Rowan's voice was soothing.

"You can fold your wings now," stated Pikeman.

Asalue slowly and painfully folded his ruined wings, supported by Ryan and Rowan. When they were tucked against his back, he sighed in relief. "I suppose *Homo sapiens* would not consider it a sin to hear the story of a heretic?"

"You may as well tell her. Because of this religious stupidity, the treatment is going to take a while." Pikeman moved to the side of the room where the nanobot manufacturing unit was situated and started pulling up stock design segments. "Antiquated garbage. Captain, could you assist me? Ask Tim to come down as well. With even a nanobot manufacturing unit type seven, this would be so much simpler."

"Certainly. Henry, ask Tim to join us." Ryan moved to Pikeman's side.

"When I think of the money I'm losing having to supply medical to this collection of sad acts." Pikeman started the process of designing custom nanobots.

Asalue watched the two *Homo sapiens* as they worked.

"You were going to tell me your story." Rowan reached out and stroked the scales along Asalue's neck.

Asalue's eyes went wide, then he flicked his tongue. "You have read the entry on batzoids in the *Encyclopedia Galactica*, haven't you?"

"Yes, I haven't had time to get to the *Space Traveller's Guide to Batzoid* yet." Rowan stopped stroking the batzoid's neck.

"There was false information in the older edition of the *Encyclopedia*. Stroking the neck is not just a way of showing support and comfort. It is primarily a prelude to mating."

Rowan blushed and looked sheepish. "Sorry."

Asalue let out the hiss that served his species as a laugh. "At least you bothered to read the entry. Most sentients do not."

"You were going to tell me what happened with your wings." Rowan went to holding the batzoid's hand.

"Do you know the legend of Jakonee?" Asalue flexed his fingers and stared at the wall.

"No." Rowan ignored the way the crippled sentient's hand trembled.

"Without the needless big words and grovelling the

servitors put on it, it is something like this.

"A royal guard in the city of Hi-asss named Jakonee rescued the prince and eggs from two of the noble families when Siss, the god of corruption, destroyed Hi-asss with a volcanic eruption. Jakonee supposedly flew at incredible heights for a day and a night, finally landing by the blessed river Ratwaaa and starting a civilization that adhered to the winged way."

"It sounds like an interesting myth," remarked Rowan.

"The theocracy considers it fact. Myth can inform science, but it always has to be taken in the light of evidence and reason. That is why I will never fly again. You see, I thought there was more to the story. I took the seeds of the myth and studied them.

"I accepted that Jakonee was a historical personage. Then I wondered about his life. The legend says only that he came to Hi-ass in his young adult years. I asked myself, where would he have come from?"

"Another city?" encouraged Rowan.

Asalue flicked his tongue. "Originally. I believe he was hatched in the city of Sliss. We know from archaeological digs that Sliss was destroyed by a volcanic eruption roughly the same time Hi-ass was. I postulated it was a few years earlier and that Jakonee was a child when it happened. He escaped the city and joined the bands of merchants carrying goods between the settlements. He would have wandered the deserts, learning how to survive. Coming to Hi-ass as an adult."

"It's an interesting origin," agreed Rowan.

"The theocratic council thought so. You see, it matched with the legend. They exalted about how the Great Flyer of the Skies had led Jakonee from the start, and the prophet had been the great he/she's chosen one. They even did a children's sensory entertainment. *Young Jakonee*, the *Stories of Jakonee as a Nestling*. Of course, in the series Jakonee was a servitor, which I found no evidence for, but by and large, the episodes did show ancient life accurately. Every episode, young Jakonee would face a moral dilemma that would be surmounted by following the winged way."

"Hold on." Rowan looked incredulous. "Are you telling me batzoids have cartoons?"

"What better way to indoctrinate, excuse me, educate, the young? In any case, I received my Standing One, what *Homo sapiens* call a doctorate, on the strength of that early work.

"If I'd only left it at that and studied something safe, but I felt I owed it to Jakonee to look deeper.

"The legends said that Jakonee became a guard to the Royal family of Hi-ass. You see, Hi-ass was not ruled by the servitors but by warriors who took their place by force of arms. The city allowed many faiths and had an open view of sexuality and lineage."

"*Homo sapiens* and batzoid seem to have a lot in common. Calling the other guy a pervert has been a common way of vilifying people for us as well."

"As I saw in my studies. It is good you see it for what it is." Asalue flicked his tongue. "Through several adventures, Jakonee rose to be the captain of the guard. This is where my work began to annoy the theocratic council.

"I dared to say that the Great Flyer of the Skies didn't speak directly to Jakonee warning him of the impending eruption but that because of his childhood experience, Jakonee recognized the signs of an impending volcanic eruption and decided to flee.

"My next point was that the names Ratnay and Slonn were, in fact, Ratney and Slun, which in the ancient dialect of Hi-ass translates as craftsbeing and scholar. I postulated that Jakonee convinced Prince Borla, the third in line for the city's command, to lead his household of craftsbeings and scholars away from the city before the eruption.

"They would have flown into the desert hours before the eruption began, taking their tools and what other items they valued. Jakonee, having been a trader, knew where the oasis and sip wells were located. I surmised they would have stopped at these. So I set my measure at a day's flight from Hi-ass and started searching. I found an ancient oasis, dry for thousands of years.

"Jakonee and his followers would have made camp there and watched as smoke poured from the mountain. I found bits of pottery and the desiccated remains of the broadleafs they used for food wrappings at the site. I suspect they were a group of nearly sixty.

"With the dawn, Jakonee and his followers flew on. Another day's travel towards Ratwaa, I found a second camp. This one still supported a sip well that was now polluted with sulphur. There were layers of debris covering the time of Jakonee. I also found bronze tools that unmistakably came from Hi-ass.

"One more day's flight, I found the last stop, a small, now-dry lake. They must have camped there for several days. There was evidence of a battle, and I found the remains of two batzoids buried in the sand. Their bones' chemical contents matched the makeup of a resident of Hi-ass.

"A half day's flight on is the temple of Jakonee on the banks of the River Ratwaa."

"So they settled and started a new society," offered Rowan.

"In a sense. They landed on lands already claimed by a primitive people. Primitive even by bronze age standards. The primitives must have looked on the tools and skills of these intruders as near magic. The two peoples combined. Borla and Jakonee married into the locals' royal family. Establishing the root civilization that eventually evolved into the dominant batzoid society."

"It sounds like solid archaeology," Rowan nodded.

"The theocratic council called it heresy. They insisted that the myth was true and could not be gainsaid. Servitor guards snatched me from my nest and dragged me to the temple of Borla, the hall of judgment."

Tim entered the room and moved to join Pikeman and

Ryan at the nanobot manufacturing unit. The three men were soon having a discussion in whispers.

Asalue shook his head and flicked his tongue. "The funny thing, the view from there is beautiful. It is high on a mountain, so high the air is always cold, and there is snow on the ground. A green valley spreads out before it, ending in a lake. The temple itself isn't much. Just a cave with the statue of Borla at its back and the firepots. There are five of them. I was lucky. If you want to call it that. The servitor charged with painting me had read my work and thought there was merit to what I had said. When he/she painted my wings with the ointment of truth, they chose the slowest burning of them. As the sun rose, they set me to judgment." Asalue looked at the floor.

Rowan spoke in a whisper. "What did they do?"

"They lit the ointment on my wingtips. I had a choice. Let it burn all of me, or try to reach the lake below where it would be extinguished. That is the Great Flyer of the Skies' judgment. If you die, you are guilty. In my case, that would have meant the execution of my wives and hatchlings. If you reach the lake, the Great Flyer has shown you mercy, holding you as misguided. Your injuries and banishment are your penance for your sins. If you are unharmed, you are innocent, and the Great Flyer of the Skies has protected you. I had to protect my family. 'To love is to be enslaved, but love buys the only freedom that is true.' Some of the scriptures hold wisdom."

"Stardust!" whispered Rowan.

"The irony is, I received word from my second wife on Petteron. The egg in our nest when I was banished hatched. The child is a servitor. He/she is three years old now. Just starting his/her education."

The nanobot manufacturing unit on the wall beeped. Pikeman moved to Asalue's side. "You are fortunate. Though it will take several sessions, we have designed nanobots to debride the necrotic tissues. I can tailor a cell division enhancer that will cause your own cells to divide and seal over the wounds. It won't restore the lifting membrane or muscle tissue, but it will close the path to infection. We are also designing nanobots that will repair the damaged nerves, ending your pain. Is this acceptable to you?"

"Whatever you can do within the theocracy's restrictions." Asalue twisted his head around to look at Pikeman and flicked his tongue towards Ryan and Tim, who stood by the nanobot manufacturing unit.

Obert led Jessica up the stairs to Angel's third storey walk-up apartment. Late morning sunlight shone through the windows, highlighting the dirt on the walls and floor. A phone call had resulted in the key being left in a jar of disinfectant on Gunther's front step. After that, collecting Jessica from Carol's apartment had been, while not uneventful, highly enjoyable.

"I really think you'll like Toronk," said Obert.

"I don't know why you can't tell me more about this friend of yours." Jessica scanned the dingy walls of the place and sniffed at the scent of cabbage that permeated the air. "This building's a dump."

"Angel says it's cheap." Obert stepped onto a landing and followed a short hallway with plaster walls to a heavy wooden door labelled 3B.

"Brace yourself." He opened the door and motioned Jessica into the apartment.

She stepped into a comfortable living room furnished with an old sofa, two battered loungers and an entertainment console. A hall led off the side of the room. The far wall opened onto a third storey balcony. The sky beyond was a brilliant blue. Pictures of skyscapes hung on the walls, and a blanket was draped over the back of the couch.

"Toronk, we're here," called Obert.

"I'm coming," called a voice from down the hall.

Jessica looked towards the voice as the thump of crutches could be heard. Toronk came into view, leaning on crutches with his leg in a cast. The two-metre tall felinezoid swished his tail in a friendly manner.

"Obert, get back." Jessica pushed Obert behind her and glowered towards Toronk as she took up a fighting stance.

"What? This is Toronk. He's my friend. He's a felinezoid. I figured showing you an alien would convince you." Obert tried to move away from Jessica, who shoved him towards the wall.

"That's a rakshasa! They eat people. He's conned you." Jessica reached with her mind.

Toronk focused his will, blunting her attack. "I am not one of these rakshasa you speak of. I mean you no harm."

'What the nova blast is happening?' Gunther's sleepy voice intruded into her thoughts. Then he saw through her eyes.

"Toronk, hello. Do you have any symptoms? Jessica, we must try to keep our emotions under control. The stress woke me." The voice was Jessica's, but the inflections were Gunther's.

"What?" began Toronk.

"Fill you in later," interrupted Obert.

"You're telling us/me you aren't an Indian tiger demon out to lull people into trusting you so you can eat them?" Jessica could feel the Gunther part of her move against Willa.

'I'm happy for the second honeymoon, but come on. It's distracting,' thought Jessica.

'You have until after breakfast.' She got a mental image of Willa tossing the sheet off her naked form. *'At best.'*

"I'd like to sit down. These crutches are digging into my armpits." Toronk swished his tail.

The movement seemed to rivet Jessica's eyes. "Obert, stay behind me." She moved towards the door and gestured towards one of the loungers.

Toronk took a seat. "What can I do to convince you of the truth?"

"Letting me scan your mind might help, but you won't do that, will you? Demon." Jessica paused with Obert sandwiched between her and the door.

"Please keep it to surface thoughts. I do like my privacy." Toronk dropped his mental defences.

"This is ridiculous." Obert pushed away from Jessica and moved to sit in the other lounger.

Jessica's brow wrinkled. A cascade of images filled her thoughts along with an incomprehensible alien dialect. She lurched to the couch and sat facing Toronk.

"You are either the most powerful rakshasa I have ever met, or you're telling the truth."

"I am telling the truth. What is the basis of your show that you have translator nanobots?" asked Toronk.

"My friends and I defend the crystal that is the source of all magic and protect people from the monsters and demons that live amongst us. I... I guess they must have given us 'translator nanobots' so we could speak with the monsters. Are you sure you're not a rakshasa? You look exactly like one. We... He and his mates were eating people. We stopped them."

Toronk lashed his tail and shook his head. "Likely a clone brother with memories tailored to a false belief. The controllers have much to answer for."

Arlene released a mild euphoric into Jessica, making her inclined to believe Toronk while at the same time using an override code to run a loop of Toronk sleeping into the *Angel Black* board. With the *Defenders of the Crystal* board still down for maintenance and Obert being inactive, she felt she had the bases covered. Turning to a side screen, she played the encounter between Carol, Jessica and Obert, making sure that there was nothing incriminating before filing it away for the *Orgy Girls Casual Encounters* feature being compiled for later release.

"Lucky buggers!" Arlene shook her head. She then checked the other feeds. Gunther and Willa were preparing breakfast. Judging from Gunther's readings, she wasn't taking any bets on for how much longer. Blips of emotion that mirrored Jessica kept coming up on Gunther's board, but nothing so drastic that, taken out of context, it would raise suspicion. Arlene was gratified to see that the blips were decreasing in frequency.

Troy scanned Gunther and Willa's boards. "Divine, if I could only find a woman like that." He shifted the focus to where Angel nodded in a chair by Valaseau's cot. He tapered back the triggers for mucus production in the felinezoid and dropped her temperature a degree.

"Get some sleep, Angel. I'll look after the psychotic nut job for tonight." He scanned Valaseau's control board. "May as well save the resources." He halted the trickle of psychotropics that normally flowed into Valaseau's system.

He checked Carl, who was buying oxygen cylinders and a portable suction unit at a medical supply house.

"Enemies become allies against a common foe. Classic, but if anyone can pull it off, it's unc... Michael. *Angel Black* is on the rise again."

A quick check of Farley and Quinta, who were on his couch with bowls of cold cereal, reviewing a text on aquatic life forms. He focused on editing the feeds from the day before when Farley and Quinta saved the two extras from the octozoid attack. He was so involved he didn't notice that the signal from Toronk kept up a constant repetitive cycle.

RUNAWAY GROOM

Ryan stood outside Wispy's quarters and took a deep breath before pressing the entry request button.

The door retracted into the wall. Wispy lay across the sofa/bed, which was in its latter configuration. The room had a smell reminiscent of cinnamon.

"Captain, it is nice to see you. What is it you *Homo sapiens* say? Take a seat. That is a funny expression because you really don't take it. You borrow it, and a seat can mean so many things. I was talking to my father-sister once about the interesting things that other species do with language and—"

Ryan tried to tune out the babble as he walked over and sat in the rolling chair in front of the computer interface board on the wall opposite the bed.

After what seemed an eternity, Wispy stopped to take a breath.

"Is your health good?" Ryan rushed to get out.

"I am feeling well. I had not realized how tight my old casing had become." Wispy indicated a pile of cracked blue shell fragments in the corner of the room. Beside the casings was what looked like an artist easel covered with a sheet. "My casing plates are hardening. I had some concerns about that, given my age. I wrote my father-sister a question about it, but she didn't know, and—"

Ryan plastered a smile on his face and thought about which ration pack he'd pull for dinner as the waspzoid rambled on in a disjointed fashion. Finally, Wispy fell silent.

Ryan looked up. The waspzoid was rubbing the arms that flanked his mouth together. "I am sorry, Captain. Krakkeen, my fellow insectoid, spoke to me about this. On Currick, everyone knows that one chatters during a moult. It honestly did not occur to me to warn you and your crewmates. Rowan told me of the vibration of my old body plates and its effects. I thank her for the knowledge. I did not intend to be rude."

"We are all slaves to our biology. Pikeman says you should be finished soon." Ryan tried to sound friendly.

"When I was younger, my shell would harden in a day. Very little is known about male anatomy after the age of twenty-two."

"Why is that?" Ryan leaned back in his chair. He had insisted that Wispy receive visitors and that visitor stay at least an hour. This was his turn.

"I... It all has to do with why I am here. It is a long story. I do not wish to irritate."

"It is a story about someone I know. It is probably of interest. If you can tell one story from start to finish."

Wispy stopped rubbing his arms together and regarded Ryan. "It is a story in ways similar to yours and Rowan's.

"The reason I am living in an environment that is hostile to my species is I am wanted for criminal offences in the Sisterhood of Currick worlds." Wispy rubbed his arms.

"What was your crime?" Ryan tried to imagine what the annoying, but otherwise meek, sentient could have done.

"It was during a trip to a nature preservation zone. I was fifteen years old and on rest from my apprenticeship as an EVA technician on the orbital transfer platform. Males are always used for dangerous tasks. I was selected for the work when I was ten years old because I showed exceptional dexterity and am gifted with superior special perception. I even considered a life in space after the second hatching. But that was years away then. It always seems that the ambitions of youth are thwarted in some way. Do you not find that?"

"I... it happens. I always wanted to be an engineer. I never expected to become a captain or a soldier." Now that Wispy was on a topic, Ryan found himself less irritated by the being.

"At least you kept a third of your choice. My father-sister always said that I should—"

"Wispy, you were on leave and had gone camping." Ryan interrupted the waspzoid, hoping to halt another aside.

"Oh yes. I was there with my family. Buzzik, my older brother, he was seventeen and was being courted by three females. I remember hoping that Crika might be interested in me when I was old enough. She was a resplendent female. Her plating a metallic blue-green with thick legs and a huge stinger." Wispy clicked his claws. "Beautiful."

Ryan smirked and almost heard Rowan's voice commenting on the universality of males in his mind. "She sounds lovely."

"She was, probably still is. Buzzik was always cruel. He had taken a tooket from one of our young brothers."

"Tooket? The translator nanos didn't get that one," remarked Ryan.

"Tooket?" repeated Wispy, then, "To—k-et. He waved his arms. "I am sorry, there were several syllables that go outside the *Homo sapiens* vocal range. Don't you find it fascinating that—"

"Yes, the shortcomings of the translator nanobots is always interesting," agreed Ryan.

"Henry. It is amazing that you have an AI on a ship this size. I have an AI friend on the station. She told me that the expense is enormous. That is why most ships use lower density chip configurations. I personally think—"

"Yes, Wispy." Henry's voice came over the speaker.

"Oh, yes. Please interface with my personal database and bring up a picture of CreCre on the wall. CreCre was my tooket when I was little. We had such adventures together."

The wall behind Ryan filled with the image of what

looked like a millipede made of plush material and stuffing. Its body was muddy brown, and its legs were black. Ryan turned in his seat to examine it. "A toy."

"Most young waspzoids have one. I would take CreCre everywhere and imagine it would tell me stories. It was very precious to me. One of the things I had to leave behind when I escaped Currick."

"Because," prodded Ryan.

"Oh yes. Well, Buzzik had taken a small brother's tooket. He was dangling it over a chasm threatening to drop it. The small one was screeching. Buzzik was revelling in the small one's dismay. I sought to pull the tooket away from Buzzik to give it back to the small one. We scuffled. Buzzik was larger, but I was the better fighter. I took the tooket from him and gave it to the little brother who ran away. Buzzik lunged at me. I leapt out of the way. Buzzik tripped on my stinger and tumbled into the chasm."

"It sounds like an accident," remarked Ryan.

"It was, but that is not how the ruling females viewed it. Buzzik broke the exo-skeleton on his left legs. I didn't think it that important because he was going for the second hatching in a month anyway."

"That would heal him?" asked Ryan.

Wispy vibrated his wings, making a buzzing sound. "I do not blame you. I sense you have many demands on your time. My brother/aunt Biccziss always says—"

"Wispy." Ryan sighed.

"Of course. When waspzoids mate, the female takes in the male to fertilize the eggs. After that, five eggs are injected into the male at the brain and the four primary neural nodes down the spine. The eggs mature in the male, then hatch into larvae that feed on their father. The one that devours the brain becomes female and takes in all the memories and thoughts of her father. She is the second hatching. The ones at the neural nodes take in the information of how to move. How to eat, waste disposal. Things done so often and so simple they are encoded in all the nodes.

"When the father dies, the drop in body temperature triggers the larvae to pupate. They emerge six days later as small waspzoids. One female and her four brothers. The female nurtures and cares for the brothers and later trades them with other females for mating."

Ryan suppressed a shudder at the implications of this mode of reproduction. "You...emerge, waste disposal trained."

"And able to walk with some limited language skills for the males. For the female, all that was her father in mind and spirit lives on. It is a glorious thing. Buzzik would simply mate a little early."

"What happened?" Ryan was finding himself interested.

"Politics. It is a great honour among waspzoids to go for the third hatching. The best of our scientists, stateswomen and artists can be selected for the honour. Males that commit crimes are used. When they mate, the exalted female lays her neck over the male's so that an egg is injected into her. The criminal is then left to carry the male offspring while the exalted female carries the female, which takes in all she is. She is re-hatched to live again in a young body. The criminal is left to go through the agony of having its secondary nodes devoured without the numbing effect of having his brain eaten."

"They were going to do that to you because of an accident?" gasped Ryan.

Wispy waved the arms by his mouth. "The standard for being chosen for the third hatching has dropped. Mostly because those in power desire it. There is a shortage of criminals. Now any minor offence is enough. My father-sister fought to have me spared, but the one who desired the egg destined for me was too powerful. My father-sister and two of my brothers from my mother's older laying managed to get me a pass to visit the cliffs of Buzzzukbu. They are supposed to be beautiful. It was always my intent to make them my gestation voyage. You see, once you are injected and waiting for the larvae to hatch, it is a tradition that you get to do one thing you've always wanted to do. I have always wanted to see the view from the cliffs of Buzzzukbu. The pictures are lovely, and the air in the morning is supposed to smell of the flowers of the valley below, and—"

"Your family helped you escape," Ryan interjected.

"I slipped away while I was in the airport. It was an unthinkable thing for a male to do. The spaceport was close to the airport. My launch pass for going back to work on the station was still good. No one had thought to cancel it. I was on the orbital station before anyone knew I was missing. A spiderzoid ship was loading. They needed a junior EVA specialist to help repair some sensor damage. Spiderzoids can share a habitat with waspzoids. The viruses that keep our species apart do not infect them. It is such a pity they are xenophobes. They could make a fortune negotiating deals between shared habitat sectors. They can go into three shared sectors, giving them physical access to twenty-six Republic member species. Though with the third group, they have to have supplemental oxygen and insulative clothing to visit. Still, they could."

"Wispy."

Wispy buzzed his wings. "When I got to the Switchboard Station, I worked what jobs I could. It didn't take me long to get a full EVA rating. I started taking classes on exo-sociology at the Republic school of higher studies. I kept writing back to Currick, begging them to reconsider the verdict. The Republic heard the case in their court and decided I could serve a level one sentence doing an EVA maintenance on a shared area. That was long ago. I was starting my second advanced study certificate in exo-sociology when my father-sister messaged me. Several males inspired by my escape had tried to run away from the second hatching. The ruling females were negotiating deportation agreements with the other species with which

I could share an environment. I had a little money saved, so I hired a physician to do modifications on my body so that I could survive in your shared area. I moved to your area, and the best work I could get was as a bartender at Wesnakee. I think it was because a waspzoid is exotic in your shared area. Saggal and Kate recognize that it is the exotic nature of species that draw in their customers. One time I was telling Kate—"

Ryan checked his watch. "Why Murack Five?"

"Oh, that. They need an exo-sociologist to map out what the kangazoid societies were like before the contamination so that we can steer them back to a culture approximating what existed before their premature contact with other species. That, and it is interesting work. It will allow me to earn my advanced standing degree. I keep hoping that if I can get enough education and prove myself valuable, the ruling females will change the order so that I can go home and participate in a full second hatching. To be honest, I am nearly thirty. There have been few males that have lived past twenty-five. Most go for the hatching before they are twenty. Buvina, the oldest male ever, now there is a story. He was crossing the great sand desert on a wind sledge back in the days before—"

"How old was he?" interrupted Ryan.

"Oh… Fifty-three. The legend says it took him twenty days to recover after moulting. When he was rescued, he only moulted once before he went to the second hatching. I can see why. I am so stiff sometimes, and my wings ache. Sometimes I think it wouldn't be so bad to go back, but I am afraid of the pain of being aware of my sons eating me from the inside out."

Ryan sighed. "We are all slaves to our failing forms in time."

"You've read Waszzzil?" Wispy rose, looking impressed.

"No, I've just had time to reflect on the nature of freedom and slavery. I have to go. My watch on the bridge starts in ten minutes."

"Everyone says that. I am so glad I'll be out of this room tomorrow and free to explore the ship. It will be such fun. I…"

Ryan stood up and left the room while Wispy's babble continued in the background.

⌁

Gunther pushed a capacitor home on a circuit board that sat amongst densely packed equipment filling a large roller suitcase and soldered it in place. Quinta mentally snaked a wire between two graphite rods and onto a junction. Standing on her hind legs, she brought a pen-like soldering iron to the wire and connected it to the junction. Gunther's basement stank of flux and burnt insulation.

"This is an impressive construction." Quinta stepped back from the suitcase.

"If it works, it will mean I can bring the 'telepathy booster' onto the street. That could prove very useful," agreed Gunther.

"Let us share information. There are questions I feel enhanced understanding could solve," suggested Quinta.

Gunther nodded and moved to his 'telepathy enhancer', turning it on.

⌁

"Nova blast! That accursed fakey is playing with his toy again," spat John from where he sat in the *Angel Black* controller's chair. "Gene, note. The interference from Gunther's science experiment is becoming problematic for production. Suggest that a telemetry line be placed inside the field of effect to maintain continuity. End."

John shifted his attention to the other screens. Angel was asleep in Gunther's guest room. Farley was at work. In her study, Willa sat behind her computer supplying phone-line tech support to some other fakey whose computer had been infected with a virus. John checked the crossover board and saw that the computer failing was an element in one of the other shows.

Sighing, he spoke. "Gene, message *Dance Academy*. Be advised. The virus on computer DA seven is about to be invalidated by cross-show contamination."

John shook his head and shifted his attention to Carl, wiring in solar panels on a new addition of one of the set region's homes. The sun beat down on him, and he had the beginnings of a stress headache. The fakey that thought it owned the house was an overweight middle-aged woman that kept up a constant stream of vitriol about the price of the installation and her opinion of how Carl did his job.

"Nothing worth recording here."

John moved on to the antagonist's boards.

Chelaa moved between felinezoids lying on their sides on cots using the new suction unit Carl had supplied to clear their airways. All of them had masks hooked up to large oxygen cylinders.

A cruel smile crossed John's face. He scanned the records for the felinezoids. One of them indicated that the cancers induced by the quick clone process were becoming severe.

"Dead in a few months anyway. Perfect for upping the dramatic tension. They can't fault me for that." John adjusted the controls for the felinezoid.

Mucus production increased, and the temperature spiked in the pirate. Her throat closed. Chelaa rushed to the felinezoid's side and struggled to clear her airway. John adjusted the electrolyte levels and triggered a chemical release from the built-in drug pack. The pirate convulsed, gurgled, then arched its back in agony. Smiling, John backed off the controls, stretching out the moment. Chelaa struggled to save her crewmate, pushing her skills to the limit and beyond. With a final convulsion, the surrogate died.

John sighed with satisfaction. "Well, that killed ten

minutes. I am so stardusted bored. Gene, record, Antagonist Felinezoid Four, non-active in keeping with studio executive policy to focus necessary deaths on surrogates who are developing terminal conditions."

"Recorded," stated the computer.

Quinta felt the static discharge of the jammer sweep over her. "The new jammer is ready. All we have to do is integrate a handheld."

"I'll ask Medwin and the kids to try and steal some the next time they go out of the set region. I couldn't have miniaturized the unit without you."

Quinta made a splashing motion with her front paws. "Sweet clams. Now, will you be telling me what lobster-like crustacean has grabbed your tail?"

"I... What am I doing?" Gunther looked at the otterzoid with a perplexed expression.

"Your mind is swimming distant streams. And while I'm no expert on *Homo sapiens*, you're walking like you had a sea urchin down your pants." Quinta shifted so she could look Gunther in the eye.

"I... There was a problem the last time I tried to recruit more rebels. I've been... off ever since."

"What happened?" Quinta used her telekinesis to pull over a large cushion and settled herself on it.

Gunther sat in one of the folding chairs he kept in the basement. "The woman I tried to recruit, Jessica, was a telepath."

"Useful." Quinta clapped her front paws and regarded Gunther with her beady black eyes.

"I don't know why, but our minds merged. It's getting better, but half the time, I don't know if I'm me, or her, or some mix of both."

Quinta looked at Gunther with an intensity he'd not seen before in the otterzoid. "Have you had sex with her yet?"

"Of course not." Gunther blushed.

"With Willa?"

"She is my wife."

"And that is a good thing. How often?" Quinta stopped pacing and looked Gunther in the eye.

"I... we lost count. As much as I could." Gunther blushed crimson.

"But you still want this Jessica. Still feel her emotions. Hear her thoughts even when you do not try. Your body longs to join with her. You physically respond to the thought of her."

Gunther hung his head. "That's the problem. It's getting better. Time and distance seem to help. I love Willa, and Jessica is too young for me, but I can't get her out of my head. I'm obsessed. I know it would hurt Willa if she found out I was thinking of Jessica when we make love. But I can't help myself." He looked up. "Do you know what is going on?"

Quinta huffed through her nose. "I am otterzoid. When they made me, they gave me many things otterzoids know. They had to. Does this Jessica look like you?"

"Come to think of it, there are similarities."

Quinta groomed her muzzle. "There are stories from long ago. They all involve two males, but that could be because it takes two telepaths. Since genetic testing, we have avoided it."

SLAVES OF MIND

Ryan lay in Rowan's bed, holding her close. The sweat of passion was drying on their skin.

"That was an hour well spent." Rowan kissed him.

"Definitely," agreed Ryan.

Rowan snuggled in. "Now I have to fill the rest of them."

"Space travel is good when it's boring. It's when it gets interesting that you have to worry." Ryan snuggled in closer.

"I know that. I know I said I wanted a break after I got the navigator's rating, but I'm thinking of taking an advanced rating to kill the time. Besides, I don't like only having the minimum in things."

Ryan kissed her neck. "The higher ratings are just for larger ships. It won't do you any good on the *Star Hawk*. If you really want a rating that might be useful, go for your GOP. The course is in the library. Kitoy has started it."

"General Operating Procedures, right?" Rowan sounded curious.

"Once Henry can move off the bridge, I'll need someone with the rating there at all times. Right now, we're squeaking by on Henry's, but once he's fixed, and I get a new operating system, we won't be able to rely on that."

"You are going to fix him for real?"

Ryan shifted so he could look Rowan in the face. "How could you ask me that?"

Rowan looked ashamed. "Sorry. It's just having a full AI operating system is so useful, and I know how you feel about the *Star Hawk*."

Ryan sighed. "I love my ship, but Henry. Henry is a brother. I'll keep my word to him because I gave it, but more than that. I'll keep it because, in a brotherly sense, I love that pile of circuits. He's family, to both of us."

Rowan smiled. "The inappropriate brother you can't take to parties. Funny thing is, that has a certain symmetry with my mom being a cyborg. Tell me more about the GOP."

Henry sat on the bridge using the overrides Mike had installed to monitor Ryan and Rowan despite the privacy setting. The undamaged side of his face looked contemplative. "I love you guys too," he whispered. Inside, a segment of his ram worked through the shame he felt for spying on his shipmates. "We may still need Michael's help. They'd agree if they could see it clearly."

"What?" asked Kitoy from the communications station. Her station screen was filled with the wiggly lines of felinezoid script.

"Just ram leakage from a show I'm experiencing."

Kitoy lashed her tail. "You really should let Ryan adjust the run speed on your sex drive. There's more to being a biologic than mating."

Henry sounded chipper. "Sure thing, hotty cat, wanna join me?"

Kitoy rolled her eyes, lashed her tail, and returned to reading.

Medwin stood on the grass, surrounded by saplings, wearing his father's ill-fitting blue suit. The late afternoon sunlight lent his surroundings a park-like atmosphere. Penelope and Tom stood to one side, supporting each other. Obert and Carol stood side by side on the other side of a hole blasted into the rock. A pile of milorganite mixed with stone chips stood at one end of the pit. Medwin could almost feel Kendra and his mother behind him. He could see Gunther and Willa standing a stride back from Armina's parents. Armina's corpse, wrapped in a hemp sheet, lay on a wheeled platform at the base of the pit.

A distinguished, dark-haired man in a black suit stepped to the side of the open grave and spoke.

"There are no words that ease the passing of one so young or fill the empty places in the hearts of those that loved her. Grief is natural and will not be gainsaid. The only way out is through. We must let ourselves feel the loss. What you must also do is feel the joy, the joy of having known Armina, having held her in your hearts. For if you did not hold her in your hearts, if she did not enrich your lives, there would be no pain. Remember that nothing can take the memories, erase the laughter and the joy that you had together. That is always yours. You must never let this break cloud those precious times."

Medwin felt his anger mounting. He would remember, and he would make them pay. They would know this pain, not from some sanitized entertainment. They would know pain like this and more before he was done. His fingers itched for his bow.

The minister continued. "Funerals are for the living. The dead have all they need.

"The living may find comfort in a simple truth. We are all the dust of stars, lesser fires spat out from those great fires that lit the cosmos long before our sun was born. Drawn together in patterns and complexities that enlighten the cosmos in its quest for self-understanding. And in that pattern, we can hope that the lesser patterns may persist. I say death is not an ending. It is the freeing of a pattern that will join the cosmos and may once more draw matter to itself and manifest in our world, a little wiser for its passing. It is a transition from a vessel of dense matter to energy that will return to once more shape matter to its needs. In that transference, it will carry all the love it has known, for love is the greatest power. Like gravity, it draws us together over the vastness of space and time and makes us whole with those we love. Rest well, Armina. May the universe bless us all."

"May the universe bless us all," echoed from the crowd.

"Do any of the loved ones wish to speak?" asked the minister.

Penelope and Tom looked up with pleading eyes straight at Medwin.

Medwin let his tears fall. Rage and loss were at the fore of his being, but he could see it in the older couple's eyes. They wanted, needed, words to be said by someone who loved their daughter, but they didn't have it in them to speak.

Medwin took a step to stand beside the wrapped corpse. He tried to find some remnant of the woman he loved in that bundle of cloth but couldn't. Armina was gone.

"I..." His voice broke. He swallowed, then, taking a deep breath, tried again. "I loved Armina. I know many thought it was puppy love. We met in high school. I will never forget seeing her walk into the science fiction club. So beautiful and, funny as it is to say at nineteen, so young. She stood beside me when my father died. Held me up when I was at my lowest. I regret that she didn't allow me to do the same for her. Penelope and Tom, you don't know this. We were waiting to tell you until I could save up enough to get a proper ring. Armina and I were going to get married after college. We had such plans. It is little comfort, but we shared the perfect fantasy that love will go on without trial and tribulation. We... I will always love her and what might have been. I... I..."

Medwin's chest heaved. He found himself embraced by friends and family with no further need to speak.

The body was laid in the bottom of the rocky grave, and the soil mix shovelled over it. Penelope, Tom and Medwin carried a sapling to the middle of the infilled pit and planted it as a living memorial to she who had meant so much to them all.

Everyone left, and still, Medwin remained staring at the grave.

"We didn't intend this," remarked a voice from behind him.

He jerked around to see Ulva in a black dress, carrying a chrysanthemum.

"I should kill you for this." Medwin glowered at Ulva.

"May I?" Ulva held out the chrysanthemum.

"They were her favourites. What happened? Why didn't you stop her?" he demanded.

"I tried." Ulva knelt on the grave and planted the flowers. "She seemed all right, so I was working on something else. By the time the automatic system warned me about her, it was too late."

"You admit?" Medwin looked shocked, then he spoke in a near whisper. "You... You know I know."

"S.E.T.E. isn't only one thing. Many of us want to make it better for the surrogates. Some of us even consider you human. Forces are working for change. You and your friends are part of that."

"Supplying emotions for the *Freedom's Run* show. Some change."

Ulva stood, dusting off her knees, and looked Medwin in the eyes. "That is only a small part of it. My friend working the control board has given us a few moments to really talk. We can't keep it up for long or do it often. I just didn't want you to feel no one cared."

"You created us to suffer for you, to be puppets." Medwin went red-faced.

"Yes, but in the end, we created you. You wouldn't exist without us. We may be lousy parents, but, in a way, that is what we are. Some of us are trying to be better."

"Why are you here, really?" Medwin stared at the grave.

"In part, to pay my respects. In part, because I've seen

your rage. Medwin, if you take your bow and go to kill somebody in vengeance for Armina, we won't have any choice but to kill you. All it would take is the flip of a switch. Then Armina's death will mean nothing, and nothing will change. Nothing will get better."

"And if I do nothing?" Medwin looked into Ulva's eyes.

"Nothing will change. Nothing will get better. But if you and your friends are smart, the United Earth Systems may change, may get better. It won't happen in a day. It might take years, but it can happen."

Medwin's lips thinned as reason and rage fought, then found common cause.

"What should I do?"

"First, take this." She passed him a handheld. "You'll need it for your next reconnaissance. Do that next Saturday. There is a map and five hundred credits in the onboard bank. Bring Kendra, Obert and Carol. Follow the directions. We'll know if you buy weapons. Stay under the radar. You're going to a party; appropriate clothing will be provided."

"A party?" Medwin looked confused.

"My boss wants you to see what you're fighting for and who you're fighting against. By the way, Michael has gotten the do not assist order removed from your mother. She's going to get a job offer. Encourage her to take it. If you help Gunther, we may just win this."

"For now." Medwin looked at the image of all he hated and saw compassion and perhaps a glimmer of hope.

"I have to go. Remember to keep things secret. Oh, and open your eyes. You need time, but you might be surprised about what you see." Ulva walked away. Medwin hid the handheld in his suit pocket and went back to watching the grave.

Ryan checked the engineering readouts. "Grav laser to

zero, all systems in the green."

"Course is dead on for the Murack stargate." Rowan sat at the navigator's station.

"Life sciences are all green," remarked Tim from his station.

"Computer, unless you count my lack of hips, is green. Hotty boss, when you do my new body, could you do a chameleon skin? Some fleshies get off on exotic skin tones. Green, blue, purple."

Ryan rolled his eyes. "Weapons?"

Ziggy scanned his board. "All systems look good."

"Communications." Ryan turned to Kitoy.

"Just normal chatter. Ziggy, you owe me an extra protein. It just came in. Mirrmirr Fish-catcher won the three hundred and twenty-seven metre." Kitoy swished her tail.

"Not during a safety review." Ryan's voice was firm.

"Sorry, Captain. All communications optimal," stated Kitoy.

"Ship is within parameters. It looks like we can let Isaac Newton drive for a while," said Ryan.

"Who?" asked Kitoy.

"Isaac Newton, a famous human scientist from the start of our technological age. He codified the basic laws of motion," explained Tim.

"Ahh, Muehiss Trapsetter. I understand. I had such a crush on Muehiss Trapsetter when I was little. Forget that he'd been dead for seven thousand years. Smart males are sexy." Kitoy looked at Tim while she spoke.

"Very subtle, hotty cat," remarked Henry.

"Finish your checks and lock down your stations, then go back to the watch rotation." Ryan moved to sit in the command chair.

Greg rubbed his tired eyes. The balcony window of his set-region, support-town apartment was dark. He focused on what looked like a book cover displayed on his living room's wall. A keyboard and mouse sat on a tray over his lap, where he sat sideways on a decrepit couch. His eyes flicked to the chronographic display on his wall. 01:27.

The book cover displayed was of an otterzoid female holding a spear, diving towards a creature that looked like an orca, but instead of fins and a tail, it had four stumpy legs ending in broad webbed feet. The background was a swamp. A pair of small otterzoids, with pelts banded in various brown shades, huddled in the background. At the top of the cover was written 'Myths from the Swamp,' and at its bottom in large print 'Qintama Deep-diver,' and in smaller print below that, 'translated by Elizabeth Franks.'

"Computer, sscan text for referencse to identical twinss." Greg closed his eyes. The human studies on telepathy between twins were easy to find. The otterzoid references were veiled.

"Reference found."

"Bring me to the referencse." Greg straightened on his couch and read a footnote.

'*1 This is a literary reference to monozygotic twins. It must be noted that while otterzoids typically have two pups in a litter, there is a social stigma attached to pups of a unisex litter that intensifies to the level of social condemnation for identical twins, and in the case of male monozygotic twins, can lead to the infanticide of one of the pair.'

Greg nodded as he felt his enthusiasm rekindling. "Computer, take me to the top of the chapter thiss footnote iss in."

CHAPTER 27

How Mormse and Qumsasa Earned the Couch of Rulership

In the year of the 'orca-like swamp hunter' during the reign of queen Quiplia of the southwestern swamplands, a litter was born to Seasa Wetwalker. Seasa loved her litter and thought little that both were male. Quilla and Blippane seemed normal, healthy cubs. If any noticed how alike they were, it was put off to them being brothers and no more.[1]

There were few signs of the horror that was to come until the pups turned from the play of childhood to embracing the joys of the adult. Though the brothers were well-muscled with shiny mahogany pelts, they showed no interest in the females of the tribe. Days came, and days went. They would hunt the deep marshes, always returning with nets full of fish but showing no interest in the mating mat.

The people of the village began to speak. Several males who swam the female's river[2] approached the brothers, fearing what might come if perversity took hold. But it was to no avail. Quilla and Blippane kept to their own company, and day by day, they changed. Always alike, it now became impossible to tell them apart. Word, thought, and action, they drifted closer and closer. Now the other males of the village began to share thoughts, but the two youths were already a mind

---

1 *This is a literary reference to monozygotic twins. It must be noted that while otterzoids typically have two pups in a litter, there is a social stigma attached to pups of a unisex litter that intensifies to the level of social condemnation for identical twins, and in the case of male monozygotic twins, can lead to the infanticide of one of the pair.*

2 *In a social development parallel to the Norse and several North American First Peoples cultures on Earth, otterzoids of this period and region defined gender by the personal predilections of individuals. One was expected to express a gender by deportment and choice of labour and stay consistently within that choice, but the choice was left open to the individual.*

more formidable than steel-wood. None could penetrate their consciousnesses to confirm the fears that they were abomination.

One day, Seasa was in the deep marsh gathering herbs when she happened on her sons. They had made a hutch and lay within it, but not as brothers.

Seasa tried to speak with her sons. They dismissed her and continued their unnatural embraces, drifting closer in mind until the two were one.

"Computer, next page." Greg felt relief that he'd finally found the hook he needed to extract information. The page changed.

That was when the horror began. Their minds together were more powerful than any otterzoid. Their will was unshakable. One would sleep while the other woke, but they were still one, and no one could approach them unawares. They would turn their thoughts on their neighbours and relatives, controlling the other otterzoids. Within a year, they forged their village into an army and conquered the neighbouring villages. One would stand on a rise of land and watch the battle. The other speaking with the same mind would direct the troops. None could stand against them.

Then came the greatest horror of all. They decided that if they were to be a king, they would need a successor. They picked the most beautiful female in all the lands. Qumsasa, whose name meant 'clear water'. She did not come willingly, for she had already paid a husband price to Mormse, a humble guard she loved. The brothers who were one had Qumsasa brought before them. When persuasion failed, they turned their will on her. How long she resisted is lost to time, but soon she shared their bed. The brothers found that they could increase their gestalt. Like planets around a sun, they brought others to their hutch, adding their powers of mind and knowledge into the whole.

Their hordes rampaged over the swamplands. Queendom after queendom fell before them.

In the end, the champion Sallandra Blackwater[3] came from a distant land where she had been defending a village from giant crab-like animals.

As Quilla slept, Sallandra had her band attack the camp of Quilla and Blippane.

Blippane, not wanting to disturb his brother-self, left the hutch as Quilla and several of those enslaved to their gestalt slept on.

Disguised as a camp follower, with a belled collar and fur died in stripes of brown and orange, Sallandra snuck into the hutch of Quilla and covered the twin's head with a bag soaked in the juice of Bunjab weed.[4]

Pulling Quilla onto her back, Sallandra bound the conqueror's wrists around her neck and raced from the hutch, diving into a deep stream that cut through the camp.

In seconds the alarm was raised. With neither Quilla nor Blippane to direct them, there was confusion in the camp, for the brothers had forced all those with the ability to lead into their gestalt

---

3 Sallandra Blackwater is a recurrent hero in the otterzoid sagas appearing in different time periods. The character is likely an amalgam associated with heroic deeds committed by various individuals.

4 A potent naturally occurring sedative.

so that none would gainsay them.

Blippane, feeling his other self moving away, left the battle with Sallandra's troops and rushed to his hutch.

Sallandra raced through the waters using the full power of her body and mind, but with the burden on her back, she was slowed. The forces loyal to Blippane and Quilla soon overtook Sallandra in the stream.

It was then that a young male, Mormse, leapt into the stream. Mormse, beloved of Qumsasa, saw the chance to avenge his betrothed and perhaps free her from the slavery of her mind. Mormse fought as only one possessed by love may fight. He held the stream against a thousand otterzoid. Darting left and right with spear and knife, his mind open so he could know from whence the thrusts of his foes would come, his mind guarded against the gestalt only by his rage, his passion, his love! He fought for love. He fought for freedom. He fought for all who would come after him, and he held the stream! Blood flowing from a thousand wounds, he held the stream! Lungs screaming to draw breath, he held the stream! All who came, be they joined to the tyrants or willing servant, did in him see the spirit of Fish-seeker.[5] He was as a golden light in the dark waters.

The mind of Qumsasa awoke within the gestalt. She saw through others' eyes her true beloved beset by the forces of Blippane and Quilla. Mustering her will, she set herself against Blippane. Their thoughts clashed. Blippane was all-powerful in the land of the mind, but Qumsasa loved Mormse and hated what she had become.

---

5   *A demi-god of the hunt, see chapter 2.*

So ferocious was her attack that she distracted Blippane, causing the spears of his followers in the gestalt to strike wide of their mark.

Sallandra swam on using the current and pushing herself to the limit. When she feared she could go no further, Quilla thrashed and screamed. Sallandra had travelled a thousand body lengths from the camp. She surfaced and dragged Quilla onto the bank, removing the bag from his head.

Quilla looked up with wide eyes and blood flowing from his nose. He spoke a single word, "Alone", then passed into the land of calm waters and rich streams.

Blippane amongst his troops clutched his head, screamed, and collapsed, calling out the single word, "Alone," as he left his life behind.

Those who had been trapped in the gestalt released a gasp and fell unconscious.

Mormse rose to the surface. He was wounded a thousand times, and the golden glow of Fish-seeker's favour had left him. Painfully he climbed onto the bank as the troops of Quilla and Blippane, now without direction, milled in confusion.

Filling his lungs, King Mormse, for at that moment he became king no matter that his coronation was still a year away, did speak. "All of you. See to the care of those freed from the tyranny of mind. Find me the rightful rulers of the conquered lands, if they yet live, so they may reclaim their swamps and streams. I will hold all in trust until this is made so."

And so it was done. From the ashes of fanaticism came forth the rule of King Mormse the wise, and Queen Qumsasa the kind, for free of the gestalt Qumsasa returned to herself with the help of

Mormse's love. As to Sallandra, she rejoined her warrior band and, after a brief time supporting King Mormse in consolidating his power, moved on in search of other adventures.

Greg nodded to himself.

"Computer, hisstorical data, otterzoidss dictatorss."

The screen filled with names that spilled off the page.

"One hundred and ssixteen." Greg shook his head. "Reducse to paired dictatorss."

This list shortened to one hundred.

"Match with twinss," stated Greg.

The list shortened to ninety-two.

"Match homossexual and/or polyamorouss."

The list didn't shrink at all.

"Eliminate pairss not dying in unisson."

Only one pair of names dropped from the list.

Greg nodded. "Computer, get me a hisstory for the individualss lissted."

He started reviewing the history.

THE BROKEN HEARTED

Yipya stood in the *Star Hawk*'s hallway, hoping his cybernetic leg wouldn't give out under him.

Ryan and Rowan held each other outside her quarter's door.

"I have got to get my swim in, but Divine, this feels nice," said Rowan.

Ryan sighed. "I need to pull a fresh uniform then get to work on Asalue's surprise. Tim is meeting me in my workshop."

"I hope you can do it. I feel sorry for Asalue. Batzoids can be savage," Rowan said aloud. Yipya felt a wave of compassion for his batzoid shipmate.

Ryan held Rowan gently at arm's length. "Read our history, my Little Mountain Tree."

"Don't call me that. Whoever at the studio picked my name was either clueless to how translator nanobots work or had a sick sense of humour!"

"I worked with those techs. I'm betting on clueless." Ryan kissed Rowan, then stepped away. "See you at mess."

"Captain." Yipya hurried to join his shipmates.

"Yes, Yipya." Ryan turned to face his passenger.

"I was hoping to converse with you. Henry told me where you were." Yipya stopped a metre away from Ryan and Rowan.

Ryan unclipped his handheld from his belt and checked the time. "I've got about five minutes. What do you need?"

"Rowan," the k-no-in dipped his head to her, "suggested

that you or your son might be willing to look at my artificial leg. It has become unreliable."

"I'm no expert in k-no-in tech, but I'll give it a once over. Cybernetic integration is Tim's speciality. We can probably figure it out. When's your next sleep cycle?"

"20:00 to 05:00 hours ship's time." Yipya looked up hopefully.

"I'm up till 02:00 today. Drop it off at my workshop before you sleep."

"What will be the price?" Yipya shifted from side to side nervously.

"You're aboard the *Star Hawk*. This is medical." Rowan sounded shocked by the question.

Ryan touched her arm. "We'll work something out. What is your advanced standing in?"

"Veterinary medicine." Yipya shrugged.

"Perfect! How up are you on batzoids?" Ryan smiled at the hulking k-no-in.

"I work on non-sentient species."

"But you work on many forms of life. Better that than a specialist accustomed to only one, and Pikeman is a pain in the backside. You can help with a project Tim and I are doing, and we'll call the work on your leg as even."

"Thank you, Captain. Rowan, you have chosen a good and generous male for your primary client."

"I..." Rowan shrugged, "think so."

Ryan kissed Rowan, then walked towards his quarters.

Rowan turned towards Yipya. "See how easy that was?"

"Yes. The more I see of your Ryan, the more he makes me think of Gunther."

Rowan sighed heavily and shook her head. "I've noticed. I'm a cliche. But I've got good taste."

Yipya looked confused, then shrugged. "Are you going for your swim?"

"If you can call it a swim, no water. Still, I have to do something to stay in shape." Rowan smiled and gestured. "I need to get by."

Yipya looked about himself in dismay. "I am sorry. I did not realize I so blocked the passage. K-no-in ships have wider corridors. I will back up. May I join you for your swim? I am finding it hard to stay active myself."

Rowan shrugged. "How will you use a rec chamber designed for *Homo sapiens*?"

"It is not impossible. If I stand on my back legs, take off my cybernetic leg and use a hack that a programmer associate of mine developed for me."

Yipya reached the gymnasium door and hit the open button. Asalue had slung a strap across his middle, and with some clever knotwork, attached it to the human press bar and was doing four-legged squats against the resistance.

"Do you need the resistance unit?" asked the batzoid as Rowan and Yipya entered the room.

"No, swimming," replied Rowan.

"It is a regret that the simulation chambers are too small for my anatomy. I dislike the pointless lifting and lowering of mass. Sadly, there is little else to do for maintaining a batzoid body on this ship."

"It will be better when we reach Murack Five," comforted Rowan.

"Yes." Asalue closed his eyes. "Have I told you that I have followed your show?"

Rowan nodded. "Yes." She raised her voice for the benefit of both her companions. "I really don't like to think of it as a show. They are my family; it was my reality. It's hard to think of all those wasted years."

"Hush." Yipya moved beside Rowan, stood on his hind legs, and gently gripped her shoulder. "They weren't wasted."

"I must agree with Yipya." Asalue tentatively flicked his tongue. "When my wings were taken from me, I thought I would die. I had nothing and no one. No batzoid would associate with me. I managed to get work with the Republic university as an assistant scholar demonstrating archaeological techniques. A *Homo sapiens* colleague befriended me. William is, by nature, a kind sentient. He saw my pain. One day, he invited me to his nest chamber. He had an e-entertainment system with an adapter to make it compatible with batzoids."

Asalue's tongue flicked from his mouth, and his finger claws tapped the deck. "At first, I demurred, but finally, I gave in to my friend's urgings. He played the speciality cut of *Angel Black*, Angel's perspective. As Angel, I could fly again. I could feel the wind on my face and the weight of air on my wings. It wasn't as good as soaring the skies of Petteron, but it was flight. I have experienced every Angel speciality cut of *Angel Black* and the Isis cuts of *Defenders of the Crystal*, so I could have those moments of flight."

Asalue hung his serpentine head. "They make it bearable."

Rowan stepped forward and gently touched the batzoid's furry shoulder. "I'm sure Angel would be happy to know she helped."

"It will probably be even better when the episodes with Croell are released," said Yipya.

Rowan snorted. "That hunk of stardust almost killed me." She then sighed. "But you're right. The flying should be impressive. How do you know about him?"

"There was an article in the information dispatch. It just said that batzoid were being added to the *Angel Black* antagonists and that Farley was going to regret laying with Angel and want you back." Yipya fell silent at the look on Rowan's face.

"I…" Yipya tapped his finger claws together in contrition. "I should realize that those experiences were different for you. I have not experienced those episodes. The last episode I experienced, you were waiting to find out if you were accepted to the master's program. You and Farley were happy."

Rowan forced a smile. "Only sort of. Did they edit out my doubts?"

Yipya tapped the foot of his artificial leg on the deck. "They may have been in the Rowan speciality cut. I only did the general cut and Gunther's perspective. We should start our swim."

Rowan looked at the k-no-in, who moved to one of the coffin-like interface chambers. He spoke to the air, taking a data cube from a pouch hung on the belt about his waist. "Henry, this is the program you examined. Do I have your permission to add it to this unit's system?"

A series of yips and yaps came from the wall speaker.

Yipya shifted uneasily from foot to foot. "That is very flattering, but I don't know how it would work." The k-no-in put the data cube into the receptor jack. Lights flashed on the controls by the recreation chamber's edge, then Yipya removed his artificial leg and brought himself to a standing position in the booth. He closed his eyes and walked on his hind legs in place.

"Have you ever seen something like this before?" asked Rowan.

"It is a big galaxy." Asalue tapped his claws and went back to working with the weights.

Rowan stepped into a recreation chamber and entered the pool simulation.

⊂═══▷

Rowan looked over the simulation of an Olympic-sized swimming pool. A huge man with a lot of dark body hair and an angular face stood on the deck. He was easily two metres tall and constructed like a barrel with limbs attached. His blue boxer-style trunks were on backwards.

"Yipya?" asked Rowan.

"It is me. The program adapts my simulacrum to the recreational environment I enter." Yipya swaggered unevenly towards Rowan. "It is an impressive piece of programming. A gift from the owner of a patient whose life I extended."

"Let's swim. I need to start studying for my GOP later." Rowan slipped into the pool.

Yipya smiled and did a huge leap into the deep end, landing chest first. A moment later, he was doing a dog paddle up and down the lane. Rowan picked her own lane and started swimming lengths.

An hour later, Yipya clambered from the water.

"I can't believe how fast you dog paddle. You almost kept up with my crawl." Rowan examined the k-no-in's avatar.

"The avatar is only cosmetic. I am built to swim like that. I could not even attempt most of the strokes you *Homo sapiens* have developed. My musculature will not permit my arms and legs to reach behind me."

"Won't this simulation neglect your middle..." Rowan shrugged. Truth was truth. "Arm?"

"I will do work with the weight machine for my middle arm. The one on the left is for others to maintain." Yipya lowered so that his avatar stood on hands and knees. "Excuse please, in the real world, I was getting a cramp."

Rowan smiled at the k-no-in. "I'm glad I met you."

"That is nice of you to say." Yipya looked into Rowan's face.

"You can probably guess that I had a questionable opinion of k-no-in. For most of my life, the only ones I knew were pirates. Then the first time I went to Wesnakee, one tried to hire me to pull a train."

"Pull a large surface vehicle?" Yipya's face filled with consternation.

Rowan blushed. "Have sex with multiple partners in succession."

"Oh. He was probably on his first assignment. Most learn that our customs do not translate well in most cultures. To set your mind at ease, I am not attracted to *Homo sapiens* in that way."

"No offence, but that is a relief. Is it common for k-no-in to, well... In most *Homo sapiens* cultures, prostitution does not lead to stable, lasting relationships," said Rowan.

"I always found your mating customs odd when I experienced the entertainments. Among my people, as one ages, one usually becomes the regular client of one or two females. They each will have a clientele, but by my age, it rarely exceeds three or four. If a male passes the breeding examination, it is not uncommon for him to be part of four or five clienteles. Breeding females, by law, have at least one breeding male in their client list." Yipya curled his lip in a snarl. "Some selfish males from wealthy families that have breeder status demand their breeding female have no other clients. It is a sadness to the good males who did service to their species to have survived war and whatever other humiliation and slavery the directorate saw fit to sell them into for their term, only to have no female willing to take their money." Yipya's head drooped. "I was a client of Grrrrale. I can see her still. Fangs as yellow as a flower, her pelt tinted golden in the morning sun, and she was smart. I spent half my earnings on her for years, then Yapgra came into her client list. Rich and in the top ten percentile for breeding. He demanded she reject all her other clients when she became with child. It is bad for the young to not have a stable false-sire in their lives to raise them. Yapgra was always too busy with his other females to be a father to his young. I always wanted to raise the young. I like children, but when Grrrrale rejected me, there was nothing for me to do."

Rowan shook her head. She could see the k-no-in's pain in the posture of its avatar. "I… I am sorry. It is a different way, but even with *Homo sapiens*, some men were made to be fathers."

Yipya's avatar's features pulled into a smile. "That is why I so enjoyed *Angel Black*. Through Gunther, I could imagine myself a father. He was father to the young of your group, even though he supplied the genetics for none of you. It was much like being a false-sire."

"He was a great dad," agreed Rowan.

"After Grrrrale rejected me, I lost interest. It seemed unlikely that I would find another female to accept me as their client. Not with my disfigurement. K-no-ins are very conscious of looks. Grrrrale only accepted me because I had a big income, and she was a friend of my mother's. I decided to come to the Switchboard Station, but it was worse here. Only those who fail their breeding test are allowed to leave Srill. All the females here are infertile, and most of them are stupid. Not what I would seek in a companion. Also, there is little demand for veterinarians on the station. So, with little money left and no hope of being a parent to a k-no-in child, I signed up for the Murack Five Reclamation Project. I can nurture a world, even if I cannot nurture a child. They need k-no-in with zoology and biochemistry because of the similarities in ecosystems." Yipya grimaced. "You must forgive. My back is cramping from being in such an unnatural position in the real world. I must leave the simulation."

"I need to go as well. Thank you for joining me. It was nice to share the pool and... I hope you find a child to raise. If you follow Gunther's example, you'll be great at it." Rowan patted the k-no-in's avatar's arm.

They blinked out of the simulation.

Medwin sat in the recliner, Kendra sat in the next chair, then Obert, then Carol. A phone call had added the slightly older woman to the focus group. Yet another instalment of Rowan's escape played, and they all tried to watch it as if it were just a show, not the slightly dated chronicle of real events they knew it to be.

Medwin could feel his rage bubbling. The grief and rage came like waves. Sometimes he could almost feel normal. Not happy, but like life was worth living, then someone would walk by wearing Armina's brand of perfume, or he'd hear a turn of phrase that was something she might have said, and the wave of grief and anger would crash over him. Then his father; he thought he'd put his dad's death behind him, but now it rode in on the waves, leaving him blinded with a red-hot rage for what the studio had done to him. Because he had no choice, Medwin focused on his job and bided his time.

The episode paused where a commercial marker would be placed.

"You okay, Medwin?" Kendra turned to her friend.

Medwin sat with his eyes closed and spoke in a near whisper. "Armina just couldn't take reality. It was all too much for her, but I've been thinking about my dad. The com… I snuck a look at his medical record. He had cancer. Maybe…" Medwin's chest heaved as his voice squeaked. "Maybe, dying ended his pain before he stopped being himself. Like Ryan did for Kadar."

Kendra got up and hugged Medwin. He stiffened for a second, but this time collapsed into the comfort. She felt his chest convulse and heard quiet sobs.

Obert glanced at Carol, then pressed the pause button. They sat in silence, letting their friend grieve. Grieve for his father long passed, and for the woman he loved, for friends taken and for the cruelty of fate. Grieve for all that made up the wave that crested over him so it might truly recede.

⊶

Arlene sat in the *Freedom's Run* control room, dashing tears from her eyes. What she saw on her monitor was gold. The studio would never use it. The pain was too complete, it would be edited down into a sanitized pablum of mediocre emotion, but even without an e-rig, it touched her. It was something so human it reached inside her and drew out her own tragedy. Tapping a well of grief she'd carried for nearly four years. Medwin would understand. She knew that the lie the studio told, that clones weren't human, was the worst of fallacies. She was proud to stand against it. Medwin's pain spoke to the core of humanity.

"I'm sorry, Medwin." Arlene dashed tears from her own eyes again. "Divine, Velma, why didn't you talk to me? Why didn't you let me help?" She took a deep breath and opened her handheld, bringing up a picture of a copper-skinned woman with large eyes and black hair. The resemblance to herself was striking.

"Gene."

"Yes, Arlene?" spoke the computer's even unemotional voice.

"Put a call through to my mother. Secondary screen, please."

Thirty seconds later, the bewildered and sleepy face of Arlene's mother stared out of a screen.

"Arlene?"

"Hi, Mom. I know it's been a while. You once said that when I was ready to talk, I should call you." Arlene let tears flow down her cheeks.

"You're ready." Her mother's voice was even and soothing, her attractive Navajo features reflecting compassion and acceptance.

"I… I was wrong to blame you. What Velma did, she did to herself. She's the one that jumped off that cliff. You didn't push her. I guess I just needed someone to blame, and you were convenient."

"I loved your sister. I love both my girls. Look, a vid is no way to do this. Come home so we can really talk."

"I'd like that. Will Dad be there too?"

"For you, my little chipmunk, he wouldn't miss it."

Arlene smiled at the use of the old endearment. "I love you, Mom, and I love Dad too. I'm so sorry for the things I said."

"I'm just happy that I can get one of my daughters back. Come home as soon as you can."

"I will. I'm off in three hours. See you for breakfast. Gene, close channel."

A LARGER WORLD

Ryan stepped into his workshop to see Tim and Yipya looking at a collection of struts and membranes on the work counter that dominated the far side of the room. A similar counter with a series of robotic arms on trackways above it filled the wall to his right. The wall to his left contained a nanobot manufacturing unit, a large three-dimensional printing system and a computerized drafting-board, schematic display system.

A large table filled with tools dominated the middle of the room. Drawers and cabinets occupied the spaces below the cabinets and under the table.

"Problems?" asked Ryan.

"It is the restriction against using a biological interface. The batzoids fail the breeding exam by a large margin to limit themselves so. The suffering they could avert." Yipya thumped the counter with his foreleg in frustration.

"Asalue would agree. He's between a rock and a hard place." Ryan moved to the counter.

Yipya let out an amused huff. "That one translates very well." His voice shifted to the gravelly intonation. "Rumping a stone."

"Gotta love k-no-in," Henry's voice came over the speaker.

"How is the leg doing?" Ryan inspected some gauges on the automated manufacturing system.

"The new control interface Tim designed is amazing. It feels. The original system only gave a sense of pressure.

And the replacement joints, magnificent. It's like having my leg back. You *Homo sapiens* are so advanced." Yipya shook his head.

"We traded for most of it. If it wasn't for having planets to trade, we'd only be a few hundred years ahead of k-no-in," observed Tim.

"It would have been nice to have a planet to trade. My people paid a high price for the consequences of our origin." Yipya sighed.

"No species asks to become sentient. We all do what we can," remarked Ryan. "So, how is the wing interface coming?"

"I think we can lick the control issue," began Tim.

Yipya huffed in amusement, but this time didn't choose to explain the joke.

"How?" Ryan moved to the bench and looked at the artificial wing. It was jointed exactly like a batzoid wing.

"By laying what is left of Asalue's wings into trackways on the cybernetic unit's leading edge, we can use microsensors to translate his movements to the wing. Pikeman is regenerating the nerves and sealing skin around what's left of the organic wings, so we don't have to worry about infection. The cybernetic wings will have a limited sense of touch, but they will respond to commands. There will be a learning curve, but it should give adequate control. It's a system the k-no-in were using up to about… What was it?" Tim turned to Yipya.

"It was superseded by direct neural interface a hundred years ago. It's still used in some cargo handlers as a control interface. One of my client kin did maintenance on cargo handlers. He told me about them when we were on a client's trip to the environment preservation zone."

"The rest is just straightforward mechanical engineering." Ryan nodded. "Henry, have you got those servos put together?"

"Unit three on the cyber bench, oh captain mine," replied Henry's voice.

"I must ask, Henry. With access to all this, why have you not made yourself a new body?" Yipya moved to examine the mechanical pieces, marvelling at their size.

"Because I will never be a slave again!" stated Henry.

Ryan nodded in agreement. "Henry and I could make him a new body, provided I could afford the raw materials, which I can't. But the designs are all patented. The moment I integrated Henry with the system, we'd have to pay for rights and usage to either the UES or Hedonism Incorporated, or his debt to them would be back, and he would be an indentured servant again. The fees for the intellectual property are enormous."

Yipya looked confused. "So, you could?"

"We could, my sexy k-no-in friend, but the second the new system became active, I'd be the property of whoever holds the patents we'd need to infringe to do it," explained Henry.

"I believe I see, but that still leaves the question of why not rebuild him into a different form?" Yipya flared his nostrils.

"I got this way because I liked emulating a *Homo sapiens*. I want my hips back. And the other species with shaggable forms all have similar laws. I won't be owned again," stated Henry.

"If I could get a Luba, let's say, I could adapt it because I'd be using a premade unit that I own. I'd invalidate the warranty, but frankly, given most Hedonism Incorporated's tech staff, I wouldn't trust them to fix a toaster anyway. But that would mean buying a chassis to begin with, and that runs into credits."

"A Luba might be a nice change." The voice that came from the speaker was female and pitched so that it caused both Ryan and Tim to shift uncomfortably where they stood.

"Let's get to work doing what we can for who we can," suggested Ryan.

Greg sat in one of the loungers in Michael's office. The younger man snored softly as his boss worked at his desk.

"The fact that you seem to be incapable of getting adequate supplies to fulfill your contracts is of no concern to me. This is the second time you've told me that catering my event was beyond your capacity. If you couldn't do the job, you shouldn't have accepted the contract."

"But sir," pleaded a woman's voice.

"No. You will have your wait and bartending staff at my residence tomorrow for the launch party, along with however much of your contract you can fulfill We will discuss your partial remuneration after the event. Furthermore, I told you that my wife was handling the catering arrangements. I resent your attempt to get around her by contacting me directly. When I trust someone to do a job, I am confident in their abilities to perform the task. Something it would seem you need to add to your management style. Send extra serving trays for pizza and spiced chicken wings. Can you manage that much?"

"Yes, sir. I'm so sorry. No one expected pirates to intercept the shipment of lobster," said the woman's voice.

"Things happen in business; one must have contingencies for the unexpected." Michael sighed and shook his head. His voice became gentle. "Miss Jackson, you dropped the ball. Go back to catering weddings and the like. Get some more experience before you try to play the big leagues. I won't pay full price for half a job, but if the service is good at the launch, I'll make sure this doesn't bankrupt you. Fair enough?"

"Thank you, Mr. Strongbow."

"Goodbye." Mike closed the channel, then spoke to the air. "Gene, audio line to the set region, Garlic Palace."

There was the sound of an old-style phone ringing. A moment later, the line opened.

"Garlic Palace, where your taste buds sing, how may I

help you?" asked a youthful male voice.

"I need a takeout order for tomorrow afternoon at 15:00 hours."

"What is the order?" asked the voice.

Mike did some mental math. "Twenty-five jumbo pizzas, assorted toppings and combinations. No anchovies! Twenty extra-large chicken wings packages, assorted spice levels, mark the boxes. Fifteen garlic bread with cheese."

The line was silent for a moment. The voice came back sounding overwhelmed. "Yes, sir. Do you want that delivered?"

"I'll send someone to pick it up. Have it ready on time."

"If you require servers, we have a list of catering firms willing to supply personnel," added the voice.

"Just the food, but thank you."

"May I have your credit card number?"

Mike pressed a button on his keyboard. The studio's account for on-set transactions linked to the Garlic Palace.

"The transaction is complete. Thank you for your business."

Mike closed the line with the press of a button. "Giuseppe is one man who knows how to train his staff. It makes me wish I could tap the set region for real-world personnel."

Mike silenced when he saw Greg in the lounger, mouth open and snoring.

"Lots of talent out here." Mike walked over and shook the younger man's shoulder.

"What, I, oh ssorry." Greg started out of sleep.

"Ex-military. You sleep when you can, if you can. I'm assuming you were up all night researching the Gunther-Jessica situation?"

Greg nodded. "It iss bad. I uploaded my findingss to the *Freedom'ss Run* sstaff coordination board before I came in."

"Give me the short form." Mike settled into the other

lounger.

"Monozygotic twinss have a heightened awarenesss of each other in both *Homo Ssapienss* and otterzoidss. In *Homo Ssapienss*, telepathy is weak enough it doessn't causse problemss. In otterzoidss, mosst of the time, there are no isssuess. Femaless aren't overly telepathic, sso they don't have the problem. With identical male twinss, the connection is sstrong enough that they can enhancse each other. Sstill, for an otterzoid, it iss not overwhelming. Think adding ten and ten to get twenty in a world where fifteen is common. The problem comess in when monozygotic twinss are alsso homo- or bissexual. The combination of identical geneticss and ssexual attraction drawss them together. If they conssummate their union, the natural dropping of the barrierss between them caussess their mindss to merge. It'ss no longer ten pluss ten. It becomess ten timess ten."

"So, overwhelmingly powerful. That could prove useful to me in the coming months," remarked Mike.

"The ego alsso increassess. They become megalomaniacss intent on enforcsing their will on otherss. With otterzoidss, they can alsso mesh their gesstalt with otherss, overwhelming the lessser powerss' free will and making them asspectss of the perssonality, adding their telepathic sstrength into what becomess a group mind dominated by the initial pair. The otterzoidss call it mind-death. I couldn't find much on it."

"So, because Gunther and Jessica are both ASH series, they are in effect genetically identical except for the XY chromosomes. And because the retrovirus that gave Jessica her power is based on the gene splice that created Gunther's, there is little or no difference there."

"We have to keep them apart, or they will become a totalitarian dictator, and they will losse themsselvess to the gesstalt, two becoming one. The otterzoidss haven't had a dictator for ssix thoussand years. Not ssince they developed gene tessting. By law, monozygotic male twinss are sseparated. Ssince they've had sspace coloniess, they've alwayss houssed the infantss on sseparate planetss. Before that, sseparate continentss. That iss how much their ssociety fearss the effect. With what Gunther and Jesssica have been up to ssince they met and didn't even touch each other, we could be looking at the casst of *Angel Black* amalgamating into one masss mind intent on concurring the universse."

"Unlikely given that most of the abilities aren't psi-based, but even so, it would be best to keep Gunther and Jessica apart. Nova blast John. Even in ignorance, he's making things worse."

"How?" asked Greg.

"The Willa-Carl affair. It's still a fresh wound. Part of Gunther wants payback, even if he doesn't admit it to himself, and now potentially the best sex of his life walks into the room. A level of intimacy that Willa is physically incapable of giving him. What a mess." Mike sighed and shook his head.

"What can we do?" Greg blinked his slit-pupiled eyes and tried to force his weary brain to think.

"For now, you can go home and get some sleep. I've brought Stan from *Defenders of the Crystal* in early to take the board. With Jessica joining the active team, it will be good to have someone informed about the crossover on both boards. We have the launch tomorrow. I want you on the board at your best."

"Becausse of how I look." Greg flicked his reptilian tongue.

"Divine, no! Because you're the best person for the job. You have a real sense for Medwin and his group. I trust you to do what you have to, if you have to, but not to act prematurely out of panic."

Greg dipped his head. "I'm ssorry. When you grow up looking like... me, you—"

Mike gripped Greg's arm. "Talent is too rare to ignore because of inconsequentialities."

Greg smiled. "About Gunther?"

"For now, we must trust in his devotion to Willa. Never underestimate what a man in love is capable of."

Greg chuckled. "Ryan provess that."

"It does seem to be a theme surfacing on the series. Funny that. Go, get some sleep. I need to arrange for a pickup from the Garlic Palace."

Tim pressed the call button by the door to Kitoy's quarters.

"I will be there shortly," Kitoy's voice came from the speaker.

Tim waited. He was dressed in a pair of slacks, a nice shirt and a sports jacket from his luggage and held what looked like a rose in his hands. It had taken him an hour to program the parameters into the nano-assembler in the workshop.

The door retracted into the wall, revealing Kitoy. The felinezoid was straightening the red sash she wore across her chest. "Come in. Is it time for mess already?"

Tim stepped into the felinezoid's quarters. The charcoal sketch of her and Kadar stared at him from her wall.

"I'm early. I… Kitoy, I wanted to give you this. I programmed it myself." Tim held out the simulated rose.

Kitoy's tail swished, then she froze, and her nostrils widened. Her eyes were drawn to the picture on the wall, then she hung her head. "I… I know what bringing flowers can mean to a *Homo sapiens*."

Tim stared at her. "Did I misread things?"

Kitoy looked at her visitor. "Probably not. I…" Kitoy moved to the sofa/bed in her quarters, which was currently rolled up on the wall serving as a sofa. She sat on it sideways so her tail wouldn't be squished. "Tim, sit down, please."

Tim sat on the couch angled to face her.

Kitoy's nostrils trembled, and her nose ran a little. "Kadar has been away for years. Our only contact messages. I also knew he was dying. I should have been prepared, but I wasn't."

"No one ever is." Tim's voice was soothing.

"Perhaps. I loved Kadar, but he had his faults. Sometimes I felt like I needed a leash whenever a compatible female species walked by, but all in all, he was a good male."

"Ryan's told me some stories. I met him once when the *Star Hawk* put in at the Earth shipyards for a retrofit." Tim stroked the fur on Kitoy's arm.

Kitoy swished her tail. "When I put on the red sash, I was almost relieved. I know that's horrible, but I was so lonely for so long. With him being there, but not there, and waiting, knowing he would die. Always expecting that final message. It was hard."

Tim nodded to show he heard, hoping the gesture would cross the species barrier.

"What I'm saying is... Tim, I like you. I like you a lot. I know the business with turning Rowan over to the UES was you trying to do right by your father. It was a mistake, but good people make mistakes. I've made more than my share. Good people forgive. I don't want to miss out on something positive because of ghosts, but I'm..."

"Not ready." Tim filled in the silence. "We can just be friends until you are. Stardust, I've got some adjusting to do as well."

"I..." Kitoy took Tim's hand in hers and gently rubbed the back of it with her thumb. "It isn't as big an adjustment as you might think. *Homo sapiens* and felinezoid. If the time comes, I can teach you. Do you really understand what you'll be getting yourself into if we, well, if, when the time is right, we become more than friends? I've had enough hurt in my life; I don't want any more."

Tim looked at the cat-like alien and saw only Kitoy, warm, sweet, a little insecure, kind, and smart. "Kitoy, I was married to a *Homo sapiens* for twenty years. I understood her less well than I understand you after a month. I can't promise a lifetime, but I can promise two things. One, I will give you the time you need because you are worth it. And two, I won't let something stupid like species be a problem between us, whether we are friends or lovers." Tim gently rubbed his thumb on the back of Kitoy's hand, the short fur forming a kind of dry lubricant.

Kitoy dipped her head and swished her tail, then rubbed her thumb on his hand. "Just a little while. I think we both need that." She released his hand and stood up. "We'll be late for mess." Moving to the nightstand at the side of her bed, she set the rose on top of it. "One good thing about artificial flowers is they do fine without water."

Tim rose. They walked together to the mess.

Medwin led Kendra, Obert, Carol and Jessica through the woods. He had his bow and a quiver of hunting arrows tied to the backpack he wore. There was the sound of a distant explosion.

"Are you sure we aren't going to run into any tree planters?" Obert glanced around nervously.

"They're all south of here. Besides, we won't move past the established forest until we're in the river."

"We could leave after shift and still make it to the studio support town in time," observed Obert.

"I want to get to the address Ulva gave me and check out the grounds."

"Case the joint," remarked Jessica. "Thanks for including me. It's good to get away from the city. It... It clears my head."

"No charge," said Obert and Carol in unison as they each took one of her hands.

"Do I want to know?" asked Kendra.

"Probably not." Carol smiled at the younger woman.

"We can use you, Jessica. When we meet people, scan

them, get all the information you can. If this studio executive deigns to speak with his slaves, keep your mind on him. Make sure he's telling the truth." Medwin came up to where the trees broke, revealing the Stewart River. The hydroelectric dam was upstream, and the waters were rushing by.

"This isn't safe," observed Kendra.

"We can't afford to be spotted. By people or satellites." Medwin shucked his backpack and opened it.

"It should be a rush." Carol dropped her pack and immodestly began to strip.

"Who wants to live forever?" Jessica, with a moment's hesitation, followed the other's example.

Soon they were all clad in black wetsuits with fins, snorkels, masks, and weight belts. Each held a pressure cylinder about as long as Medwin's forearm with a built-in regulator.

"Medwin, what do we do if they are lying?" asked Kendra.

Medwin reached down and picked up his bow and hunting arrows. "They owe me lives."

"Stardust, man. This is recon. I'm not going to war. We're not ready," objected Obert.

"Then hope Ulva isn't lying about our invitation," stated Medwin.

Kendra sighed. "These mini tanks will only give us about ten minutes bottom time. I've used them before. The river isn't that deep, but don't hold your breath, especially when you're coming up. You could blow a lung, and that will kill you."

"Clip the line to your weight belts so that we don't get separated. Get in, get under, and let the current carry us out to and across the Wolf River."

"How are we getting back?" asked Carol.

"On the other side, we'll hide the water gear under some rocks, then we can recharge the air tanks with the hand pump and swim across the Wolf," explained Medwin.

"Because that worked so well the last time," griped Obert.

"We have wetsuits this time. If you have a better idea…" Medwin glowered at his friend. "Armina died because of them. I can't go back to living like normal. This is the best plan I have."

Jessica reached with her mind, smoothing the turmoil of Medwin's emotions. *'Feel with your heart. Lead with your head. Your friends look to you. Serve the living.'*

Medwin glowered towards Jessica, took a deep breath, and spoke. "You okay?"

"The further from Gunther I am, the less I feel him and other things."

"Kendra, you've dove before, so you take point. Everyone, keep to your place. No passing."

Ulva leaned back, excitement running through her. Her charges were, except for Jessica, all normal people. Kids just out of high school, and they were taking insane risks for what? For freedom, for a thing she wasn't even sure she had a good definition for.

They filed into the river, each with a pack on their back. The cold shock of the water as it entered the wetsuit almost caused muscles to cramp, but the water quickly warmed with their body heat. Kendra went under, then Obert, Carol, Jessica and Medwin.

The river bottom swept by at what seemed an impossible speed. All except for Kendra fought down a panic response and tried to keep their breathing steady. Ulva's fingers itched to adjust their biologies, take the edge off the fear and let them focus on the wonder.

"Oh, why not? Life can be beautiful too. Maybe if Armina had realized that, she'd be with them right now." Her fingers played across the console, reducing the stress response in her charges. She then turned her attention to the otter drone waiting on the rocks by the river and set it to follow and relay the signals from the swimmers.

Kendra kept them to the middle of the channel and a metre above the bottom.

A secondary screen blinked on. A tree planter extra was relieving himself by the river. He looked at the flow and caught the merest hint of shadow sweeping by. He looked again and saw nothing. "I'm going loopy. Next, I'll be seeing the Wolf River serpent," he muttered to himself.

The Stewart River disgorged its flow into the Wolf. Kendra glanced at the compass strapped to her wrist, seeing they were now travelling north. She angled to the east until she came to a shallow bank that she climbed up on and braced herself.

The rope connecting the team pulled taut, dragging them to the shore where they scrambled out. Doffing their fins, they bolted away from the border of the set region. The water drained from the wetsuits, and they became stifling. When Carol fell, Obert and Medwin helped her up, and they all huddled by a large boulder on the barren.

Ulva watched Medwin's readings. He was in pain. But something was growing. A quiet resolve. He didn't lead his band because he was the smartest or strongest. He led them because, at the end of the day, he was the most determined.

"If the kid was three or four years older, I'd pull a Ryan. Divine, Ulva, talk about a Pygmalion delusion."

Medwin spoke again. "Good work. Especially you, Kendra." He undid the zipper of his wetsuit and stripped. Soon they were all in the old clothes that they'd put in their packs, walking across the barren to the studio support town.

"How are we going to find the place?" demanded Obert.

"We know it's east-northeast of Sun Valley, so we just follow the compass until we reach the hills. We get some height and look for buildings. Pretty obvious," said Jessica.

"How did you know that?" asked Carol.

"Defender of the Crystal here. You pick things up. I hope you guys are wrong. It would be so much easier to deal with everything if this was just some plot by a bunch of demons." Jessica closed her eyes and took a deep breath. "I can't sense Gunther and… Wow, colour me pink." She looked at Carol and Obert. "Sorry guys, I couldn't help myself."

"We're not," they said in chorus.

Ulva laughed.

THE OTHER HALF

Ryan sat at the engineering console, scanning the readouts from the gravity laser drive.

"Pull points for deceleration manoeuvre in the pilot's file," stated Rowan from the navigation station.

Ryan pressed a button on the engineering board and stood. "Drive lasers prepped and ready for deployment." He walked to the piloting station and sat. Scanning his board, he focused the grav laser on the pull points and activated it. "Pull is good. All systems green for piloting."

"Deceleration according to revised flight plan, all angles good. Navigation is set," said Rowan.

"Computer still needs hips, but optimal," remarked Henry.

"Life support checks green," added Tim.

"Communications optimal," reported Kitoy.

"Weapons systems look good," remarked Ziggy.

"Nice transition, people. Everyone, do your safety checks, and we'll call it a day. Rowan, what's the status of our friends?" Ryan started the pilot's checklist.

"The *Chimera* is still off our forward port, and the *Mary* aft starboard. Both just outside legal range."

"Kitoy, any luck on our enquiries about the *Mary* or Croell and Zandra?" Ryan finished his checks and locked down the piloting station.

"Star Searcher just keeps quoting the regs about the right to privacy." Kitoy lashed her tail. "That crab is as bad as ear mites!"

"No argument." Ryan shifted to the engineering station and began the deceleration checks.

"Life sciences is green across the board. Can I go? I need to adjust the humidity in Asalue's quarters again."

"Go. If you see him, ask Pikeman how Asalue's wings are coming along," replied Ryan without looking up from his control board.

"Aye." Tim sauntered from the room, making a brief detour to lightly touch Kitoy's shoulder.

She swished her tail but kept her focus on the communications board. "Captain, the *Chimera* is receiving an encrypted message from the Switchboard Station."

"Can you crack it?" Ryan turned his chair so that he could watch his communications officer.

"It's a low-level encryption. Henry, can you translate it?" asked Kitoy.

"It's a text document," said Henry.

"Put it on the big screen." Ryan did the final check on the engineering board and started locking it down.

Rows of numbers appeared on the screen. The first row was separate from the rest and set in two groups of two and one of three. The other lines were groupings of six with a lot of zeros in the first two places at the beginning of the file.

"I can't believe you monkey descendants are still using that old gnawing leather," remarked Kitoy.

"It must be low priority. You have to admit, it works for most situations." Ryan moved to the command chair.

"Navigation is checked and on course. Can we work out the title, and do we have the edition?" asked Rowan.

"The hotty gets it," observed Henry. "Title's easy, *The Art of War*, 697 PC edition."

"Weapons checked and operating as to current specifications. And how the nova blast did you get that?" Ziggy's complexion was now a healthy shade. The coverall uniform fit a little more loosely than when he'd boarded.

"First row, my organically slow friend, 20 is T, 08 is H, 05 is E and so on. After the title, it shifts to straight numbers for the date. Notice it's the only group of three in the row. The lower rows are page, lines down, then word in that line."

"If this were a serious secret, they wouldn't include the cipher. It would all be pre-arranged," added Rowan, taking pleasure that for once, she wasn't the one scrambling to catch up for lack of knowledge.

Ryan shook his head. "This is just an inconvenience to keep some hack from trying to sell it to the news dispatches. Henry, do we have the edition?"

"Negative, hotty boss, but I can do a workaround. It will take up a lot of RAM. I'll have to drop oversight on the control systems and shut down the *Orgy Girls-Station House* crossover I'm experiencing. Captain Philips really knows how to use his hose. He—"

"Henry, not on the job!" Ryan's voice was firm.

"Yes, my captain," snipped Henry.

"Pull the RAM. Let's find out what our friends are chatting about. Everyone, pay attention to your boards. Henry won't be there to catch mistakes. Kitoy, let Tim know I want him back here when he's done with Asalue's quarters. We can let environmental coast for a few minutes, but I'll want it rechecked afterwards." Ryan moved to the pilot's station and re-checked its feeds.

Henry closed his android eyes. The computer board lit up as all its auxiliary RAM units were turned to the problem.

"What's he doing?" asked Rowan.

"Looking at the copy of *The Art of War* we have on file. Doing page, paragraph, and word in on it, then shifting forward and backwards to find sentences that make sense with the coding in the message. Using those sentences as a basis, he'll form a compensation pattern that will speed up matching later sections until the message is translated into comprehensible sentences. We organics could do the same thing, but it would take days."

All eyes turned to Kitoy.

"I was felinezoid intelligence. I learned more than how to chat on a sleeping cushion." Kitoy twitched her ears and lashed her tail.

"That's going to take a long time without the cipher," observed Rowan.

Henry kept his eyes closed and his focus inward. Five minutes later, he opened his eyes. "It's no *Orgy Girls*, but at least it wasn't boring."

"Put it on screen, please," ordered Ryan.

> To Command Officers *Chimera*.
>
> From Admiral Yvonne Carlotta LaFleur. UES Space Services Command.
>
> Effective immediately.
>
> Once the *Star Hawk* leaves the Switchboard System, you will proceed directly to the Sol System stargate, where Captain Graham Crapper will take command of the gate monitor and transfer vessel *Postman*. Commander Adler McKenzie will assume interim command of the *Chimera*.
>
> Regards.
>
> Admiral Yvonne Carlotta LaFleur.

Ryan laughed.

"They're rewarding that idiot with a new command. Talk about failing up," snipped Rowan.

Ryan kept chuckling. "The transfer ships are backwaters for officers waiting out their retirement. Most of their crew have lost their edge. If they ever had one. The ships are small, antiquated, and only hand out speeding tickets and transit information through the gate. In short, they've put Crapper where he can't do any harm and has about zero upward mobility. He is now a slave to his own incompetence with no one else to blame."

A conniving expression came to Ryan's face. "Why not? It will make me feel better." Ryan moved to the command chair and sat like a king on his throne. "Kitoy, please contact the *Chimera* and put it on screen." Two seconds later, the bridge of the *Chimera* filled the *Star Hawk's* main screen. Crapper sat in the command chair looking like a dog about to pounce on a rabbit. Commander McKenzie stood behind and to the right of the chair.

"Do you require assistance?" Crapper's voice dripped venom.

"Not at all. I simply wanted to congratulate you, Captain Crapper, on your new command. I'm sure the *Postman* will prove a post well suited to your talents." Two seconds passed as the message sped to the other ship, and the response reached the *Star Hawk*. On-screen, Crapper went pale.

"What are you talking about?" demanded the big man.

"We intercepted the standard communication blip from the Switchboard Station by accident. It happens all the time when ships crowd each other. My system decrypted it automatically. I couldn't stop myself from reading your new orders. As I said, I wanted to congratulate you on your new command." Ryan's smile nearly split his face.

Two seconds passed. The faces of the bridge crew on the *Chimera* seemed to light up.

"Communications, what is he talking about?" demanded Crapper.

"Sir, new orders in the daily dispatch. I hadn't reviewed it yet."

"Put it on screen," snapped Crapper.

"I must be going, but I also want to congratulate Commander, acting Captain, McKenzie on his field promotion. Acting positions have a tendency of becoming permanent if the officer is competent. Good luck with it."

On the screen, Crapper leapt out of the captain's chair red-faced and screaming. Commander McKenzie heaved what looked like a sigh of relief.

"Thank you for your good wishes, Captain." McKenzie shot the screen a salute before it went blank.

"Kitoy, kill it, please."

Rowan laughed out loud.

Ryan returned to the pilot's station. "Henry, bring up the next dispatch. Let's see what else we're not supposed to know."

Greg settled in the chair in the *Freedom's Run* control room.

"It's too bad you need to work the board. This is going to be one nova blast of a party," remarked Arlene.

Greg shrugged and scanned Medwin's readings. The surrogate was stressed with a side of rage. The rest of the team were edgy.

"I dialed back Carol to her natural settings. We don't want her seducing a show producer to take the edge off. Jessica is running at default. The *Defenders of the Crystal* board is reading her as asleep. There's a new controller on it, so she probably won't notice the loop in the feed. I haven't seen a blip from Gunther all shift. Medwin had them crawling over Mike's estate. If that kid does get out, he has a real future in security, or as a second-storey man."

"Or a hitman," added Greg.

Arlene moved to the door. "Let's hope not. Any idea what's up with Gunther and Jessica?"

"They're probably too far apart. Telepathy functionss with a field sstrength dynamic. Could alsso be the curve of the planet iss blocking the 'ssignal'. I learned more about pssi in the lasst forty-nine hours than I ever wanted to know. If they'd sslept together, the sseparation would likely have killed them. At leasst that'ss what the mythss ssay."

"Stardust happens when you don't know what you're doing."

"Truth."

"I need to get changed for the launch." Arlene ducked out of the door.

Greg set the main monitor to show Medwin's inputs. He was in a large bedroom done up with a king-sized bed/couch rolled against the wall into its second function, two chairs, and a coffee table. A desk and a dresser sat against the wall. An e-rig sat in one corner of the room.

"My apartment isn't this big," observed Carol.

"Rich bastard!" grumbled Medwin. He scanned his compatriots. Kendra was in a black dress that bared one shoulder and showed off her lean muscular legs. She'd combed out her hair, and it fell like black satin to between her shoulder blades. Her makeup was minimal. Medwin's monitors showed attraction mixed with mild surprise, then confusion, then guilt.

"At leasst he noticsed," remarked Greg.

Obert was wearing a black tux that matched Medwin's. Jessica and Carol were both in black dresses that conformed to their figures and fell just below the knee. The clothing had been waiting for them when they arrived.

"I wonder why we're here. What's in it for the controllers?" mused Obert.

"Ulva didn't know. I don't think she's big on the planning side. She thinks that her boss wants to make things better for clones and that he's gone as far as he can without coordinating with our side. She... I scanned a lot of minds today. Most people only know that *Freedom's Run* is a show but nothing about it past the name," added Jessica.

"So, this really is a show launch," said Medwin.

"Probably. Ulva also let it slip that Michael's wife, Marcy, is like us. She started on a show."

"And he still enslaves clones," blurted Kendra.

There was a knock at the door. Obert moved to open it, admitting Michael and Marcy, who were dressed in conservative formal wear.

"Hello. I'm the rich bastard you came to meet," opened

Michael.

"Bastard is a debatable point," remarked Marcy with a smile.

"You're…" began Jessica.

"Michael and Marcy." Mike became serious. "Medwin, let me offer our condolences. No one intended what happened with Armina."

"What did you think would happen?" demanded Medwin.

Mike sighed.

"We thought, we hoped, to get a better deal for clones on and off the set region. What you have seen in *Freedom's Run* is true. It is very bad for clones. I wouldn't be alive today except for Mike. I'm like you." Marcy smiled reassuringly.

"So why are we here?" Kendra stepped forward to better see her hosts.

"Let's sit. Old knees don't like standing as much as they once did." Mike and Marcy took the couch, Jessica and Carol the other chairs while the others stood close by.

"You were going to tell us what this is about?" demanded Medwin.

Mike nodded. "Ulva's deduction that my plans have gone as far as they can without a dialogue between our groups is largely accurate. Maintaining secrecy with both your group and the studio is becoming cumbersome. One of the secrets had to go."

"So, you know we've been out of the set region before?" asked Obert.

"That trip will come up in season three." Marcy smirked a little.

"You look like Willa," observed Jessica. "And your mind is… It's not her, but there's something."

"Think of us as twin sisters."

"Season three, you mean…?" Medwin went red in the face.

"You are all principles on *Freedom's Run*. Starting the day that Gunther recruited you." Mike looked a little embarrassed. "As soon as your episodes come up on the timeline, I'll change your official status. For the time being, I've cancelled any do not assist orders regarding you and your immediate family and friends."

"My mum," blurted Medwin.

"Is as safe as she ever was," answered Marcy.

"Wait a minute. Are you saying the jammer doesn't work?" Obert leaned against one of the loungers. His head was spinning.

"It works well enough. Only *Freedom's Run* has any idea of what goes on in that room, and I intend to keep it that way," explained Mike. "By the way, I've purchased a dozen handhelds for you to take to Gunther for his jammer project. I've instructed those in red jackets at the party to let you 'pick pocket' them. I'd rather not have you stealing from my guests to meet his needs. Just try to put on a good show. You will be recorded, and we'll likely need the sequence later."

"What's the point of all this? Ryan, Rowan, us? If you don't like how clones are treated, why not just set us free?" Medwin glowered at Mike.

"One, I don't have that kind of power. Two, the emotional surrogates are just the nasty tip of an extremely nasty iceberg." Mike looked at his wife. His features grew soft as he spoke. "Over fifty years ago, I fell in love with a dream, a fantasy that I had conjured to let others touch a moment of life. To feel and see through the eyes of the other. I'd hoped that seeing through those eyes, people would awaken to the fact that the other had merit."

Mike sighed.

"Some did." Marcy took his hands in hers.

"Some. Sadly, there are always those who must hold the other separate. Must have a focus for their hate and dissatisfaction. After many years, the powers that be determined that my dream had run its course and that newer fantasies would garner a greater following."

"They were going to kill you." Jessica stared at Marcy.

Marcy nodded. "Back then, they killed all the principles from cancelled shows." She looked at her husband. "We put a stop to that." Turning back to Medwin, she continued. "I know your pain. Every one of my friends from high school is long dead. Killed by the studio without even the bad excuse of a plot device."

"I tried to save you all." Mike looked down. "I rigged the vehicle that was removing the cast to malfunction. I didn't have a way of helping them all, so I picked the one I loved the most, while I gave the rest a chance to run."

"I didn't know what was going on. Swept thousands of years into the future. No friends, no family, and just a very sexy, very strange man as a guide. Sound familiar?" asked Marcy.

"*Freedom's Run*," remarked Kendra.

"Cycles repeat." Mike nodded to himself. "Human nature remains human nature. Once I was sure Marcy was safe, we decided that we could do more working from the inside to amend the system, so I came back."

"Since then, we've slowly worked to change things. The right to life legislation that ended the blatant killing of emotional surrogates was the first big step."

"My father and the do not assist orders?" asked Medwin.

"Your father had cancer. There's a heightened incidence just from the quick clone process. To make matters worse, a group of anti-clone fanatics poisoned part of Sun Valley with radioactive dust. Even with our advanced medicine, many clones developed cancers that couldn't be cured. Rather than make them suffer, we used them for the necessary deaths that propelled the dramas."

"You're sick. We're people!" blurted Carol.

"Everyone in this room knows that. That's the point of *Freedom's Run*, to teach the people out there." Mike gestured to the universe beyond the room.

"Then what, a civil war?" asked Obert.

"Accomplishes nothing for the price paid," said Marcy. "Activism. For the clones like Ryan, equal rights, antidiscrimination legislation, the right to keep their status to themselves and an extension of the cloning age limit based on science, not an arbitrary number. For clones like us, the right to join the real world as citizens if we discover the truth. An end to the 'do not assist' orders. An end to the extreme quick-clone procedure that only gives a thirty-year life expectancy."

"There is a slower quick-clone procedure that gives about sixty years of life. It costs more, but throughout human history, sixty years was pretty close to an average life expectancy," added Mike.

"And you keep making your shows," demanded Medwin.

"They won't stop. The UES needs the money. S.E.T.E. is a major employer. Change must come in steps. If I try to bring down the system, Obert's big red button will be pushed."

"What?" asked Carol.

"They'll kill everybody," explained Kendra.

Carol went pale.

"And dear, Medwin. How many of the surrogates would follow Armina's example? How many could not accept what they were? Like my Trevor." Tears brimmed in Marcy's eyes.

Mike hugged her.

"It's all right, Mike. It was long ago. You see, Medwin. Trevor was my first love. He, like your Armina, couldn't deal with the reality of what he was. He slit his writs. It still hurts, but life goes on."

Medwin stared at the couple on the couch and wanted to hate them. Wanted to let anger consume him, but he couldn't. "What do you want from us?"

"Go on as you have. We will contact you. Don't let on that we've been in communication. We'll edit out what we need to make it seem like you stumbled into the party with no more encouragement than the rogue controller, Ulva, tipping you off. Talk to people at the party, learn about this brave new world. Keep Gunther and the rest in the dark. It will be better for the drama if the audience thinks you're doing it all yourselves."

"We're still a show," observed Obert.

"My greatest show. How else can we get the message out? We need to sway public opinion, make real change. Are you with me?" asked Mike.

"What choice do we have?" challenged Jessica.

"We could slip away. Just vanish into the world," suggested Obert.

"Don't try that," pleaded Marcy. She looked at Mike. "Without a guide, it just won't work. Trust me."

Medwin turned to Jessica. "You're the telepath. What do you think?"

"I think... we're among friends." She turned to Mike and Marcy.

"Then let's party. Red jackets beware," quipped Obert.

"Enjoy yourselves. If anyone asks, you are student interns from the university working the control boards. If they ask which show, mention *A Cat's Life* or *Detective Dave*."

"You have got to be kidding," said Obert.

Marcy smiled. "They should be serving the banquet."

"I need answers," objected Jessica.

Mike sighed. "I don't have many. The situation with Gunther is an unforeseen development, but I'll share what little I know."

"I smell pizza." Obert started for the door. The rest followed him, Medwin in the rear.

DODGING A BULLET

"Greg, this is Michael. Our lost lambs can now be found."

Greg closed his handheld and adjusted the *Freedom's Run* board, reactivating Medwin's group's feeds.

The party was lavish, with well-dressed people spotted over the palatial estate. The sounds of splashing and play came from a pool situated by a large manor made from native stone and topped with solar panels and tulip wind turbines.

Medwin's perspective made a beeline to the food table where various kinds of seafood were matched with pizza and chicken wings, all on silver serving plates. Waiters in red jackets walked through the crowd carrying trays with drinks.

A willowy woman with medium brown skin and luxuriant hair dressed in a blue sequined evening gown used silver tongs to select chicken wings from a platter labelled 'suicide' onto a plate. She was speaking to a blonde woman with a golden tan dressed in a light blue pantsuit.

"She adores Fluffy from *A Cat's Life*. But I just don't agree with clone kittens when there are so many unwanted pets in the world. So, I took Cassie to the shelter. The kittens were so adorable. I wanted to bring them all home. Cassie just fell in love with Midnight and Tiger. They're littermates. We went from having no cats to having two." The dark-skinned woman sighed. "And I went from no cats on the bed to Cassie, Midnight and Tiger sleeping together most nights. They're just too cute together."

"Cats find a way in. When Lynx showed up at my door, I just couldn't turn her away," remarked the blonde.

Medwin collected a tray of mixed food and moved away from the table, circulating through the crowd.

"Jason, I'm not saying the dirty bomb was a good thing. All I'm saying is having more surrogates to fill victim roles has allowed me to up the pace on *Homicide Investigations*. Stardust, there wouldn't be a *Vampire Chronicles* at all if it wasn't for the dusting. Mike is squeamish with the fakeys' deaths."

Medwin moved closer to the men and listened.

"Each surrogate we replace costs. It just makes good sense to get the most out of what we have. Especially with the production facilities being turned over to the new set region. All that prep is credits out of the bank, Zack."

"How is Mike planning on handling the transition? With the right to life act in place, it won't be like last time."

"That's why he's starting early. From what I hear, he will circulate a story of a global pandemic that causes sterility. Sun Valley will be a quarantine zone. The population can drop naturally while we play out some dramas against that backdrop."

Greg watched as Medwin's board showed heightened anger, then a cold hatred.

"Sstardusst!" Greg's hand hovered over the button that would release a sedative into Medwin.

Medwin approached the men. "Pardon me, but are you Zackery Smith?" he asked.

Zackery turned to him with a smile. Zackery was of average height and build with pale skin and blue eyes. His sports jacket and slacks weren't new but were in good repair. "I am he. And you are?"

Greg watched hatred surge on Medwin's monitors but also a will like iron that held it in check. "I'm Medwin. I just wanted to tell you how much I enjoy *Homicide Investigations*. It is my favourite show."

"Well, thank you. I try to supply a compelling drama." Zackery smiled. It lent his face a fatherly quality.

"I'm just curious, do you recall the case of Frances O'Hare?"

"Frances O'Hare, I can't say I do. There have been so many cases."

"He was the beat cop." Medwin forced himself to smile.

"Hmm." Zackery Smith seemed to consider. "Sorry, but if you visit the museum, I'm sure Gene, the computer system, can answer any questions you may have."

"Thank you for your time." Medwin slipped away. A minute later, he'd deposited his plate on the collection rack and was heading for a hill overlooking the party grounds.

"Nova blasst, kid. Don't do thiss." Greg scanned the other boards.

Obert was conversing with an attractive, statuesque woman who looked old enough to be his mother. She laughed and touched the younger man's arm suggestively.

Carol was in the centre of a cluster of men of various ages holding out like a queen and her court.

Kendra put her plate in the collector and rushed to where a waiter had draped his jacket over a chair while he unjammed a dish collector. She slipped the handheld out of his pocket. The waiter, a young Asian man, turned. His eyes tracked over her appreciatively, then he winked at her conspiratorially.

Kendra's emotions registered a mild embarrassment and a flattered self-awareness that the man so obviously liked what he saw.

Jessica moved silently through the crowd with a plate of mild wings and two slices of pizza. The drink in the holder at the side of her plate bubbled slowly. She took a sip to still the burning in her mouth. The readings said it was root beer.

"Ladies and gentlemen. If you could all make your way to the e-interfaces under the marquee, Michael Strongbow will be proud to present to you episodes one and two of his latest creation, *Freedom's Run*. The second course will be served at the buffet tables after the premiere." The voice came from everywhere and nowhere.

Greg followed his charges as they moved to the tent, which sheltered four long rows of lounger-like e-interfaces. Most of the crowd moved to take a seat. Obert and the older woman slipped away from the others.

Greg shook his head. "UESS councsillor Abebe. I guesss the rumourss about you and younger men are true. Not bad, Obert."

As his other charges entered the e-rigs, and Obert became engaged with the councillor, Greg shifted his attention fully to Medwin. The screen showed a grassy hill that afforded a view of the grounds. A line of oak trees topped the hill, affording cover. Medwin's emotions were conflicted. He was in pain, confused and angry.

Reaching the top of the rise, he climbed one of the oak trees. His bow and quiver were where he had left them when he cased the place.

Greg sighed. "Doping will take too long if I wait. The choicse is, knock him out and put it off for another day or facse the crississ." A few adjustments to the board, and Greg was ready to stop Medwin's heart with the press of a button. "Don't make me do thiss, buddy."

"*Star Hawk*, this is dichrostigmazoid Murack stargate control. We have noted your approach and advise that the Murack system is currently contested. Be warned that we cannot assure safe passage." The rich feminine voice filled the bridge.

"*Star Hawk*, this is sycamorezoids Murack stargate control. We will not be held accountable for your fate," stated a bass rumble.

Ryan sat at the piloting station of the *Star Hawk*. All the stations were manned. The main screen showed the distorted image of half a gas giant with banded clouds forming stripes along its upper atmosphere. The image was about the size of a golf ball. It occupied one side of a starscape inside a dull silver-coloured ring.

"Back off the view. Interesting coincidence that Murack Seven lines up dead centre with the gate when Star Searcher's original flight plan would have had us transiting," remarked Ryan.

The magnification on the main screen tapered back. Murack Seven became a bright spot in the starfield inside the dull silver coloured ring. The ring diminished in size until it was a dot in the centre of the screen. Two flecks of light, one to either side of the disc, came into view.

"Kitoy, open a channel to both controllers." Ryan moved to the captain's chair. "This is the *Star Hawk*. Be advised that I am flying under a Republic writ of passage delivering relief supplies to Murack Five. At no time in my flight plan will I be passing through dichrostigmazoid or sycamorezoids territorial space. You have no grounds for blocking my passage. Supply approach vectors and prepare for gate insertion."

"The entire Murack system is our space," challenged the deep voice. The screen filled with the image of a sycamorezoid. The cilia at the base of its bulbous brown body waved furiously, and its green backswept wings vibrated, making a buzzing sound. The room beyond it looked like it was made from varying shades of glass run together.

Ryan bared his teeth in an unpleasant smile. "Be corrected. The territorial space of a species extends to ten light seconds from their inhabited planets and three light seconds from artificial habitations. This is Republic law. I will be travelling through only Republic and unclaimable space. Please transmit approach vectors."

"The sycamorezoids of Murack Six take issue with oppressive Republic regulations," snapped the male voice.

"Take issue with what you want. I'm following the law.

Dichrostigmazoid control ship, please transmit approach vector."

"We cannot guarantee your safety, good sentient," spoke the female voice. There seemed to be a mildly pleased tone to it. The screen split to show the image of a dichrostigmazoid on one side. The dichrostigmazoid folded and unfolded its back sail, which was nearly completely red, and its wasp-like body with its elongated neck and triangular head seemed to vibrate. Its slit-pupiled eyes shifted back and forth nervously. The background was a wall full of spirals and triangles seen through a yellow-tinted haze.

"Unless someone is planning to violate Republic law, why would I need protection?" asked Ryan.

"Your ship is a *Homo sapiens* design and a warship," snapped the deep voice.

Ryan sighed. "Sycamorezoids control. The *Star Hawk* has been reclassified as a civilian vessel. Furthermore, the *Homo sapiens* contract with the dichrostigmazoid was cancelled the day of the Murack Five disaster. Would one of you please give me my approach vector?"

There was a long silence. "What of the other *Homo sapiens'* vessels?" demanded the sycamorezoids.

"They are independent craft," stated Ryan.

"The *Mary* is sending a message," stated Kitoy. "The signal from the controllers is off as well."

"How?" asked Ryan.

"The dichrostigmazoid are at normal strength for local transmission. The sycamorezoids are blasting out strong enough that the Switchboard Station should pick them up." Kitoy kinked her tail as she considered.

"Methinks he doth protest too much," mused Ryan. "Everyone watch for other oddities. I think the game is afoot."

"You read too much, hotty boss," observed Henry.

"Play the *Mary's* transmission." Ryan steepled his fingers as an audio-only message played.

"Murack stargate control, we are a civilian craft en route to Murack Five with relief supplies. We travel under a Republic writ of passage."

"*Mary*, be advised that there are pirate elements active in the Murack system, and the dichrostigmazoid cannot guarantee your safety." The being on Ryan's screen tapped its six legs beneath it in emphasis. A row of fleshy tissue along its lower body inflated, and it floated, reaching outside the image's frame. Then the tissue contracted, and the dichrostigmazoid descended to the floor.

"We have given our word under the Great Flyer of the Skies and must fulfill our obligation," replied Croell.

The channels went silent.

"Will he turn back?" asked Tim from the environmental station.

Rowan snorted.

Ryan sighed. "Not a batzoid on a geis. He'll keep coming until he makes his kill or is dead."

"What we gonna do about bug girl and tree sperm?" asked Henry.

Ryan sat in thought. "Kitoy, record this. Transmit it first to the control ships, then to the Switchboard Station on a tight beam."

"Switchboard   Station.   Be   advised   that   the sycamorezoids and dichrostigmazoid control ships at the Murack stargate are refusing passage to vessels flying under Republic writs of passage. I, Captain Ryan Chandler of the *Star Hawk*, wish to lodge a formal complaint and suggest that a review by a full Republic court be initiated. End Message.

"Kitoy send that on the open channel to our friends out there. In five minutes, transmit it to the Switchboard Station, tag it, and send a copy to the *Chimera*. They're obliged to carry it as a dispatch in case it doesn't get through."

"Then what?" asked Rowan.

"Then we wait. Four hours for the message to get to the

Switchboard Station, a couple of hours to do the paperwork, four hours to get a reply. But it probably won't come to that."

Rowan focused on her instruments.

"Incoming," announced Kitoy. Her tail wagged enthusiastically.

"*Star Hawk*, we do not dispute your legal right. The dichrostigmazoid simply wanted to protect you from possible destruction. The situation in the Murack system is volatile. Some fractions do not respect the Rule of Law."

"Protecting other species is also the goal of the sycamorezoids. If you are determined to continue, we may not stop you."

"We are providing coordinates for a standard gate insertion. Please follow all stargate use regulations. May the Divine watch over you," said the dichrostigmazoid. "*Mary*, please follow the *Star Hawk* at a distance of ten thousand kilometres."

"Rowan, please give me my pull points. Log points for emergency diversion." Ryan watched the main screen.

"Captain." Rowan's voice was grave.

Ryan focused his full attention on her and emotionally braced with the use of his rank. "What is it?"

"I'm not sure. There is a cluster of random gas leading from the sycamorezoid ship through the stargate. I think an invisible horse may be kicking up dust."

"Replay the reading on the big screen." Ryan moved to the command chair for a better view.

The black of space filled the screen, dominated by a large ring.

"I'll highlight the heightened gas density in blue," said Rowan.

There was a blue line formed by micro-particles passing through the gate. The density was too thin, and the light it refracted too dim for anything but the most sensitive of instruments to detect, but it was there going from the bulbous sycamorezoid ship through the stargate.

"Could just be an anomaly," suggested Henry.

"Could be, or it could be an ion trail from a cloaked probe," said Ryan.

"What are we looking at?" Kitoy swivelled her chair so that she could stare at the big screen.

"Cloaked vessels draw ionized gas particles towards themselves. Gases build up around stargates because of all the traffic. Nothing by planetary standards but enough that the attraction effect can be visible. You might not see the ship, but you can see the gas trail. If the sycamorezoid are running a cloaked vessel in the Switchboard System, let alone this close to a stargate, they're up to something. If they get caught, their grandkids will be paying the fines."

"They're pretty long-lived, hotty boss. Probably just their kids." Henry closed his eyes, and the computer board lit up. "If there is something there, the displacement is small."

"Should I shoot along its course?" asked Ziggy.

"This close to a stargate?" Ryan shook his head. "What could it be?"

"A messenger pod," suggested Kitoy.

"Why cloak it unless..." Ryan stared at the screen.

"*Star Hawk*, please follow the approved stargate approach," spoke the sycamorezoid's voice.

"What do we do?" asked Rowan.

"We follow the flight plan with a slight change." Ryan worked the piloting board. The *Star Hawk* stopped decelerating relative to the stargate. "Rowan, Henry, watch for another probe."

"Maybe they sent a signal to be sure no one else was coming the other way," suggested Tim.

"No. All stargate insertions are at a ninety-degree angle from twenty thousand kilometres out. That way, you can see other vessels approaching straight ahead of you. The law is whoever is further away will divert and go through later when it's clear. That way, you can avoid any chance of collision. That's part of the reason that cloaks are forbidden in all Republic territories, especially the stargate exclusion zones. They constitute a navigation hazard," explained Rowan.

"They wouldn't," blurted Kitoy.

"What wouldn't they?" asked Henry.

"Henry, look up what would happen if there was an antimatter release at the transit point of a stargate?" Ryan's voice held fear.

"Hotty boss, no one's crazy enough to try something like that." Henry went silent for a second, then spoke with a quaver in his voice. "Quick search turns up... The theory is that the rings on both sides would collapse, releasing all the energy used to create the gate in twined beams of high energy plasma. It could destabilize a sun if it hit one and..."

"Trigger fusion in a gas giant if it hit one," finished Ryan.

"You've researched this?" Rowan looked and sounded shocked.

"Always assume that no matter how stupid and crazy something is, some idiot, somewhere, somewhen, will try it." Ryan shrugged.

"Why wait?" asked Kitoy.

"If the goal is to take out the dichrostigmazoids, the orbits have to line up. Planetary gravity gives a small margin for error, but space is big. This is sharpshooting at its most challenging. That's one. For two, deniability. Human ships have lost antimatter containment before. Only once, and it took more ordnance than it would take to pulp a moon, but it has happened, and it was a Hawk class."

"So, the gate blows, kills the dichrostigmazoid by turning Murack Seven into a sun, destabilizes the Switchboard System by blasting its sun, and they blame it on a malfunction," said Henry.

"You know what Republic courts are like. If you have a choice of answers, one means you can sweep it under the rug, blame it on pilot error and anyone that might mount a defence is dead. The other means you will be obliged to mount a costly real-time interstellar military expedition to punish a member species whose population is cut off from the Republic anyways. Which costs less?"

"What could the sycamorezoids hope to gain?" Rowan's eyes riveted to her instruments.

"The isolationists get what they want. Rid of the stargate and the system to themselves," observed Ryan.

"We should turn back," suggested Kitoy.

"We can't prove anything, and if we go back, they'll send Ryan to the UES," countered Rowan.

"Besides, if they are bringing a cloaked missile through to hit us, they planned this for a long time. We're a target of opportunity. They'll just pull the same stunt with the *Mary*. At least we're watching for it, and our sensors are better than a space yacht. Add that we're early to the party because we amended Star Searcher's flight plan." Ryan gripped the arms of the piloting chair so hard his knuckles turned white.

Rowan worked her console. "If we'd stayed with Star Searcher's original transit time, a beam would hit Murack Seven dead on. As is, maybe a glancing blow, partial environmental destruction from heightened radiation."

"Rowan, work out the fastest legal flight plan for gate insertion and give me the consequence to Murack Seven of a plasma beam if we get hit transiting then," ordered Ryan.

"Should we tell someone?" asked Kitoy.

"Transmit our suspicions to the *Chimera* and the Switchboard Station," ordered Ryan.

"*Star Hawk*, this is Murack Stargate Dichrostigmazoid control," came through the speakers.

"Go ahead, Dichrostigmazoid control," answered Ryan.

"I am showing your vessel deviating from flight plan," said the high-pitched voice.

"Dichrostigmazoid control. I am altering the approach for possible safety considerations. Rowan, send them the revised approach ASAP. I hope this doesn't affect any plans you or the sycamorezoids may have."

There was silence on the channel before the deep voice

came on. "Sycamorezoids are adaptable."

The dichrostigmazoid voice sounded concerned. "The new flight plan is within regulations and acceptable to traffic control."

Several minutes passed, then Rowan spoke. "There's another line of concentrated gases coming from the sycamorezoid ship and going through the stargate."

"That confirms it," remarked Henry.

"For us, but not for the Republic." Ryan sat in the pilot's chair, stroking his chin. "Kitoy, get the *Chimera*."

Two seconds later, Commander McKenzie appeared on the *Star Hawk*'s big screen. "Captain. I've looked at your suspicions. I'll keep my monitors on you until you transit. I'm also moving away from the gate, but I can't do anything more than that. Your suspicions are exactly that, suspicions."

"At least you acknowledge the threat. Commander, there is something you can do. Pick a spot a hundred kilometres forward of the stargate and focus your gravity lasers on it with maximum pull when I near transition."

"What would that do?" asked McKenzie.

"If there is a cloaked missile and if I can drag it to this side of the gate, you could pull it out and away from the gate. Accelerate it so that if it blows, the energy and debris would be expended into space."

McKenzie nodded. "And if we do contact something, we can pull away fast enough to avoid the blast ourselves. I hope you're wrong, Captain, but I've fought against you enough to know better than to assume that. Suppose there's a remote detonation system?"

"I'll put out a broad-spectrum jamming signal. That should hold things up until I transit the gate."

McKenzie nodded. "I'll have us in position and transmit the point for the gravity laser's line of attraction. I've spoken with the *Mary*. They're flying in behind you at ten thousand kilometres. They won't budge. They say that whatever happens is the will of the Great Flyer of the

Skies."

"Nova blasted religion!" grumbled Henry.

"Thank you, Captain."

"How will you see a cloaked missile through the distortion of energy passing through the gate?" McKenzie looked concerned.

"You mean, how do I see something that is practically invisible at the best of times through the equivalent of filthy glass? I'll call you back." Ryan stared at the big screen as it clicked off.

Rowan took a deep breath. "I may be able to help with our vision problem. You won't like it, and I'll need Krakkeen and Ziggy's help."

Two hours had passed. Medwin still sat on the rise of land, his bow lying across his knees. Below, people filed out from beneath the marquee. Mike and Marcy stood to one side, shaking hands with people and seemingly receiving exuberant praise. A small group of people strode away from the party. Others rushed to the restocked catering tables.

Zackery Smith appeared in the line to speak with Michael. Medwin watched him through his binoculars. The man was smiling. How could he smile after killing his father, a good man who tried to make the world a better place?

Setting aside the binoculars, Medwin picked up his bow and came to his feet. Seconds seemed like hours as he nocked an arrow and took tension on the string.

Greg watched through Medwin's eyes. "Don't do thiss." Greg's hand hovered over a nondescript button on his console that would mean Medwin's end.

"Come on, kid. What would your father have done?" Greg pleaded to the empty air.

Zackery Smith was a clean shot, then the dark-skinned cat lover from the overheard conversation moved into the field. Medwin let off the tension on the bow. The woman embraced Zackery. She kissed him and said something. They both laughed. He touched the side of her face. Medwin looked at his palm.

He spoke to the air, and it came through the speakers in the control room. "I touched Armina like that. You wouldn't let me do it anyway, would you? Maybe I just wanted to join her. Maybe it's not about my dad. Maybe, maybe, maybe. Whoever you are, you can take your finger off the big red button. I'll play Michael's game, for now."

Medwin returned his bow and arrows to their hiding place. He then started down the hill towards the party. "Controller, get someone to save you some of the chicken wings. They're incredible."

Ryan sat at the pilot's station, his fingers poised over the controls.

"So far, so good," said Henry.

"Kitoy, how's Ziggy doing?" asked Ryan.

"He reports that the net is deployed. He's returning to the airlock," replied Kitoy.

"Ask Pikeman how Krakkeen is doing. That net took a lot of silk." Ryan's voice held a note of concern.

"Medical reports that Krakkeen is sore but will recover with a few good meals and rest." Kitoy's tail lashed. "Ziggy reports that the net is in place."

"It's up to you, love. In ten seconds," spoke Ryan.

Rowan closed her eyes and reached with her mind. She could feel the atoms in the *Star Hawk*'s hull vibrating. Just beyond that, she felt the silk-like strands of a massive net that had been spread over the front of the ship. She could sense the flow of the subatomic particles. With an effort of will, she pushed the gossamer mesh of the web forward of the *Star Hawk*, splaying it out so that it stretched nearly the width of the stargate. "Net away," she announced.

Ryan triggered the grav laser drive to slow the *Star Hawk* at eighteen Gs, letting the net drift out in front of them. "Slowing velocity to insertion speed."

"Thirty seconds to insertion," said Henry.

Rowan kept her focus on the net, maintaining its spread while keeping it centred on the stargate, then it hit the gate.

"I've still got the net. Oh, my head." Rowan clutched her head as pain shot through her, but she held onto her sense of the mass of the net through the gate. "I've got something!"

"Henry, fire lasers, minimal intensity. We want a flashlight, not a cutting tool."

"There," blurted Kitoy.

On the big screen, the near-invisible gossamer threads of spiderzoid silk lit up with laser light. The web had wrapped itself around something speeding towards the centre of the stargate.

Ryan directed full gravity lasers on the tangle of web, pulling them and what they encompassed back through the stargate.

Rowan was only vaguely aware of her shipmates as she reached forward. Matter was a pattern of atoms. A thing to be moulded, a thing to see and touch. Her heart raced as her breathing became ragged. The missile in the web tried to pull away from the course the grav laser dictated, but her will held it steady.

"Ten seconds," said Ryan.

The net of silk containing a thing of dense matter with a core that repelled Rowan's perceptions, antimatter, passed through the stargate, becoming clear to her senses.

"Kitoy, full jamming. Henry, cut grav lasers."

Three hundred kilometres ahead of the *Star Hawk*, Rowan felt the missile jerk away across the field of space in front of the stargate.

A second later, the *Star Hawk* jerked as it passed through the gravity laser where the missile had been seconds before.

"It's a missile, port up," observed Henry.

"Kill the boost to Rowan." Ryan worked his controls, correcting for the *Chimera*'s pull on the *Star Hawk*.

The *Star Hawk* entered the stargate just off the centre point of the trans-matter ring.

The universe blinked.

"We aren't dead, so I think it worked." Rowan massaged her temples, then looked at her instruments as they scanned the Murack side of the stargate. "Oh, stardust!"

Pause.

Acknowledgements

Afterword

Thank you for reading *Freedom's Myth*. I hope it brought you pleasure. I will mention that *Arming Freedom*, the next instalment in the Freedom Saga, should be out in December of 2023. This saga, initially envisioned as a trilogy, has grown in the telling. Ryan and Rowan, not to mention Mike and the rest, are demanding and have started calling the shots.

If you could please review this work, it would be greatly appreciated. Remember, the power's in you, please review.

About the Author

Stephen B. Pearl is a multiple published author whose works range across the speculative fiction field. Whether his characters are wandering the wilds of a post-oil future, braving a storm in a longship, or flying through the interplanetary void in an army surplus assault lander, his writings focus heavily on the logical consequences of the worlds he crafts.

Stephen's inspirations encompass H.G. Wells, J.R.R. Tolkien, Frank Herbert, and Homer, among others. In writing the Freedom Saga, he has, among other factors, drawn on his diverse background and broad general knowledge garnered from preparing for and serving on seminars and panels at numerous shows and events. These panels and seminars range from Intelligent Spacecraft Design to Building Better Aliens. His training as an Emergency Medical Care Assistant, a SCUBA diver, and his long-standing interest in environmental technologies have factored into all his science fiction books, be they on or off the planet Earth.

For more about Stephen and his works visit: www.stephenpearl.com